A Pretty Age

Barbara Mueller

WESTBOW
PRESS
A DIVISION OF THOMAS NELSON

WestBow Press books may be ordered through booksellers or by contacting:

WestBow Press
A Division of Thomas Nelson
1663 Liberty Drive
Bloomington, IN 47403
www.westbowpress.com
1-(866) 928-1240

Because of the dynamic nature of the Internet, any web addresses or links contained in this book may have changed since publication and may no longer be valid. The views expressed in this work are solely those of the author and do not necessarily reflect the views of the publisher, and the publisher hereby disclaims any responsibility for them.

"Names, characters, places, and incidents either are the product of the author's imagination or are used fictitiously."

"Scripture quotations are taken from The New American Bible. Catholic Book Publishing Corp., N.J. 2010."

Any people depicted in stock imagery provided by Thinkstock are models, and such images are being used for illustrative purposes only.

Certain stock imagery © Thinkstock.

ISBN: 978-1-4497-7955-9 (sc)
ISBN: 978-1-4497-7956-6 (hc)
ISBN: 978-1-4497-7954-2 (e)

Library of Congress Control Number: 2012923609

Printed in the United States of America

WestBow Press rev. date: 1/7/2013

Contents

In memory of
my grandmothers,
Julia and Mary,
and
for my
beautiful
granddaughters,
Sabine, Sela, and Jada.

Acknowledgments

I prayed, and prudence was given to me; I pleaded, and the spirit of Wisdom came to me.
—Wisdom, 7:7

Prayer is the language of heaven.
—Julia Mumm, pocket notes 1910

In writing this book, I am grateful for the assistance of my siblings, Frank, Mary, and Tim, in gathering our grandmother Julia Mumm Knopp's notes and records and to Anita and her husband, Michael, for writing suggestions, African adventures, basket weaving, and bird watching. A special thank you goes to my good friend Charlene Musgrove for reading the raw manuscript and offering valuable insights. Memories of great teachers Sister Lucille, Sister Alexine Marie, and Sister Alexina and experiences of convent life have been kept alive thanks to continued emails and reunions with my band of sisters: Katie, Connie, Vicki, Sister Barbara Ellen, Theresa, Annette, Rose, and Carlene. Thank you to my publishing team at Westbow Press. I am also grateful to the Dennis Prager radio show for weighty discussions, especially thoughts on failure.

As always, though, my biggest debt is to my husband, Gary, who is a good failure spotter, and to our children and grandchildren, who give me lots of good reasons to tell stories.

Chapter 1
Out of Place

Sophiny Mumm opened the door to headmistress's office and disappeared inside. She was aware of the eyes of the other academy students watching as they filed downstairs without her.

"Can you tell me about this?" Sister Louise asked as she returned the pages of sums and measures Sophiny had worked on haphazardly for the past week. "Convert your figures into *dollars and cents* and your measurements into *large and small units.*"

When would I have a use for menu planning at a boarding school? Sophiny thought pretending interest in the grocery list for 1910: one pound of apples, eleven cents; one pound of roast, nineteen cents; one pound of bread, five cents; one pound of butter, thirty-nine cents; one pound of chicken, nineteen cents; one pound of coffee, twenty cents; one dozen eggs, thirty-six cents; one gallon of milk, thirty-four cents, one pound of sugar, five cents; one bushel of potatoes, forty cents, and the items continued.

Unfortunately, Sophiny again seemed to have entirely misunderstood the direction she was supposed to have taken in Sister Louise's latest assignment: plan one day's menu of breakfast, dinner, tea, and supper for fifty-five students. Calculate quantities. Calculate costs. Ask for assistance from the sister cooks about serving sizes. Provide a final tally. In effect, the unit needed to be completely redone, and comments in the margins stated as much. On the last page was a bright red, *"Please rethink this."*

"Somebody gave me that influenza that was going around. I have not been feeling well ..." Sophiny replied with her prepared defense. It was true. She had been thinking how much easier it would be to die of spotted fever than to finish this project.

Sister Louise looked at Sophiny as though searching for the moment when her words would best take hold. "Your failures will not hurt you until you start blaming others." The bell interrupted the long pause that followed. With a sigh of resignation, Sophiny mumbled the expected apologies, promised to do better, and then waited for the obligatory, "You are dismissed." Sister Louise had made her late for chapel on a day when time most mattered.

All Sophiny could do to make up was take the stairs at a run. No one was looking. Her eyes were already on the sewing and storage room door where the altar supplies were kept when she made a last surge to increase her speed and hurl herself through the opening below ... and then *smack*. The impediment in her path had not been dislodged in spite of the full force of her moving body. Instead she felt herself bounce backward from the impact and nearly lose her balance. He should not have been there. At Mount St. Mary's, there was a place for everything, and everything was in its place. Did not the signs in the dormitory say so? Stunned, she opened her eyes to see what she had not seen coming ... an impenetrable outcropping of rock suddenly appearing on a flat plain.

Sophiny's confusion lingered until her best friend came to collect and steer her into place in the processional line. As Antoinette handed her a lighted candle and fitted a veil headband over her hair, she commented, "You look smitten."

"As in struck with a hard blow ... he ran into me," Sophiny was suddenly aware of surrounding whispers and giggles, an added humiliation. But as she turned to confront her classmates, she noticed they were not looking at her but at the progress of a visiting monk into the chapel. "We are all smitten ... as in very much in love," Antoinette reassured her. The girls' gazes had been focused before the collision—before Sophiny had intercepted his course.

The procession began to move.

Chapter 2
Call of the Missionary

In the chapel, Sophiny's concentration worsened. She neither heard the cantor's "Ave Maria" marking the beginning of the special blessing nor saw the monstrance encased Eucharist, its starburst of golden rays, the divine portent of grave misfortune, on the altar before her. The kneeling missionary clothed in sludge-brown robes had captured her attention, and she felt again the rock-solid impact from the vestibule. Father Brownell, the chaplain, had introduced him as Brother Claude. He had just returned from a mission in Brazil to preach and solicit funds from the surrounding parishes.

Now the visitor knelt at a prie-dieu in side profile, head bent over clasped hands, eyes closed. His face glowed from the embers of a divine inner fire. The jeweled light coming through the stained glass overhead cast pools of emerald, ruby, sapphire, and citrine all around him. Sophiny envisioned him suffused with a golden halo on the bank of a forested stream in Brazil, as on the holy card of a saint. To one side, calm waters lapped in a green hollow. On the other side, off in the distance, the village woke from slumber, and at his feet early morning worshippers sat on a terraced knoll transformed by the sound of his voice breaking the stillness. As a missionary, he would live among but be marked by a simpler, purer way of life than the people. A cloud of scented smoke from the burning incense filled the sanctuary.

What is it like to receive the call of a missionary? Could I be one? As she studied him, she did not recognize his order from the habit. Without warning, his eyes, suddenly alert, focused directly on hers. The wilderness landscape she had pictured but a moment before suddenly darkened, as when a cloud blots out all but a few rays on a bright day. The lapping of the water turned cold and wild. His eyes were the color of the burnished metal on the upraised monstrance. Gone was the golden halo. Gone the marks of purity. His form turned into shadow, but the embers within still burned. She felt the scorching of an unholy fire, and unquiet thoughts made her want to neglect spiritual matters.

Father Brownell moved to the center of the communion rail in anticipation of the special blessing for the Virgin's acolytes on February 2, 1910, the Feast of the Purification. Each of the fifty-five boarders of the Mount St. Mary's Academy wore a starched white veil of tulle, which stood out like a nimbus over her navy jumper and white blouse. One by one, the girls proceeded with lighted candles up to the railing separating the altar and its ministers from the congregation of students and sisters in rows of pews. Sophiny told her eyelids to stay lowered as Brother Claude rose to assist. Visiting clergy were not unusual. Father Brownell's quarters were spacious. He graciously hosted religious travelers who stopped off for a night's lodging before continuing their journeys to other destinations. Usually the visitors reciprocated by preaching a sermon or assisting at services. But never had Father Brownell had so handsome a guest. This missionary was tall and broad-shouldered, and even the heavy robes could not conceal the strength and ease of his movements.

With a start, Sophiny realized her eyes had disobeyed. Her heart began to pound like a huge, swollen thing in her chest. She was staring—actually staring—openly at Brother Claude. But her first blush of mortification was stilled in the throes of another emotion: envy. Brother Claude was no longer looking at her but was intently studying the girl standing before Father Brownell. Antoinette Dominguez recited the prayer of dedication to the Virgin in honor of the feast day. Her voice was low and even; her gaze was seemingly oblivious of the attention she was receiving. When she finished, Father Brownell pronounced the words of blessing. Brother Claude, at his side, sprinkled Antoinette liberally with holy water and as he did so, studied her in a most analytical manner.

By this time, Sophiny's entire body had stopped listening. When her own time came to recite the prayer, she gave him her best withering gaze. The return look of his spectacular eyes was amused and unwavering. It was she who lowered her gaze. Her intention to guilt him into looking away seemed to intrigue rather than intimidate. And the cold dousing of holy water from the aspergillum that she was subjected to at the end of her recitation left her limp. She was glad when the familiar strains of "Laudate Dominum" sounded from the choir loft, signaling the end of the benediction.

As the students filed past the great mass of sisters in black-and-white habits out of the chapel, Antoinette slipped a folded paper into her hand and smiled through sly, thin slits covering her bright eyes. Sophiny waited until she was beyond the range of other curious eyes to read the note.

My friend, health and benediction,

Nourish my soul with discourse on the source of your meditation

4

this afternoon. The blossoming of spiritual ardor upon your face at Father Brownell's blessing seemed the very essence of beatitude. Oh sweet mystery, unfold at your leisure. The tombstones have no ears.

Lead us not into temptation

As usual, Antoinette did not use names and took precautions to foil interception. Sophiny easily translated the message: "Walk in the cemetery during afternoon recreation." She was about to be subjected to Antoinette's enquiry. Sophiny pocketed the note and went to the cloakroom, thinking about how she could best correct her friend's mistaken perception. It was that or Sister Louise and the sums and measures all over again.

"Let's walk fast," she said once they were outside. Her annoyance propelled her several paces ahead as the two, bundled in heavy winter wraps against the crisp brightness and freezing temperatures, made their way up the hill path to the sisters' cemetery on convent grounds. The wind whipped her long hair into her eyes, and the cold bit at the back of her neck.

"Slow down, Sophiny …"

"It is cold out here. Why couldn't we talk inside where it is warm? Do you want to end up under one of those tombstones moldering in a grave yourself?" Sophiny complained. A bitter gust snatched her breath momentarily.

Antoinette's own intake of breath was as startled and unexpected as was her change in direction. "Let's go back then."

"Now what? Are you upset with me?"

"No, it is just …"

"Just what?" Sophiny, in turn, found herself running to catch up.

"I felt the cold breath of death pass through me," Antoinette said, pointing to her late-afternoon shadow moving over the gravel path.

"It was not death, Antoinette, believe me. The temperature must be near freezing, and there is snow on the ground."

"Let's go to the trunk room. It is not heated, but at least we will be out of the wind." They were walking side by side.

Sophiny remained silent. She well knew that the students were allowed in the trunk room only on two days: the day they arrived at the start of the school term and the day they left at the end of the term. But the entrance was out of sight and the door usually unlocked. When they entered the room, her original annoyance mounted as she observed Antoinette's selection of the best leather-bound trunk on which to seat herself, her finicky attempts first to blow away a fine layer of dust and then to dust the surface with her gloved hand, her disgust at the dust that remained, and finally, her disdainful, resigned perch. Antoinette seemed to like the rustling sound made by the layers of her clothing as she settled on the cold surface. Then she studied the open beams of the ceiling overhead as though to make sure no spiders were listening. What a flair she had with her deep, dark eyes and swift movements.

Antoinette's attention soon turned from her petticoats. "Sophiny, sometimes you remind me of one of those cherubic children on chocolate boxes. You are just so sweet with your turned-up nose and your freckles … I have been wanting to tell you about something, but I am afraid that I might shock you."

"Tell me what?" Antoinette had changed direction on her again. "What?" What had she missed? What had happened? She seemed to be stuck in a snowdrift, blinded by flurries, and pushed back by the wind. Only moments earlier the two had been going for a walk to talk about another of Antoinette's mysteries. "Does this have something to do with the missionary?"

"Do not get carried away, Sophiny. You have been devouring too many travelers' tales. This has nothing to do with the missionary or at least nothing to do with the missionary and me. But I did see the way you looked at him, as though you were ready to pack your trunk and run off to Brazil. And I have been thinking about journeying across the wilderness myself."

Sophiny gazed around the trunk room, sorting out the plain from the fancy in an effort to diffuse thought and imagination, avoiding Antoinette's intrusive eyes, which she knew would be demanding a confession. Next to the back walls were the flat-topped trunks, which were stacked three high. Her own was here, the cheapest steel-bound trunk in Mr. Sears' catalogue, fifth back. At this moment, she wanted to crawl in. There were familiar things inside her trunk: the print dress her mother had hand-sewn for her when she turned fifteen—a bit snug when she last wore it—a saved stack of her mother's letters, and an extra quilt made by her grandmother. Was Antoinette making fun of her for the way she had looked at the missionary? Did Antoinette think she was an infant? If she had to call her a cherub, why was the reminder from a chocolate box? Why could she not look like the cherubs on the stained glass in the chapel? Her fingers plunged deep into the pocket of her coat, and she felt and gripped the key tightly, for her coat pocket had seemed a safe place to secure her key.

"Did he make you feel something?" Antoinette looked at her, absorbed and serious.

"Who?" What insight was she lacking now? Strangely, Sophiny felt that the trunks were watching her. Were they laughing?

"The missionary … you know who. I am trying to make a point. Just say that he made you feel something."

A twinge of pain shot from Sophiny's head to the pit of her stomach. She could not give up this secret that a stranger, the missionary, bringer of other world messages, had wrought. "Why is this so important to you anyway?"

"Because I have to know if you have ever felt the way I feel. Spill."

A numbing cold crept over Sophiny even as she wrapped a muffler around her neck and mouth and pulled her knitted hat over her ears. The act of breathing in the winter air was almost audible. Was Antoinette playing a cruel joke? Would the sisters and the other girls all stop at supper and stare at her because she was somehow different? Antoinette's pointy, black leather lace-up boots caught her attention. "What do you want me to say? He was staring at me. I was staring at him. Yes, something seemed to pass between us. After all, I did run into him."

"I thought you said he ran into you?" Antoinette seemed oddly relaxed, in spite of the cold. "Seldom does truth come without disguise. Without disguise, truth would be destroyed."

"What truth? What disguise?" Again she was coming up short in Antoinette's exercise of connecting the dots. Was Antoinette expressing concern or condemnation?

"I had to test you to know that I could trust you. What I am about to do would make no sense to you unless you knew," she rambled on.

"Knew what? Antoinette, sometimes your mind seems to stick in a rut like a wagon wheel after a rainstorm. Just tell me what you are talking about … Why all the secrecy?" Sophiny was furious.

Antoinette scooted to one side of the trunk and patted the spot next to her in a decidedly nonhostile move. "I have an understanding with … well, I will not tell you his name. It is not important that you know whom … just that you know we have an agreement, a mutual pledge. We are going to elope."

"Elope!" Sophiny gasped. "From here? But your family? Your friends? The sisters?" *What about me?* She did not speak her thought but felt the depth of the loss.

Antoinette nodded. "You must know, dear Sophiny, what a chill went through me out on the cemetery walk. When a young woman loses her family's protection or if her family can no longer provide the restraints of civility … well, I too shudder to think what might happen."

"Elope …" Sophiny grasped her cheeks in dread. "What are you talking about now?"

Antoinette and her search for forbidden knowledge. Antoinette and her secret messages. She was going to get caught someday. Where would that leave her? The mail went to the secretary's office to be sorted and dealt with by one of the sisters. Outgoing letters were left unsealed and incoming letters to be passed out were slit open at the top. Certainly any notes passed among the students were confiscated. Did the sisters read these communications? One could never be too careful. But Sophiny was noticing a disturbing increase in the regularity of strange phrases in Antoinette's speech.

"What do you mean by restraints of civility?" Now who was lacking in density of details?

"Nothing that either of us needs to worry about, I am sure. But when I leave, I am going to take your trunk, and you are going to keep mine. First, promise me ..." Antoinette scrutinized her without a hint of her usual mischief.

"I promise," Sophiny relished the intrigue, relieved that the focus of the conversation had shifted away from the missionary.

"Promise you will not tell anyone about our trade or about my elopement!"

"Promise!"

Antoinette continued, "Also, you are not to look at or go through my things or let anyone else look at my trunk."

"Promise ..."

"If anything happens—if I am found out by my mother or Sister Louise or if something goes wrong—you are not to give my things to anyone or allow anyone to take my belongings from your possession. Do you understand?" When Sophiny hesitated, she added another hurdle. "If you do, you will probably be accused of stealing anyway. Vow to me?"

"Vow?"

"It is more serious than a promise."

Sophiny hesitated then added, "I vow ... but what if your trunk falls open and everything spills out? If I have to pick it up, I am not going to close my eyes."

"Fine ... only if it cannot be prevented. But you must not tell anyone what you have. I cannot risk losing the part of my life that connects me to my past."

Sophiny's curiosity was bursting, and this third request already weighed upon her. *Friends are few ...* Was she about to lose her best friend? Winter was such a rotten time.

Antoinette's injunction to caution and silence both distressed and enchanted her. "Of course you can use my trunk. Here is the key." Sophiny reached out teasingly, swinging the braided black cord back and forth. "Now tell me, is he very handsome? How did you meet? When are you going to elope?"

"To your first question—yes ... very handsome. We have known each other since we were children. And it is better that you do not know when. All the details have yet to be worked out anyway." Antoinette snatched Sophiny's key before hiding it away in her own pocket. "But we must seal the vow. Give me something of yours in case I cannot see you in person and must send you a message. Then you will know that the correspondence is from me and all is well."

"What could I give you?"

"Think of something, and just put it into my hand. I will know what it is for." She turned to look around as though studying the row of trunks before her. "You know which is mine, don't you?"

Of course Sophiny knew which trunk was her friend's: the ornate steamer stamped in a black and silver metal-leaf pattern with bent oak trim over each seam and a barrel top. It stood in the double row down the center of the room with other mostly barrel-stave-topped trunks that could not be stacked. Goaded into motion at her friend's query she went right to it.

"Will you be all right? Truly all right?" asked Sophiny, picturing fate flinging a path of sunshine and butterflies before Antoinette and her rogue hero. She had no doubt that her friend would carry off an elopement with her usual flair, and all who heard her story would love it.

"Do not worry about me, Sophiny. There are ways of doing things you do not even know about. I will get married. My husband will adore me. We will plant lilacs and peonies in the front yard. I will clean the coffee pot every Monday, bake a pie every Friday, and write you a letter every Sunday, just like the sisters do here at Mount St. Mary's. My life will be in order at last. Just thinking about it makes me long to be with him. Oh, how I miss him so."

Sophiny turned her head to make certain she had not missed something, but Antoinette looked perfectly serious. Just as they secured the trunk room door, a bell sounded, marking the passage of the day.

After supper, evening recreation, quiet study time, and night prayers, Sophiny felt exhausted. Antoinette had extracted two promises and a vow from her. How had what Antoinette wanted changed so radically? Before the Christmas holy days, they had even talked of joining the convent of religious women or going on to college to learn to run a business, such as Antoinette's father's. Acceptance for women's paid work and greater entry into new female professions beyond teaching and nursing, as the sisters practiced, was gaining ground. In some states women were even getting the right to vote, and Antoinette had been excited that the movement of votes for women was growing in Kansas as well. *Marriage*! What had happened to change her friend's plans so drastically? It seemed their brief walk to the trunk room had taken hours, days. She had expended a year's worth of energy just to live a brief moment. And she still could not quite fit in the stranger at the dedication service or account for her own behavior. Maybe it was a kind of lapse; there was little chance of ever running into him again. She knew nothing about him but his name, Brother Claude—and what did he have to do with either of them?

Chapter 3
Rite of Passage

At the clang of the rising bell, Sophiny groaned inwardly but arose quickly, knowing the little time Antoinette remained at Mount St. Mary's Academy was borrowed time for their friendship. Already her friend's perception had changed, and once she put her plans into action—lifted and lowered the reins to signal the horse (so to speak)—the commitment would give her the resolve and courage to overcome her fears of what lay ahead. As she began to pick up the speed it would take to cover the distance to her future with her beloved, she would leave behind the comfortable, secure world of the academy, childhood, and Sophiny. What was her urgency? Why not wait for the semester to end? But Antoinette would not answer Sophiny's questions.

While brushing her teeth and combing her hair in a dormitory alcove of communal sinks with running water, Sophiny was grateful that the motherhouse had been brought out of the age of wax candles and into the age of incandescent lighting. She paused to look in the mirror over the sink at the someone watching her: pale blue eyes, "the color of heaven," and long hair that was multihued with streaks that lightened in the summer to the shade of harvest wheat, "sunlit from heaven," in her father's phrases. Was that really a turned-up nose under all those freckles, a candy box cherub lacking in enigma and mystery? But what change had Antoinette seen in her? As she turned away, the familiar Latin axiom stenciled over the archway separating the sink area from the dormitory's row of beds caught her attention, "*Principiis obstra, sero medicina paratur,*" for which all the students knew the translation: "Watch over the early beginnings of passions and apply remedies in good time."

Each morning the young women dressed in silence and knelt for morning prayers along the aisle separating the curtained rows of beds extending the entire length of the fifth-floor dormitory. Afterward, still in silence, they filed in double rows down four flights of stairs, past a larger-than-life (as if one

11

knew how large angels were) statue of a guardian angel with outspread wings, past the sainted Little Flower clutching her lily, garbed in Carmelite white and brown in a niche on the forth floor landing, past a gold-etched icon of Our Lady of Perpetual Help gazing in adoration of her child on the third floor landing, past the print of a flock of sheep lost in a blustering snowstorm, and finally into the chapel, where more images in statue, stained glass, and human flesh awaited to give instruction. The building that housed the academy for young women also housed a motherhouse for the Sisters of Mary, whose early-morning hours were occupied with chanting the Divine Office and meditating. Sophiny was grateful that at least Sister Louise's sums exercise did not include all the convent inhabitants. How much butter? How much soap? How much electricity did they all use? How much would be subtracted because of their vows of poverty?

In the few minutes before morning mass, Sophiny had developed the habit of recording entries in a pocket notebook small enough to conceal in the specially made large pocket of her skirt. Past entries indicated celebrations of feasts, daily refectory specialties, snatches of news from letters back home, bouts of homesickness and occasional sickness among the boarders, breaks in the schedule—picking apples, critiques of the practice of virtue, her own and other girls'—and weather: "pleasant," "rained," "snowed," "blustering," "another cloudy, dull day." This morning she was having difficulty not because of a dearth of material to write upon but because now she, like Antoinette, had secrets to keep. She must be careful not to punctuate her sober entries with cries of longing or other indiscretions such as she had heard Antoinette voice: "Oh! If I could only see him," or "I feel so lonely," or "Oh! How I long to be with him." Her diary might be subject to prying eyes if Sister Louise, the headmistress, were to question her after Antoinette's disappearance. Yet she could not let this day pass unrecorded. Her prescient insight into Antoinette's mind made her want to track her own unruly thoughts before they required correctives. Was Antoinette's passion going to cause her to commit a transgression that prayer, penance, and silence could not rectify?

Or was there no illness to cure? No cause for remedy? In school, Antoinette was well liked for her love of mystery, and she employed mystery as a cloak that rendered her more interesting to her friends and teachers alike. How could Sophiny condemn what she did not understand? Her day's entry was short and confusing even to her.

February 3. Yesterday was the feast of the Purification:
Candlemas. The gospel tells of a pilgrimage to offer a pair of
turtle doves, and the flame of the candles represents a new
light in the temple. If one person uses the words, "I promise,"

is she still bound if the other person does not act according to the terms agreed upon? Weather: clear and cold.

Just asking

She made a duplicate copy for Antoinette, intending to slip it to her after breakfast and then bowed her head, beseeching the Virgin to protect and guard her friend from harm. But a disquieting thought arose. *The Virgin, a sublime model of chastity, demands chastity from her votaries. A votary who abandons purity of mind and body to lust severs an intimate bond. The Purification, which we celebrated yesterday, signified the cleansing of the Virgin of her own impurities after childbirth. Will Antoinette any longer be under the protection of the Virgin?*

As Sophiny pondered these questions, the familiar grind of the organ began the processional and brought the congregation of women to their feet. Father Brownell entered the chapel to perform his office. The missionary from the day before followed close behind. An unfamiliar tingle shivered along Sophiny's spine at the sight of him. A grayness that was scarcely light crept through the sanctuary. Gone were yesterday's pieces of paradise collected on the chapel floor. This interval between daylight and sunrise was an unreal hour. It seemed to Sophiny that she moved between night and day, and when the sun rose, she would awaken. This fluttering in her abdomen would vanish and with it Brother Claude. She consoled herself with the thought that when it was all over—when Antoinette and Brother Claude were both gone—she would go to confession to make sense of her ambiguous feelings. At least *her* bond with the Virgin had not been so damaged that it could not be repaired. Weaving together strands of fantasy, tradition, and religious duty, Sophiny's reflections were all about tending to her friend, securing the help of the saints, and dealing with the upheaval that Antoinette's leaving would cause.

"How could the Virgin feel cleansed with the blood of two turtle doves on her hands?" Antoinette questioned after she heard Sophiny's concerns about her changing state and read her note. "Death resulting from a violent sacrifice is intended to warn us all against romance."

"You sound like one of those heretics Father Brownell warns us about."

"Sophiny, I know you think my actions very strange," Antoinette said, voicing her impatience as they gathered writing materials before religion class. "But I will not be an accomplice in my own slavery just because I was not born

13

a boy. I will be eighteen in a few months, for Kansas women the age of an adult. If I had been born a boy, I could have inherited my father's land. Men are allowed, even expected to declare their independence from childhood, from guardians, from tradition. Why can't women? I am about to carry my theory into practice." How poised she was.

"What if your plans don't work out? What if you are caught? What if your understanding was not his understanding?" Sophiny paused briefly, pushing back her hair. "What if your mother won't forgive you?"

"Forgive me? My mother deserves no special consideration; she has done nothing but try to get rid of me for the past two years. Who would refuse to see her own daughter, send her to a boarding school, and now threaten to arrange a marriage without even a discussion? Besides, it is premature to talk about what to do should this plan fail."

"You may come up against some complications ..." Sophiny turned and walked toward the stairs, wondering how many steps she would take before Antoinette said anything. *Three.*

"I am planning for that ..."

Shocked though she was by Antoinette's denouncement of her own mother, Sophiny knew it was unlikely her friend would change course, so she hoped for the least damage to occur. After a day of thought, Sophiny was not so charmed by the plan she had heard about the day before. How frustrating, aggravating, and irresponsible could her friend be?

Signaling Sophiny to silence in observation of the rules, Antoinette led the way down two flights of stairs to the St. Cecilia Music Hall and their usual back row seats to wait for Father Brownell's weekly religion class. The pastor had told them many times about his priestly mission, which charged him with handing on the faith. But edifying young women did not have nearly the import of Brother Claude's missionary commission. Father's lectures of late were mostly on Pope Pius X's encyclical against modernism and the evils of trying to reconcile Christianity with science, especially Darwin's theory of evolution. The movement, according to Father Brownell, subjected the Bible to study by modern standards of literary criticism and "a degenerative tendency to treat religion as a myth." But Sophiny had a more immediate, unsubstantiated theory to be concerned about.

So Antoinette thought her mother had already abandoned her. "Do you believe in evolution?" Sophiny penciled on her notepad.

"I believe in my evolution ... having the ability to react to sudden predators or adapting to changing circumstances comes in handy where staying alive is concerned." She wrote in return, interrupted by the appearances of Father Brownell in his black cassock—a sort of black dress right down to his feet—and Brother Claude in his hooded missionary drab. The missionary would be addressing the young women on the history, geography, and people of Brazil, Father Brownell announced.

In all of Father Brownell's lectures, he had never bothered to learn the girls' names, much less look at them. He focused instead on some seemingly huge text written on the glossy oak panels at the back of the hall. Brother Claude insisted that each girl stand, introduce herself, and name the town or city she called home. He seemed to be taking his script from each face before him. Antoinette, ever alert to possibilities for mischief, hurriedly scrawled a note: "You say you are me, and I will say I am you when we stand up! He will never know!" Antoinette's recitation was slurred, and Sophiny's name was barely audible, followed by Prairie Dog, the small town where Sophiny was born. Even so, faint gasps of surprise could be heard around the room as Antoinette collapsed in her chair in a fit of coughing.

Neither Brother Claude nor Father Brownell noticed. At her turn, in spite of her pounding heart that threatened to reveal all, Sophiny looked directly at Brother Claude and announced Antoinette's name as though it were her own, followed by "Wichita," challenging the clergyman to contradict her identity. Though Sophiny had never set foot outside of the state of Kansas, she had a suddenly intimate understanding of what the ocean must be like as wave after wave of turbulent phosphorescent sea flowed over her in the look that he returned.

After the name recitation, Brother Claude began to talk of a terrestrial paradise: the intensity of the light, the brightness of the colors, the richness of the vegetation, the vastness of the landscape, and the beauty of the people. But Brazil was also a land whose potential had been undermined because of the ineffective leadership of a dying monarchy; nature was corrupted by politics.

"Everything in human affairs seems to rest on politics. If we don't get it right, our very survival is at risk," continued Brother Claude.

Sophiny wondered if he was talking about the same kind of evolution Father Brownell referred to. Simplicity and complexity existed side by side. The land and its people had many problems, which made it necessary for the church to maintain as careful a vigil as possible over its flock. The young women of the academy could help by prayer offerings and the parishioners of surrounding churches by monetary contributions. He allowed questions. Antoinette was the first to raise her hand.

"Yes, Miss Prairie Dog, is it?" The students laughed.

Antoinette mumbled Sophiny's name inaudibly and then asked, "Have you ever felt like your life was in danger, like the saints who suffered martyrdom for their faith?"

"No, we follow certain safety measures."

A chattering of voices begged him to tell more, to which he responded, "Such as traveling in pairs to watch out for each other, agreeing on a code word or words that seem innocent in ordinary conversation, having a diversionary tactic in mind."

"What would be a diversionary tactic?" asked Sophiny, not to be outdone by Antoinette.

"An action that reduces threat to another, like acting sick. You especially want to do something that would be against the norms of social behavior—rude or disagreeable; throwing up works. Or look apologetic, nonaggressive, nonthreatening, just a touch of friendliness but not overly familiar. Sometimes it is better to make a socially accepted rather than a defensive gesture, such as, in this culture, putting out a hand to shake. In a tribal society, acceptable gestures would be different. Or when the threat is real, catch the enemy off guard by using a leg or a foot instead of a fist to defend yourself." He gestured with a swift kick that sent the front row into gasps of surprise followed by giggles.

"By tribal society, do you mean you have to worry about raidings and scalpings?" asked Mary Clare.

"Well no, not exactly," he said, shaking his head in animation, "just like we do not have to worry about that in this country any longer."

"Have you ever been imprisoned like St. Paul?" Theora questioned.

"Yes, but I know how to pick a lock, so I didn't have to wait to be sneaked over a wall in a basket."

"How … how do you pick a lock?" asked Antoinette without raising her hand.

"How much of this will be on the test?" interrupted another.

"Your attention to details is a test. If you flunk the life-threatening ones, you could die." His eyes were sharply upon them.

The front row looked stunned. Their pencils stopped moving.

As other hands shot up, Brother Claude smiled and turned his palms outward to stay their questions. "I am afraid this discussion has gotten somewhat off track."

Father Brownell came to his rescue and dismissed the session. "We will continue next week."

Then they were gone, the heavy paneled doors closing in their wake. Female voices buzzed like insects and rang with the hoots, cackles, and caws of subtropical birds.

Sophiny moved through the day, worked on sewing up a pair of child's drawers for the orphanage project that Antoinette had initiated after Christmas holidays, and completed the embroidery sampler of "A stitch in time saves nine," which she considered giving to Antoinette as the return sign that all was well. As she walked about after afternoon prayers, she tried to learn more of Antoinette's history, but Antoinette would add nothing to what she had already communicated—that she was shunning "an atrocious persecution by my family." Antoinette's conversations increasingly referenced oppressions inflicted on her by her mother: denial of her father's legacy and affection, refusal to let her come home for school holidays, lack of economic support. Were her family's atrocities myth or real? Instead Antoinette wanted to talk about a code word to signal danger. They finally agreed on the word *missionary.*

On another walk around the grounds, Antoinette teased, "Even now I can see the peril your heart is in at the very thought of him." Her next topic of conversation was what name she should give to the new person in her own life. She had used terms such as "my intended," "my sweetheart," or "my lover," rejecting each in turn as being too evasive, too emotional, or too vulgar, until she finally settled on "my betrothed." As she said the word, she stopped for a moment and frowned tenderly, like a little girl revealing a secret. The schedule of the day only served to remind Sophiny of how much she had become attached to habits, customs, rules, and the expectations of others. How could Antoinette laugh in the face of propriety and decorum and make this decision about eloping entirely on her own?

A few mornings later, Sophiny raised the same questions as she twisted the oiled dust cloth around and between balusters and handrails of the doublewide staircase outside the chapel. It was a task she had performed every morning after breakfast for the past week. Each student was assigned a house-cleaning chore, which changed bimonthly. The woodwork gleamed with the patina of daily rubbing—allowing no sticking surface for even a mere speck of dust. She supposed that the discipline of daily dusting had the same effect on her own soul.

How had Antoinette known the words to say to a man, much less become betrothed? How curious that she did seem to have difficulty in finding a comfortable word to describe her relationship. Sophiny counted the number of men she had had dealings with. She had four brothers. They talked about food and weather, wheat and livestock, and argued among themselves about costs, about seasonal planting, about land and animal productivity, and most of all about work to be done. Rarely did she listen, much less respond. James, her eldest brother, was slow and deliberate, though never unkind. Andrew, next in line had the accepted role to apply new ploys to tasks at hand. Henry, third in order, seemed unable to resist the urgency of his own thoughts, especially regarding the extraordinary grace and beauty of female creatures he chanced to meet, and he took great pleasure in giving lengthy accounts. Richard, next in age to her, was a pure mercenary with his easy scheming nature and half-baked plans to make money.

All she remembered of her father was his continuous commentary on mortal pains uttered without expectation of solace, much less relief. And conversations Sophiny had with Father Brownell were by approximation. One need only greet him with a simple, "Good morning, good afternoon, good evening, Father, God bless you" in his general direction. She could not remember that he ever said anything in return. There was nothing in this discourse of the nature of true passion. An irresistible desire to know her future significance to another seized her. *What or who ... am I fated for?*

Suddenly the chapel doors swung open onto the landing above, and Brother Claude began to descend the very staircase she was dusting. A thrill of alarm ran through her as she noted his slight start, heard the clatter of a book escaping his hand, felt the vibrations of the perilous heave of his whole person leaning over the rail, looking after his lost book. For a moment, her body hung motionless and slack; then she returned to her first purpose, rubbing the newel on the starting step as though to erase it. *Don't fall. Don't fall. Don't fall,* she said to herself while the heat of excitement burned within her deep enough to send a tremor through parts of her body she was not accustomed to thinking about. A profound silence returned, and when she looked up again, he had continued his descent. She was struck by his energy, his well-proportioned figure even in his monk's robe, and the disciplined independence of his manner. His Remington-like, sinew-in-sculpture poise made him noticeable. She knew about Remington because she had long stared at one of his sculptures in the sisters' guest parlor and wondered what it was doing there with all the pictures of saints.

An agonizing misery, disorder, and delirium raged through her mind until Brother Claude loomed over her as he neared and he was close enough that she could touch him. She heard herself saying, "I was thinking of your mission in Brazil just now, Brother Claude, as a matter of fact offering up my dusting for the conversion of souls." With an acute pang, she was stabbed to the heart by the thought that ten years, twenty years would pass, and she would remember with loathing and humiliation this most ludicrous, most awful moment of her life. No one could have gone out of her way to degrade herself more shamelessly.

"Uh … uh, bless you, my child," he responded; but she noticed the way he lingered with his hand close to hers on the newel post. "Look, would you like to perhaps correspond with one of the young women who attends the mission school?"

"I … I do not know the language." Her eyes locked onto his mouth. His lips were perfect, neither too full nor too thin. Portuguese wasn't the only language she did not know.

"Your reader will not know yours either. Someone will translate." The corner of that fine mouth quirked upward.

"Yes, if you could translate, I would like to write very much, and I could share news of you with students here. Our prayers for your work would have added fervor." Without thinking, she ran the tip of her tongue over her own lips.

"Good … why don't you compose a letter, and I will take it with me when I return."

"When will that be?" She envisioned carving a secret tunnel to Brazil to bring back his saving message.

"Not for weeks yet, and return mail will be even slower. Promise you will not get impatient for a response. God's work cannot be rushed," he said with a slow, gentle smile one would use for a scared child or injured animal. Then he shrugged, glancing around the staircases and hallways moving like filaments of a giant web from the chapel to other parts of the convent. Lowering his voice and drawing even nearer, he said, "But we all have to rely on each other."

Sophiny frowned and floundered, looking for his meaning, "Of course, Brother Claude, and I will look forward to mail time with new anticipation." Sophiny was suddenly struck by the thought that to Brother Claude she was Antoinette, not Sophiny, and Antoinette was almost a newly emancipated being. She reasoned a justification that it did not matter what she did or said. None of this was real. She was playing a part and, like her model, testing her own declaration of new freedom. The thought that her letters would first be read by Brother Claude gave her a convulsive start. "What do you think my reader would like to know about me?" she asked, hoping her question did not reveal her fugitive thoughts.

For a fleeting moment, Sophiny caught a wistful smile, but his response was solemn. "You know that better than I. What do you and your friends talk about? Are you here of your own choice? What is your schedule like? What subjects are you studying? What is your family like? Do your parents support your education? What will you do when you leave school? What are your plans for your future? Are you happy? I am sure a young woman in Brazil could relate to your concerns."

Bumpkin, an inner voice cautioned with a grim flash of self-derision. But some portal in her mind had opened, and caution could not rein in the runaway that escaped the once-secure corral. "I will tell her of the handsome missionary who preached about the mysteries of the Amazon and that I hope to learn a great deal more about Amazon women."

When he tried to reply, the sound stuck in his throat and seemed to take some effort to clear. Sophiny felt her real triumph when she saw the effect she had on him. Instead he turned away to retrieve the book he had dropped over the banister. Waving the book in the air as though to scatter her words and dissolve their meaning, he said, "Reverend Mother requested that I see her this morning. Could you direct me to her office?"

"Of course, this way." Sophiny was actually walking with him down the long hallway to the west wing. What a distance off it seemed. She moved like a woman in bonds: past the music practice room, past the priest's dining room, past the guest parlor, past the bursar's office. But too soon they arrived. She pointed to the correct doorway with the sensation of dealing with dream vapors, and then at the last moment he extended his hands to cover hers. She was aware that she was the object of his graciousness.

"Well, there you are, appointed official missionary to solicit prayers on my behalf. Remember to sign your name and include an address in your letter." His eyes penetrated hers in a very unbrotherly fashion, and his hands were warm and strong around hers. Then he released her hand and gaze and turned away. "I am looking out for your interests too, you know."

It seemed as if all of a sudden a pair of wings had grown on her shoulders. She skimmed along the polished floor to return to her dusting and with great effort, focused on another character-building joy of all students, the scheduled handwritten exam, this one on the morality play *Everyman.* God, discouraged by mankind's neglect of spiritual matters, demanded a reckoning of Everyman. *What would it be like to go on a journey with death? Would he talk to me or just look grim?*

After a half hour of fevered scribbling, she felt the peculiar slight ache in her forearm as she struggled to find answers to questions such as, "Does this sixteenth-century play still have relevance to us today?" Her first response had been a firm and uncompromising *yes,* but it soon became clear that there were not enough of these thoughts to fill the allotted time or page length. So she deliberately made her handwriting deteriorate to appear that she could have written much more if only she had had the time, but unfortunately she did not. She doubted Sister Margaret would be taken in, but it was all a rite of passage, a kind of game. What if Everyman had a sister? How different would the story have been?

Chapter 4
Acts of Deception

At the end of the school day, Sophiny trudged down the stairs. With scant solace, she replayed fragments of her exchange with Brother Claude. Instead of a beam of approval when she related the incident, she was subjected to a critical review. "You goose, have you taken leave of your senses?" demanded Antoinette when told of the plan to communicate with Brother Claude. "He thinks you are me and I am you. If you use my name, all those letters will be read by Sister Louise, especially after I am gone."

Sophiny flinched. She had not considered this complication. "I will have to tell him my name."

"No, you will not. Promise you will not tell him your real name. Sister Louise will get involved in all this …. Let me think. What can we do? How can we use this? How did you do on the written exam?" Antoinette asked, suddenly changing the topic and signaling Sophiny to silence as she began to pace up and down in the cloakroom. Then she stopped, looked around for eavesdroppers, and led the way through the thick, heavy door to the front of the five-story building. They walked for some time, distancing themselves from other girls who were shivering in clusters or briskly striding around the grounds in pairs. From outside, Mount St. Mary's resembled a fortress, impregnable, built on the rise of a hill amid a great expanse of lawns, gardens, and orchards, all surrounded by an iron-gated stone wall at the foot of the hill. The solidity of the building conveyed an aura of stability that suited the convent's purposes. It allowed the inhabitants inside an unhurried pace and unworried approach to all questions, knowing that time and earthly travail would not erode the linking of heaven and earth, time and eternity from one generation to the next.

But solidity was not Antoinette's concern on this winter afternoon in February. Sophiny suspected that Antoinette was about to hatch a new plan. She was a changeable girl, multicolored like a fire that could leap in any direction at any second, unaffected by the chill of winter. For Sophiny, time was fleeting, and in her hurry to keep up, she generated her own heat, bouncing up and down on the balls of her feet to keep warm. "We'll write letters and sign every girl's name. When Brother Claude goes back to Brazil, he'll have a whole packet. Then I could write to you and be your Brazilian correspondent. You will be sure to get my letters because they will be good for your spiritual growth, and I'll tell you all about the geography of Brazil. No one will suspect. Oh, Sophiny, you are my dearest friend."

Sophiny thought how difficult it was to spend just an hour a week writing letters home; her nails necrotized after all the blots, smudges, and fingerprints. She would even smell of ink. "It would be easier to ask Sister Louise for each girl to write a letter to a Brazilian girl. We don't have time to write fifty-five letters."

How was it that Antoinette always managed to usurp her ideas and bandy them about as though they were common property? It was not fair. Antoinette was going to get what she wanted. Sophiny was not. Even if Brother Claude wrote to her, she would never get his letters now.

"How is Brother Claude going to translate them all?" Sophiny grumbled. "Sister Louise will probably decide that is a good reason to make us all learn Portuguese, and she will find someone to give us lessons. You know how she is about keeping us well rounded, and you will not be here for the torture. I am so awful at Latin. How can I learn Portuguese? Besides, what will Brother Claude think when I hand him all those letters?"

"All right, but you got us into this, and you have to work it through. I cannot be involved. It would be better if we didn't go directly to Sister Louise. We will tell …" She corrected herself, "You will tell Sister Louise that Sister Mary Charles is letting us do a special geography lesson, and we can write the letters in class tomorrow."

"Maybe Sister Mary Charles will tell Sister Louise."

"Even better! That will work if she does. In any case, Sister Mary Charles will give the letters to Sister Louise to give to Brother Claude, so you won't have to talk to him again." Antoinette looked at her with satisfaction, as if awarding top marks.

Sophiny listened with her mouth open. At Antoinette's last words, she exhaled in startled protest; a billowing white breath hung visibly between them in the cold air. Like her objection, it was soon brushed aside, "But I *want* to talk to Brother Claude again."

"You are an idiot. I am saving you from being completely stupid. He is a religious man who has taken vows, celibacy included. Go find Sister Mary Charles right now. Tomorrow we will just say we had her approval today."

Sister Mary Charles was a permanently benevolent woman who never remembered from one day to the next what lesson she had covered without checking her notes. But when corrected, she easily and graciously shifted to another lesson as though all her lectures were filed away in her brain and needed no preparation other than retrieval under a keyword. Aging only enhanced her long-term memory. Sophiny found her in the main kitchen dunking a cookie in a hot, steamy mug of coffee thick with cream. As she raised the cookie to her lips, it broke, leaving a soggy lump and brown stains on the white half-circle of gimp that covered her breast. "Sit down, my child, and have a cookie," she commanded, unembarrassed at being observed. She called all the young women "my child," probably because she could not remember their names, but each of the girls felt a special endearment to Sister Mary Charles and forgave her memory lapses as a result.

Sophiny reached for a cookie—oatmeal molasses, her favorite—and sat down. After swallowing a mouthful and allowing time for Sister Mary Charles to sponge herself off, she began talking about Brazil, using phrases she remembered from Brother Claude's lecture. "It would be so wonderful to find out about Brazil and Brother Claude's work. Maybe tomorrow during class, you could let us write letters that he could take with him and exchange with his students at the mission school in Brazil." There, she said it!

"Are we on the unit about South America right now?"

"Just about, I think, but Brother Claude will be gone by then. May we cover it earlier? Brother Claude said he needed our prayers and …"

"Yes, my child, a most delightful proposal. I will make arrangements with Sister Louise. Would you write that down for me?"

"Can I go with you … to talk to Sister Louise, I mean?"

"Now is not a good time. I will talk to her this evening at recreation. Perhaps she could have Brother Claude come and write some Portuguese phrases on the board for us."

Sophiny could not believe her luck and quickly scribbled the reminder. The plan was falling into place, and she would see Brother Claude when he came to her geography class. "You will not forget, will you, Sister?"

Sophiny was embarrassed at her own boldness, but Sister Mary Charles's eyes twinkled as she shook her head in response. "Now scoot, and don't tell anyone I spoiled your supper with cookies. Tomorrow we will talk about Brazil."

"May I have one more cookie?" Sophiny asked even as she scooted, and anticipating no objection, helped herself.

The soil has been cultivated and promises
to yield an abundant harvest.

Your vassal

Sophiny penciled a note along, with the extra cookie, to slip to Antoinette.

The next morning Sophiny hurriedly finished her tasks and then waited impatiently through two classes. The exhibition of student work suspended upon the wall in long rows—essays, examination papers, drawings—represented their work in the subjects taught: religion, reading, math, geography, grammar and composition, drawing, history, Latin, chorus, decorum, and Bible history and Scripture. The total effect was that the academy's pupils did very neat work, intended to arouse a sense of pride in the school as a whole.

Sophiny had an interest in neat work. Order had always intrigued her—especially how other people managed to arrange things with seeming ease. She even thought that by coming to the academy, she would become orderly. But order evaded her, and so did getting her work hung for all to see. She soon turned her attention elsewhere. Her assigned desk by the door allowed her a view of the hall, on which she vainly focused, hoping for a glimpse of Brother Claude in passing. He had given her a long, studied look at communion during the early-morning mass. To her great disappointment, Sister Mary Charles entered the third-period classroom alone. Had she forgotten? Antoinette was looking at her, a curious contest emerging on her face.

"Young women, I had a most interesting request for a special unit on Brazil," Sister Mary Charles announced. "I spoke to Brother Claude, our visiting missionary, about coming this morning to talk with us, but he has another engagement elsewhere." After listening to a brief summary of Brazil's mountains, rivers, seas, and rainforests, the girls were encouraged to write letters. Just as Sophiny had paused after the comma in the closing, wondering what name she should use, Brother Claude walked through the door. A strange, exciting sensation fluttered within her, and she started to leave her seat before she recollected herself and dropped her gaze, holding her ground. What was it about him that made her feel all giddy and silly? She reread what she had written:

To my dear new friend in Brazil,

We at Mount St. Mary's are all in the highest spirits about making new friends and learning something of your far away country. I do hope Brother Claude has some kind things to say about his stay at our academy and meeting us, as he has many positive things to say to us about you. However, he did not tell us exactly what your life was like, and so I have many questions for you …

Brother Claude apologized for not being able to arrive sooner but assured them that he would be happy to take their letters. At that he turned to Sophiny, smiling and reaching out his hand to take hers first. She liked the smooth bronze skin of his arm. "You forgot to sign your name." An amused grin curled his lips—amused and just a little devilish as he proceeded down the aisle collecting other letters. Sophiny felt an ache in her core, unexpected and unstoppable, which prompted her to turn around following him with her eyes until Antoinette's insistent glare focused her attention elsewhere. "Sign my name," she mouthed and pantomimed writing a signature. With resignation Sophiny signed *Antoinette Dominguez,* not even attempting to imitate her friend's ornate script, and handed over the letter. She dared not challenge Antoinette's plan. But it seemed forgery was not all that was required of her.

During the Saturday-morning chore of hand-washing her drawers and the cotton squares that she had to scrub once a month, Antoinette not so subtly slipped a note into Sophiny's pocket. As Sophiny arranged her garments on the clothesline, she wondered guiltily, *What would it be like to watch a public hanging*? Furtively, she waited until no one was around to read the message:

We well know how to remove spots, whiten linen, protect
from moths, and wash laces, but what we have not learned
is a remedy for the misfortune of getting burned. Fire itself
is remedy and protection. For your sake, you must ignite
a fire that will burn away memory of our friendship.

Fire in the belly

"Fire in the belly?"

What was Antoinette asking her to do now? Bewildered and unable to get an explanation, she thought about the morning reading for the saint of the day. February 12 was St. Eulalia's feast day. St. Eulalia was a thirteen-year-old Spanish girl who suffered martyrdom at the hands of a Roman emperor. Some of the thirteen tortures included putting her into a barrel with knives stuck into it and rolling it down a street, cutting off her breasts, crucifixion on an X-shaped cross, and finally decapitation, during which a dove flew from her neck. The reading, followed by a breakfast of scrambled eggs, toast, and dishes of prunes washed down by coffee or milk, provided the day's fortification. It was after all a remarkable account of the marvelous constancy, strength, endurance, and virtue of women. No man could call St. Eulalia fickle, flighty, weak-hearted, or least of all, lacking in stamina even though she lacked the protection that, in lieu of the law, her society promised for women. Everyman could learn a great deal from this woman. These outrageous acts perpetrated on Eulalia effectively demonstrated the malice and vice of her accuser.

"Please, St. Eulalia, help my friend," Sophiny prayed, even as she savored the saint's story. She took extra care to make notes, mindful that she might be asked to surrender her pocket notebook in future.

St. Eulalia, a Christian maiden of Barcelona, Spain, suffered martyrdom under Emperor Diocletian. Her day in the calendar is February 12. If the sun shone bright on this day, the ensuing season would be rich in fruit. The sun is shining. Hope we shall have a good fruit crop. If it is water you need, for fires or crops or for doing laundry, she is the patron of drought.

Fire out

Though Sophiny attempted to pass on her note, she did not get a chance to ask exactly what Antoinette's earlier communication meant. Instead Antoinette turned abruptly and unfurled, "I need you to throw a major hissy fit." Noting that several girls were within hearing distance, she raised her voice, "Really, Sophiny, your ignorance is breathtaking. I am afraid I might catch it if I talk to you much longer."

Sophiny was astonished by her snub, as were the other students. She noted that Sister Louise had moved within hearing distance. By the inquiring eyes and lowered voices of the students around, she knew their attentions were shifting. Antoinette signaled with her eyes and said under her breath, "Fight with me."

Sophiny could only think of the saint story still on her mind. "So you do not think St. Eulalia really went through thirteen tortures? It is a fable—a lie? Is that what you think?"

"Not a lie exactly. It is an allegory. Did we not just finish reading *Everyman* about the battle between opposites, questions of conscience or choices between extremes of good and evil?"

"It is a saint's story. It has to be true."

"*Simplicio.*" Antoinette jabbed Sophiny's forehead with her outstretched fingers.

"*Paganus.*" Sophiny jabbed back at Antoinette's chest.

"Are you questioning my faith?" Antoinette's raised voice, forward lean, and clenched fists had gained Sister Louise's entire attention.

"Are you questioning my intelligence?" Sophiny mirrored her friend's decidedly accusatory gestures.

"What is this all about?" interrupted Sr. Louise.

"Ask Sophiny; she started it," deflected Antoinette.

"Sophiny?"

Reluctant to take responsibility, Sophiny took a second to answer. "Don't you want to do this by seniority?"

Sister Louise suppressed a look of impatience, "I assure you, I suspect both of you. Let us take this a step at a time. Sophiny, you first since you are younger."

"Since when did being younger count in firsts?"

"I was giving you the presumption of innocence, but if you would rather …" She did not like evasions.

"I am sorry, Sister Louise, I did start it. Why is Antoinette questioning the lives of the saints? Perhaps Brother Claude, who is a missionary expert at working with mind battles of this sort, could save her."

"Antoinette?" Sister Louise nodded, giving her a chance for correction. Sophiny noted with satisfaction that Antoinette was too shocked to respond, but a second glance revealed she was suppressing an explosive case of the giggles. "I am waiting."

Antoinette raised her head still choking, "Perhaps Sophiny is right, I should talk to someone about my doubts. Send me to Brother Claude then."

Sister Louise was not easily surprised but paused as though seriously considering the suggestion. "Let me remind you, it is unworthy of a student of this academy to call another names."

Sophiny, dismissed, silently turned one way as Antoinette turned the other. The students around them noticed but pretended not to.

After supper during recreation, Antoinette was called away by Sister Louise and remained absent for the entire hour.

Sophiny sat at the library table in evening study period not studying as she waited for Antoinette to return. As soon as Antoinette appeared on the stairs, she pretended interest in the library shelves, forcing herself to scrutinize the titles of the novels. Was there one she had not yet read? Antoinette hesitated momentarily near her chair. "*Paganus*?" she hissed at Sophiny.

"*Simplicio?*" Sophiny hissed back. Antoinette spun around before her eyes and headed for one of the empty classrooms. Sophiny was disappointed to see that Mary Clare and Theora rose and followed. She was being replaced.

Somewhere during the rotation of turning back bedspreads, taking baths, replacing uniforms with nightgowns, and night prayers, Antoinette had managed to leave a note on Sophiny's pillow.

Fair, sweet friend,

I am sorry for blaming you for starting a quarrel, but I couldn't think of anything. How did you think of that story so fast? Meet me in the toilet alcove after lights are out.

Oh brilliant flame

Sophiny stilled the pulse of anticipation by counting Sister Mary Charles' *God bless yous* as she made the night rounds, checking each bed before she turned out the lights. Then she counted to sixty five times before slipping her feet onto the cold floor.

"What happened?" she whispered as soon as Antoinette made certain the alcove door was closed and the stalls were empty. A nightlight in the toilet area was just bright enough to see by.

"It was so much fun being you, Sophiny. I told Brother Claude I was in love with him."

Sophiny could feel the blood drain from her face as a small *oh* escaped her.

"You should see your face … but I shouldn't be teasing you. Actually I asked him how he knew he was meant for the life he had chosen. He asked me, 'What is this about your crisis of faith?' I told him I should have faith because in fact most of my life I have been taken care of and surrounded by those who love me and support me, but I was having doubts about my future."

"What did he say?"

"Blind faith is not always a good thing. *Doubt is the beginning of wisdom.*"

"And then what?"

"He said that anything I tell him, he would consider a total confidence."

"Like the seal of confession?"

"Like that, I guess … but I could not tell him. Nothing he can do or say can drain the vast pool of my doubts. Besides, what if he thought it was his duty to say something to Sister Louise?"

"I was kind of hoping he could change your mind or help you find a way to—"

"Is that what you were up to?"

"What *I* was up to? You could have warned me about what *you* were up to. That is the best I could do on the spot. We could have really been in trouble. How did you like the distraction?"

"Dear, sweet friend, you were stunning. Now that I think about it, our visiting missionary does not seem like he belongs to a religious order. He asked me about my friends, about Antoinette … how well I knew her. How odd. When I asked which saints were his order's patrons, he didn't seem to know. I wonder why he is really here. It was like he wanted me to doubt him."

Sophiny was relieved, on the one hand, that she did not have to worry about a rivalry with regard to the missionary; on the other hand, Antoinette intended her surprise thumping to set the stage for a prolonged and messy fight that would burn away all memory of their friendship for the students and so protect Sophiny from questions after she left. To that end, the quarrel continued in the days following.

"How could you embarrass me so? I had to sit and listen to Brother Claude's lecture on faith until I was in tears. It was humiliating, and I will never forgive you." Antoinette's next confrontation created the full-blown spectacle she had promised.

"I am your friend. I love you, and I care about you." Sophiny's sincerity was real.

"Some friend. It is nice to be so loved," Antoinette said bitterly. "Did you hear the devil screaming when you ratted on me?"

"How right you are to worry. One hears such horrors. But do not forget to close your own mouth as added protection."

"I will do that where you are concerned." Antoinette covered her mouth with her hand.

"Just because you are two years older than I am does not mean you too cannot be an idiot." Sophiny was still smarting from the time Antoinette had so labeled her. The two looked at each other in a staring contest, aware that they had the attention of all in the room. "Is that it then? You are not going to talk to me anymore?" Sophiny made clear Antoinette's meaning.

Though Antoinette removed her hand, her lips remained pressed together by way of response. But as she turned her back, she flung her hand in the air.

31

"How many here are in love with Brother Claude?" Sophiny was at first angry at the exposure, but almost every hand in the room went up.

Intended instruction for Antoinette's crisis of faith became remedy for others as well. "Sister Louise, I am having some doubts about my faith. Do you think I might speak with Brother Claude?" Sophiny overheard several students make particular requests until Sister Louise became suspicious and announced a general lecture to be given by Brother Claude on topics for their edification.

Antoinette was either surrounded by other girls during recreation or bent over, scribbling in her pocket notebook. Sophiny knew the distancing strategy was part of her plan to make their friendship appear estranged, but even so she felt like she was shuffling on uneven ground.

Sophiny watched her friend busily obsess over her writing. Antoinette sat facing the window, holding herself straight on the edge of her seat. First she would lean slightly on her left elbow, and with head somewhat bent, watch her dip-pen, its nib forever bending and breaking, as it moved over the paper until bled dry by the straight lines of angular handwriting. Then the little glass inkwell on the top of her desk with watery blue ink became her fixation. What was so important that her whole world had turned inky? Her desktop was soaked in ink. It got into her skin, under her nails, and even into the white sleeve of her uniform blouse.

Sophiny felt Antoinette's touch as she went quickly past her down the stairs on the way to afternoon tea and mail call, Mary Clare or Theora in her wake replacing her as Antoinette's number two and number three.

"Look at my callus," Sophiny heard Antoinette say with a certain pride, indicating to Mary Clare the skin of the side of her middle finger that rubbed against the wooden handle of the pen. Sophiny felt her own finger and knew that the measure of her diligence by the thickness of the callus did not equal her friend's, and she longed for it to grow bigger.

After mail call, Mary Clare, Theora, and Antoinette linked arms to stroll around the grounds as they read lines from *Romeo and Juliet*, their reading assignment for the week. When the walking began to interfere with their understanding of the play, they stopped near a statue in the big, rocky, cavernous grotto, becoming even more dramatic, attracting other students who wanted, at first, to listen and then to participate. Theora returned to the classroom for more books, while Mary Clare began to assign reading parts. She gave herself the part of Romeo and Antoinette the part of Juliet. "You can be the nurse," Mary Clare indicated to Sophiny, "or would you rather be Mercutio?"

"Who are they?" Sophiny asked in all innocence.

"The nurse is a traitor, and Mercutio a subversive."

"I'd rather be the traitor."

"We thought you would be best in that part too."

The cluster of girls held court, circled around the grotto statues, entertaining each other with a story of true love on St. Valentine's Day. The place was damp and cold, but Sophiny could feel the excitement of the staging and even a little jealousy at being bumped to the sidelines. The fading sunshine and creeping winter haze roused in her a bit of wistfulness as she read the nurse's lines following Juliet's mother's reflection on her daughter's "pretty age." Fourteen was Juliet's age of marriage. For Antoinette, fourteen had been the age she had been separated from her mother though by her father's death, not her own marriage.

Mary Clare's comment about the traitorous nurse troubled her. Studying the lines did not ease her mind; clearly the nurse had a dark, hidden nature. The dramatic reading of *Romeo and Juliet* continued throughout the week, as did discussions of the meanings of lines. Antoinette, Mary Clare, and Theora planned a Sunday-evening performance and found an audience by enlisting Sister Margaret, who invited the convent residents. The students would have costumes but not sets or memorized parts. *Will Brother Claude be there? How will Antoinette manage to conceal her identity if the hand-printed program identifies performers?* Sophiny wondered even as the players continued to argue about the role of the monk and whether they could get Brother Claude to play the part.

The image of Brother Claude as he seemed to be pleading with her kept popping up unbidden but clear and distinct in Sophiny's mind. One morning while she was dusting the stairs, he had come to her with deliberate purpose. "If you need to talk or if I could be *of use* to you in any way, please contact me. … I know I am a stranger to you, but I am aware of your situation." He had handed her a card handwritten with his name and a telephone number. Then he strode away before she could respond or ask what he meant. She felt the exhilaration that came from his touch, immediately followed by a fit of pique. What was this longing that clouded her brain and confused her perception?

When Sophiny tried to convey Brother Claude's message, Antoinette turned her back and said in a loud whisper intended for all in the classroom to hear, "Sophiny, you know I cannot forgive you. Do not think I have forgotten what you did." With a small shriek, she then tossed aside the book Sophiny was trying to hand to her, her note about Brother Claude inside. She had had to scramble to retrieve it. On Saturday as she stood in a line of penitents in chapel waiting to be purged, she wished that Brother Claude could hear confessions. She would tell him all, even about her vow. But he was a brother not a priest, and so could not absolve her or ease her conscience. Should she place her note under Antoinette's pillow or wait until lights out? Perhaps Antoinette had changed her mind about eloping. It had not worked very well for Juliet.

On Sunday, the congregation rose as one at the entrance of Father Brownell dressed for sacrifice in the purple vestments of the first Sunday of Lent. Brother Claude, in his dung brown, coarse-wool frock, did not follow him into the sanctuary. The realization that she even held her breath with anticipation startled her. Why did the absence of that mysterious man so disappoint her? Had he gone back to Brazil, taking the Mount St. Mary's Academy students' letters with him? And why would anyone want to spend months tramping around a reptile-crawling, bug-infested coast in South America in unimaginable hardship, strife, and oppression, getting swallowed up by a jungle or surrounded by tribesmen in face paint pointing arrows at him? His extinction would be a tragedy, but Antoinette's identity was safe for the present.

Not only was the dramatic reading of *Romeo and Juliet* a great success, with standing ovations for the cast, but the essay exams that followed also resulted in high marks for most of the students. Once *Romeo and Juliet* was dispatched, the assignment for *Frankenstein* commenced.

By this time, Sophiny and Antoinette had arranged a regular after-lights-out meeting time near the toilet alcove nightlight. "You know, I think I would make a good lawyer," Antoinette said when the subject of their futures came up again.

Sophiny regarded her for a moment. "If you really want to be a lawyer, you should start practicing your argument skills. You did such a good job with *Romeo and Juliet*. I think you should put Dr. Frankenstein on trial."

"Who brings charges? The victims are all dead." Antoinette sat on the floor with her back holding the door closed.

"How about the monster? Is he not a victim as well?" Sophiny kept her face turned to the wall, not looking at Antoinette. "Dr. Frankenstein tried to bring various pieces of corpses back to life in that strange creature he engineered and then just abandoned him, endangering all of society."

"But the monster committed the murders."

"Yes, but he is a monster because of how he was created—an unnatural being. He didn't know his own strength; he didn't have a place in society or protection under the laws of the land; and he didn't understand how to communicate without harm. So Dr. Frankenstein, as his guardian, is the one responsible for the evil of his actions."

"Guardians … who cause us to lose our way …" Antoinette sat with her head bowed for a moment.

"Brother Claude gave me a card of how to contact him. I think he meant to give *you* a message," Sophiny said gently, and she placed Brother Claude's card in Antoinette's hand.

Antoinette shrugged and gave the card back to her. "I don't trust him."

"Where are you, Antoinette?" Sophiny asked. Her friend seemed far away. "Where are you going?"

"I will not know until I get there … kind of like what happens in a trial."

The next thing Sophiny knew, she was being called *the Monster* and made to submit to a ghastly makeup session. She was happy to pay the premium of being delegated to silence just to be among her classmates. Antoinette was leading the team for the prosecution. Mary Clare was acting lawyer for the defense of Dr. Frankenstein. Theora was the judge. The players were only fairly nice to her so they could better tease her about being a monster. She was filled with a furious admiration for the way Antoinette had pulled everyone together for the project.

The staging of the Frankenstein trial took place before the congregation of sisters and academy students and gained rousing applause, for which Antoinette seemed genuinely happier than Sophiny had seen her in a long time. Before the production, she wished them all well and announced, "I read in a newspaper story that a silent film is being made about Frankenstein. Maybe we can all go see it when it comes out in the movie theater. But it will not be as good as our version."

Theora, acting as judge in a black robe, walked to the seat behind the broad library table at center stage of the St. Cecilia Music Hall. The third- and fourth-year students already crowded onto benches and side chairs murmured among themselves, comparing defense and prosecution notes as they awaited the beginning of the court session. The second years playing court officers and acting roles stood at the ready to enter on cue. Off to her left a knot of first years acting as jury were seated in a row of straight-backed chairs waiting to pass judgment on the spectacle provided by the upper-class women. "All rise," a second year acting as clerk announced, and the commentary ceased as the participants obeyed. "The people on behalf of the monster versus Dr. Frankenstein for murder!"

Theora cast a magisterial gaze over each watching face. When she had their attention, she seated herself, elbows propped on the table, arms folded. "The people acting on behalf of the monster shall render your deposition." At this point Sophiny, charcoal-blackened scars upon her face, hair in a wild tangle, and covered by a black-and-red-stained shroud cast over the lumpy pillow bound to her shoulders, was led by the rope belt tied around her waist and binding her wrists. One after another of her classmates came forward with folded sheets of paper. She gave each a threating stare and an occasional growl. Each speaker spread out a page of copied notes and read aloud a particular passage from the novel, along with a passage from one of the law texts Sister Margaret had been able to locate for them or that Antoinette herself had produced.

"Lawyer for the defense," Theora announced, "you shall examine the defendant."

"Thank you, your honor." Antoinette was confident. "My pleasure. Dr. Frankenstein, defendant, shall submit to examination!"

"Dr. Frankenstein, you stand accused of the following charges. You have sworn an oath, and I expect you to tell the truth."

The exchange of arguments, of readings for evidence, and of citations from law codes went smoothly until at last the focus turned to the jury. But as the first-years began debating the merits of the arguments from both sides, Sophiny saw trouble ahead. This part had clearly not been worked out. Their debate seemed to be going nowhere. Time was almost up, and neither a guilty nor a not-guilty decision seemed eminent. The third and fourth years were beginning to look nervous, as this unpredictable ending marred their performances. The project lacked climax. Sophiny rose as though sleepwalking, her bound hands stretched out before her, until she reached Dr.

Frankenstein's chair. The stage banter ceased. She had their full attention as she placed her hands around Dr. Frankenstein's neck as though to strangle her. Her classmate cooperated with this impromptu conclusion and slumped to the floor as though dead. The monster had secured its own justice. As the chaos on stage grew, gasps from the audience exploded into laughter and applause. The jury unanimously shouted, "Guilty." And "The monster is guilty too." Then they surrounded Sophiny so she could not escape. The shocking ending had been found pleasing.

Chapter 5
Way of Discipline

Being inflamed by the fires of earthly desire, vexed by the passions of carnal nature, and consumed by temptation, I abandon the way of discipline. Unworthy to receive the crown of martyrs, this day I go to seek the consolations of this world. Gentle reader, I warn you, love shall not be my downfall, but pernicious ownership keeps me on my guard and is the source of my disparagement. This journey and contemptuous treatment, hardship, hard work, torments, and opprobrium, all these will I bear with calmness until that day of maturity when I can again return to my own domain.

I entreat and beseech you to destroy all communications between us. Let no word of what you know pass your lips until I correspond further.

Love and legacy

"Love and legacy," mused Sophiny as she read Antoinette's most recent note, passed as she was busy at her new charge, cleaning the toilet alcove in the dormitory. Was Antoinette leaving soon? Reading and rereading the note triggered a succession of images.

Promises Antoinette had extracted from her: "You must say that your trunk is mine and mine is yours if anyone asks. You must not look at what I have put in the trunk. Do not let my important papers fall into anyone's hands but mine. Vow to me, upon our friendship."

Secret meetings after lights out in this very toilet area: "Antoinette, are you sure you want to elope? You are such a good student, so good at everything …"

"How can I do something so wrong? It takes a good girl to be bad." A smile had tugged at Antoinette's lips. "Remember, I am pretending to be you, so in a way *you* are doing these things, not *me*."

"I would not do these things," Sophiny had protested.

"But you would. You always act, especially the *you* I know would act. Just like the *Antoinette* I know would be too terrified to act."

Antoinette had a way of always making places more interesting by her very presence, for even the dimly lit toilet alcove had suddenly taken on a secretive, seductive atmosphere surrounding Sophiny in an exotic intrigue. She had waited for Antoinette to go on, but the teasing light in her bright eyes faded, replaced by a serious, somber intensity. Her friend seemed to have come to the end of her negotiations.

Fear and sorrow over Antoinette being left without protection: "Vow to me that you will not keep me in the dark for too long about your whereabouts," Sophiny had demanded.

Antoinette had nodded her agreement.

"Say it out loud! The way you made me vow."

"I vow to let you know my whereabouts as soon as I can. I would hate to think of you sitting in chapel, day after day worried about me."

"I will not see you fainting, terrified, screaming … but I will imagine it, do not forget." Sophiny sought to impress on her the distress she would cause if her absence endured.

Omens and portents: the initial exchange of trunks and keys was to conclude with the return of Sophiny's sampler. Antoinette's signal that all was well: "A stitch in time saves nine."

"Love and legacy"—Antoinette's closing message from the note Sophiny had hastily slipped into the cuff of her sleeve as she followed the other girls downstairs to morning classes. It wouldn't do to be late. On March 15, Sister Louise's feast day, a special tribute had been planned for first period. Perhaps the celebration would assuage her growing unease that Antoinette had not told her all. Could there be something else to her plan? But try as she might, her unease grew throughout the day. At afternoon mail call, she observed Antoinette sharing the *Concord Chronicle* society page with Mary Clare and Theora. But most of Sophiny's attention was on her own letter from her brother James. Her mother was getting worse.

The coming of night did not provide respite. As Sophiny put her head on her pillow, she felt something hard inside the case next to her ear— Antoinette's key—the signal that she would be leaving soon. *Is this the night?* The fantasies that kept crowding in upon her increased her anxiety and made sleep impossible. She got out of bed and looked down the center aisle extending the entire top floor dormitory of the five-story building. The rows of beds on either side were separated not by walls but by white curtains, now pulled. Carefully avoiding squeaking floorboards, lest she rouse her sleeping classmates, Sophiny grabbed her blanket and tiptoed to an alcove window, where she could look down over trees and walls to the street bordering the front of the academy. The night was clear and fine. There was a moon as cold and distant as the barren grounds upon which it shone. She wanted to think of Antoinette's safety, of her mother's illness (she could pray for them both), of the Latin vocabulary list that she needed to memorize: *periculosus:* hazardous, dangerous; *infestus:* aggressive, hostile.

As she sat by the window wide awake, a most unexpected thing happened. Out of the shadows below her crept a cloaked female figure. Ever so slowly from the edge of the wall near the entrance gate emerged a taller figure, distinctly male. The two moved toward each other in the moonlight. They embraced briefly and then melted into the shadows and were gone. Sophiny pressed her face to the window, blinked, and strained her eyes in the darkness. This is how love for Antoinette should be, an extravagant gesture: elopement on March 15, the feast day of St. Louise de Marillac, in the middle of the night. In the distance she heard the sound of a horse and buggy and caught a brief glimpse of its passage beyond the barred gates. Was Antoinette in the arms of her betrothed?

Then as she was about to turn away, a slight movement in the darkness across the street caught her attention. A tree blowing in the wind? But the trees were skeletal, spring leaves barely in bud stage and not easily blown. Could it be a man, disappearing into the shadows? Her overactive imagination again! She shook off her unease. Still she cast an uneasy glance back across the street. The figure was not from her imagination. The sound of a motorcar on cobblestone preceded the headlights through the wrought iron gate of a driver heading in the direction of the horse and buggy.

Though wrapped in a heavy blanket, Sophiny began to shiver uncontrollably. The darkness of the high-ceilinged room closed around her as if waiting for the end of the story. She hoped the lovers' destination was not far. Throughout the night she felt ill. At times she was feverish, at times she ached all over. And she didn't seem able to get warm. In the early-morning hours, she felt as though she might really fall seriously ill. Alternately she wished that morning would come soon and that morning would never come.

But the morning came on schedule. When the rising bell sounded and the electric lights went on as if connected, she lay in bed as though this were her first day in school, that awful day when she didn't know the schedule, where things were, or the other girls' names. Worst of all she missed home. That day Antoinette had become her sister and Mount St. Mary's her home. *How had it happened?* When the long school day had finally ended, the girls had gathered in the refectory for afternoon tea, cookies, mail, and conversation. Sophiny held back, watching the others, fearful of the dam of tears ready to overflow. When she at last approached the refreshment table, there were only three molasses oatmeal cookies on the plate. Just as she timidly came forth, Theora and Mary Clare swooped in, leaving only one. Antoinette and Sophiny looked at each other over the one that was left. Sophiny quickly picked up the plate saying, "This must be yours. I do not much care for molasses oatmeal cookies."

Antoinette had laughed a magical sound, given Sophiny a hug and said, "I doubt that, but I'm going to take care of you, new girl. Do you like chocolates? Your picture is on my candy box. What is your name?" Like a spark on dry wood bursting into flame, Sophiny adjusted and became established at the academy all at once.

Somehow she did manage to get out of bed, dress, and line up with the other girls in the queue wrapping around staircases and hallways down four flights of stairs in sinuous movement like a serpent to the chapel on the second floor. When she looked at Antoinette's place in chapel and saw it vacant, an intense loneliness acted like a dampening cloud on her brain. She had a morbid vision of Antoinette frozen to death, laid out on frost covering the front grounds, of Antoinette floating upward from a well, of Antoinette white and still in a coffin. Why had she not tried to stop her? Had Brother Claude been trying to give Antoinette a message that could have saved her? Her guilt weighed so heavily that she supposed she would surely arouse suspicion. Perhaps she could yet right the deception by telling Brother Claude she was not Antoinette. As the academy students in two-by-two formation filed down the center aisle, the pipe organ filled the foot-shuffling silence until the cantor's voice joined in. Sophiny blocked out both at the thought of Sister Louise mercilessly pricking, probing, and prying at her secret until all was apparent.

The image of Antoinette dead was replaced by the vision of Antoinette cloaked and muffed, rushing past dark rooftops, closed doors, shuttered windows, and trees barren against the leaden skies. Men in greatcoats and hats hurried about their business; Antoinette hurried about hers. At breakfast, Antoinette was missed. Sophiny waited with creeping dread to be called into Sister Louise's office and asked what she knew. Paralysis overtook her; the debate with herself over Brother Claude's revelation and absence and the long night without sleep had drained her.

Mary Clare was the first to be summoned. She came out with her eyes reddened and dabbing a handkerchief at her nose. Theora was next. Had Antoinette shared her secrets with other classmates? When Sophiny was called, she looked at the preternatural sharpness of the ridge of the headmistress's nose, the deep cavities in her cheeks, and sensed the disembodied spirit of a woman mastering her flesh for the greater good of her soul. Sister Louise (tall, angular, quiet) was a woman who burned the candle at both ends. Absent was the usual prim smile of greeting that she allowed herself in discourse with her charges. She questioned in a solemnly hollow voice devoid of emotion as she prepared to dissect the veracity of her response, "Sophiny, do you know anything of the whereabouts of Antoinette Dominguez?"

Life could hold horrible moments; Sophiny's repressed guilt set her face and made her voice curt and unemotional while she issued her declaration that the two of them had not been speaking for the past weeks because of an earlier argument—a fact that the other girls could attest to. The staging of the quarrel had been such that any further interaction was noted and much discussed. Furthermore, Antoinette's supposed interpretation of St. Eulalia's story as allegory had led to even more lectures on faith and the dangers of modernism, a movement attempting to tear down structures that had been put in place to safeguard them all.

"I must ask you to release any correspondence or journal entries you have made over the past several weeks. You and Antoinette seemed to be very close in the past. I am sure she has let you know something, even if not consciously." Sophiny had prepared for this request and quickly handed over her pocket notebook titled "Memory Gems," her collection over the past month of autograph verses. As soon as she had heard of Antoinette's plan, she had begun to copy all the verses she had seen students write on saint's cards, on bookmarks, on Valentine's greetings, and in memory books, trying to cheer herself. She had had to search through her notebook for most of them. A few she remembered, some she had received herself. Others she had solicited from classmates. Next to each verse she had written a different student's name until she had collected fifty-five. For Antoinette she had selected her favorite verse:

Sweet! Oh sweet the estimation
When true friends together meet
But the thought of separation
Brings the bitter with the sweet.

Sister Louise absentmindedly fingered Sophiny's pocket notebook, reading the verse. "What exactly happened between you two?" At just that moment, fortunately, a loud, disturbing noise came from the grounds below. Sister Louise stepped to the window and then looked back at Sophiny, saying, "I will speak with you again later. Go back to your charge." Sophiny, relieved that there had been no censure, no accusation in Sister Louise's manner, and having no wish to disobey, fled.

Idle gossip was generally viewed as a useless and demoralizing pastime at the academy. But as Sophiny neared the cleaning closet after her encounter with Sister Louise, she could see evidence of rumor flourishing.

"Young girls, without their mothers to take care of them, are very apt to get into mischief," Theora was saying.

Sensational plots along with the smell of cleaning agents spread throughout the school as each girl gathered around her cleaning task, freshening it and divining the reasons for Antoinette's disappearance. It was as though each knew exactly what had happened as Antoinette's moral constitution, her practice of virtue, and her exposure to forbidden knowledge were explored. So great a relief did Antoinette's disappearance provide against the dull routine of the daily schedule that her flight was taking on epic proportions. Someone claimed to have seen her get into a car drawn by a pair of winged dragons and carried away in a fiery trail. The saints might even be involved in her disappearance or more likely a demon.

A certain moth-like fatalism kept Sophiny fluttering in the vicinity of the storytellers. She had a great desire to know what the other girls were thinking. At the same time, she vigilantly guarded her own responses and facial reactions. "I do hope she went off to marry someone very rich so that she can just sit from morning to night and never turn a hand unless she has a mind to do it," said Mary Clare. "I think her family is already very rich."

"What if she lost all her money and could no longer pay the tuition to stay here, but she couldn't bear the shame and so left in dead of night in the dead of winter?" ventured Julia, not so optimistic.

"Maybe her disappearance is an act of Sister Louise's pruning," speculated Grace, thinking even darker thoughts.

And Viola voiced another thought: "She probably just got the chicken pox and public health had to quarantine her. She will be back."

After hearing these comments, Sophiny wished that Antoinette had thought in advance to cover up her swift departure with a story that did not include such possibilities for scandal. Was there not something about human erasure that merited serious thought? Intent on adding a more benign explanation, she cleared her throat and sighed in an audible way, thus announcing that her response would be innocuous. "Maybe her mother just came and got her."

"How would you know anything? As I remember, Antoinette was not talking to you … or her mother," Mary Clare reminded her with a certain acerbic tone.

"Maybe she went to Brazil to join the pagans." A twitter of laughter followed Theora's comment.

"She will be writing soon to tell us all about the raidings and the scalpings." Grace gave a whinnying little snort, like a horse.

"*Simplicio.*"

More snorts and more laughter followed as the girls remembered the deception. Sophiny decided not to engage her schoolmates further. But she noted that her theory had been quickly rejected, and suspicious looks were cast in her direction as though she had caused Antoinette's disappearance. The students could hardly be blamed: cannot live with it, cannot live without it. A relationship—broken—was a compelling spectacle and a satisfying topic for their embroidered delectation. Noting the disagreement, Sophiny called upon her patron saint to help her quietly accept the criticism, hold her grudge, and keep on walking. Only the click of rosary beads against Sister Louise's swirling skirt in the hallway could and did deter the heaping helpings of catty remarks and reckless conjecture. They all knew better than to talk about Antoinette where their teachers might overhear.

During the next week, Sophiny was aware of how time crawled. In geography, she thought about how the length of time she waited for a letter might be justly attributed to contrary winds and hostile environments. She could not bear the delay and was twenty times upon the point of hazard, going to Sister Louise and demanding that she release Antoinette's letters. She was very sure that Sister Louise had concealed correspondence, especially after a lecture on Sunday cautioning against writing frivolous and idle gossip to general correspondents. In mathematics she wondered if there was a formula she could use: *average elopement wait time equals average number of couples eloping divided by their actual arrival rate?* But she did not know anyone else who had eloped. All she had thought about for the past month was Antoinette's impending elopement. Now that Antoinette was no longer near, she experienced the strangest sensation of loss and lack of direction. In religion class she wondered, *Has my friend found sanctuary?* The only consolation she received was that Antoinette would be saved, but not in this life, and then she was haunted by the notion that one usually did not meet with the dead again on this earth. The literary works in her reading class did not favor happily-ever-after endings either. Sister Margaret had moved on to Edgar Allan Poe's short stories and poetry.

How is it possible to live when life is so incomprehensible? The longer she stayed at the academy without word from Antoinette, the greater the chances of three things happening: one, the letter might have been or might be intercepted and its contents examined; two, she herself would give something away; or three, tortured by her own thoughts, she would lose her sanity. She was beginning to look on Antoinette as a defector, irrationally perhaps, but because of her relationship with Antoinette, all else was undermined. She had to remain stoic in the presence of the sisters, who now seemed to view every action of the students entrusted to them with suspicion. She had to remain friendless among the other girls because she could not confide in them without deceit. But worst of all she had to monitor her own outrageous imaginings. Every hour that passed was tedious in its lapse; every scheduled activity irksome. She barely spoke to anyone. No longer did prayer afford her the blessed solitude of the past but only increase of worry. She felt herself unworthy to address supplications to the Lord or to the Virgin and instead began to call on all the saints represented in shards of glass in the chapel windows, in the statues in recessed corners, and in the painted images hung on the hallway walls and so cease her suffering. She knew the stories of a hundred saints, their temptations, their bravery, and their final martyrdom. Of them all, the story of St. Eulalia's perseverance, allegory or fact, was strangely comforting.

In her present state, destitute of tranquility, the wait felt endless. Her entire association with Antoinette demonstrated the immeasurable wickedness that flowed from imperfect discipline. Sister Louise turned one of the classrooms into a sewing room/typing room and ordered a room full of new machines. Sophiny found she liked sitting at the typewriter, often spending long study hours taking notes on her reading. As she pecked and poked at the keys, even occasionally smudging her way across the pages with erasure marks, she had the feeling that, for good or evil, what she had done was her own and unique, and with growing satisfaction, she noted her speed and accuracy was getting better. Who needed a writing callus? Her marks on exams improved without it. The written comment from Sister Margaret on her Frankenstein exam pleased her: "Your answers to essay questions reflect a new maturity in thought from earlier work."

It seemed there was something really important about manipulating the machine. From her brain, to her hands, to the machine, her thoughts and ideas were composed on a piece of paper. But her paper had not been placed on the classroom or study hall wall for all to see as an example of outstanding student work. In fact, all the student work, including Antoinette's compositions, had been removed. In their place was an expanded chart of the virtues coming out of a large fountain, along with corresponding vices pictured as though coming from a crater of mud below. How long had Sister Louise and Sister Margaret worked on this?

Sophiny stared at the stream representing hope. The sentiment that distracted her was anything but hope. The longer the troubling silence endured, the more worries came in its wake. Sophiny began to worry about everything in her life. What would she be doing the following year, especially if she were sent home in disgrace? Was Sister Louise satisfied with her protestations that she knew nothing of Antoinette's plans? And what about Brother Claude exposed to the perils and hardships of his missionary journeys? Would she ever hear from him again? Her own mother's illness did not seem to be getting better, as the latest letter from her brother James attested. She longed to go home to see her. Hence arose a thousand scruples to which she had hitherto been a stranger. She was alternately agitated by fear and fatigue. Backsliding into the danger zone, she imagined herself beset by the snares of a spiritual foe, and her only security lay in … virtues? "Virtue is weapon and prize in the warfare of life," Father Brownell was fond of saying, a good first line for her new pocket notebook. Her secrets drained her energy and made her feel a specter of herself. *Has Antoinette been reduced to living in the shadows? Why is she not communicating as she promised?*

What should she write next? She flipped through the blank pages. Her spells of paralysis were increasing in regularity. In a minute she would make herself get up and study the chart more closely. To gather energy, she looked around the common area where the students finished most of their schoolwork. One side of the room was lined with book shelves, another with windows, a third open area of staircases leading up and down and a hallway into the interior of the convent blocked from view by swinging glass doors. A fourth was broken up by the doors leading into classrooms, the bulletin boards where student work used to hang, and the framed chart titled "Virtues" presently hanging in the most prominent position. The virtues, after all, were intended not only as a help in the road to perfection but also a safeguard and protection against faults and delinquencies. What false impressions and erroneous opinions had she fallen into? The theological virtues of faith, hope, and charity formed the top division, followed by the cardinal virtues divided into four principal channels: prudence, justice, temperance, and fortitude. Each of the cardinal virtues was subdivided into several rivulets.

She could not let her whole afternoon slide by in idleness. It was best to ignore the impending sense of chaos and instead cultivate one of those very virtues that perhaps might act as a successor to the anxiety that made her feel like she was living in a habitat for dragons. This thought propelled her into action and gave her a second line for her pocket notebook—the quotation beneath the virtue most closely aligned to her name: "Prudence, the knowledge of what to seek and what to avoid," which was a quote from St. Augustine. She was thinking about giving up her hand-written pocket notebook in favor of binding together her typed notes. Where could she get some string?

Chapter 6
Fodder of Rumor

The days of Lent passed in a fitful way. So intermittent were the signs of spring that the poor sun only made a cameo appearance. And still Sophiny had had no word from Antoinette. Had Sister Louise received anything? She wondered. The academy students and Sisters of Mary stood around the open grave in the cemetery reciting funeral prayers for Sister Bonaventure, whom Sophiny remembered as elderly and wheelchair bound. Earlier a storm had begun to hover over the town with threatening intent. Now, just as Father Brownell assisted Reverend Mother in tossing the first symbolic shovel of earth onto the casket, a clap of thunder broke. A brilliant flash illuminated the whole sky by painting jagged, live filaments. The young women and sisters alike bolted for the motherhouse a quarter of a mile away. But before they could reach the safety of the building, the heavens began a fusillade of pelting rain. Under the sky's assault, heads bent, arms, hymnals, and clothing extended upward as shields, and the dignity of the funeral ceremony gave way to whoops of uncontrolled laughter in sharp contrast to the solemnity of the scene only moments before.

As they entered the vestibule to the St. Cecilia Music Hall and shook off the rain, the girls removed their wet coats and ran to the windows to watch as rain turned to hail and pummeled the earth even more brutally. Spring hail was a worrisome phenomenon for farmers. Sophiny's brothers watched over the tender heads of their newly growing wheat, which in the course of an hour could be wiped out by wind and hail such as this. All of the family's name saints would be called upon to protect them from the devastator that assaulted them. Sophiny's mother would light candles, and the prayers would continue until the threat ceased. "St. Anthony, keep your namesake safe from all the dangers that may befall her," Sophiny prayed, hoping that the age of miracles had not passed.

Her present companions did not share her fears. They were looking out at the storm as though at a delightful amusement. In the midst of the hail, the lightning continued. Each time it came, she could see the trees in the front yard—wind whipped and clinging to the earth as though in danger of being blown away. Her classmates were also looking forward to the special dinner that was prepared on funeral days. The tables would be awash with white linen. Funerals for the sisters were a cause for celebration because in death the soul was rescued from the powers of darkness and transferred into the kingdom of eternal light. Another blessing of old Sister Bonaventure's funeral was that it provided a respite from schoolwork. The privilege of departing from the normal order as well as a special menu somewhat inverted the schedule of the day. Since the storm did not permit outdoor activities, one of the visiting sisters was engaged to give the students a drawing lesson. Spatial ambiguity—trickery—was the topic. Each student was allowed to select an appropriate subject.

After the lecture, Sophiny cloistered herself in the small reading library set apart from the common study area. First she dismissed the thought of penciling in St. Ephraim's advice stenciled over the doorway: "If you apply yourself to reading … after the manner of a wise bee busily gathering honey from flowers, you will draw fruit for the healing of your soul from what you read." *Too long.* Instead, she quickly sketched the bookshelves, receding in the distance, the reading tables getting smaller, and the window at the far end. Her subsequent focus on the ceiling led to thoughts about what a ceiling did: *a ceiling hides or covers or protects or reminds one of limits.* Next she thought about what a floor did: *provides a foundation, a grounding, some kind of stability to move about.* All this thinking was making her feel numb, so she began to thumb through the titles of the books on the shelves and found herself reading *Ramona*, a story of forbidden love by Helen Hunt Jackson. The novel probably was not what Saint Ephraim had in mind. Sophiny felt a melancholic detachment from her own surroundings spread through her as she followed Ramona's tragic romance from page to page into the late afternoon. A good cry was good medicine.

It must have been about three o'clock when she rose to stretch and rest her eyes from reading by peering out the third-story library window, overlooking the front lawns. Though the rain had stopped, the threat continued. She saw a gray squirrel sitting as quietly as a sculptured stone. For a moment it was lifeless; then it hurried noiselessly for cover. A few potbellied pigeons came to their senses and took flight as well. As she heard the muted sounds of activity through the window, she expected to see a deliveryman had startled the squirrel and the pigeons. Instead, she was surprised to see two men emerge from the path and push open the unlocked wrought iron gate.

As they came up the path to the front door, she noted the similarity of their street clothes. They weren't speaking to each other, and their steps didn't match. Both wore black, shapeless hats, overcoats, dark pants, and boots. The first man was slight and quick, weathered of face, with restless movements and sharp, strong features, and was about her father's age when he died. Every part of him was defined: strong hands, thin, bony nose. The other had a familiarity about him, taller than the first, younger, and broader of shoulder; his muscular stride reminded her of ... it was ... could it be? Brother Claude? What was he doing back at the academy and without his religious habit? A shocked, icy chill engulfed her, followed by a wave of heat as the blood rushed to her cheeks. The two men moved under the protective overhang of the front door, and she could see them no longer. The peace of the afternoon fled, as if in the wake of another torrential assault. The vision of this man shattered her being as so many hailstones on a stalk of wheat.

She stood, unmoving for she knew not how long, until the door to the library opened. "Oh, here you are," said Theora. "Sister Louise wants to see you in the guest parlor right away."

"Me? Why does she want to see me?"

"She did not say. Maybe you have visitors."

Her throat tightened against a sudden lurch of her stomach. She had never been this frightened. "But who?"

"Sophiny, are you all right? You are as white as a ghost."

"Just walk me down to the second floor, will you?" she asked, hoping Brother Claude was not waiting for her in the parlor. Increasing dread made her heart hammer as she descended the stairs, and the fingers of her right hand clutched Antoinette's trunk key in her pocket as though it were a talisman that could ward off evil.

Sister Louise drew her into the room and held her by the shoulders, as though to make sure she did not escape. "Is this the student you were speaking of?" she asked, and Brother Claude in disguise stepped forward.

"Antoinette?" asked Brother Claude. Their eyes met, and even in her present terrified state, Sophiny noted that, for the moment, he was too interested to look away.

"No," Sister Louise answered. "This is Sophiny Mumm." Then she turned to Sophiny with a stern look of disapproval. "It appears you and Antoinette were playing some sort of game with Detective Tyler."

"Detective ...?" Sophiny made a slight sound of protest. "I was playing a game? You told us you were a missionary ..."

"That is what we wanted the students to think; my agency was hired to investigate Antoinette's whereabouts, her state of mind, her stay here, and to obtain a copy of her signature … Which I thought I had," here he produced Sophiny's letter addressed to "Dear Miss from Brazil," written and signed by her with Antoinette's name.

"Where is she?" Sophiny's voice was a murmur.

"First you will answer my questions. Did Antoinette suspect she was being watched?"

"I do not think so. But she did wonder if you were a true missionary."

"What aroused her suspicion?"

"You did not know anything about your order's saints …"

The two detectives exchanged looks. "When was this?"

"When Sister Louise sent her to you about her doubts …"

"Ah, yes, and she said her name was …"

"Sophiny." At last he knew her name.

"Sophiny … Sophiny," his eyes flicked to the side, repeating himself. "From Prairie Dog, right?"

"Right." How did he remember where she was from, Sophiny wondered.

"Why was she using your name?"

"Remember that day you came to our religion class? Father Brownell never asks us our names; Antoinette just wrote me a note to say each other's names when you asked as a prank … at least that's what I thought. Is she all right? Have you found her?" Sophiny felt a spark of hope that made her realize how debilitated her fear had made her. Her long weeks of waiting were over. She would soon see her friend.

But Detective Tyler dashed that hope as quickly as it had arisen. "We lost her trail the night she disappeared from here. Perhaps you could tell us where she was going?"

So he was the pursuer in the shadows, and Antoinette had escaped him. Now he wanted to know what she knew. Antoinette had sensed that he was not what he seemed, even dangerous, from the first moment she saw him, but never would she have guessed that he had such diabolical motives. How dare he, a detective for hire, show his face here and pretend friendship for Antoinette on behalf of his client? Was he the cause of Antoinette's disappearance? If he had not pursued her, she would not have had to change her plans, and Sophiny would have heard from her by now. His secret mission might have cost Antoinette her life.

"Please, anything you can tell us might help in her recovery." He stepped to her side and took her hand in a warm, firm clasp. She stared at his hand in revulsion and then raised her eyes to look up into the dynamic features of the deceitful face that had crept about the fringes of her mind since the first smiting in the chapel vestibule. What a cold, cold thing it was to look at him through eyes now scraped clean of the film of delusion. If he had been the one following Antoinette and her betrothed that night, he must know that she had intended to elope. She would not be giving away any secrets or breaking any promises if she admitted that much, and it was better to pretend to cooperate with such a villain than incur further suspicion. "Antoinette was going to elope, but I do not know where she was planning to go." She thought about the meanings of the word detect—*to unmask, to expose, to apprehend*—as she settled on the import of Brother Claude's new identity. Was his name even Claude?

"Elope?" Detective Tyler seemed genuinely surprised. "With whom?"

How could he not know about the elopement after all the fodder of rumor his very appearance had provided and from which she might never recover? But he was a master of disguise himself. He did not know, nor would she tell him, that someone other than she had observed Antoinette's elopement. Had she given too much away? Would she harm Antoinette with this disclosure? She resolved to say no more. "I don't know. She would not tell me anything else, no matter how many questions I asked. Is your name really Claude?" Antoinette's actions had not been empty dramatics after all. She did have enemies, and Detective Tyler could be one of them.

"Yes, it is, Claude Tyler." Detective Tyler dropped her hand abruptly and began a tight circuit of the room.

Then he stopped as the other man spoke for the first time. "Why did she go to such great lengths to conceal a marriage?"

In spite of her resolve to say nothing more, Sophiny could not help but blurt out, "I think her mother was arranging a marriage for her that she did not want."

"She told you this?"

"Her mother wrote her a letter saying as much in November." Sophiny said looking at Sister Louise for confirmation.

Detective Tyler's attention turned to Sister Louise as well, considering her. *Is he wondering if she read the letter? Has Sister Louise revealed Antoinette's history? What other messages has she intercepted?* wondered Sophiny.

But Sister Louise was a closed book; her expression gave nothing away. Instead she turned to Sophiny. "It is time for afternoon prayers; we must join the others. Is there anything else?" she asked Detective Tyler.

"Just thought you might want to see this," he handed her a newspaper clipping dated March 21, 1910, which she subsequently handed to Sophiny.

Mysterious: Young Academy Student
Disappears in the Middle of the Night
A puzzling enigma was presented to the sheriff's office yesterday
when faculty from the Sisters of Mount St. Mary's Academy
Boarding School of Concord where Miss Antoinette Dominguez
(seventeen years old) attended reported that she had disappeared
suddenly. She is the only daughter of the late Antonio Dominguez
and Mrs. Antonio Dominguez of Wichita. Her mother is
unavailable for comment. "Behind her mysterious disappearance
lies a story of domestic unhappiness and a separation from her
mother," says Mr. Thomas Stillman, her guardian. She is rumored
to be the wealthy heiress of her late father's estate. A search
was made for her, but no trace of her movements was found.

Strange how Mount St. Mary's showed no sign of cataclysm, no melee, only the memory of someone once there now absent. *Please give her back*, Sophiny spoke to the *Mysterious* that had caused her disappearance and could so easily cause her return, as though she had simply been borrowed.

"Yes, I am aware of that article. Detectives, if you will excuse us … Sister Margaret will show you out."

"Do you know who put this in the paper?"

"No, I am afraid I do not. Not the sisters, certainly. Mr. Stillman may have had some part in it. The reporter seems to have spoken to him."

"We don't ask these questions lightly. We do not ask to damage anyone's reputation. We ask because we need the whole picture. Contact us if you think of anything more," Detective Tyler said, giving a sigh of disappointment.

Though Sophiny was exploding with questions, there was nothing she could do but comply. *Was Sister Louise' dismissal an attempt to divert attention?* Sophiny wondered as her lips repeated the prayers that she had long ago memorized. *Sister Louise must have read all of Antoinette's incoming and outgoing letters. Did she have her own suspicions about Antoinette's elopement? If she suspected anything amiss, had she warned Antoinette's mother? Antoinette, you did not tell me you were in this much trouble. Why?* Sophiny was frustrated at the futility of asking questions of empty air. *Is there reason to suspect Sister Louise for having a part in the disappearance? Had Detective Tyler suspected abduction? Had she eloped or been kidnapped? But why?* "Love and legacy," Antoinette had signed her last note. *What had she meant? How can I find out?*

Sophiny's hand strayed to the key in her pocket, which she now found herself clutching. She had not checked Antoinette's trunk since her friend left, mindful of her promises. But if Antoinette were in harm's way, should Sophiny not use any means at her disposal to discover what had gone wrong?

She determined to take the first opportunity of privacy to search the trunk for clues. *I tell you*, she confided to Antoinette's key, as though some magic in the connection could convey her message to its owner, *I had better hear from you soon, or I will come after you myself.*

But that opportunity did not come until Sophiny was accompanied to the trunk room for purposes other than her original intent.

The black of Sister Louise's habit melted into the shadows surrounding her as she stood over Sophiny's bed at the rising bell early a few mornings later. The day was March 28, the day after Easter, nearly two weeks after Antoinette's March 15 disappearance. Awakening from sleep, Sophiny heard Sister Louise's steely voice as though from a great distance. The words came out measured, separated, and defined, as though coming through a sieve. She felt her body was being battered as so many peaches in a fruit press and was reminded of her mother turning the handle to squeeze out the distance between the top and bottom plates, thus reducing the fruit to juice and pulp. All that remained in the press were empty skins and pits. "Dear, your mother passed away. Your brother is here to take you home. He arrived late last night, but we did not want to awaken you, and he needed rest himself. Dress and come with me to the kitchen."

Sophiny dressed hurriedly and followed Sister Louise to the kitchen, where her older brother James stood mute and still. "Sister Margaret will help you pack. Make sure to take all of your belongings. Your brother does not wish you to return."

When Sophiny looked at him, James could only nod his confirmation that Sister Louise had interpreted his message correctly. She must have had to piece his words together like so many fragments of broken china. "It is better that you say nothing to the other girls about leaving. It would disturb the schedule needlessly. We will tell them at breakfast, and we will remember you and your mother in our prayers. Sister Margaret is preparing breakfast for you and packing a lunch for your journey; then you can pack as your brother prepares the horses. The other girls will be in the chapel."

If Sister Louise kept her word about praying for Sophiny's mother, at least she wouldn't be dropped into the pit of silence that had enveloped Antoinette two weeks ago. Before yesterday, Antoinette's name was never again mentioned by any of the sisters though the girls continued to speculate about her disappearance. Sophiny found it difficult to eat the bowl of oatmeal set before her, but she knew she must give the girls time to rise and go to chapel before she commenced packing. James ate hungrily and without comment.

The dormitory was deserted and Sophiny's possessions were few: two towels, two sets of sheets and pillow cases, seven hankies, seven sets of drawers, seven pairs of stockings; seven vests (the students did not wear corsets to minimize dressing time); two dark underskirts; two muslin nightgowns, one of each set was clean, the rest dirty; two pairs of shoes (one for Sunday, one for everyday wear); two blankets; two uniforms, which she would leave with Sister Louise after changing into her own clothes; one heavy wool coat, one light jacket, one dark sweater, one laundry bag, her toiletries; a statue of the Virgin; and a small crucifix she had kept on her pillow in the daytime. She had her belongings neatly folded and stacked when Sister Margaret arrived to escort her to the trunk room.

"I am so sorry to hear about your mother," Sister Margaret greeted her. "Do not forget us in your new life."

"Thank you, Sister, Mother was ill for the last year, but she didn't want me to stay with her. She wanted me to have an education, and now I will be taking care of my brothers, I suppose."

"You have a very hard cross to bear, but the Lord will give you strength. And your mother can now guide you from heaven."

Sophiny took consolation in Sister Margaret's words, anticipating the best in the next world. There were no secrets in heaven. Her mother would know where Antoinette was. She and Sister Margaret arrived in the trunk room, arms laden. Sophiny placed her burden on another trunk and then reached into her pocket for the key to Antoinette's stamped-metal, black with silver where the leaf was stamped, barrel-topped trunk. She glanced up to note that her own trunk was missing from the stack where she had last seen it. What if something of Antoinette's lay revealed so that Sister Margaret questioned her? She positioned herself in front ready to shield the contents with her body if something drew Sister Margaret's curiosity. As she lifted the lid, the smell of new paper greeted her senses. Antoinette must have repapered the tray. She removed the top tray, which was empty. Below she saw a packet of something wrapped in tissue, over which she quickly spilled the towels and sheets she had stacked on the adjoining trunk.

"Here, let me help you," said Sister Margaret freeing one hand to straighten the linens. Sophiny felt her heart stop.

"Thank you, Sister, I have it. If you can just put those toiletries in the tray. I will straighten things out in here." She busied herself packing the trunk, quickly sorting her belongings. She noticed that the tray did not fit smoothly when she tried to put it back, as though it were new and did not have the newly-papered corners pressed down. She adjusted the contents for a more perfect fit, realizing the impediment was not from what was in the trunk but on the underside of the tray itself. She quickly closed and locked the lid. Now was not the time to investigate. "Sister Louise wants you to come to her office before you go," Sister Margaret said after helping her carry the trunk to where James could pick it up in the buggy.

"Thank you, Sister," she managed, grateful that more was not expected from her. As Sophiny walked back up the stairs, she mentally said good-bye to all the rooms through which she now passed and had spent the previous two years. She missed Antoinette. *Antoinette would have hugged me. She would have cried with me about my mother, and we would have made promises to write and see each other.* Another thought struck her. *How will Antoinette get in touch with me if I am no longer at the academy? What if a letter comes from Brazil? Antoinette does not know that Brother Claude was not a missionary; Sister Louise does. But what am I thinking? That Sister Louise is in on a conspiracy against Antoinette?*

Sister Louise solemnly closed the door behind her as she entered. "Please be seated, Sophiny. I am sorry that you will not be able to finish the term. Your teachers and I have agreed that if you will finish some assignments and mail them, we will be able to promote you to the next level at the end of the term. Your marks of late have been very good. You have applied yourself diligently in spite of … in spite of everything." She handed Sophiny a large mailing envelope, which included the assignments from her classes. Her eyes were mixed blessing and blame. "As for the other unfortunate occurrence, Miss Dominguez's disappearance, your schoolgirl antics did not take into account how precarious was her situation. Perhaps Antoinette did not recognize it herself."

"What do you mean? Have you heard from Antoinette?" Sophiny blurted out. She had to know. "Did she write?"

"Yes, my dear, two days after her disappearance, I received a letter stating she had left to look for her mother, but so far she had been unable to locate her. I gave this letter to our local police. I have since kept a close watch on the mail. Three or four other letters have been short, with no significant information given. I am sorry, there has been nothing for you."

"I did not mean … I just … what could have happened to her? Does anyone know where she is? Her mother?"

"The Wichita police have been unable to locate her mother. So it seems there may be two missing persons." Sister Louise shook her head. "But I shall forever feel responsible. Her mother placed her under our protection, and I am afraid we have failed her."

"Um … what do you mean?"

"Antoinette and her mother had problems, yes. They did not communicate frequently in the past year or so … I do know Antoinette was very upset by the lack of contact. Did Antoinette say anything to you?"

"Yes, but what kind of problems were they having?"

"It is not for me to divulge family confidences," she said, but her voice was gentle. "I have told Detective Tyler all that I know; unfortunately, it is not enough to bring her back. Pray for her. She is a very troubled girl. May the Lord give her direction." Sister Louise folded her hands out of sight under a cloth panel over the front of her habit in what Sophiny knew was a sign of dismissal. She would learn no more from the headmistress. "And now you must be going. I am sure your brother is waiting." She walked Sophiny to the door and closed the heavy oak panels behind her.

James had secured Antoinette's trunk to the family's conveyance for the long ride home. "I do not remember your trunk looking like that," he commented. Sophiny looked around quickly to make sure he was not overheard, but they were already alone.

Chapter 7
Stretch of Road

S ophiny looked back for a last glimpse of the cocoon-like village where she had been sheltered for the past two years. Her heart was sad to leave. She loved the building and its inhabitants. Stone walls and a slight rise as well as rules and ordered behavior insulated this community of women from their Concord neighbors. The high-pitched roof protected alcoves, decorative brick pilasters, the grandeur of a rose window and a central tower, neat rows of molded windows, the heavy doors of the five-story brick building, and the sisters and students who lived there. The wings of the building itself formed an inner cloister, not visible from the front. In summer, gardens, lawns, and orchards flourished on the surrounding grounds and provided reclusive areas for exercise and meditation. The sisters had brought many refinements from their homeland, including architecture, needlework, and devotion to music and education. They had fled persecution during the French Revolution to cultivate a small portion of the Kansas plain. What use would these refinements have for Sophiny now that she was returning to her family farm with her four brothers?

As she watched Mount St. Mary's and the outbuildings recede in the distance, the tall laundry smokestack sent curling white steam diagonally across the sky, signaling the convent routine. Today was Monday, laundry day. The sisters were firing up the incinerators for the weekly washing. This was the day of the week she would have exchanged her soiled sheets and towels for clean ones. It was comforting to divide infinity into repeating units of time with distinct qualities. Dawn was breaking, an indication of the six o'clock hour, but she felt herself to be between time, and the white vapor instead of signaling the repeat of a cycle signaled change. She watched for miles the pillar of smoke rising over the rooftops and gradually dispersing into the early chill. Thus they left the city, the schoolgirl with her trunk, the farmer with his rig and horses.

Had Antoinette also given this imposing edifice of towers, walls, and gates with its huge, castle-like splendor one last look? Or was she gazing only at her betrothed, her lover, her intended, her soon-to-be husband? Had they followed the same street out of town past the new two- and three-story houses, many of them constructed with the new style tower rooms, past the railroad station, past the construction site of the sisters' new hospital with its medieval battlements and turreted towers out to the flatland of the prairie? Antoinette was a woman now. She would have a woman's things to do. Did she take time to sleep that night? Did she remain in the town? Or had she gotten on the train? It was as though she had been locked away in a secret prison someplace like one of the saints who would not obey. The thought caused Sophiny to shiver in the early-morning light. Such despair was unfitting for beginning a new adventure. After all, to risk, to dream, to grow were inherent to youth. Should not those who came before encourage that, not stifle it? In the weeks since Antoinette had left, it was as if she did not exist at all, never owned anything or left anything behind. Only her trunk, now in Sophiny's possession, indicated that she was not completely self-contained.

As the horses advanced onto the plains of cultivated fields and enclosed pastures where men wrote history with plows and sweat, barbed wire and post-hole diggers, James became more communicative. He spoke of his own lapse of duty on the farm because of his two-day ride to collect and deliver Sophiny. "A pity to waste light like this. I wanted to leave earlier. Now we will be lucky if we make it home before evening chores. The neighbors will probably come over for rosary too. You know how our mother was about going to funerals."

Yes, she knew her mother was religious about attending every neighborhood celebration. It was her respite from the monotony of hearing menfolk worry about the wheat going to seed, turning to rust, getting hailed out, or shriveling up from lack of moisture. The loneliness and drudgery of the hidden country life could only be borne with so much dignity and silence. Sharing other families' celebrations and tragedies was her mother's escape.

"Things will be different now that she is gone," James continued. "You will have lots of space to strut your refinements for the chickens and the cows and the weeds, but all we care about is if you can get dinner on the table, wash our clothes, and take a broom to the floor now and again."

Great, white, billowing, feather-bolsters of clouds rolled together across the blue background of the spring sky. A light breeze from the southwest stirred the first blades of what Sophiny knew would soon become dense brush crowding the roadside ditches. The thick growth was a sign that spring rains had been heavy. "You sound more and more like I remember Dad used to, always talk about the weather, the seasons, the work to be done. I am not going to sit home and spend my life taking care of livestock and siblings. I will burn everything I cook for you," Sophiny heard herself say in fine squabbling voice, one she had not used since leaving home.

"Better think again. You know town is a way away. It could get mighty lonesome for a girl out on that farm. You will have trouble going anywhere by yourself," James answered in the manner of a slow-talking farmer that she had grown unused to, living among adolescent females at the academy.

Kansas prairie spread flat before them. The sweet smell of new grass after spring rains was heaven's best gift to the earth, she thought. The quails and meadowlarks were nesting. Their mating calls came clear, sweet, and insistent. *Is Antoinette a woman now? Was she responsible for doing woman-things, which previously constraints of the academy controlled?* A hawk flew low, quartering. Now and again a rabbit darted along fencerows, or a pheasant took startled flight. Cattle and horses grazed on buffalo grass in pastures dotted with cactus plants and marked by winding cow paths and deep ravines. An occasional farmhouse, outbuildings, and windmill spaced miles apart broke up the frontier.

James pushed on toward the horizon. The two of them had been alone on the road for some time now. They passed a cemetery on the outskirts of a small town. All together they had seen only two other rigs on the road and a handful of motorcars. According to James, she was to find compensation watching her brothers subdue the prairie, tied to the harvest cycle, and do it stoically. What was her barbed wire, that brilliant invention that made farming on the open plains possible for keeping wandering cattle away from crops? Rather than spend the next few hours clashing with her brother, she decided she had better act now to groom him as an ally, "James, let me drive."

"What for?"

"You must be tired coming all that way yesterday and driving all morning. If I take the reins, you can rest. You can eat the fried chicken Sister Louise packed for us, and I would guess she found a piece of pie for you left from Friday."

He ignored her. "Wonder what that farmer is planting this late in the season. He's not going to get enough rain, whatever it is." James studied the field to try to figure out from the type of work what the crop was going to be, and because he couldn't be sure, he dismissed the farmer. "Probably a greenhorn easterner."

"Maybe he just likes to break crust; you know, flaky, melt-in-your-mouth crust." She could tell he was thinking.

"Could be, I heard that they had bad spring rains through here. Maybe it flooded out his wheat." James was all too familiar with the ways nature could destroy the bounty of the land, which—just like the state's hardy people—must endure harsh nature and weather conditions from carnivorous grasshoppers, to invasive grain bacteria, to devastating drought, flooding, hail, or even land erosion.

"How is our wheat doing?"

James shrugged. All he would say was, "Depends ... we will just wait and see." Sophiny knew what "depends" meant. For farmers producing their own food, weather was critical.

"We helped pit the cherries last year ... bushels of them ... so sweet, yet tart ... so good."

"Roads are good along here. Bigger towns have more cars, and cars need better surfaces than the horse and buggy. I heard some towns are having good road days. Local residents bring teams of horses to grade and gravel roadbeds. They even have guidebooks to help motorists. I want to get me an automobile someday."

After James made this uncharacteristically long speech, he handed Sophiny the reins and ate his chicken, buttered bread, and pie with an economy of effort. "Try to stay on your side of the road, will you? Just give me a little kick if anything happens," he directed and nodded off.

Driving meant handling the reins. If the horses became spirited, she would have to employ her arms and chest, besides pulling hard upon her back. But for the most part the animals in harness required a minimum expenditure of strength. Sophiny held the reins until she felt herself relax into the rhythm of the horses connecting to the road. As she narrowed her focus from the continuous swath of land before her onto the confines of dirt road ahead, she knew she had to take care to avoid rocks and eroded sections of roadbed. The rhythm of the horses became a litany soothing her troubled spirit and making her unmindful of the taunt and springy seat where she and James were wedged together. Occasionally she nudged James awake to ask where to make a turn or where to stop to water the horses. Once they stopped to let the horses graze and rest. In the afternoon, the breeze weakened, then failed altogether. The rolling hills sent up waves of heat they had gathered from the day's sun. The air became parched and visible with flecks of fine dust. At one point she was overcome by a wave of loss so great it seemed to fill up the entire horizon to draw her in a journey to the heavens. If she had worked on her own holiness, perhaps she could at this moment have raised spiritual eyes and seen there a burning flame to illuminate her path, or at least her mother's face smiling down on her to pioneer the direction of her future. Instead she was left without even her mother's footprints to make their mark on earthly soil, or feel her sheltering arms, or hear her voice.

Because the sky revealed nothing but a ceiling of clouds and sun, and the horizon nothing but carpets of green in fields and pastures, Sophiny's gaze fell on the stretch of road ahead, which now appeared to be below her and up the descent of the next hill. Like folds of fabric, parts of the road were lost behind the next stretch and picked up again on the other side. On that distant hill, she saw a silhouette wagon slowly pulled by a silhouette horse.

For a time it was swallowed up in the dip of the hill like a stick-puppet behind a curtain. Squinting against the light, she watched the place where it would reappear again. *When a dragon-pulled wagon of substance came into sight, the strange navigator bowed and said, "Your fame is spread over all the Earth. Are you not the queen of all enchantresses, wisest of monarchs from the Wheat Kingdom? Welcome home."* With that image, she smiled brightly at the famer, who raised his straw hat in greeting and said, "Howdy," as he passed. Could she see her mother again just as she had seen the wagon when it came over the hill? Not able to conjure up this vision on her own, she pressed James when she noticed he was no longer sleeping. "Tell me about when Mom died. What did she look like? What did she say?"

"Dunno … I was out in the field." There was more emotion, compelling storytelling, and entrancement in a single flutter of foliage than in James' communication. Thus ended her probe.

Sophiny realized she would learn more from the horizon or even from the thuds and rebounds of the horses than from her brother, and so her life in the Wheat Kingdom was about to begin—what of "love and legacy"? From the height where she sat enthroned behind the horses, and with the reins in hand, she began to collect the scraps from her memory. What did she know? Antoinette, though not an orphan, had essentially been entirely motherless the past two years since Sophiny had known her. She lived with a mystery. *Who was she? Her father died four years ago. Sister Louise said that she had been sent to Mount St. Mary's for her own protection. But from whom? From what? She eloped on Sister Louise's feast day with a childhood friend. She was followed. A detective had been hired to do what? Observe her? Get her signature? What exactly did Antoinette know? Had her marriage been sealed by a priest in a hallowed, religious ceremony? Or was her life in danger? Who wanted to harm her? How will her story end?*

Sophiny thought of all the endings of the saint stories read for edification in the silence before breaking morning fast: for their disobedience, young women suffered many punishments of being locked in towers, of having heads chopped off, of being raped, of being stabbed, of being burned alive, of forced marriage or forced entry into a convent.

Following the flight of a red-tailed hawk, Sophiny was struck by a dark thought. Was Antoinette's betrothed part of the plot? What if Sophiny had witnessed an abduction rather than an elopement? "Dear St. Anthony," she intoned to Antoinette's patron, "Please come 'round. Antoinette's lost and cannot be found." She hoped that possessing miraculous powers would not prove to be a terrible burden to the saint, as recovering her friend was beyond her own power.

Chapter 8
Flash of Images

L ight was fading fast as James and Sophiny arrived at the Mumm farmhouse and were soon overwhelmed with the funeral, the farm, and the family that had to be immediately addressed. A wake was in progress. Stepping from the buggy into the circle of mourners, Sophiny felt herself being handed from one to the other like a package until she arrived at the casket. It took some time before she could stop thinking about the soreness of her backside from all the hard bumping on the road.

Sophiny looked down at her mother in the wooden box, her skin so pale, nearly translucent. "She went quietly, just faded away, a blessing really," were Andrew's, her second brother's, first words since her return.

"We are glad you made it for all the fuss tomorrow," said Henry, the third of her brothers. "Mom would not have wanted you to miss her big shindig."

In spite of the comments from neighbors that her mother looked natural and at peace, Sophiny thought she did not look peaceful; she looked empty and in a state of gray. But instead of focusing on these thoughts, Sophiny simply said, "Isn't she beautiful?"

"Indeed she is. Your mother was such a dear and always so proud of her and your father's pioneering success," said Martha Shaw, one of her mother's closest friends, who came to stand beside her. "The best proof is this flock of healthy and sturdy youngsters before us." She continued, indicating Sophiny and her brothers, "Could we take a photograph now that you are all here and before the light fades entirely?"

At that Richard, the youngest of her four brothers and next to her in age, came to fling an arm around her. "We're depending on you to hold us all up."

The priest's text for the funeral sermon the following day was that "the angel of death has placed a period at the end of a long season of much suffering." After burial, visiting neighbors, family, and friends filled the Mumm farmhouse with a high-spirited mix of food and general merriment as no previous event ever had before. Sophiny knew her mother would have appreciated the town's collection of society on her behalf. It was not exactly a festive occasion, but Sophiny noticed her brothers taking full advantage to engage in a freedom of conversations.

A young woman by the name of Janet Adamy was talking about a magazine article she had read on advice to young men to gain a position in the "better class society."

"Does being onerier and meaner than a distempered mule count?" Richard, the youngest of the brothers though older than Sophiny by two years, said with some sarcasm.

"You have to possess something that has value in the society."

"Like what?" asked Andrew, intrigued.

"Can you dance? Can you sing? Act in a charade? Tell a story well?"

"Seems a rather superficial society," interjected James in a tone to squelch the subject.

Janet shook her head. "Okay, how about this: have you traveled? Can you be pleasant in telling about your adventures?"

"I do not think she is talking about you, James." Andrew clapped his brother on the shoulder. "Can't knock the hayseed out of that hair," he said, his attempt thwarted as James shielded himself. "But where does education, information, and being able to come up with ideas fit in?"

"Yes, yes, those things do give one a claim to social recognition."

Another girl whom Sophiny recognized as Glenda Sommers interrupted, "A man who wears a good coat, dresses with style, and can be an ornament of society has my eye."

Howls and groans followed her contribution, but Glenda's sunny outlook was infectious, and surely mankind did have remarkable powers of adaptation and problem solving, even those so simple as changing clothing to fit in. Sophiny noted that her brothers were getting admiring looks, reward enough for all the effort and all the dreaming. She began to notice certain masculine features that she had not been aware of before: wrist bones and hands with knuckles and nails, clothing stretched over taunt abdomens and belted to designate upper and lower regions of the torso, facial features hardened by weather and work and defined by hair.

"Oh, and good teeth … I like a man who shows them in wit and good conversation," Glenda continued, looking at Andrew. "And you do have a contagious smile."

"Contagious …" howled Henry, "as in hoof and mouth disease?"

"Ignore him, but I think you have described me with some accuracy." Andrew gave his brother a shove and flashed his teeth at Glenda.

"Of course, James, we recognize you as a true, straightforward, manly fellow, whose nature it is healthy for society in come in contact." Janet smiled up at him with an inexplicable, unfamiliar tenderness while she spoke. "It is the characteristic of a gentleman that he never speaks of himself at all." James listened, watching her in silence.

"Strike while the bug is close, my brother," Sophiny heard Richard whisper in his ear.

"Enough about James. Anybody for cards?" yawned Henry as the conversation slowed, but the group seemed unwilling to break up.

"By the way, I think being able to play cards was on the list too," Janet added.

"Aha … I have arrived … I invite anyone who wants to be in my better class of society to join me," Henry declared, emboldened.

The game continued throughout the afternoon, and as she passed Sophiny heard Andrew and Henry planning a bicycle outing once the weather warmed up and the drugstore began serving ice cream for the season. Sophiny felt a tiny hitch inside her chest, a moment of enlightenment. In spite of their mother's long illness, her brothers' farm's isolation did not mean insolation. They seemed to be comfortable and their behaviors even seductive. Was this exchange representative of most young men and women? Certainly James was showing signs of becoming Janet's warmest admirer.

March became April, the month of awakening. Trees began to bud in earnest after the spring rains. In the next week, Sophiny took up the arts expected of her: sweeping floors, washing dishes, laundering and ironing, making beds, kneading bread, shaking blankets and rugs, and lending a brisk hand to the outdoor chores as well. She pulled weeds and even planned a garden arrayed in the print gowns her mother had made for her. This uniform was suited to the employment of brawn and sinew, the scene of unmixed desolation that she had escaped for some time but was now required of her by her new responsibilities. She set to her tasks doggedly, traversing a routine for routine's sake. When night came she longed for the sweet sleep of the laborer to overtake her. What other satisfaction could she derive? World explorer of uncharted mystery was denied her.

Hers was a smaller story: to arise each morning to begin all over again. Her work conjured up childhood images, good images involving her mother. She picked up her mother's Fannie Farmer *Boston Cooking School Cook Book,* and in the absence of her mother as teacher, was grateful for the clear instructions with exact measurements and timing as she settled on a recipe for making bread. "Bread is the most important article of food, and history tells us of its use thousands of years before the Christian era," she read. "Considering its great value, it seems unnecessary and wrong to find poor bread on the table." Just maybe she did have some use for Sister Louise's sums and measures exercise.

Gratefully, she did not have to measure solids by egg size, liquids by teacups, or gauge the measure of a gill, a pint, or a pound. The "mother of level measurements" was her friend. "Okay, Fannie, it is you and me." She began to collect the ingredients for the milk and water bread recipe. Her mother had had an almost visceral passion for bread making. Sophiny plunged her hands into the dough, kneading the living substance of yeast, releasing the smell of gestation. When she finally set it aside to mature, an ineffably fulfilling sensation came over her. About mid-morning she heard her name. "Oh, Sophiny, come outside," James called from the kitchen door shortly after returning from a trip to town. "Look what came by train this morning," he said, nodding his head toward a chirping box containing a row of holes along the side.

"And they are all yours too, except for the eating part," Richard huffed, unloading a second box.

Baby chick hatchlings had arrived in crates, transported by railroad. She knew there was money in chickens. It was a way of income her mother had used. She could trade the eggs for food, provisions, and even have funds left over for her own discretion. Chicken and egg management was now her business. She could sell them at the general store for twenty-five cents a dozen: the grocer in turn would sell them for thirty-six cents a dozen. Should she keep a record of the sums involved, she wondered? But first she had to find a place to keep them warm through the chill of early spring so they could grow up to be healthy hens laying the eggs. "You might need this too," said Andrew, handing her a bag of cracked grain. In a few minutes the birds swarmed at her feet pecking at the grit. As she reached down to pick one up, Richard commented, "You know a bird in the hand is going to poop on you," but too late. When she went to the pump to wash her hands, she saw the mail had brought something else.

Along with the chicks came a bundle of letters from her academy classmates—who now seemed far away. She shuffled quickly through the stack, looking for Antoinette's name. Though disappointed at not seeing a letter from her friend, she welcomed the news from her schoolmates—

their expressions of sympathy heartfelt, their eagerness for school to be over universal, and their accounts of summer plans pleasant and entertaining.

But most curious: Over and over they wrote about a break-in in the trunk room, first discovered by Sister Margaret. Someone had gone through all the trunks, turned over some, broken a few, spilled contents of others, and in general had created havoc that took a full afternoon to clean up. Nothing much seemed to be missing. Most trunks were empty anyway, as the contents were in use in the dormitory. But the locks were broken. A sheriff's deputy came and asked questions, but no one had seen anything suspicious, other than a new gardener working in the orchards. New locks and new rules somewhat soiled the memory of the frenzied adventure. There was no mention of Brother Claude or Antoinette. But the pie on Friday was lemon meringue, the weather spring like, and the saint of the day martyred. Some things did not change.

A week from the day of her mother's funeral, Sophiny welcomed the sight of a pair of horses and a couple in a buggy emerging from the swirl of dust off the hard-packed, country road. She remembered Martha Shaw had told her she would bring the photographs as soon as she had them developed. This reminder of her mother was bittersweet. Paul and Martha Shaw, brother and sister, were her first guests. She straightened her dress, put away her apron, looked around the kitchen with quick scrutiny, and went to the door to invite them in for coffee and the few cookies remaining after her brothers had attacked her baking session of the day before. Not having children of her own, Martha had adopted the families of the farm community and appeared at weddings and funerals, reunions, and disasters alike to record events. Most people did not have the money for a camera or for film to record everyday lives, but they wanted memories of special events.

Martha laid out photograph after photograph along with an accompanying story. "Here is the wife of George Spangler, who committed suicide in her kitchen by cutting her own throat with the bread-slicing knife. She had been deranged for some time. Here is the fire of the Souza store. He burned it down and used the insurance for a new one. Everyone knew. Here is the new hearse, purchased in Kansas City, just arrived last month. These are the farmers that organized a vigilance committee to scare off the tramps that were raiding farmhouses in the county last year. Here is the Jacobs' baby, only nine months old and the third one that death has taken from them. The loss of her children has affected Mrs. Jacobs very deeply and made her partially demented. This is

Henry Johnson, an old bachelor who imagines his neighbors visit his house at night to poison his cattle and try to injure his property … seems to be rational on all his business affairs, though, and he wanted this photograph to advertise in the newspaper for a wife. Here is a wedding picture of Isabel Farrell, aged fifty years, married for the fifth time. Here are the graduating classes … Your brothers should be here … this one of 1907. Such a tragedy what happened to the Gunson boy. They say he gets drunk and then beats his mother—helps transport alcohol from Missouri where companies operate legally and ship by train to towns along the route. Here are your brothers and the two girls at your mother's funeral, Janet and Glenda."

The flash of images was so modest they hardly seemed equal to the bloody grandeur, the luck of the draw, or the spin of the wheel as told in Martha's accompanying narrative. "She could go on like this for hours," said Paul, teasing his sister.

"It is true. Just this morning while sipping coffee, I glanced at this picture of you after your first couple of weeks of school when you were about six or so. You and your mother had stopped by. It will forever be paired in my mind with the shooting of President William McKinley at the Pan-American Exposition in Buffalo, New York, in 1901. The fair was in darkness; the country was suspended. The newspaper later quoted the assassin who said he was an anarchist just doing his duty. The president died eight days later."

"How terrible."

"Yes, those were terrible times and a reminder of the dangerous people living among us." Martha paused, as though thinking over a riddle.

"What was his campaign slogan?" asked Paul, remembering the historical event as well.

"The full dinner pail!" both said together and laughed.

"Remember how we used to joke about that," reminisced Paul, "the government feeding us all when thirty percent of the labor force in this country are farmers. Are we children?"

Studying the photographs, hearing Martha's accounts became an exercise not only in sharing the misery and the hopes of strangers but also an adjustment to a world where photography was a new and growing technology to keep visual records of patterns, textures, and forms by the mere turning of a knob to wind a frame of film into place. Martha's collection of photographs, and the years and places they evoked, spoke of something deeper: the interplay of images and the landscape of her life, the visual record of a search for a spark of pleasure or insight, wisdom or truth. Disposable portraits, snapshots, were becoming increasingly inexpensive, and most everyone owned a few. Sophiny's sorrow over her own mother's death was turned inside out as she was not only horrified by but strangely comforted by these scenes of desperation that mirrored her own life. "May I go along with you sometime when you take pictures?"

"Can you drive a buggy and manage a horse?" Paul injected himself into the conversation.

"I have four brothers, don't I?" She caught Martha's look.

"School may be out for you, but learning continues. I do need someone to go with me when Paul has to take care of farm business. You could be my driver and my assistant; that is, if your brothers can spare you." Martha smiled, a professional serenity in her manner.

"Could I? James let me take the reins most of the way from Concord."

"Tell you what, I cannot pay you much, but I have a camera, a Brownie, you can use. I'll teach you what I know of photography and how to develop the photographs so that you get some practice. We will make up a calling card, something with your name and a design. You can write appointments on the back, and you'll be in business."

Sophiny's brothers had few objections, as the two families had a long acquaintance. Martha brought out her calendar and began to talk about scheduling events. "On Mondays, I call on certain townsmen: the funeral parlor, the clergy, city officials, the newspaper to see if they have something for me. Friday and Saturday are usually my busiest days. I was thinking about posting notices to take appointments in my home one day a week, maybe Wednesday."

Sophiny felt aspirations for her own future as she examined Martha's camera. This little miracle that transformed the energy of a moment of a life like so many exhalations crystallized in silver emulsion on glass would transform her life, she was sure of it. The photographs spread out on the table revealed open secrets that everyone knew, but maybe people should pay more attention to what they know. After Martha had carefully gathered up the images and the Shaws had gone, Sophiny studied Martha's photographs of her mother, relishing the memories and her new friends.

Nature at work in the fields, Sophiny thought as thunder wakened her the following morning. Farmers needed rain, surely, but in the gray dawn, she saw the first churning clouds above and behind the sullen, solid bar of the true storm, a gray wall with bullets of rain and flicks of lightening. No robins appeared. New growth of the giant elm near the front of the farmhouse jumped as the first swollen drops began to fall. A fitful squall lashed out then died. The fields had been plowed, harrowed, and seeded the previous fall with winter wheat. Now that nascent grass, like a green haze, colored the earth. Sophiny made her way into the kitchen. Mud had been tracked across the floor, her warning of, "Remember now, ya'll, wipe your feet" ignored. She felt badly to think that she was destined to be in such a place. She wept for a while and then commenced chanting and made up an antiphon as she set the table, fried the sausages and eggs, toasted the bread, and stirred a pot of oatmeal.

I thank you, Lord, for these fears
I thank you, Lord, for these tears
Let these sausages and eggs
Give strength to my resolve and to my legs
Carry me past this sorrow
Until the soil is tilled by time's harrow
Let there be wages to reap in the marrow.

And then she finished with a resounding chorus of, "Alleluia, alleluia, alleluia."

"It is a gully washer out there. Save the sausages." Richard, the youngest of her brothers, barged into the kitchen grabbing the plate out of her hands and shoving one down his throat.

"Hey ... how about hands off, swine? Wait for the others."

He squealed when she punched him in the arm and snorted for effect when she retrieved the plate. "What if I fill you in on what James has been up to with—you know—Janet."

He had her full attention, but she still refused him the plate of sausages. "So sorry ... I guess the news will have to wait too," he teased as their other brothers, James, Andrew, and Henry, took their places at table.

By this time she was ten days deep into the Wheat Kingdom. Conversation began with the fields and effects of the rain, moved on to the livestock and the newborns, litter sizes, gestation and farrowing pens, from there the condition of outlaying buildings and farm tools garnered attention, and finally steadily climbing corn prices and upcoming grain, dairy, and produce markets excited their imaginations. Then the men were back to the weather, always the weather, which this morning kept them at the table longer than usual until James reminded them, "Chores won't do themselves. Can't just sit here or the moss will start growing, and you know what that does."

Yes! Stagnation was death! They saw it in the scum-topped water of the windmill tanks, in the rancid grain of feeding troughs, and in the soured milk left in dairy pails. Everywhere about the farm and her brothers' activities were examples that action was life and health and growth. Immediately upon being born, farm creatures demonstrated their robust physiques by springing into action. A physique lacking development of muscle and tissue or grown feeble was soon destroyed. Not so much as a head of asparagus ever presumed to poke itself out of the ground without being subject to terrible calamity if it did not show its verdure.

As soon as every morsel on the breakfast table had been demolished, which took all of ten extra minutes given the rain, the four men of her household moved outdoors to take on their appointed tasks. The porcine quality had not entirely gone out of Richard, for as he left the table, he took the last remaining piece of toast off her plate and stuffed it into his own mouth. "What I like to eat most is the food on someone else's plate … good bread, almost as good as Mom's."

"I wonder why I waste my culinary talents on you. A bowl of slop should do just as well to put you in swine heaven."

"I do not have anybody to fill my lunchbox, you know. So isn't eating my way through everything you make the greatest compliment I can give? And bread has been a rallying cry for revolutions throughout history. I'm wounded that you think I have no taste."

"Better put a poultice on that wound—might turn into a pustule … and your mouth too," Sophiny felt her spirit lighten.

"Things will get better if you just imagine that things will get better." Richard paused and looked almost sympathetic. But when she shook her head and rolled her eyes, he continued, "Oh, I get it. This is what's wrong! You have no imagination!"

"Get out!" she yelled with a certain satisfaction.

But he had not finished tormenting her. "Don't you want to hear about James and Janet?"

"What about James and Janet?"

"He is seeing her." And Richard went, sharing no details, entirely too pleased with his exit. Though Richard did not possess a decent degree of sense, he could talk decent nonsense. Was that a quality that could give a man social recognition and privilege? Unlike Glenda and Janet, what she wanted was a man who could make himself useful to a lady on occasion. Perhaps Richard's usefulness would come through on other occasions. With a sudden start she thought of Brother Claude/Detective Tyler. "If you need to talk, or if I could be of any use to you, please come to me." Again she regretted that she had been unable to convince Antoinette that he might be sincere. If only she could put a poultice on her sadness. She missed the scheduling of her life that had begun with celebratory responses and antiphons in the chapel. She missed the excitement that her friend brought to each day. She missed the layers of security provided by her mother's protective prayers.

She thought about these things while heating water, clearing the table, and washing the breakfast dishes. She also thought about the letters she would write to her former classmates. They would be pleased to have mail; surely they were waiting for an account of her trip home, her mother's funeral, and how she was getting on as they munched their afternoon snacks of cookies and drank their glasses of cold milk. As she sat in the now-quiet kitchen finishing up her letters, she fell into a stupor watching the thunder and lightning display outside the window like being on the brow of a bluff promontory that dips into the bosom of a lake, drifting between sky and water without conscious effort. It gave her a feeling that she was drizzling away, getting swallowed up. Before she knew what she was doing, she found herself in her bedroom staring at the blanket-draped profile of Antoinette's trunk in the corner of her room, letting her imagination run riot at what would happen if she broke her promises to Antoinette: *Then sprang up through the earth, with the red fire flashing before her, Brimo the wild witch-huntress, while her mad hounds howled around. She had one head like a horse's and another like a ravening hound's, another like a hissing snake's and a sword in either hand …*

Chapter 9
Means of Conveyance

I n the dark silence, atop her bed Sophiny felt the chill morning air settle, enfolding her even as she swaddled herself in a blanket. She picked up Fannie Farmer's cookbook and read an introduction on soup making. Time … how she wished she could make it appear from nowhere. She knew she had to make time, and that meant giving up something else. Her list of tasks scrolled through her brain even as she took in the familiar objects in her bedroom. Like a monstrance, *what would it show? What proofs would it offer?* Sophiny knew she was struggling with the encroachment in the corner; there was something in Antoinette's trunk that merited her attention above the disconnected images, quick takes, and memory fragments that added up to her increasing anxiety over not hearing from Antoinette. What was the meaning of the trunk room break-in? She was seeing Antoinette's large, dark eyes staring straight, eyes that saw things other people did not. Her mouth, unusually serious, demanded promises. Antoinette was alive. She was not sure how she knew, but she knew. Was it possible for her to connect her mind to Antoinette's? Antoinette had promised to contact her; she was smart and would have made every effort if she could. She must be frightened and her fear paralyzing. As Sophiny stilled, she felt a ripple of awareness touch her, move away, and circle back again.

This shifting awareness was gradual, like a shadow. No, not a shadow. A figure in the shadow. Sophiny felt a sudden, ferocious fear—frantic and violent. Her ankles and wrists paralyzed. Her chest and head felt about to explode from the chaos. Whatever was holding her fast began to change. The fear softened, the cacophony waned, and in front of her she saw clearly Antoinette embodied in a dark place, her eyes wild—her hair straggling around her face, her clothes rumpled and dirty, her feet bare. Sophiny saw her head jerk up; Antoinette was alert now. *Help me, Sophiny. Help me.* Then, as though someone had blown out a candle, she was gone.

Sophiny started: her mind cleared of gothic cobwebs, her ankles and wrists free. But a sharp sense of strangeness remained, as vague, yet as distinctive as ... as ... Sophiny realized that she must have fallen asleep. But was the dream's image the work of her imagination? Had poisonous substances accumulated in her brain? Was it a conversation with herself? Was it a different mode of thought in allegory? No, she thought not. This was Antoinette's contact as much a miracle as the images on Martha's photographs. Antoinette was in danger as confined as the contents of her trunk. Was the trunk a means of conveyance? Did the trunk hold the key to her whereabouts, even to her disappearance? Was Antoinette a persecuted maiden, trapped, violated, and dying? "I promise ... I promise ... I vow," Antoinette had extracted from her. How could she betray those promises? The art of locking devils inside of boxes was ancient. Like Pandora's Box, the trunk in the corner of her room, under its covering, drew her magnet-like. Sophiny's hand was already grasping the key on the cord, which she now wore around her neck. She knew there would be no stopping the next sequence of her actions. Would she unlock a dark family secret? Would hope remain after she removed the contents?

Time to go to work. Time to find out where Antoinette was. For nearly three weeks Sophiny had honored her promise not to investigate. On the stormy April spring morning in 1910, her search began with a feeling of heartache and desperation and a longing for something solid, such as turning a key in the lock and hearing the creak of the heavy lid opening. First Sophiny carefully removed her own clothing, sheets, and towels (the dirty and the clean), just as she and Sister Margaret had placed them the day she had left Mount St. Mary's. She set them aside so that there would be no mix-ups.

For a moment as she removed the tray, she felt the paper beneath, turned under but not secured. The new paper was concealing something. She would get to its contents later and begin with the items packed beneath the tray: Two stylish shirtwaist dresses of current fashion—much finer in fabric and cut than her own homemade print dresses—a bundle of letters, another of photographs, a purse with money, more and larger bills than Sophiny had ever seen together in her life, and an address book including some telephone numbers written in Antoinette's own hand. Sophiny saw her own name. A small leather case included a diamond cross and chain, a silver medallion on a necklace of turquoise beads and matching bracelet, a beaded necklace of a translucent amethyst stone, silver rings, and a pearl rosary. Yellowed envelopes contained obituaries and more letters. A small packet of books included Antoinette's Bible, some novels, and what looked like law books as well as the familiar pocket notebooks, which most of the students, including Sophiny, used for journal writing.

She began by reading what she thought was an obituary of Mr. Antonio Dominguez from the *Concord Chronicle*. Antoinette's father was born to a family of ranchers in Texas and died in Concord, Kansas, of an apparent heart attack. It appeared Dominguez was too restless for the family ranch or anything else, for that matter. He had dabbled in turn at three professions— ranch hand, warehouse manager, itinerant well digger—and to a certain extent succeeded at each. But after a belated stint and intention to study law in a Kansas institution sputtered out quickly when he was suspended for failing his first-year exams and faced with the alarming prospect of a dishonorable expulsion, he had turned to real estate and farming. This roster of private enterprise turned out to be the best possible resume for the major achievement of his life. His large real estate holdings included his home near Wichita, his farmlands in the outlaying region, and many business warehouse properties housing mostly farm machinery in and around Wichita.

Sophiny was aware that obituaries were a staple in newspapers, mostly following the principle, "Do not speak ill of the dead." Usually bereaved families wrote them to recapitulate the deceased's life story, which included loving memories, lessons taught, examples set by the person, and in effect, canonized their family members. A second Dominguez story did not seem to follow this pattern. Who would have written this one, also from the *Concord Chronicle*? Mr. Dominguez was painted as a disagreeable capitalist with little time for his wife or young daughter, whom he repeatedly transplanted as unfeelingly as he would any sapling. He was, the article said, an unethical opportunist who prospected in businesses, stripping the community of resources, made purchases on speculation—a veritable carpetbagger.

A third article told quite another story. Someone had been a crusader, creating a historical record for a future researcher casting a searching light, welcoming exposure to the possibility of public corruption. The sheriff had been called in following a report of a man found deceased at the Stillman address. Details of the cause of death could not be known until an autopsy was conducted, according to the news story. But by later in the week, the cause of death was reported as a heart attack. He was thirty-nine. Already the man had so much potential and so much to show in the farming and farming-business community of Wichita. He had left behind a wife and daughter.

According to the article reporter, the investigation of Mr. Dominguez's death was very poorly conducted. "The circumstances of his untimely passing remain murky," the article said. A catalogue of failures included charges that the Concord Sheriff's Department deliberately thwarted the original investigation—refusing to ask the right questions, silencing reports on this story, favoring community paragons who wanted the story hushed, discounting the suspicious nature of the death and Stillman's conflicting roles of friend and host as well as beneficiary through the death of his friend. The cozy relationship between investigators and Dominguez's so-called friend

Stillman resulted in a premature ruling of Dominguez's death from natural causes, "a serious misjudgment," quantified the reporter.

Furthermore, the reporter wanted to learn more about the medical emergency that resulted in Antonio Dominguez's death, so he filed a Public Records Act request with the city for its report on the case. The city denied his request, giving two reasons officials often use: The records are protected by attorney-client privilege, and they pertain to pending litigation. Both arguments, the reporter claimed, "were not only bunk but clearly self-serving for the secondary partner in Dominguez and Stillman co-owners of real estate holdings in Concord and surrounding areas. The two men had had a falling-out the year previous and Dominguez wanted out." His interest in the company was supposed to be bought out, but instead he died. And the agreement between the partners filed through Mr. Stillman's legal office stated that the demise of either partner would result in the properties going to the living partner. "Stillman has effectively enveloped the whole business with an attorney invisibility cloak."

The writer called the Concord sheriff a "shrinking violet who lacked a nose for real investigation for fear that a city scandal could distract him from his pseudo job of poser for the society pages." The city was criticized for not releasing the results of its investigation, and a hint of foul play was left hanging in the air. The sheriff's department spokesman responded, "We are standing by our investigation." The report climaxed with a stern warning: "This community needs to see themselves and think about the meaning of local events instead of hypocritically talking about decency and standards to cover wrongdoing. Their day of reckoning is yet to come." Anyone with information was asked to contact the *Concord Chronicle*. Contact name of J. Canon and offices for a Concord address were also included.

Why did he die in Concord? The family lived in Wichita.

Sophiny began to read a packet of Antoinette's letters from her mother. The first of the series was dated some three years previous, filled with Mrs. Dominguez's memories of her late husband, and expressed increasing retirement from the world as the burden of grief and aching pain made self-control most difficult. "I am so worn out with grief, there is no strength left to compose my soul." Eventually her mourning became more abbreviated.

The second packet of letters contained her reemergence into a world of making purchases—some handkerchiefs, a package of hairpins, a bottle of attar of roses, new undergarments and shirtwaists to begin repairing her wardrobe of widow's black—and becoming involved in charity bazaars, hospital benefits, fund-soliciting, and prayer meetings. She seemed to be regaining self-sufficiency, managing her house, making repairs, and looking at business accounts with Mrs. Weaver, the family bookkeeper. Her attempts to run the businesses, however, were followed by self-recriminations that she lacked her husband's business acuity and so had mostly turned accounts over to Mrs. Weaver and a new foreman suggested by Mr. Stillman. One letter even mentioned a possible visit to Concord for her daughter's seventeenth birthday, which apparently had not happened since the next letter had a marked difference in tone, with sharp criticisms.

The third year contained one shockingly abusive letter to her daughter in which Antoinette's mother accused her of being selfish and paying little attention either to the comforts or distresses of her mother and that she was always decidedly vulgar and a glutton in her rush to attach her father's affections to herself by her own outpouring of grief. Furthermore, she was hereby cast off and disinherited, and any further communication would only be through her lawyer, Mr. Stillman, who was now her court-appointed guardian. The letter marked the start of a journal entry in which Antoinette responded:

> This letter so poisons my thought and paralyzes my actions
> that I know it cannot be true. A mother cannot be so devoid
> of duty or affection as to cause her only daughter to lose faith.
> Why would she create this wasteland between us? What lies
> behind her bizarre immolation of my claim on her? I can no
> longer trust Mr. Stillman to manage my father's financial
> affairs prudently, nor trust that his account of my mother's
> life and activities is accurate. I think he is at the heart of a
> serious threat to my mother's and my own security. But what
> can I do? I cannot contact my mother except through him.

Included was Mr. Stillman's account of the status of her mother's affairs at year's end. All seemed to be in order, with purchases and debts, rents collected, crops produced, and market returns listed in neat columns, totaled at the bottom of the page, and signed by Mrs. Weaver.

On page after page Antoinette asked questions and responded with her own speculations as to what had happened to her mother. These accounts seemed to reflect her various moods of the day—some saw her mother happily living in luxury on her husband's legacy, others saw her as committing suicide, going mad, being imprisoned, dying, getting remarried, starting another family, or going from one lover to the next without consequences. Each page was illuminated with Antoinette's doodles that included faces, flowers, hearts, spirals, meanders, whimsical animals, mythological beasts, and her own distinctive flourishes spelling out her initials, A. D., which she liked to associate with *Anno Domini*—in the year of our Lord.

Antoinette's second pocket notebook, to Sophiny's surprise, was addressed to her, "My dearest friend Sophiny." The intimacy of the greeting in Antoinette's handwritten script took her breath away even as her interest quickened. The note had been pinned to the first page. What might the slant and shape of letters reveal as she sought to examine the tangled knot of Antoinette's story? Would her own words offer a cord for unraveling the knot or become a security line for crossing boundaries? Would her tour through the contents of the trunk give insight into Antoinette's mysterious disappearance? Antoinette's introduction came immediately to the point.

Chapter 10
Figures of Influence

Antoinette's Pocket Notebook: December 1909–January 1910

My dearest friend Sophiny,

If you are reading my diary, it must be because you have not heard from me in a reasonable amount of time, and I am not in a position to contact you. I want to acquaint you with the events that led up to my decision to "elope," as you may need to uncover more than one mystery to find me. As you recall, I was invited by Mr. and Mrs. Stillman to spend the two-week December 1909 Christmas holiday with them, since my mother could not be located. As soon as I came downstairs with my reticule, I was greeted by Mr. Stillman, who told me I was looking well and that he and his wife had made plans they hoped would make my holiday memorable.

Mr. Stillman's conveyance and the topic of conversation for the short trip to his house was his automobile fresh off of Mr. Ford's assembly line. How different the town looked from a motorcar. When I showed interest in its workings, he told me, "It is more of a novelty than a genuinely useful device. Breakdowns are frequent, fuel is difficult to obtain, roads suitable for traveling are scarce, and rapid innovation means that a year-old car is nearly worthless. But this revolution will change … is changing everything."

My first outing in such a convenience was an excitement that I had to suppress, as I did not want to appear such a rube. But to my question of whether I might drive, he answered in the negative.

A.D.

December 20, 1909, Monday, day 1: The Stillman family home is a sort of mansion, I suppose, much admired and envied by neighboring families who live in less-pretentious homes. It has three impressive features on the outside: the native white magnesium limestone, a porch that curves around two sides, and most especially, a half-story tower with a flat roof and ornamental-stone guardrail. This widow's walk in the middle of a Kansas town seems an odd construction. But it was the latest fashion of the 1890s when the house was built, or so Mr. Stillman informed me. With seemingly genuine affection, Mrs. Stillman greeted me in the parlor, a beautiful room featuring a large, ornate fireplace with oak mantel and variegated tile. We had tea. Theirs was a serene and polished little island of crystal and silver and mirrors, of hard woods and exotic area carpets, of brocade furniture and matching drapes, tastefully furnished and decorated, with the convenience of electric lighting and many luxuries. The amalgamation of soap, furniture oil, and a faint hint of cigar was pleasant. She told me of tickets to see a theater production in Concord's new theater, of attending Christmas church services, of plans for a Christmas party, a New Year's party, and a visit to the orphanage. She also said that I would have occasion to shop for appropriate wear for the parties.

By this time, Mr. Stillman had excused himself to return to his office. "Antoinette, I trust you will take an interest in subjects proper for a young woman," he said upon leaving.

Instead, I tried to ask Mrs. Stillman about Mr. Stillman's law business and his acquaintance with my mother and father. She thumbed through *Harper's Bazaar* and *Woman's Home Companion,* commenting on the current vogues. "I do not get involved in my husband's affairs, as that is his wish." When I persisted, she encouraged me to take a little rest in my room and read the stories from a stack of her magazines, work on my needlework, or select one of the novels on the bookshelves in the library. She was stitching some garments for the children in the orphanage. "Any of your talent would be welcome as well," she said, showing me how to sew a pair of tiny drawers. I took the cut pieces, a spool of thread, and a needle with me to my room.

Instead of taking any of her suggestions, I captured my impressions and determined to learn what I could about my father's real estate and my own future. I began to formulate questions directly that I wanted to have answered. In the late afternoon, an A. B. Seelye Medicine Company wagon from Abilene made rounds door-to-door. Mr. Stillman had also just arrived, and he spent at least half an hour talking to the peddler at the back of the wagon. I watched from the window as he made several purchases, which he then carried into the basement of the house. I asked Mr. Stillman if I might make some purchases as well of toothpaste and soaps and hand creams, to which he agreed, and

I asked to have a brief tour of the vendor's other products, mostly medical remedies for one ailment or another.

I dined with the Stillmans. He dressed carefully, in blue serge trousers and matching vest, a starched shirt-front and an open, white handkerchief in his vest pocket. She wore a stylish silk and velvet shirtwaist blouse over a dark, well-fitted skirt and low boots. I had nothing so suitable to wear. Both were very elegant in their manners. They have a good-natured Irish housekeeper named Eaglan, somewhat attractive with grey streaks in her hair, a ready smile, and a big pillow kind of chest. She lives in, as Mrs. Stillman is not well. During dinner he sat at the head of the table by the window and read the newspaper. From time to time he read an article aloud to Mrs. Stillman and to me about Mr. and Mrs. So-and-so's institutional philanthropy and Mr. and Mrs. Such-and-such's cultural patronage, along with the reporter's gushing praise of their doing far more than their share in charity and social service to promote the city's prosperity. Other than reading and eating, he remained very detached. The delicious tomato bisque soup, braised beef, scalloped potatoes, winter squash, and citrus salad elicited no comment other than my enthusiastic compliments to the cook.

Mr. and Mrs. Stillman asked me if I knew how to play bridge. Mr. Stillman was intent on helping me master the rules of the game. I took the opportunity to say that I wanted to have some time for a serious discussion with him regarding my future and my father's businesses. I wondered if I might visit Wichita and my mother's home as well as our family businesses to know firsthand their state. He in turn examined me about my studies. "We must take every care, my dear, that your splendid cerebral development has not been paid for by neglect to … to other organs."

Mr. Stillman insisted that if I had a glass of apple cider, I would sleep better. At first I refused, saying I was unused to drinking before bedtime. Mr. Stillman countered, "Mrs. Stillman and I take your refusal as an affront to our hospitality. It is only apple juice, after all. You must not be so inflexible."

As I did not wish to appear ungrateful, I drank the entire glass, though it was the nastiest thing I had ever tasted, nothing like the cider made by the sisters from their orchard apples. Shortly after, I was ready when Mr. Stillman suggested that I retire. "Do please take your glass to the kitchen," he said. "A home should never be cluttered." Did he forget to add that children or pets should also never be allowed in a home, for they are messy and sometimes emit unwanted odors? The apple cider seemed to have impaired my thinking. I did not like it.

A.D.

December 21, 1909, Tuesday, day 2: I rose early, as we do at Mount St. Mary's Academy, and went down for breakfast. I learned from the housekeeper that Mrs. Stillman often took breakfast in her room, usually reading or taking care of her correspondence until mid-morning. When I asked to speak to Mr. Stillman about my father's affairs, he at first seemed amused. But after he finished his breakfast, he called me into his library and asked me to be seated. He was pleasant and cheery. I was tempted to let down my guard. "I know that you are a smart and studious girl who wants to please your parents," he said. "But I do believe you need help to channel your efforts."

Then he mentioned several times that my father's business dealings were quite complicated. I responded that I was on the verge of uncomplicating them, as I would soon be of age to act without a guardian, reminding him of my eighteenth birthday on March 31, when I would be of legal age for a female in Kansas. I assured him that as my lawyer, he could help me in this process by explaining what had happened to the farms and warehouses since my father's death. He merely said, "There is nothing for you to be concerned about. Your mother has wisely followed your father's good sense and left that to me." Then he added as an afterthought, "Of course, I will not be around forever. And when you marry, your husband will advise you."

I nearly choked. If he thought marriage would snatch away my dream for uncomplicating my life, he was mistaken. "But you must have documentation, a ledger, a business record that I could look at now," I countered, again to no satisfactory end.

"I am happy to help in any way I can." At this point Mr. Stillman seemed to feel that he did his job by using his entire vocabulary of legal terms to prove how confusing his topic was. "What constitutes necessaries," " *in Loco Parentis,*" "jurisdiction of courts," " statutory provisions," "defraying expenses," "deed of conveyance," and "adjudications" were some of his favorites. At no point did he arrive at a resolution or indicate a transition point at which I could begin to be involved in my father's affairs. "Frankly, Antoinette," he said with a pained expression and tone that was anything but frank, "it is my duty to prevent your unnecessary exposure to the intricacies of the courts. But you could be of great assistance," he added, "if you could tell me where your father might have kept certain … ah … important documents."

"Why would I know about that?" His request surprised me, but I did my best not to let on, even though I could see he was studying my reaction.

He abruptly cut short the discussion, saying he had to be in court. When he stood up, he unlocked a desk drawer, took out a roll of bills, and thrust them into my hand, seemingly as proof of his generosity as my guardian. "Of course this money will be added to your expenses. Ask Mrs. Stillman to take you to the shops today. One has to be sensitive to the requirements of society." Was he buying me off with my own money?

I determined to make one last effort to plead my case: "Every day I want to go home. The pain in my heart to see my family—my mother—again does not get any smaller. Please, I am begging you, bring me home."

He sealed his lips in a strategic silence, removed my hand from his sleeve as though it were a dog hair, and backed out of the room. "You must take care not to appear so unpleasantly singular," he said and was gone.

When Mr. Stillman left his home, I took the opportunity to study the titles of books in his legal library to improve my own vocabulary, looking up the terms I had heard him use. His words, instead of providing clear thought, had set up barriers to the truth I sought. Actually the book that helped demystify his use of terms I later "borrowed," and it is included in my trunk. I have marked passages that I think apply to my case regarding property guardianship. What was most astounding as I was looking through his library was that I found a hand-written letter from my father in one of his books. It was peculiar how a hazy ghost of him appeared from my memory between the pages of the book.

Dear Thomas,

I dislike reminding you yet again, but it has now been six weeks since I lent you $5,000 "for just a few days." If I could just forget about it, I would, but as it happens, I need that money myself—right away.

I will be arriving in Concord on the Thursday-evening train and expect to pick up the funds. At that time, I should also like to go over some irregularities I have noticed in your account of the Concord properties for which I cosigned.

Sincerely,
Antonio

I bent my head to smell the letter, knowing my father had touched it. A cold draft blew through the passageway leading to the stairs. I thought to ask why the letter was there, but "Dear Thomas" would probably accuse me of snooping. I confess, I did not recognize myself as I searched through the papers on his desk, the pages of his logbook, the contents of his drawers, the files in his cabinets. Names of clients, particulars of cases, actions taken, and arguments proposed all flashed by in a sort of blur until I saw the file with my mother's name. I did not know what I was looking for, but a voracious appetite seemed to have overtaken me to gather as much information as I could. In the file were several bills for medications, for doctors, for surgery … her leg, for facilities used and services from a hospital in Wichita for someone with my mother's maiden name. The particulars of her case I made notes of. Two doctors' names and addresses were listed, along with charges for her care. Both charges and care seemed excessive. At least I now had some contact information. I even looked in his wastebasket. Here I was surprised to see my signature written several times, with increasing likeness to my own style. I felt a chill along my spine.

Mrs. Stillman appeared before lunch but spent much of the afternoon going over the details of her upcoming holiday party, with her housekeeper and a caterer. I heard them discussing lima bean soup, roast goose, duchess potatoes, and chicken croquettes with green peas, as well as holiday decorations for the house. Two of her friends called on her and engaged in the conversation. I did not wish to disturb her with Mr. Stillman's shopping directive.

At dinner Mr. Stillman again read the newspaper. Accounts of Concord society figured in the stories he selected. "Do pay attention, Antoinette, you may be meeting some of these people at the party." He was most concerned with the activities of members of his Municipal Improvement Club. "Take note of births, deaths, and weddings so as not to be a total social infant." I watched the arched black brows and chiseled planes of his face move in the shape of the words that came from his saturnine mouth. "Get a grip on opinion. Read the letters to the editor. Often they are quite witty, and they tell you what current obsessions may be." Outwardly he was the soul of tact and had the solicitude of a good tutor. "Do not neglect finding out about who is in government: the city, the state, and the country. It looks good if you can pretend to hold an opinion, not that you have to believe it yourself. For a little fun reading, this page: criminal trials … murder, robbery, and other mayhem make people talk. There," he shoved the newspaper at me, "do you think you can manage?"

"Thanks very much." I intended to act on what he suggested.

Later he and a late-night visitor isolated themselves for some time in his library. The smell of their cigars and the clink of crystal first drew my attention. As the house was quiet, I stationed myself in the parlor to read Mrs. Stillman's magazines and Mr. Stillman's newspapers and heard parts of the conversation about getting a business declared illegal and finding a pliant judge to invalidate a law. At this point, I selected one of Mrs. Stillman's novels and crept up the stairs before Mr. Stillman came out of his office. I could not sleep. Raging thoughts furnished my fevered brain, and I determined to confront him again about my situation. Reading *Wieland or the Transformation* by Charles Brockden Brown, I was "lulled into grim repose."

A.D.

December 22, 1909, Wednesday, day 3: At breakfast the following morning, I was still not fine. Mrs. Stillman appeared at the table in her dressing gown, cordial but stumbling, as though she could not see very well, and she just sat there smiling and sucking peppermints.

"Lucretia, could there be a more perfect way to ruin a morning?" her husband commented unsympathetically. "Had you not subjected yourself to unnatural stimulants of excessive mental effort and neglected the development of bodily functions when you were an adolescent, you would not be suffering now." She refused anything to eat, but Mr. Stillman insisted that she drink her special medicine. She was slow in complying. "It is the law of periodicity." Mr. Stillman focused his attentions directly at me.

"Pardon me?" I thought I had not heard him right until his look subdued not only my attack of giggles but also the courage I had originally brought to the table.

"Indeed it is unfortunate that you do not have a diligent mother to supervise the menstrual cycle of her daughter and protect her against over-work of brain and of body. Take care of yourself during your cycle for your own future health and beauty, or suffer from lifelong invalidism, as does my wife."

I made no response, but he did not seem to require one and returned his attentions to his wife, whom he studied. "I see you are wearing your usual monthly ornaments."

"What is that, dear?" She looked puzzled.

"Your sick headaches and your tiresome laziness. I suppose we should all consider ourselves fortunate that you are lazy, or you might have killed yourself by now."

"Yes, Thomas, sometimes I feel you would like nothing better than that I kill myself to prove my innocence, as did that other unfortunate Lucretia."

Shocked by the violence of her words, I was reminded of the victim of Wieland, but Lucretia, Mrs. Stillman, smiled as the explosion went off neither insulted nor intimidated—though even she seemed to be brought to the end of her tether.

"A man likes the women of his household to be smart and up-to-date in dress and appearance," he said, folding his napkin with precision. Then he turned to me. "I hope you do not tend toward sulkiness, Antoinette," he said, as though he expected me to make a fuss. When I said nothing, he continued,

87

"All this holiday planning is a draining business. You must conserve yourself as well; otherwise, neither of you will be of use. Read something soothing to her, see that she does not harm herself and takes her little helpers—a half glass every hour." He placed two bottles in front of me as he rose from the table. Before going out the door, he further cautioned, "You must lie down yourself after lunch and take a dose of prickly ash bitters."

The first bottle was labeled prickly ash bitters. The label claimed the potion would cure all diseases of the liver, kidneys, stomach, and bowels and purify the blood, invigorate and cleanse the system. The second was Seelye Medicine's cure-all labeled Wasa-Tusa. After taking one sniff, I determined not give her any more "little helpers," as I had been instructed, but insisted that she sip some tea. Within a couple of hours, she became more herself. I asked if she was ill. She complained of being very thirsty, and as I looked at her, the black part of her eyes was very large. She seemed to know neither why she felt so poorly nor why her spells of confusion were becoming more frequent. As I studied her reactions, I noticed that she was wearing a diamond cross, similar to my father's gifts to my mother and to me. When I remarked on its beauty, she said her husband had given it to her a year ago on their anniversary and that he was a most generous and forbearing husband. I searched for more evidence to determine whether she and my mother merely shared the same tastes or in fact there was a more sinister connection. In my brief exploration, I found several ornate snuff boxes that looked like items from my father's collection, a small ornamental clock like one that had adorned my father's desk, an ornate dressing set like my mother's, and a ruby pendant and earrings set. Mrs. Stillman soon returned to bed. The housekeeper set about cleaning from top to bottom in preparation for the Christmas party. I added these notes to my study of the Stillmans. How did my findings relate to the stories in the *Concord Chronicle*?

A new kind of fire burned in my brain that would not let me rest. I told Mrs. Stillman that I wished to take a walk and got a less-than-convincing lecture from her about wearing warm clothing and being careful about going out alone. From our many student walks around Concord, I knew the location of the train station and determined to purchase a ticket to Wichita. When I arrived a half hour later, I found Mr. Stillman in his automobile waiting for me. Was he spying on me? He insisted that I get in, and he seemed more upset that I had gone out unaccompanied than that he had found me at the train station. Since I did not want him to suspect that I was on my way to see my mother, I made up a story about meeting a boy to add fuel to his concern about my lack of development according to the laws of periodicity. Though he tried to get a name out of me, I could not come up with one, and so I hoped the mystery would distract him from my true purpose. Then he gave me a lecture on silly frivolity and disagreeable blundering, that I was set on enticing, seducing, and entrapping a man at the price of ruining my own reputation. He threatened that for my own protection he would have to deprive me of the money he had given me the previous day. Instead he drove to the downtown shops to look for new dresses for his parties.

The session began with a corset fitting. "No woman wants to look like a shapeless dowdy," said the proprietor. For half an hour, I listened to a speech about the merits of whalebone versus coralline as stiffeners. "Whalebone from Greenland needs no defense," she said. Coralline had the advantage of whalebone in being light, though not quite as stiff made from a Mexican fiber, when flattened and tempered is unbreakable and indestructible. The next best material is the black horn of the buffalo from India, which has long been used as a substitute for whalebone and supposed by many women to be real whalebone. When new and fresh it has good wearing qualities, but when a year or two old, it becomes brittle and breaks like a dry bone. After this geography lesson, I picked the lightest corset in the shop, made of whalebone, double the cost of the coralline and four times the cost of the black horn, to prove my competence in arithmetic. Other articles of undergarments to augment outer coverings were discussed: the chemise, corset coverings, a one-piece union suit for colder weather, various petticoats to conform to fashionable dress shapes and hosiery and garters.

"Comparatively few women have fine taste in dress," continued the attendant for my edification as we moved on to outer garments. "Of course, Mrs. Stillman's taste is impeccable, as she knows how to focus on the higher art of dress versus capricious fashions."

"The art of dress should be part of a woman's necessary education," replied Mr. Stillman. The next topics for review were my defects, my complexion, my eyes, and the tints of my hair. As though dressing a doll, the two of them discussed each dress's tightness, shape, and trim before deciding that I would have at least one carefully made, tailored street dress, two party dresses, several dresses for home evening wear, and three ready-made dresses from the shop for day wear. In their expert opinion, my nut-brown hair and eyes would look lovely in golden brown, which suggested the glints in both. The shop tailor was educated to do this work carefully and consistently. After selecting material for and taking my dress measurements, boots, gloves, and hat to match followed. "One must not have shabby gloves or half-worn shoes with a fresh street dress." She glared at my present attire. "It is enough to destroy the reputation of being a well-dressed woman."

For evening home-wear, they favored light, delicate, and picturesque dresses in attractive fabrics with slippers dyed to match in case friends dropped in for a chat. "After a day's toil, it is easier for a man to forget courtesy with an unattractive woman than one daintily and becomingly dressed," agreed Mr. Stillman. I got the distinct impression that Mr. Stillman and the shop proprietor had engaged in numerous discussions of this kind and made a mental note to keep his presumptions in mind in future. I had not forgotten his brusque and irritating tone of the morning. As of one mind they next focused on what I should wear for the two social events Mrs. Stillman had told me about earlier. "No color suits her better for evening wear than the rose that glows in her cheeks under strong excitement," said the shop owner. Their educated tastes agreed on one party dress in rose and another in blue with "the lines, drapery, form, and fabrics to suit her personality and use as well as regard for eternal fashion consistencies."

"And remember, fashion is something that comes after style," was the attendant's parting wisdom.

For the proprietor's benefit, Mr. Stillman acted the generous guardian in promptly paying for the charges, but he reminded me that this money was being charged to my own expense account. I am sure it cost the eyes out of my head.

When we returned, I was exhausted and begged to retire with the half dozen or so layers of undergarments that separated me from the sunlight. "Take care to straighten out the creases and folds when you hang your dresses," cautioned Mr. Stillman. It seems that I was not the only one going through drawers. My sheets had been changed, my clothes rearranged, and my traveling case unpacked. Fortunately, I had taken my pocket notebook and other valuables with me. What kind of horrible people are they? I have been reduced to a position of complete dependency and trickery.

A.D.

December 23, 1909, Thursday, day 4: On the day of the Stillman Christmas party, I composed a very messy draft to my supposed lover explaining why I had missed our meeting time and place. Words crossed through and badly spelled, smudges, and doodles attested to my supposed state of distraction. Should anyone go through my traveling case again, she/he would have something interesting to read. I volunteered to assist the housekeeper and help hired for the occasion in hopes of discovering what other hypocrisy and treachery he was capable of.

Eaglan was beginning preparations for decorating the tree. I did appreciate those hours of perfecting details and wandering through the house before the guests arrived. It was a pretty sight and a seasonable one. The tree ornaments were exquisite: sequin stars, golden moons, crystal snowflakes, miniature angels of blown and spun glass, porcelain and china figurines, and gaily-painted baubles. Beneath the tree were brightly wrapped packages, which reminded me that I had not thought to bring a present for the Stillmans. Perhaps my needlework on matching pillowcases and a dresser doily would suffice; at least, they could sell it for one of their charities. The rooms were pungently fragrant with juniper and bayberry and spice and an air of anticipation. The beginnings of an elaborate buffet including a traditional Yule log cake, English plum pudding, and sugared fruits and nuts were being set up. The table included an abundance of knives, forks, scintillating glassware, and white napery. Logs were already burning in the fireplace. A pianist was arranging music with Mrs. Stillman for the evening's entertainment.

When I was sent to the basement for another box of Christmas trimmings, I made the most of the opportunity. I wished I knew how to pick the huge padlock sealing off a room at one end. There was also a safe large enough to walk into. Provisions for every possibility were stacked on rows of shelves. At least a half year's storage of cleaning supplies, soaps, oils, paper products, baking products, intoxicants (absinthe in the largest number), canned vegetables, and fruits in jars took up one wall the length of the back of the house. One shelf held Seelye Patent Medicine purchases: Insect Die, Killa-Germ, Ner-Vena's, Compound Extract of Sarsaparilla, Cough and La Grippe Remedy, Seelye's Fluorilla Compound, more bottles of Wasa-Tusa Home Remedy, as well as other bottles labeled astringent, tonic, stimulant, sedative, narcotic, alterative, diuretic, diaphoretic, expectorant, and set off to one side: alcohol, arsenic, quinine, strychnine, aconite, and mercury. Any pharmacopeia would have been proud to have such a collection. It seemed secrecy and mystery were the backbone of the patent industry as they were of Stillman's practice. I did not want to neglect any detail of this place. I thought of Stillman's concoction for his wife. Finally I was sent to my room to dress for the party as I was getting in the way

By putting together bits and pieces of information, I gathered that Mr. Stillman and his associates had made it their lot in life to gain a record of contributions to the city's significant economic, voluntary, and political institutions. The Stillman Christmas party was a fundraiser for a local orphanage operated by the Sisters of Mary. Members of Concord society were invited and expected to contribute to the cause. Poised and affable, Mr. and Mrs. Stillman stood in the hallway, showing particular favor to some honored guests by introducing them to others and passing them drinks from a special tray. During the progress of the party, they courteously accosted and chatted with their friends and took care that the ladies were furnished with seats and brought refreshments.

Dressed in the rose gown with the big bow in the back that Mr. Stillman had selected for me, I felt all wrapped up like a present. When the guests arrived, it became clear that I was a trophy of the Stillman charities, a basket case left on their doorstep—variations of this story I heard over and over throughout the evening. Sisters from the convent were there, including Sister Louise. Mr. Stillman hustled around the packed room as though seeking a coveted hospitality honor amid his symbols of wealth and virtue. I was introduced to a judge, a lofty presence with a placid smile and a thin mustache. Was he the pliant one? Other introductions followed in quick succession: the president of a bank, the mayor of Concord, a state congressman, a hospital administrator, a newspaper editor, a financial advisor, land investors and developers, more lawyers. But what concern did I have with Mr. and Mrs. Stillman's collection of ladies gowned in silk, challis, chiffon, crinoline, satin, and voile and gentlemen in elegant dark ties?

I had made up my mind to find a suitor to make true the lie that I had told. I narrowed my choices to three candidates—toys for my temporary diversion. I know my thought was indecent, but my host and his friends had made such a toy of me. The first was an impressive, indomitable man, tall and spare of frame with shrewd hazel eyes under flaring, sand-colored hair and brows, but he was too quiet and would probably take too much work. He bowed his head slightly when he caught me examining him. The second was robust and vigorous, his skin ruddy from the cold, his teeth perfect and set into jaws built for wear and tear, his movements quick and controlled—too controlling, perhaps, as he began to move in my direction at my notice of him. The third definitely a smart young man with charm, surely on the rise. His black hair waved extravagantly. His eyes were a brilliant blue, a shade that seemed not quite real. His flamboyance was already attracting a following, which would not come without harm. *Attached most definitely,* I thought observing a female companion move in to take his arm in a show of familiarity. I sidled over to a septuagenarian who seemed to recognize what I was about and who urged me, "Try setting your sights on older men." Just in time, too, for wear-and-tear jaws was almost upon me.

"Antoinette Dominguez," I said, taking the opportunity to introduce myself and so deflect an unwanted encounter. "And why is that?"

"Crescentia Gottfried," she responded with a sly smile. "They are more mature."

"Right. So any ideas?"

Mrs. Gottfried looked around the room. "This is an unusual crowd. Unfortunately, there seem to be several people not from Concord that I do not know."

My eyes followed where hers were directed. That's when I saw him, unruly hair, confident in his stylish jacket, starched collar, silken cravat carelessly tied, and knew that my options had suddenly expanded. I thought providence had smiled on me by teasing my old childhood friend into existence with a few staccato brush strokes in the Stillman parlor. Such a miracle could happen after all. Had I not been praying for direction? The sight of Mark Weaver lifted my spirit. I excused myself to Mrs. Gottfried and made my way across the room. The moment our eyes met and our hands touched, the gap between our childhoods and our futures was bridged.

"Can you spare me a moment of commiseration?" he pleaded in the most charming manner.

"Mark Weaver … is that you?"

"Antoinette Dominguez … you are—you are sheer perfection all grown up."

"And you, so handsome, sprouting a mustache."

"Makes me look older, don't you think?" He laughed, and all those lost moments in-between suddenly filled.

Mark's mother had been my father's trusted accountant for as long as I could remember, always at his office, frequently at our house, with Mark often in her company. We had practically grown up together. Finally, a direct tie to my past, he could answer what Mr. Stillman would not. "What are you doing in Concord? Where are you staying?" I pondered the possibilities and waited for an opportunity to engage him in my search. He informed me that he was working for Mr. Stillman's law practice as a sort of law clerk.

"Can we meet again?" he asked, as though reading my thoughts

But to my most specific question about the whereabouts of my mother, he had no answer. He had heard that she was traveling, possibly that she had even remarried. He never saw her anymore and did not think his mother was any more enlightened than he. When I asked how the farmlands and businesses were doing, he murmured something vague. I was surprised at my own forwardness in extracting his promise to remain in contact. He promised to call at the Stillman house the following afternoon.

We were watched by Concord society, most specifically by Mr. and Mrs. Stillman and Sister Louise. So I very carefully made certain that all three knew of our previous acquaintance and that there was no impropriety in our familiarity. I couldn't help but notice the interest of Mrs. Crescentia Gottfried, the pillar of society whose opinion was so freely given on my behavior earlier. "What about this one?" I asked, leading Mark to her for approval.

"Does he have the lineage factor?"

"The what?" we asked together.

"Who is your father, young man?"

At that moment, the pianist began again in the other room, and Mark took the opportunity to back away from her without answering.

To Mrs. Gottfried, I shrugged as I also moved away with Mark. "I am so sorry," I said. "She was giving me advice on prospective suitors earlier, and I was intrigued by her opinions."

Mark was not amused, so I did not continue to tease him. But I wondered if he could be as crazy as I felt I would have to be in order to get my life back on track. Should I test him? One thing I did know was that he had no father to break away from, just like I had no family to break away from, only my guardian, but for me Mr. Stillman didn't count. How much did he count for Mark?

A.D.

December 24, 1909, Friday, day 5 Christmas Eve: At breakfast, Mrs. Stillman handed me a note from Mark, apologizing that he was unable to visit in the afternoon. He had some pressing work to complete. "Mr. Stillman will be away for the day on business of his own. The housekeeper has gone to see family."

Where does she live?"

"I am not sure exactly."

Thinking of the long day ahead, I asked if I might stay at Mount St. Mary's overnight to attend midnight mass with the sisters. The train to Wichita was still on my mind.

"I was hoping you would spend the day and evening with me. I so enjoy your company." Then, as though gauging my reaction, she said softly. "Forgive me for changing the subject, but the Equal Suffrage Association is hosting a special afternoon tea. A speaker will be reviewing resolutions and grievances. I so rarely get to go to these things and … I thought you might be interested as well."

We mostly spent the morning cleaning up after the party, Lucretia and I. Mrs. Stillman asked me to call her by her first name after I asked about her saint. She went on to explain, "I am not sure Lucretia was a saint, but she has a sad story relating to the law and violence against women. Would you like to hear it?"

When I said that I would, she told me this story. "Lucretia, a Roman matron known for her chastity, was threatened and raped by a man who claimed to be a friend of her husband. Unable to address a legal court, she enlisted a social court. After telling her story to her father, her husband, and relatives who were among the most powerful people in Rome, she drew a knife from under her robe and stabbed herself before them to prove her innocence."

"Oh!" I gasped. Lucretia's account left me speechless. Was suicide a wife's only recourse to prove innocence?

"All of Rome was moved to this cause. As a result of the outrage, a law was enacted that a man would be executed for raping a woman," she continued as though she had heard my thoughts.

Lucretia seemed to know a great deal about the history of the movement for women's rights, both past and present. "You might want to review Elizabeth Cady Stanton's Declaration of Sentiments. Otherwise, the afternoon's discussion of resolutions and grievances will not make sense," she said, handing me a copy, which I immediately sat down and tried to read. Only with Lucretia's explanation did the flow of the argument make sense. "She worked at least fifty years on this cause, but still women cannot vote. It has been a long battle. Men are so stubborn. How can we ask them to vote on issues that affect us so vitally?"

One of her friends with an automobile transported us to the meeting at a church nearby. First on the agenda was the reading of a letter from the Kansas Equal Suffrage Association explaining the three elements of the campaign: membership extension, education, and press releases. The names of women in charge for each action was included, as well as a suggestion that house-to-house canvassing with membership cards was used successfully in other states and could be used in Kansas as well. Lucretia volunteered to take charge of the canvassing campaign. The speaker was passionate about the partiality of families to the boy offspring and discrimination against the girl even before she is born. "She loses social, political, and legal rights through the handicap of birth." She is raised with a "veil of ignorance." Even in past historical eras, women were allowed to wield swords and guns for protection. But in this era of peace, "the weapon of peace—the inkstand—is denied her."

"This will be our little secret," Lucretia said when we returned. "I would rather not have to explain to Mr. Stillman my whereabouts this afternoon."

My estimation of Lucretia soared at her defiance. Hidden within her, behind her quiet appearance, was a raging war against limits on actions and knowledge. I had seen the life creep into her eyes, like blood into a hand unclenching, like hope in release from captivity. "Are there things women shouldn't know, just because they are women?" I asked.

"That is a good question. Many great legends and myths warn us of the consequences of forbidden knowledge," she said, as though fixing my face in her mind.

We sat beside the Christmas tree near the fire watching the flames peal away from the logs, eating leftovers from the night before and drinking hot chocolate. I had many questions for Lucretia about the issues we had heard discussed until a chime sounded and she seemed suddenly tired.

"Happy Christmas," she said. "I have something for you." She gave me a silver medallion on a necklace of turquoise beads and matching bracelet. "These were a present from my mother. I had hoped to give them to my own daughter." Her generosity left me breathless.

I gave her my stitchery, an assortment of flowers on matching pillowcases, and a dresser doily. "These are beautiful. I will treasure them knowing every stitch comes from your fingers." She seemed genuinely touched.

My usual bedtime glass of apple cider foregone in Mr. Stillman's absence, I was still wide-awake and said I wanted to read a little when she went upstairs to bed. *Forbidden knowledge* was still on my mind, so I went to Mr. Stillman's library and took the book that had intrigued me on my first visit: *A Treatise on the American Law of Guardianship of Minors and Persons of Unsound Mind* by J. G. Woerner. Fortunately, a table of contents enabled me to turn immediately to the parts of the law that I most had questions about. Minors, no matter what age, are referred to as infants. This term made me feel quite heated as I thought of Mr. Stillman's conception of my relationship to him. In Kansas, women reach independence at age eighteen. On March 31, I will be eighteen and no longer need a guardian for my person or property. My next questions were about the particular kind of legal guardianship he had over me and over my mother. Each legal designation had a different relevance to his control and management of my father's properties.

When I tired of the law, I turned to a huge medical book. I could not help but read the sections on "Diseases of Women and Children" dealing particularly with her sexual life in *The Twentieth-Century Family Physician* by Lyman, Fenger, Jones, and Belfield. The front cover had the image of a snake eating its tail encircling a winged torch. Did these doctors know the secrets of eternity, life, and death as the symbol promised? The section began with the ominous statement, "Self-preservation is the first law of nature—in point of time only; for a second law, not less imperious, is race-preservation. Life, it has been said, is a struggle to gratify two instincts—hunger and love." What did hunger and love have to do with disease? For that matter, Mr. Stillman's basement pharmacopeia seemed a superfluous lot to treat eruptions of hunger and love. Strange, there was no chapter on diseases of men. Where else but in a library would I have equal access to the learning and erudition of the past?

A.D.

December 25, 1909, Saturday, day 6, Christmas Day: Snow had been falling intermittently all week, promising a white Christmas. The day was meant to be at leisure. The housekeeper was nowhere to be seen, but a buffet had been set with Christmas breads, cheeses, sausages, fruits, nuts, and candies. The Stillmans remained out of sight. I was not an infant, contrary to Mr. Stillman's law books, and so I determined to walk to church for the morning service before breaking fast. Mr. Stillman suddenly appeared and insisted on going with me. "How we appear in society has a lasting bearing on our reputation," he said.

As we walked, I voiced again my wish to see my mother, especially during Christmas holidays. He said she was traveling in Europe and that he thought she had met someone, repeating Mark's contention of the previous evening. She was even thinking of remaining on the continent after her tour. "There is nothing left for her in Kansas," he said, a special cruelty for my benefit on Christmas. He was sending her money to bank accounts in various locations. I asked for her mailing addresses. He said she was moving around too rapidly for the mail service to catch up with her. Then he said to me, "I do not understand you. Your mother has mistreated you and ignored you for the past two years, and now you want to visit her. Something's not right here. Why would you put yourself through that kind of abuse?"

I reminded him, "I will be of age soon."

But he indicated that would make little difference on my relationship with my mother or how she managed her business. "Your mother, who brought you up to believe that she always told the truth, has lied to you. You need to understand that this is where she is now. She does not want to hold your hand anymore." By the end of the conversation, I felt that every word Mr. Stillman said to me was a lie, including what was left and which was right. And I did not see anyone slapping a guardian on him anytime soon.

At church I happened to see Mary Clare with her family. I had forgotten that she lived in Concord. I latched onto her as though we were particular friends and begged that we might get together over the holidays either at her home or at the Stillman home. Her parents invited me to spend the following afternoon and evening with their daughter, for which I was extremely grateful. We walked part of the way home together, so I learned where the Decaturs lived.

For the remainder of the walk, Mr. Stillman began to tell a story of when my father was involved in a fistfight after a youthful bout of drinking and got arrested. Mr. Stillman claimed he came to the rescue and told the sheriff that it was he, not my father who had misbehaved and their exchange of identities had led to the confusion that started the fight. My father was let out of jail, and all charges were dropped as a result of this intervention. Mr. Stillman continued his story with his arms flung about like tentacles, punctuating his words with his gestures. My father was grateful for his kindness and showed his appreciation by his trust and partnerships in businesses. Later he had more trouble with the law stemming from his well-digging days, and Mr. Stillman claimed to have helped him with legal matters in that situation as well.

I remembered the versions my father had told of these stories. The hero of the tale was not Stillman but someone else. Was it Canon? Had Stillman simply stolen the story and put himself in the lead role? In fact, in my father's version, it was Stillman who often became intoxicated and Stillman whom he suspected of spreading the rumor of intoxication that got him in trouble at his school. My father had actually been placed on probation because of the accusation of alcohol abuse. My guardian's combination of inaccuracy and bravado stiffened my resolve. His words were downright frightening. How cunning, how capable of deceit, he had shown himself to be in just a few minutes. But was he also capable of greater harm: was he a thief, a liar, a forger?

Turning and smiling, he bumped his shoulder against mine at this point and asked in a casual voice, "By the way, Antoinette, we need to know where your father kept permanent records and other important papers in order to better oversee the properties."

"What are you looking for?"

"Some business has come up in Wichita, and we just need to verify his records, that is all."

"Have you asked my mother? She would know more about that than I would."

"Well, of course, we've been in touch about other things, but I was wondering if you knew something about a safe or safety deposit box?"

"Sorry, I cannot help you. I was only fourteen when he died, an infant," I could not help adding. "He didn't talk to me about such things. But I'm sure if I talked to Mother, we could find what you are looking for."

"That will not be necessary … at the moment." He dismissed my suggestion rather too hurriedly, I thought

I waited for Mark Weaver to call. At first Mr. Stillman seemed peevish about my caller, but after some time, he grew bored with our accounts of growing up in Wichita and sought instead to engage us in a rubber of bridge before he at last left us alone in the parlor. Mark was my first caller. The novelty did not wear off on the second or the third day, so much so that I almost forgot my original purpose. I begged the Stillmans to allow Mark to attend the theater with us. They agreed. "Mark, you must give me your mailing address in Wichita so that I can write to you when I go back to school."

To my surprise, he gave me the address of my own house. When he noticed my confusion, he quickly explained. "Your mother left the house unoccupied. My mother and Mr. Stillman thought if we lived there we could watch over the property. She has been managing the care of it."

"But why wasn't I told?" Certainly Mrs. Weaver had gotten steady work and fair wages from my father, whose contention had been that if a woman prove herself as competent and acceptable, in all respects, as a man to fill any respectable position, why shouldn't she fill it? Since my father's death, she was my mother's employee. What did it mean that she was now living in her employer's house?

"We … I assumed you were."

"Take me to Wichita," I demanded. "I need to speak to her myself."

"Well … I work for Mr. Stillman now, and I would have to ask him." Mark looked across the room at his employer. It was unsettling to see their eyes make contact. How could he work for Mr. Stillman? Didn't Mr. Stillman work for my mother? What else didn't I know? I already knew Stillman to be the wizard who made things vanish from my life using all the tricks of a sorcerer. Was he tutoring Mark in his tactics? Mr. Stillman had showed marked unkindness not only to me but also to his wife. How was he treating Mrs. Weaver, Mark's mother and my father's employee?

As my eyelids sagged with the weight of remedial layers of makeup concealing my own flaws, Mark's potential to become the man of my dreams began to descend like so much macaroon dust.

A.D.

December 26, 1909, Sunday, day 7: Since even the good-natured maid seemed to be watching me and making sure I did not go out alone, I decided to follow Mr. Stillman's directions and keep his wife company. We spent the morning in her room, looking at photograph albums and uncovering memories. As she looked at each image and collected memento, the story of her and Mr. Stillman's life together became clear. Her father had been a founding member of the town of Concord and active in getting a county seat and railroad to ensure that the town would grow. She met Mr. Stillman shortly after he first arrived in Concord and set up a legal practice. They married and lost a child early in their marriage but to her great sorrow were unable to have any more. When the orphan trains came through from New York, and the orphanage was founded, she had wanted to adopt a child or children, but her husband had refused. He insisted instead that they remain active in the city's politics, as those connections helped his growing profession.

"Men are money-making machines." She shook her head mordantly. "Women are the community builders with their fund-raising projects that help build libraries, schools, and hospitals."

Lucretia had eased her way into the public arena by gradually adding volunteer work and involvement in various clubs and civic organizations. But her work for the orphanage gave her the greatest satisfaction until her husband took over and used her charity to promote his own political rise through social causes. She did not seem to know very much about my family or Mr. Stillman's connection to my father other than that they had met while both were going to law school. She had not seen my father on that fateful trip four years previous and only heard about his death when Mr. Stillman read the obituaries to her. She had heard about me when Mr. Stillman suggested that I visit their home during the Christmas season the year previously. Only then did she learn her husband was my guardian.

Mary Clare and her brother called on me to attend the late Sunday-morning mass, followed by a visit at her house. The escape was a great relief. The Decatur family was so normal. How I envied their domestic harmony. Her brothers, who all shared Mary Clare's engaging swagger and ready grin, insisted that I join them in what they called a "craziest" contest. Each of ten feats was given a score. The first challenge was to make rude noises with their hands or by blowing into their elbows or by blowing into the palms of their hands. *Can.* The second task was to shake hands with oneself behind the back, one hand over a shoulder. *Can.* The third ordeal was to make fish lips (must wiggle them). *Can.* The fourth test was to see who could slam shut an open book with one hand and make the loudest noise. *Can.* (What a surprise, I won that one.) The fifth trial was to crack knuckles. *Can.* Sixth was touch elbow with tongue. *Cannot.* Seventh was flip eyelids back. *Eww.* Eighth was to raise one eyebrow at a time. *Cannot.* Ninth was spitting through one's teeth. *Cannot.* The final contest was to burp at will. Cannot. Mary Clare's brothers began making passing gas sounds to imitate a burp sound and then began to pass gas in earnest when they tried not to laugh at each other. In order to get our craziest scores, we simply added up all the *"cans,"* for one point each. Trying not to laugh, of course, led to even more loss of control. I cannot remember when I have laughed so hard: wheezing, bent double, tears forced from my eyes. Parts of my lungs felt like they had not gotten oxygen for a very long time. Did adults ever do this? Losing was never so rewarding.

After we cooled off by going outside and trying to make snowballs, Mary Clare wanted to dance. The parlor was cleared, someone sat at the piano, and before long her brothers and sister and even her mother and father got involved in practicing reels, waltzes, and two-steps. When her relatives—aunts and uncles and cousins—came, someone showed us the new dance called the turkey trot. Mary Clare's mother and aunts prepared a sumptuous meal of roasted beef and vegetables and many different kinds of Christmas cookies and breads. Dinner was a boisterous, satisfying, happy affair, with everyone chatting at once and platters passed this way and that. Her family is quite musical, and after their family's dinner party, entertainment included more dancing and singing. The change was intoxicating. I realized that my failures of having my own family reunion had bored even me and kept my mind returning to my fizzled attempts to get answers from Mr. Stillman. Practicing the dance steps made me realize that determining a new path in my life was not much different than learning new patterns of movement. I was happier that night than I had been in a long time. Sometimes to see the joys, one has to overcome fears, do something crazy, be disciplined, and endure the process. Which virtue is that?

A.D.

December 27, 1909, Monday, day 8: I was ready to go back to Mount St. Mary's or at least spend the day washing my hair and doing my laundry. These tasks helped me to formulate yet another plan. What were my guardian's intentions for my future? I would be graduating from the academy in the spring. My time and my endurance were both limited; therefore, I knew I could not try too much, but whatever I did try, I had to be sure to follow up on. How could I determine my own direction? My nights spent reading law books led me to conclude that I had the intelligence to follow the law. I was reading about deeds, "written instruments by which a landowner transfers the ownership of his land." Another written instrument called "the power of attorney" drew my attention. Such an instrument had to be formal as well— that is, observed, acknowledged, recorded, and sealed. Mark had been given a position in the Stillman firm, apprentice to learn about written instruments. Would Mr. Stillman do the same for me? What harm was there in asking? Yet another confrontation with Mr. Stillman occurred over dinner. It was almost as if someone could not have another opinion that was different from his. He became visibly agitated at being challenged.

"Mr. Stillman, I appreciate all that you have done for me during the holiday, but if your charity could extend to providing me with useful training, it might be better spent." I sliced a bite from the pork cutlet on my plate. "May I work for you this summer? I am a good student and will soon catch on to the ins and outs of filing necessary papers, court proceedings, and developing strategic lines of defense." I could see that he thought I was being impertinent.

"I am afraid not."

"Why, may I ask?"

"Antoinette, laws have consequences: human law and natural law."

"Why does Mark merit an apprenticeship in the legal field whereas I am denied the same advantage?"

To which he replied, "Because the two of us know it is impossible. Women have certain limitations."

"And men once thought humans could not fly, or tunnel through mountains, or go to the North Pole either …"

"The fact is that the girl has a much greater physical and a more intense mental development to accomplish than the boy, and she must complete that development in a shorter time than is allowed him. It follows that she cannot and should not be expected to devote to other functions, whether of mind or body, as much energy as may be properly required of him during the same period."

"Mr. Stillman, have you thought about what I will be doing this summer or next year, instead?" My attempt to calm the water only exacerbated the tension of the current.

"Have you?"

"Yes … a great deal. I thought I would be taking over the Dominguez Farms accounts in Wichita and maybe starting university."

"I want to caution you against such a plan."

"But why?" I should not have asked, knowing that a stream of words would follow.

"Too often the success of a girl's school life is purchased by the sacrifice of her sexual perfection. The development of a girl's reproductive organs requires the circulation of large quantities of blood in these organs. The mental activity necessary to prepare and recite her lessons demands the circulation of large quantities of blood through the brain. The girl has not blood enough to perform both lines of work at the same time. Menstruation slows her brain; study slows her menstruation. During the menstrual week, the first business is menstruation, in favor of which study and other mental effort must be subordinated."

"Really, Thomas, is it necessary to be discussing this during dinner?" Mrs. Stillman had pushed her plate back, as though losing her appetite.

"Yes, I believe it is. These facts, so apparent upon the slightest consideration, have been ignored by her educators, and as her guardian, it is my duty to enlighten her. Especially since I have directly experienced the dire consequences." He looked at his wife.

"Are you blaming me that we have not had children?"

"Educational methods of our schools are certainly not the only cause of female diseases, but they are an important factor. Sufficient opportunity for the growth of the ovaries and accessory reproductive organs and their periodical function should be a plank in the platform of women's rights to which you ascribe. Your own special mechanism of menstruation remains undeveloped, attaining at best an incomplete, unsatisfactory, and often painful process. One has only to look at your own brilliant school records to find cause."

I could not believe how Mr. Stillman had skirted the issue. And so the conversation dissolved into a muddle because Mr. Stillman had already settled on a solution to the problem I was trying to address, and that was to provide no course of future direction—and who could blame him when such a course was to his benefit? As I drank the evening's glass of apple cider, I wondered if alcohol had any effect on the law of periodicity.

A.D.

December 28, 1909, Tuesday, day 9: My brain felt scrambled from the sizzling shock of Mr. Stillman's scrutiny. Yet Mrs. Stillman showed some industry in spite of the limitations imposed upon her. She wasn't entirely content to play the passive role that society gave her, dressing beautifully, organizing parties, and obeying her husband. Knowing that Mrs. Stillman would not be at breakfast and that I would have the opportunity of dining alone with Mr. Stillman, I made my own Declaration of Sentiments in earnest, listing grievances and resolutions to assess my uncertain future. My gradual awakening with the events of each passing day, inch by inch, minute by minute, gave me the impetus to insist on my right to know, my right to participate, my right to express, and my right to monitor.

Mr. Stillman largely refused to discuss my father's holdings with me. His strategy was to talk about anything but my financial situation. And that was the problem. How could I retain him as a lawyer or financial guide in my own future, and how could I trust anything he did in the meantime? Instead he created a new crisis of a bankruptcy to overshadow these economic issues—saying the farms were not doing well, and he had had to take out a loan to keep up with machinery costs.

"You will be subject to excessive regulations because there's more work left to do as a result of new regulations, and I will be forced to retire some of your father's operations," Mr. Stillman countered to frighten me against change rather than to lead me confidently to do what must be done. Yet, ironically, his larger goal seemed to be to seize a bigger share of power over me. "And as for walking to church for mass this morning, I am afraid it is out of the question. A storm is threatening." Indeed he was right about that, but of a different kind. I considered pouting my way through breakfast, punishing him with my silences, or going to my room but wasn't that what he wanted—my silence?

Instead I spent the morning reading parts of Harriet Beacher Stowe's

Uncle Tom's Cabin to Mrs. Stillman as she and her friend worked on sewing clothing for the orphans. From time to time I looked up to see squirrels sprinting across the lawn, their tiny hands clutching sustenance against the harsh environment. Their actions provided a lesson to me as well. Hide acorns for recovery in hard times.

My thoughts strayed from the text I was reading. Should I attempt to unsnarl the tangle or wait until I was of age and hope the courts could do it? But would the courts do it? The guardians of the law were men like Mr. Stillman. And he would use every weapon in his impressive legal arsenal to convince me that he was working to protect me against insidious forces. Would he find another pliable judge? Mrs. Stillman clearly needed the ballot for women as a weapon for protection in her own home as well as for protection of her wealth and resources.

As I stood before the mirror and dressed, I knew I was smart enough to design my life. Kansas is a much more accepting place for women in occupational fields that men have worked in than most states; half of the women have been schoolteachers, for example. Kansas women have been able to vote in city elections since 1887. My father gave me the wherewithal to make these choices. Certainly my expectations of gaining leverage with Mr. Stillman had been considerably lowered from my original plans. But I did not intend to be frightened or dismissed. My claim to ownership was valid, but I realized now it would not come without a fight. I could not expect to get this given to me. I would have to go out and take control of my farms or remain a hatchling wrestling for a place in a carnivorous world. He ate my father, he ate my mother, and now he was about to eat me. Was Darwin right about the survival of the fittest? Stillman was a carnivorous beast—I was pitted against him without a fair shot. Yet I feared seeming desperate. Any debate with him in that key would never resolve what seemed his tyranny over me and over my family. After about an hour, Mr. Stillman interrupted my reading with a suggestion that I consider spending the summer as Mrs. Stillman's companion on a European tour. "We cannot have you growing up uncivilized."

In the late afternoon, Mark arrived with hard candies for Mrs. Stillman and chocolates in a little cupid-covered box for me. I felt like I was being courted. He also brought a camera and took photographs of the Stillmans and of me dressed in our theater clothes. I insisted on taking some of him as well. This venture lightened all of our moods.

Mr. Stillman seemed to like having me at his side and made a big production of introducing me to his many acquaintances visiting the theater. The sparkly chandelier and thick carpet were an elegant solution to covering up what was "uncivilized" in Concord. The word seemed to have stuck in my mind, and these were my thoughts as we settled into our seats and the frenzy of the orchestra preparing to play began. The stage appeared to be covered with cabins (though on closer inspection, I saw that they were painted onto a large canvas), and crowds of people were walking about, just like they were in a real town. The play began with a minstrel plantation scene and later incorporated a slave auction designed more to show off the talents of African American singers and dancers than to depict the horrors of the sale of human beings—scenes hardly written to encourage abolitionist sentiments and activism from audiences.

I did enjoy my time spent in the theater, but the play seemed so much more masculine than my reading of the novel. This was not Mrs. Stowe's story. The men got the best speaking parts, and the women hardly got any. On the other hand, with Mr. Stillman, I knew I had a chip on my shoulder. He seemed suddenly to want to spend time with me, trying to come across as the reasonable one with his language that belongs in a medicine bottle or a legal brief. As I sat next to Mark, his hand trailed over the back of my chair, and his shoulder leaned into mine. I did not pull away but moved closer so that Mr. Stillman could not hear our whispers.

At the intermission, Mr. Stillman, who does not suffer from modesty, made a point of boasting about his own knowledge of the theater. His credentials for saying so were his academic degrees, his case winnings, and his community involvement. I tried to remember his label-by-label criticism of the play as a "sensationalist narrative" written by "subversive reformers" intended to "collapse romantic ideals" with titillating "sadomasochistic violence" and "displays of human degradation and humiliation." No one interrupted, though he paused to allow for an objection. Giving one more example, he moved on, but so did I.

As we were exiting the theater after the play was over, I brushed shoulders with the man of shrewd hazel eyes and sand-colored hair from the Stillman Christmas party. "I would be interested in what you thought, Miss Dominguez."

"This is not Mrs. Stowe's story. The play version has a happily-ever-after ending with the death of Simon Legree. Stowe was not so optimistic. The death of one man did not cure the evil of slavery." Though surprised by his request, I was more than willing to give my opinion.

"May I quote you on that?" he asked. But before I could ask who he was, Mark had pulled me in another direction.

A.D.

December 29, 1909, Wednesday, day 10: The day did not start well for Mrs. Stillman, who seemed to have misplaced one of her "little helpers." She frantically flicked through a box, staring beseechingly at the labels on bottles, as if begging one of them to explain where the missing bottle had gone. "More delusions," her husband deprecated, finding it for her. "Too much medication, I suspect. And I understand you have also added laudanum to your tonics. For medicinal purposes, I presume?"

"My doctor prescribed it for my nerves to promote relaxation and a sound slumber," her wren-like voice piped up nervously.

I knew what she felt, getting a telling off, and tried to show my sympathy by sighing loudly, but I drew his attention instead.

"Take care not to continue this perpetual poutiness, Antoinette. It is disagreeable and could lead to the feminine tendency of hysteria. Boarding schools for girls are sometimes swept by hysteria as if by an epidemic. It is part of the innate tendency to mimic, especially as a failure to combat emotions. Too much talking about a thing can bring it on."

"I will be sure to caution Sister Louise; she will want to offer a new class on the subject immediately."

"Your sarcasm is not appropriate," he replied though his lips curled. Did he appreciate my retort?

Most unsettling about Mrs. Stillman's conduct was its eerie similarity to my mother's behavior the last time I saw her. I was fourteen when my father died so suddenly. Shortly after that I was sent to the academy. Mother, at Mr. Stillman's suggestion, thought it was best to continue my education (funny how his views on that subject have changed). My first two years of correspondence with her were very regular. She wrote weekly about the farms and my father's other businesses. She had hired a foreman, and between the three of them (Mrs. Weaver included), they were managing. That summer before my third year was the last I spent with her. I worked with Mrs. Weaver, adding figures in the ledger book. Then at Christmas I took the train to Wichita. But Mother was not the same—confused and lethargic, especially in the mornings. She no longer had access to my father's ledgers. When I asked to see the accounts, I was told I could not look at them without Mr. Stillman's guidance, as the business was rebounding from a brief decline. The strain on all involved had been taxing. Mother was always taking her medicine. I wanted to talk to her doctor but was told he was unavailable during the Christmas holidays. Before summer came, she wrote to me that she had made plans for me to travel as a stroke patient's companion. My letters to Mrs. Weaver and the foreman were returned unopened, as were the letters to my mother's doctors and to the hospital where she was supposed to have been a patient.

Most devastating of all, I received a letter from Mr. Stillman about prearrangements for my own summer activities. The experience of being a companion would be good for me and provide some much-needed education of the outside world. The woman I tended had had a stroke and went to Waconda Springs in north central Kansas. The water contained healing minerals: calcium, magnesium, iron, silica, sodium chloride, sulfate, and bicarbonate, and won a medal at the St. Louis World's Fair for its superior medicinal qualities. According to legend, it was once a ceremonial gathering place sacred to all the plains Indians for its healing powers and inhabitance by the Great Spirit. Dr. Abrams had just purchased the site and the health sanitarium, which the family turned into a hotel and resort for the relief of ailing and health-seeking people like my lady patient. Besides the bottled water, which was shipped all over the country, the spring's water was used for internal and external cleansing. My patient was daily bathed in a private stall and consumed gallons of the famous mineral waters said to cure many maladies and infirmities. Her health did seem to improve, but I believe her own will and consistent habit of walking in the pool every day helped as much as the waters. There was not much for me to do but swim and read; both were good preparation for the coming school year.

I wondered why I couldn't be my mother's traveling companion. I begged and pleaded that I missed her and even wanted to stop going to school to be with her. Her next letter insisted that I needed to grow up, that I was being an infant, and that she could no longer coddle me. It was my duty to be a good daughter and to obey her. She even hinted that she had met someone. I was prevented from going to Wichita to see my mother, nor did she make any attempt to see me. I was very angry at her last year, as you well know. Then again when I got the letter about summer travel plans as a woman's companion, I was not surprised. Though I did think of running away, I did not have the money to make the journey on my own. As a result, I began to save every penny of my allowance, should I ever have the opportunity again to escape. This Christmas here I was at the Stillmans. My fingers both ached and were numb with writer's cramp. But even my busy scribbling did not silence the nagging voice in my head. Mr. Stillman, in the very least, had become an impediment to my future.

Left on my own and alternating between submission and rebellion, I went through the trash and picked out all the newspapers. He was giving me a road map for navigating the public maze, after all. Concord society was known for the stability given by its well-mannered first level of families, its railroads linking it to the outside world, and its sustaining farming industry and political order. Peaceful images covered over the chaos and lawlessness of less than a generation ago, but even order can hang by a thread. Through the interpretation of the writers on various topics pertaining to Concord residents, I came to realize that I already had scraps of information that had a multitude of explanations. If I wanted to be a businesswoman or to study the law, I cannot walk around enraged, a threat to men like Mr. Stillman.

In the society section, I found an account of the Stillman Christmas party, including the names and civic involvement of those in attendance. What Mr. Stillman had told me about paying attention to social clues suddenly became clear. Understanding all the actors was challenge enough, but I had to figure out the balance between the actors' often-contradictory needs and between their goals and my needs and goals. My future remains murky, but this is the point where, out of the corner of their eyes, people are starting to get impressions about Mr. Stillman and about me. Mr. Stillman was counting on something, but what? In the article I was identified as, "Miss Antoinette Dominguez, ward of Mr. Stillman, student at the Mount St. Mary's Academy for Young Women," "unusually pretty," and in my "rose-colored gown displayed a fashionable style sense." Mr. Stillman was named one of Concord's most respected lawyers, serving on several boards, and his wife, from the "old family" roster, was praised for her community contributions. Could Mrs. Crescentia Gottfried further enlighten me? For I had noticed that she was the society writer responsible for describing all the party dresses in the newspaper. What could I gain by becoming her shadow at the Cloud Ball, the title given to the New Year's Eve gala?

At this time Mrs. Stillman entered the parlor and reminded me of Mr. Stillman's appointment to return to the tailor for the traveling suit that had been fitted earlier. Mr. Stillman was waiting in the motorcar. She accompanied me into the shops this time while he returned to his office, where we were to meet him at the completion of our shopping expedition. My tailored walking suit needed no further changes, so I wore it out of the shop, complete with boots, hat, and gloves as we walked down the boulevard named after Mrs. Stillman's father. Mrs. Stillman noted that heads were turning, a testament to my fashion sense and bearing.

Mr. Stillman practiced out of an office in a recently completed city building, still new-smelling with dark woods, brass fixtures, and green leather chairs. Incandescent lights and halls and lobby heated by steam were additional modern comforts. Mark was positioned at a desk in the outer office. "It is my job to keep his desk diary current with his court dates, client appointments, business meetings, and social engagements. I file his case documents. I also keep accounts of all receipts and disbursements stowed away in such order as to be almost immediately available when wanted. Best of all, I am beginning to do some legal research for him," Mark told us. As he thumbed through the previous calendar months, I could see that October, November, and December were entirely filled, as was January of the new year. "Mr. Stillman is speaking to the sheriff on a case right now, but he should be through shortly." I could hear some of the conversation.

"Yes, my office is more than halfway finished with the investigation. All involved have been interviewed. Cause of death and reports from the coroner's office have not been received, and we still have lots of work to do. Unfortunately, the scene was contaminated by townspeople walking through to have a look. But I am still confident that there is enough evidence in this case to give us a clear picture of what happened, but no … we cannot release anything publicly. It could influence potential witnesses."

"Legal haggling," interpreted Mark, "part of the case preparation." Seeing his eyebrows arch, and the wrinkles form on his high forehead, I supposed he was trying to figure out what he should do with this observation. To which he added a note in a legal file proving his dedication and commitment.

Mr. Stillman made a point of introducing us to the sheriff when they emerged from the inner office. "Miss Dominguez, it is a pleasure." He seemed to study me with more than a cursory interest, as though recalling a memory.

After a tour of the inner office and the highlights of the building, we walked past more than a few shops along a covered pedestrian walkway. In the early evening, a few citizens milled about as we crossed the street for dinner reservations at the Sternberg Hotel restaurant. This building too had been opened in the past year and featured an electric chandelier purchased at the St. Louis World's Fair, along with other novelties in the lobby seating arrangements. Mr. Stillman led the way to the hotel dining room and designated for himself a seat facing the entrance. As we were seated and waited for service, Mr. Stillman seemed obsessed with the comings and goings in the room: the pretty women, news from outside the town, rivals, and business acquaintances.

His commentary seemed to focus on one theme: how the slowness of downtown growth and progress threatened to make Concord irrelevant on the county stage. "When people ask where I am from, I do not want the next question to be, 'Where is Concord?' We need some new tactics to boost civic pride." He mentioned Abilene as a neighboring town that had risen to greatness but had quickly lost county power among local fiefdoms. Right now Concord was out in front. But it too was faced with the possibility of losing opportunities to a cross-county rival. "Concord city leaders will have to accept the risks of going into business with the state government, private business, and farmers or risk forfeiting their own leverage to woo new partners for expansion." He smiled and nodded to acquaintances in the dining room as he spoke. Was his pessimism misplaced? Mr. Stillman then lapsed into some rather crude remarks, which I shall not repeat, on what seemed to be his favorite bogeymen of Concord progress: sloppy, amateurish speculation, tired religious platitudes, and political oversimplifications, demonstrating that he was anything but fair-minded or able to maintain critical care.

When Mr. Stillman suggested we leave ordering from the menu up to him, I conceded, dulled by his vulgarity and fearing that I might be starved into submission if I dissented. Besides, after one look at the menu, I was for once in agreement. The list of fountain drinks alone intimidated me: soda water, ginger ale, lemon or orange phosphate soda, sarsaparilla, Dr. Pepper, Coca-Cola, and German mineral water. His choice in cuisine was excellent: cheese biscuits and salad (a hotel specialty), trout amandine, wild rice and mushrooms, house tomatoes in Hollandaise, and the surroundings most pleasant featuring a pianist taking requests as we dined. Dinner was interrupted by holiday well-wishers and acquaintances. At Mr. Stillman's signal, the pastry-cart was wheeled to the table. He selected a meringue filled with custard and strawberries for himself and a Napoleon for Mrs. Stillman. Mark and I both chose a slice of fudge chocolate cake. Afterward we drove through the downtown area so Mr. Stillman could point out both Concord's progress and lack of progress in building and housing projects. I could not listen to much, as my teeth were chattering in the cold night air.

A.D.

December 30, 1909, Thursday, day 11: Mrs. Stillman and I spent the day visiting the orphanage, playing with the children, working on a quilting session, craft session, and making cinnamon rolls. I think I would like to try making bread sometime. The children put on a performance, singing Christmas hymns and reading the Christmas story from St. Matthew. After that I read them a story while Mrs. Stillman showed a little girl how to hem a skirt. The child turned to her and said, "Please can I go home with you?" I could see why Mrs. Stillman worked on clothing for the children, and I determined to spend more time on needlework myself. Many of the children especially seemed in need of drawers. "Charity and service is the province for women who have proper attitudinal bent as well time for this kind of civic endeavor," she said when I asked her about the little girl. My admiration for Mrs. Stillman grew, for her motivation was quite different from her husband's. Her giving was from pure goodness, and she remained capable without using a lot of resources. I spent the rest of the day and the following morning stitching garments determined to follow her example of usefulness. That was when I thought of starting the orphan sewing project at the academy.

A.D.

December 31, 1909, Friday, day 12: The Cloud Ball was the glittering social event that marked the beginning of 1910. Mr. Stillman read the newspaper account: "Virtually all of Concord's figures of influence as well as many citizens of average status will be gathered in the recently completed town hall for the New Year's Eve Gala." Mrs. Stillman had many acquaintances from her memberships in women's clubs, especially children's charities—arts and culture, education and health, and community services—all of whom she looked forward to seeing at the ball. I came to look on this evening as a perilous adventure such as diving off a cliff or racing buggies until I reminded myself: Had we not learned all the skills of social interaction at Mount St. Mary's? I was about to implement my plan too. Since I could no longer trust my guardian's responses, I would have to find my answers elsewhere and make this party the catalyst for movement on my part. When circumstances provided, it was time to reevaluate; not just good times could lead to inspiration but the bad ones could also be a channel as well. Each party guest might have a piece of the puzzle I was bent of solving.

Mr. Stillman was acting as a waiter, along with other members of the Municipal Improvement Club, to pass hors d'oeuvres and fruit punch. Clad in starched white shirts, black ties, and black vests, club members would approach each guest with their offerings: a napkin with their club's name, a savory morsel, and a witticism. Mrs. Crescentia Gottfried, with her commanding presence and crown of white hair, was among the black-clad, white-collared elderly female regents and my first target. "Hello again," I said, stationing myself near her in a reception line. "Mrs. Crescentia Gottfried, I believe. We met at the Stillman Christmas party." I liked saying her name for the mouthful of substance and fusion of sounds.

"A very impressive event at the Stillmans … the best parties are given by people in trouble."

"Why, Mrs. Gottfried, whatever do you mean?" I was so shocked I did not know how to respond.

"I have been told I have a wicked tongue. It must come with age."

"I would so love to hear more."

She appeared to be thinking about it but instead directed her attention elsewhere. "My dear, Miss Dominguez, you do look lovely, and it isn't your dress. No fashion can make a pretty girl otherwise than pretty; unfortunately, the opposite is true, as in my case." She waved aside my protest on her behalf. "I am living on faded glory, though social connections do have a certain power and lingering mystique, which I count on. Would you mind if I held your arm for balance? These lines are so tedious, but I do want to shake hands with the mayor."

"Of course, and would you be so kind as to point out some of the notable members of Concord society to me?"

"That probably would not be a kindness. Many of these people are hideous." With that she began a whirlwind tour of the room. The influential Sternbergs were by her account the most prominent and admired family in Concord and not only the nucleus of "the social people" but founders and officers in charitable and cultural associations that came into existence during the early years of its founding. "But in this generation there have been no male heirs, only daughters. Sad, really, what often happens to these great families after three or four generations, either their children move away or they cease to have children entirely." The Steinberg Hotel was where we had had dinner and where Mr. Stillman's club met for lunch.

"What happens to their fortunes?" I could not help but be reminded of my own lack of family connections. My parents had eloped, as my mother had no family other than distant cousins with whom she had lost contact. My father's parents had died when I was young.

"The community usually benefits as acres, buildings, and estates are donated for institutions, parks, and educational and community resources." Various lawyers and doctors were pointed out, their school credentials cited, and their wives described as ladies of the "head set"—a school board member, a minister, an establishment family in furniture, those who made their fortune in the region's strength from livestock and grain. "By the way, how old are you?"

"Seventeen."

"Seventeen ... such a shame that we cannot read our own lives differently ... You do not really know your whole life until you are about seventy—and then you are too old to get it in focus or even care to."

"I am not sure I understand what you mean."

"If I could read my life backward, I would know not only how important relationships are but also how important are work and being part of a political community that makes sense. Women have to be able to vote. You are too young for this election, but at least women in Kansas can vote in local elections. Make sure you take the opportunity."

"I will next year. Is the mayor your candidate?"

"That is what I am about to see for myself." The line was moving slowly, but neither of us minded. Mrs. Crescentia Gottfried looked at me sagely and said, "You did not answer my question at the Stillmans' about who that young man's father was."

"I think his father died when he was a child. At least he has never been in the picture as long as I have known Mark."

"Even so you must find out his history. Who are his parents? What schools did he go to? Is there insanity in the family?"

I suppressed a giggle when I saw that she was speaking in all seriousness. Crescentia Gottfried would be an invaluable ally. I asked if I might write to her when I returned to the academy. "I would like that very much," she said and wrote her address on my program. "Do not keep me waiting, I have already promised a lot of people I would die soon."

From the account Mr. Stillman had read in the newspaper, the star of this show was the mayor of Concord. "Mayor Laurence Wolf had risen on the wings of patronage by serving as director of many civic institutions in Concord essential to business and political advantage or advancement of a candidate. He is a good-hearted man with a solid record backing his party's political views." Another account had condemned him as "a defender of the spoils system. Mayor Wolf's supporters are rooting for him because he promises to protect their security and wealth. Over the years he had leveraged personal connections and family prestige to secure resources, and then mobilized the same networks to protect them until ticketed for state senator. This year his campaign is on." Indeed he was the star from what I could tell. In spite of its trappings as a celebration to show off the new town hall sitting in the middle of the town common, the Cloud County New Year's Eve Gala was a political shindig.

I also observed that politics was a fleshly profession, all hugging, kissing, and shaking hands of anyone who approached. Mayor Wolf and the trusted circle of smiling friends around him were the most demonstrative touchers. There was no question where their loyalties lay. The ballroom was packed. Along with the barrage of Christmas decorations and balloons floating over the assembly hall were his posters and handbills plastered on every available wall. Everywhere there was evidence that the party was the beginning of organizing a campaign. All attendees were finely dressed and groomed, for they knew the power of appearance—the awe and respect that wealth created. They talked about the law and its instruments, the necessity of government for the peace and safety of all of us, but even a mud turtle coming out of hibernation such as I entering the perfidies of Concord society could recognize the environment arrayed in the mayor's favor.

While we sampled the finger foods being paraded past us, Mrs. Gottfried characterized the status of each as election or inheritance. Continuity in blood lines of the highest social stratum in Concord seemed primarily female, as was the case of Mrs. Stillman, whose status was inheritance, but Mr. Stillman's, whose was election by marriage. "But old families are like civilizations. One day they just wither and die." As I learned Crescentia's categories, most of the faces of the guests who began as strangers became familiar. When I looked outside the windows of Mount St. Mary's in future, I would know the people who ruled within the neat grid of blocks and streets making up the town.

And by the newspaper accounts Concord was kept going by the contributions of the galaxy of talented men represented in the evening's company, many of whom were the fathers and escorts of the beautifully gowned young women ornamenting the hall. The branches of the city government all seemed to be represented: the sheriff and the court, the charities, the public works, education and health, and building and road construction. Concord was also distinguished for the number of its churches and its good fortune in attracting brilliant and able preachers to preside over their congregations. Crescentia Gottfried knew them all. After we shook the mayor's hand, I led her back to her observation seat. "A woman is not just an ornament. A new sun is rising in the West. See that you stand up for yourself, Miss Dominguez," she said when I hugged her in parting.

"I will," I promised and began to roam around the room on my own. You cannot imagine my excitement at being part of the energy of such a gathering. I wanted to talk to everybody there about what was happening in Concord—and so I asked the only questions I knew: Do you have any women in your department? Would you hire me? What preparations would I need to make? I paid particular attention to whether I liked the people I met and whether I sensed that they were generally happy to be in their chosen profession. I needed to find a place where there were people I could learn from, a place where I would feel comfortable, and a place that was going to allow me to work. Most were as curious about me as I was about them when I revealed that I was a student about to graduate from the academy, itself housed in a recently completed five-story building that had a stately presence commanding community status.

I had choices, in spite of Mr. Stillman. I saw myself advancing in conjunction with Concord's citizen agendas through one of their institutions. All it would take was to educate myself on the available options and chart a direction for the future. This thought sent an electric current throbbing through my being.

Even so, I was not sorry when Mark caught up to me and adroitly turned my focus in another direction. The area designated for the ballroom was magically festooned with red and green flower, ribbon, and cedar wreaths and garlands, and aglow with perfumed candlelight. The orchestra opened the grand march with Mozart's "A Little Night Music." Couples promenaded ceremoniously around the waxed and buffed floor. When he took my hand and escorted me onto the floor, I could not help smiling at his extravagant compliments and flirting with him as well. He was charming and handsome and fun. I liked his smart suit. For some inexplicable reason, dignity and discretion were abandoned. The ball was a play after all, a public reprieve from the hidden lives we would return to the next day, for the next year. By some mysterious transformation, I felt my charms were irresistible and Mark totally captivated. Dancing followed interspersed with announcements of raffle winners and even an occasional cakewalk for prizes.

I had many partners, and some were names I was beginning to recognize from reading about Concord families in the newspaper and hearing Crescentia's narrative. "Is he your beau?" my partner for the new song "By the Light of the Silvery Moon" asked, nodding at Mark.

When I took a second look, I remembered him as the quiet, sand-colored-hair guy from the Stillman Christmas party and from the theater asking my opinion on the play. "I did not get your name."

"Frank Canon … is he?"

"Oh no, nothing like that," but he commented that I was blushing. "He is just someone I have known for a very long time."

"He seems a spindly, snide fellow to me," he critiqued.

I shrugged and laughed at his boldness. "And what is your interest, exactly?"

"Are you sure he is not your beau?"

"I am quite, quite sure." I suddenly wanted to learn more about Frank Canon.

"He would be a lucky fellow," he said kind of soft, in a way that made me want to concentrate on the sound.

"Is this what they call smooth talk?" I asked rethinking my first impression.

"Not at all," he said, "but I am glad to hear that he is not the one. I hope to dance with you again, Miss Dominguez." I wanted to say something memorable, but I had turned stupid all of a sudden. "Look me up when you graduate from that academy, won't you?" We had been dancing in a little square, close together and hardly moving at all. He bowed like a gentleman as the music was over and handed me a card with his name, a telephone number, and an address with the *Concord Chronicle*. "Maybe I'll do a story on you."

"And who is your father?"

"My father?"

"Mrs. Crescentia Gottfried told me I should always learn a gentleman's parentage. There might be insanity in the family."

He stopped in the middle of the dance floor and laughed heartily then became serious. "I thought you knew … J. Canon … and I have had my eye on you for some time …" He signaled with two fingers at his eyes and then at me. "But right now I have to go to work in another direction."

Why? I wanted to ask, but he was already backing into the crowd. *What did he mean his eye on me?* My own eyes followed where he had disappeared. There was something about the posture of his shoulders that would have been more comfortable sitting down, hunched over a scrawled page before him. I did not doubt his palm was gray with graphite. Was his father the watchdog who had written a story about my father? I could see Frank Canon receding to the other side of the room, where Mayor Wolf was demonstrating his gift for public speaking. It was shortly before midnight when the mayor raised a glass to toast in the New Year from the stage, giving his year-end review of achievements on behalf of the city and making promises of more to come if he were elected senator in 1910. Indeed the mayor was good-looking in a political way and an amiable fellow. Cloying scents of perfume, bay rum, pomade, and smoke from pipes, cigarettes, and cigars began filling up the room.

A few minutes later, Mark and I joined the revelers to walk outside as a countdown began, "Five, four, three, two, one …" A spew of confetti startled gasps and then giggles around the courthouse square, choked with people giddy on New Year anticipation. "I suppose I could say I have missed you like a brother so that I could kiss you like one," said Mark. "But then I would be lying because I did not miss you until I saw you standing in the Stillman parlor all grown up and not looking like anyone's sister but like someone I wanted to kiss and keep on kissing."

His arm was around my waist, and as I turned to look into his eyes, we were pushed together by the crowd. I wanted to kiss him too. All around us was the sound of cheering, singing, horn blowing, and the excitement of a new beginning. The crowd of revelers continued to press as his face bent over mine, and my arms rose to embrace him. Our lips fused. I could feel his ardor and my own. The promise of a new year took on new possibilities.

After midnight the buffet tables were set up with trays of meats, cheeses, breads, salads, and desserts. I was too excited to eat. When I said how delightful the evening was on the way home, Mr. Stillman remarked, "The point of throwing a party is not enjoyment. How little you understand of society, Antoinette."

A.D.

January 1, 1910, Saturday, day 12, New Year's Day: When Mark came over, I read aloud to him the society page of the newspaper in imitation of Mr. Stillman. "The musical entertainment earned waves of applause." The ball was declared a "spectacle of unusual brilliance," with participants listed as serving on planning committees and sponsoring various events of the evening. All told, upward of a thousand Concordians attended. A list of female attendees, what they wore, and a descriptive adjective was included: Mrs.— beautifully gowned in yellow brocaded satin with chiffon trimmings, Miss — a lovely pink silk with lace trimmings, Miss — handsome black silk with chiffon, Miss — a pretty green organdy, and so on. My own blue gown was described as "stealing attention." "Thank you, Crescentia," I had told Mark of my discovery.

"Notice she does not say anything about the seriously lumpy girls," commented Mark.

"That is the point, isn't it? Not being mentioned is like being invisible."

On the editorial pages, I found a scathing review "Concord's Town Hall Opening on a Sour Note," which I partly read and partly summarized for Mark about the attendees of the Cloud Ball. "I am disturbed that Concord's mayor would have what appears to be a private party and political benefit mostly at city expense," wrote the author, none other than my dance partner Frank Cannon, who claimed to be a watchdog for the community's interests.

> Do we really need an expensive shindig to celebrate the opening of a new building? This celebrating of every new road, city hall, and school has got to stop, especially when the city council approves contracts that are criticized in city audits for careless spending, insufficient controls, and missing records of taxpayer dollars. The people in charge of these projects—designers, workers, and our mayor and his friends—are just doing their jobs. They do not need a pat on the back every time a big job is completed.

According to the article, the mayor countered that the gala was an event scheduled to garner interest in developing serviceable roads and parking for automobiles. "The gala was part of the usual outreach to the public by Concord's planning and development officials, which provided the entertainment and co-planned with the streets and roads department, which provided the food," and that he was well within his authority to host such an event. "It wasn't Mayor Wolf throwing a New Year's Eve party," Thomas Stillman was quoted in his defense. "It was the city holding a reception. You have to have some pomp and circumstances to commemorate significant architectural achievement." Canon was skeptical about Mayor Wolf's claim that the event offered a free opportunity to educate the community on current projects and make outreach to potential donors, volunteers, and fellow organizations, as well as a valuable way to get the word out to the city. "Large and small, all those in attendance have this in common: they do important, meaningful work on behalf of the community." To which my new friend responded, "I wished them Happy New

Year, and that did not cost anything. That is the extent of the participation the city of Concord should be subjected to. The financial burden of a gala event should be theirs alone."

Mark made no reply when I finished reading the article.

I continued my defense. "Canon has a point about the mayor and his friends, you know. I couldn't help but notice how even Mr. Stillman flitted about and smiled at people shamelessly."

"Why are you so down on him? He is just doing what's good for business. I've picked up some valuable pointers on that account, even been working on the mayor's campaign, doing research, and passing out pamphlets."

"Don't be cross with me, Mark. It alarms me when you are angry and aloof. You're the only person I know here, and I hope, my friend." To change the tenor of the conversation, I read a short article about the coming of Halley's comet in 1910. The report included beginning sightings by observatories throughout the world and the fear of poison cyanogen fallout.

"There, you see. You have nothing to worry about. The world is about to end anyway." He grabbed the newspaper away from me and began to read a story from the last page.

Faux Firefighters Charge Businesses for "Inspections"
Concord Fire Department officials say local business owners
and residents should be on the lookout for a group that has
claimed they are required to enter local businesses to inspect the
electrical wiring that has been subject to rats gnawing on the
insulation, exposing wire and causing fire hazards. They wear
dark uniforms but do not identify themselves as being from the
fire department. They have someone in charge from the business
sign official-looking paperwork that requires business owners to
pay $5 for the inspection or be turned over to a collection agency.
There is really no law against what they are doing. By signing
the documents, business owners agree to pay the fees. Businesses
who get a visit should contact ... sheriff's department ...

"What incredible nerve. Who would do such a thing?"

"It's a pretty clever idea, though, don't you think? In lawyer's terms, that contract is called a legal instrument. Wish I'd thought of it ..." Mark stopped talking, and then he did a peculiar thing. He reached out and touched my cheek, lightly, as if brushing away a speck of last year. We looked into each other's eyes as we had the evening before, and he gave the same irresistible smile. "You're so beautiful, Antoinette, and absolutely enchanting. I can't help but look at this mouth. I'd like to—"

But Mr. Stillman inviting us to dinner interrupted. Our conversation thus hobbled, I asked Mark what he would be doing the following summer. He shrugged and looked at Mr. Stillman. "I suppose I will be doing research or continuing to work as a clerk. Maybe even start university." Eaglan began handing Mrs. Stillman the serving dishes.

"Why is one sex destined to reach for the heavens and the other left to drag in the earth and made to defend herself? Do women have souls? Do women have brains? Do women have strength and stamina?" I asked, shaking out my napkin.

"Do they?" Mark joked.

But I ignored his interruption. "A woman's time, her labor, her ingenuity like that of a man's should be marked. Not being able to vote has such devastating consequences." I noted that Mrs. Stillman made no attempt to express an opinion.

"Of all these narrow ideas of female identity imaginable, none of more toxic than the notion that the vote is the center of authentic citizenship," Mr. Stillman countered.

I continued, "My plan is to spend the summer with my mother when I locate her, but perhaps you could join us." I included Mrs. Stillman, who had remained silent. "I think you and my mother would have much in common."

"Holidays … a mass pretense of enjoying oneself," was Mr. Stillman's blunt assessment of the week gone by. "Christmas is the worst insanity of all."

"Yes, we suffer when we have no one to love," I could not help replying, even thinking I could forgive him, for it is usually impossible to figure out what someone else is saying if you do not speak the language. His behavior certainly indicated he did not interpret events as most other people did.

"Antoinette, you pursue this notion to your own detriment—you cannot measure yourself against parental standards set by others. I suggest you forget about your mother. Concentrate on your future in society."

"An ounce of mother is worth a pound of society." The retort came without reflection.

"Feel free to ignore my warning, Antoinette …" At one moment, he seemed earnest, as though fidgeting over my level of engagement. In the next, he seemed sarcastic, "You may well regret it."

I looked at Mrs. Stillman, who sat across from him molded to his ideal of fashion, beauty, manners, and duty simply to please him, yet not pleasing him. He was amused by the endless variety in her costume and claimed chivalry by her seeming helplessness and dependence and ten thousand fears. And she was a woman who had not married a man for a home, for silks, bright jewels, equipage … yet she now revolved around him, lived only for him, in him, with him … was fed, clothed, housed, guarded, and controlled by him, only shining in his reflected light.

"You should consider having your own guardian," I quipped trying to refresh the conversation. Too many subjects had become unmentionable. Thankfully, our game was interrupted by the housekeeper announcing some late-arriving visitors and suggesting she had enough dessert for all. After preliminary introductions, Mark and I remained in the dining room while the Stillmans and their guests moved into the parlor.

"Do you always tell the truth, Mark?" I asked, pretending to help clear the table

"The whole truth, and nothing but the truth?" he asked with a grin. "Probably not all the time, but most of the time I do my best."

"Have you ever observed Mr. Stillman in his law practice distort the truth or provide inaccurate information?"

"You are serious, aren't you?"

"On a scale from mostly honest to grossly dishonest, where do you think Mr. Stillman fits?"

"He is a lawyer, after all, whose tools are debate, persuasion, and, yes, manipulation. Right or wrong, truth or falsehood is not always clear-cut. What is true to one person may appear false to another. He is not obligated to give equal emphasis and recognition to a view opposing his own or his client's."

"But what if his view is opposed to his client's? What then? Isn't he morally bound to seek truth for his client even if it is to his disadvantage, especially if she is a minor?"

"What are you getting at?"

"Does Mr. Stillman have a file on me or my mother in his office?"

"You know I cannot give you that information."

"I need your help, Mark, as my oldest friend. I am not satisfied with the answers I am getting from Mr. Stillman about my family's affairs."

"What do you want me to do?" he said warily.

"Stop the charade. Disarm him. Lead the charge." Could Mark pass my crazy test?

"Isn't that rather dramatic?"

"Help me to get to Wichita, find my mother, and take charge of our lives and property."

"There is one way we could do that, very easily."

"What's that?"

"Marry me, Antoinette."

The sucking sound I made following his proposal startled both of us. His proposal had greatly complicated things. If I said no, he would not help me, and he might even convey my plans to Mr. Stillman. On the other hand, the protection of a husband would immediately end Mr. Stillman's guardianship over me. But ownership of my properties would transfer to my husband. It was dangerous to allow a silence to go on too long. The impact of Mark's words did not diminish in the vacuum. Instead they grew and gained in consequence. I had to say something or all would be lost.

"Do you think a wife should obey her husband in all things?" A not-so-irrational thought occurred to me.

"What?"

"Do you?"

"Two people who love each other should be able to make decisions together without one having to obey the other."

"This is so sudden … I have to think about our life together … We both do. What will we be doing during the next year? In two years?"

"I have trouble thinking about anything else."

"And what is it you think you will be doing?"

"Right now I have a boss who makes my decisions for me."

"And I have a guardian who does the same for me. Don't you see, Mark, we have to help each other break free from his control before we can marry? We are very young, neither of us considered adults."

"From what I have observed in the past few days, you seem to be doing a pretty good job of taking care of yourself."

"It may seem like that, but the life I lived before when my father was alive and my mother was the center of my world was so different. I was so happy then. I just cannot touch that happiness anymore."

"You don't think we find other people to love, not like old shoes or anything, to make us happy?"

"Are you happy, Mark?"

"I don't know, I suppose. Seeing you again made me happy."

Our conversation ended, not altogether on a satisfactory note. Mark's proposal went unanswered when the Stillmans came in to suggest that we retire and then remained in the room to make sure that we did. Our good-byes were gestures: a salute of his hand, a wave of mine. I knew he wanted to kiss me again, and I wanted him to. The moment he was gone, I went to my room and sat forlornly on the bed. I got a sudden chilly feeling that I never would do anything about anything because I could never make up my mind. I was treating myself gingerly with my situation in peril—on the one hand wanting to unleash a fury, but externally my timid actions belying the interior fury I was holding at great cost. What would happen to my father's fortune should I not marry and have children to pass it along? Mr. Stillman's prurient comments on my budding womanhood at least validated that my emotions were as complicated and ungovernable as those of any young woman my age. So while I savored the admiration and tender feelings of Mark, I was inclined to be argumentative and grumpy. Was the corset forming my new waist causing other changes to my body?

A.D.

January 2, 1910, Sunday, day 14: Mr. Stillman did not appear until the arranged time for taking me back to Mount St. Mary's. I was left prey to my thoughts or rather how I was prey to my guardian's use of both his legal power and my father's capital to enforce his will, stifle dissent, and consolidate power, even to threaten that if crossed, he could bring me to financial ruin. He controlled the payment of mortgages on my father's businesses, the payment of taxes, the management of day-to-day operations, including purchase, sales, and maintenance, the hiring of employees … For all these essential activities, he was given a wide berth. Was there a way to get my guardianship revoked? I just wished that my mother and father had other relatives. How could I search from here? Could I even get letters through the post? Perhaps Mr. Stillman had that information in his books or files. Already I was searching for a way to make Mark a lookout, reaching out for him as though a lifeline to another world … Would he be there when I most needed rescue? *Am I behaving as though my life is in peril?*

Mr. and Mrs. Stillman lived in a state of tension, which I was only too happy to leave. But Lucretia seemed genuinely saddened to say good-bye. "I might have had a daughter like you," she said. "I am sorry I have not gotten to know you better. Do come to stay with us again." When the automobile stopped in front of the academy, Mr. Stillman patted my arm awkwardly. Abruptly, I felt awkward, too, embarrassed and glad of the prospect of being away from him, away from his control.

My homecoming, for this was my home, was a day earlier than the return of most of the other students. In spite of the isolation, my spirit lifted. This place was Eden compared to where I had been. I arrived first. Mount St. Mary's was quiet in secret, delectable waiting, with no one but the saints to hear me. Climbing the five flights of stairs to the dorm would be, I hoped, a detoxifying remedy, but instead left me weak and breathless. I immediately removed my dress, petticoats, and corset, and as the tight waist fell away, so did the paralysis of nerves and muscles around my ribs. Fashion design should aim to please and be useful, not torture and make wearers unable to function. Clad only in my step-ins, vest, and hose, I was able to take deep breaths, restoring the free circulation of blood and action of my heart and lungs. Mr. Stillman's point about the relation between scholarship and clothes was clear, though not his interpretation. As my deep breathing continued, I felt a newfound vigor and enthusiasm. Elizabeth Cady Stanton was right, "The cunning girl is to have health." The cut and cloth of my school uniform was remedy indeed. I thanked Mrs. Stillman for the introduction to the work of this truly great woman.

Always when I thought of Mrs. Stillman, Mr. Stillman came to mind as well. The best way to beat Mr. Stillman's surveillance was to abandon patterns, to make enigmatic decisions. The process of discovery was anything but a linear narrative leading to the present. Instead it was the false starts, dropped threads, and contrary lines of thought that best seemed to lead to Mr. Stillman. His was a very crooked path.

I tried to read a book of quotations to give my thoughts a more positive direction. There was not much for me to do, and I did enjoy the quiet. Then I came across this quote from Emerson: "Do not go where the path may lead; go instead where there is no path and leave a trail," which started me thinking about my situation again.

What was Stillman really about? I could solve the puzzles if only the pieces would stop moving, if only my thoughts would stop racing, if only I could breathe … He had outlived his usefulness to my mother and to me. First of all there was the direct obstacle of the law, which saw me as a minor, an "infant," and a woman. This I could stand up to when I reached the legal age of eighteen. But I also lacked knowledge of the current standing of my father's holdings and management. Both of these obstacles could be quickly remedied by time, my birthday in a few months, and proximity, going to Wichita and speaking directly to accountants and business managers.

My main challenge was Mr. Stillman. He had made himself difficult to fight with. While he did not seem a direct threat—not fanatical or irrational—he had accused me of both when I made the attempt to discuss business matters with him. Was he a parasite destroying the host he preyed upon? Was he a tyrant martialing an arsenal of power? And was name-calling the worst I could do anymore? I had to stand up to him and not be frightened by him. But I might be in for months, even years of the Stillman threat. Did I have the fortitude for that? I determined not to speak of my pains or to distract my mind by gathering sympathy from my friends but to martial my own giant's strength to encounter the trials I might yet have to meet. My memories of Christmas celebrations of years past with my family intact were no longer distinct. Even as I stared at a photograph, fuzzy images of expensive gifts and party dresses that seemed important at the time now merged into one dim, blurry haze. In the silence came the realization that this year, Christmas itself was the present. It was the tool kit I had been praying for.

If the past year of uncertainty and dread had given me purpose, it was all I could have asked for. Mr. Stillman was the key to fixing what was broken in my life and the focus I had lacked for my previously wasted energies. At first writing this account was merely a side project. But the process has proved to be a true revelation. I was confused and discontented. But the more I thought about how my confusion and sadness made me turn inward, the more I felt compelled to stop hiding and connect with people on the other side. This journal and my journey began over pain, and what is pain for but to find the cause of injury (to my mother and me) of the loss of her husband and my father, softened at times but not diminished? The difficult problem of finances remained perplexing. My only requirements were those imposed on me by the execution of Father's will. He is in my heart forever. That's why I know that my mother's grief did not end either. She still has the broken heart of a wife who has suffered the worst kind of pain. Was this not a virtuous endeavor and daughter's duty to make what restoration I could?

As I began writing about the events of the Christmas holiday, my plan developed. I wanted to tell my father's story, his hopes and dreams, his trials, and what my mother and I experienced when that telegram arrived telling us he was gone from our lives. We were in shock, the news so devastating, our minds shut out its truth. Our only protection was disbelief, until we went to the train station to claim his body and faced the reality that the bad dream was not a dream. We would not awake from the nightmare. As time passed, more questions than answers began to arise, yet queries led to dead ends.

A.D.

(Tear along the dotted line)
****

Sophiny, if you are compelled to share my pocket notebook with anyone, destroy this page and keep the documents under the trunk tray hidden. You can only give them to me. I must hold you to this final promise.

My last memory of my father was when I went to his library to make some request, a bicycle, a dance lesson, a new dress—he never refused. After it had been granted, and I was leaving the room, he became very serious. "Antoinette I have a request to make of you as well. I wish I could give you wings to make you fly, but since I cannot, you will have to learn to fight. If anything should ever happen to me, you are to make sure you never let my

124

trunk out of your immediate possession," and he put his hand on the trunk to which you, dear Sophiny, now have the key but was then standing on one end and used as a lamp table in the corner of the room. He was gazing at me with an expression of particular affection. "Remember, you might have to fight for what is yours."

But I was in a rush to celebrate my conquest, and so I hurriedly agreed to avoid further engagement. My father left that day for Concord and what ended up being his final journey. Sometime before he left, he had placed the locked trunk in my room under a throw, the key left in my jewel case with a note to keep the contents close and secret. I didn't realize all this until several days after we had buried him. After Father's death, the house seemed empty, shorn of his smile and his guiding spirit. It was then I first knew that uncontrollable things were happening beyond the surface of my life.

A.D., in the Year of Our Lord 1910

Chapter 11
Crux of the Traveler's Tale

Antoinette's passion was not the kind Sophiny had been expecting to come through in her pocket notebook. There had been no plan for elopement. This was an entirely different Antoinette from the one she knew from her last weeks at the academy. Antoinette's journal revealed an induction into the adult world that she had so longed to join, but these were rites new to both herself and her friend. Antoinette's composed schoolgirl exterior had given no evidence of the turmoil simmering beneath or that she was on the brink of an unforeseen crisis. What, then, had run her plan off the rails? Her predictions about her own future of living happily ever after were deflected by the snapshots she had created:

- Her father a victim of his friend's treachery—Antoinette's whole world had been about seeking her family's "love and legacy." How far did that treachery extend?
- Her widowed mother pushed out of her home and off her farmlands by an aggressive lawyer who she discovered was not on her side. Did her protests result in her disappearance?
- Antoinette a fatherless daughter sent to a convent without the consolation of her mother and at his mercy as a court-appointed guardian—alone and without legal protection. Would she become lost where there was no path?

Antoinette had in the months before her disappearance been collecting information, studying the characters, calculating actions and reactions, and plotting her course. The past month, though, things must have looked far different than they did from afar and taken a turn she had not expected. How much of the information was inadequate or irrelevant? Even now the mystic in her was probably improvising solutions, relying on wits, guts, adaptability, and prayer.

The banging of the screen and the slam of the front door abruptly ended her prospecting. One of her brothers had entered the house. With a start, Sophiny realized she had made a sudden, abrupt return to her own reality. In fact, the trunk containing Antoinette's pocket notebooks and other treasures had managed the neat trick of making the world inside the trunk supremely vast and mysterious. Antoinette's narrative read as though penned by a skilled sleuth disguised as a uniformed schoolgirl. Study halls, cleaning charges, and passing notes had much more ballast and heft in the written account than in her fleeting memories of the academy. She carefully locked the contents back in the trunk, unwilling as yet to share the secrets, and quickly went downstairs to think about the mundane subject of what to put on the table for a midday meal.

The crux of the traveler's tale was whether Antoinette could fulfill her quest for specific knowledge to reclaim her family and her inheritance. Her first challenge was the very safety of her surroundings. The connection through reading her words, though unsettling, gave Sophiny a very intense sensation. The harrowing ordeal that Antoinette had gone through—was going through—was directed by the passion of her pursuit. Sophiny was reminded of Sister's Louise's sign over the library shelves: "Do not bend, fold, mark, or mutilate." Would Antoinette be returned in one piece, whole and undamaged?

Was Antoinette's story one of tragedy, of shock, or simply an accident? Was she an innocent and virtuous person in distress? If so, her friends ought not to leave her until they had delivered her out of her troubles or helped her triumph over her enemies. Was her elopement a mere spectacle and her own action the cause of her adversity? In which case, chastising her bad choice, punishing her for a time, excluding her from virtuous society would be in order. Or was the elopement a comedy of errors, a game of hide-and-seek, inside-outside, a childish prank, a scandalous catastrophe less fatal than either of the above? Dear Antoinette could be forgiven for such folly after a good laugh, a hot bath, and a cup of tea when one saw her graceful motions, her pretty face, and listened to her merry words and peals of laughter as she told her story.

But there was more ... How had Antoinette been lured into eloping? What would her travel/touring guide look like on a map? What action could Sophiny take from Prairie Dog? Antoinette, her father, and her mother had originated from Wichita. Antoinette's father had died suddenly in Concord. Antoinette had gone to school for the past four years in Concord. Antoinette had last seen her mother in Wichita. Antoinette's guardian, with whom she had spent the Christmas holidays, lived in Concord. Antoinette had eloped from Concord. Antoinette had disappeared from Concord. Lawyer Stillman's law practice was in Concord. What was his connection? What if Antoinette herself had been lied to? How could she rely on a legal system so riddled with exceptions and holes that those who should be prosecuted were largely exempt or used the very instruments of the law to conceal the evidence against them, whereas, the true heirs were exiled, dispossessed, and threatened?

Antoinette's written revelation of her troubles had expanded Sophiny's own life. But because of the rain and dim lighting and Antoinette's ornamental though neat handwriting, Sophiny could only engage in a slow reading. In the dim light and silence, reading became an act of contemplation, allowing her to merge with the consciousness of her friend. Her patience in giving each narrative line space and time to prevail surprised her. Withdrawing from the world she now lived in, stepping back from the noise, the tumult of the Mumm household, she regained a transmission with her friend that had a deeper impact, a more intimate connection, than any she had experienced. Antoinette did have big reasons for writing. *If you lied about that, what else did you lie about?* she seemed to be asking over and over again of Mr. Stillman. Her story made an art of uncertainty by uncovering how her guardian had twisted things.

Above all Antoinette's dominant motive was doubt not curiosity, as Sophiny had first thought. Whenever limits were placed on her ability to know something, she was driven like Pandora, like Psyche, like Eve to doubt the knowledge she had received. Sophiny was reminded of great discoverers: Did Columbus fall for the flat-earth theory? Did Galileo stop thinking about gravity? Did Descartes credit humans with having the highest intelligence in the universe? It was doubt that gave energy to Antoinette's reasoning. Her doubt had spared nothing, not even the curiosity that led to her first investigations. Thus, curiosity, though a starting point, had to be acknowledged as having limits. Did doubt too have limits?

The rain had stopped, the sun was out, and little evidence of the early-morning torrent remained. Her brothers brought a faint tang of the outdoors with them: the smell of hard work in the fresh air. Richard brought something else. "Remember this morning when you told me about poultices? I need one now."

"Why, what happened?"

"I think I sprained my wrist moving all that equipment. Do you have something I can put on it?"

Sophiny did not, but she knew where to look: Mrs. Child's *The American*

Frugal Housewife "dedicated to those who are not shamed of economy," another of her mother's indispensable resources. "Wheat bran and vinegar—which we have. Can you make it yourself while I get the food on the table?" she asked, locating the items.

Fortunately, leftovers from the previous evening's beef stew and thick slices of buttered bread satisfied her brothers' appetites. Richard commented that his sprain felt better with the poultice. She did not wish to share her morning's preoccupation—not knowing how her brothers would interpret or translate the events of her friend's disappearance or her own role in searching for her. Who could she turn to? Between the "Pass the …" and "Is there any more …" Sophiny managed to get in her own requests. "Remember, I told Martha Shaw I would go over this afternoon so she could explain a thing or two about photography. I need one of the riding horses."

The Shaw house was a modest, clapboard structure, with some charm thanks to its long front porch and a fine showing of spring bulbs—tulips and daffodils—just beginning to bloom. Some steep, rickety stairs led to the porch entry where Martha waited to greet her as they had planned on their last meeting. "Is this your maiden voyage since you have been home?"

"Yes, James didn't want me to come alone after the rain and all. Almost as complicated as sailing to a new world," Sophiny said with a laugh.

"It doesn't do to complain, but make no mistake, women's advancement, though slow, is steady. Do not let the obstacles cause you to waver."

"I assured him that you were expecting me, and you didn't live far."

"Good girl! Paul will take care of your horse. Come inside."

Sophiny followed Martha into what she deduced was her sanctuary. The tone and furnishings of the room delighted her instantly. "You have a very comfortable home."

"Feel free to come over anytime. Your mother wanted you to be educated and to continue your reading. We had many long talks this last year. She had dreams for you her youngest and only daughter, and she asked me to keep an eye on you. I have a few books you might like to borrow, and there is a circulating lending library that comes to town once a month," said Martha as she took Sophiny on a tour of her dining room, which was not so much for eating as a library-photography studio. Against the right wall was a floor-to-ceiling bookcase in three sections. Bound volumes of history, biography, informational texts, and many novels lined up at attention. Martha's Bible was on a stand by itself. The titles testified to Martha's personal interests. Here was a universe of reading acquired for her own education.

Other furnishings included a small, ornate pillar, a large wicker chair, hats, canes, and various other props that Sophiny had seen in many photographs. Her dining table was covered with the tools of her trade, and on the left wall a china cabinet was filled with glass photo plates, jars of chemicals, and cameras. "I still use the dry-plate negatives and process them in my kitchen and the fruit cellar has become my darkroom. The photographs are much clearer, especially for the postcards and photo albums." Obviously precautions were taken to have materials for general use in readiness—tripod, various cameras and their cases, notepad and pencil, filters in a filter case, chemical equipment bag, and established routine saved time and prevented disorder. An artistic arrangement of photographs—reminders of places she had been, things she had seen, and people she had met—were mounted, framed, and hung for public viewing.

"How are you able to have this space all to yourself?" Sophiny's eyebrows arched with interest, if not surprise.

"And not feel obligated to do needlework on the side?" Martha asked, nodding sagely.

"Exactly!"

"I'll show you. Now you will take a photograph of me."

One hour and ten shots later, Martha asked for a summary of what she had learned. Sophiny demonstrated the procedures to her satisfaction.

"Enough for today." Martha had doled out the information like candies to small children: one at a time, and not too much. It might make them sick. "I have to make a delivery tomorrow afternoon—not far, and by that time I should have your photographs developed. We can review your work."

Sophiny was at the point of saying something about her morning exploration, but Martha seemed rather in a hurry and indicated, "Paul has your horse ready."

When she arrived home, the house was surprisingly quiet. On the kitchen table she found a note.

Soph,

Andrew says Richard's sprain might be a break.
We all took off to town to see the doc. Can't take

his complaining—might have to shoot him.

Henry

Poor Richard, but the absence of brothers could not have worked better for Sophiny. In the time it took to climb a flight of stairs, she was back in her room

The second journal was written after Antoinette's return from the Christmas holiday and did not include specific dates.

Chapter 12
Aid of Chance

Antoinette Dominguez 1910: Pocket Notebook

Here I am a decade into the twentieth century, still with no clear pathway forward. Instead, I am tethered to a past that isn't even my own. My ruined life has been suffocating in night terrors of a figure with a missing face. I never intended to write about how to cope with my emotions because I still don't have any answers. The words in my mother's letters telling me about "moving forward," "healing," "getting over," and "burying the past" did not happen for me, nor do I think they happened for her. The voice was not hers! Just like the voice in the *Uncle Tom's Cabin* theater production was not the same as the voice in the novel. I want my mother to tell me herself. My thought in the beginning was to write just for my father—to tell this story, wrap it in words, and put it away for now. Surprisingly, writing helped me to stop focusing on my personal failings, the things about myself I did not particularly like and wanted to change but didn't know how. I saw a different Antoinette emerge in the telling of events of the Christmas season, and found I wanted to be her. For that to happen, I would have to head into the wilderness: alone.

Sister Louise found me sitting alone in my cell after I had come back from the Stillman household. When she asked about my stay, I decided to find out what she thought of Thomas and Lucretia. "Fine, I guess. I can't quite make them out."

"What do you mean?"

I felt like such an idiot, but I started crying. I knew my tears were weakening my cause, but I just could not stop myself. She sat quietly and waited while I found my handkerchief and tried to stop sniffing. "I am not exactly sure what a guardian is supposed to do for a ward. When I asked him about my future, about my mother, about my father's properties, he tried to distract me, saying all was taken care of."

133

"And you don't think it is?"

"Well yes, it might be, but without me. Why can't I be a part of my own life?" I heard the tremor of frustration in my voice.

Sister Louise must have heard it too. "What did you expect him to do?"

"I am about to leave school in a few months. Where will I go? I want to fit back into my old life. What comes next?"

"What can I do to help you?" she asked, finally taking me seriously.

When she asked that question, I sobbed uncontrollably, hiccupping so rapidly that I couldn't speak. All the grief I had been holding back overflowed, as though an obstruction had been lowered.

"I have to find my mother. I have to talk to her ... see her ... know that she is all right." Then I told her all I had learned over Christmas from Mr. Stillman's files, from Mark, and my own foiled attempts to take a train.

"It does seem that you have cause for concern. We have a sister order in Wichita. Perhaps I could ask one of their members to investigate the institutions you mentioned to see if your mother is a patient."

Incredibly, my tears stopped at the very mention of taking action. Sister Louise, I am sure, did not want to raise any false hope, because she hurriedly said, "I cannot promise anything. But we will make inquiries."

A.D.

One moment I felt hopeful that I would be reunited with my mother, the next I felt angry and resentful. But I worked hard on my studies. Through January, every time I passed her in the hall, saw her in chapel, sat in her classroom, watched her in the frugal, regular, and strict performance of her duties, I had to force myself not to burst out with questions. The foundation of my happiness was in her hands those days.

Only later was I able to truly formulate the questions I needed to answer to stem my growing uneasiness. Had my guardian ever publicly proposed a single significant structural investment in my future independence? After my father's untimely death? *No.* After the commencement of my attendance at the academy? *No.* After my mother's distancing strategy? *No.* To my proposal of an internship? *No.* To my pleas for future direction? *No.* In fact he had pounced on my father's gross "misallocation of capital," my mother's "sense of entitlement" and "failure to care a whit" about reducing her expenses in a time of straitened finances, my investigation as "an obsession," "an inherited character failure that would dim my own prospects for a future in society."

A.D.

Apparently news travels even more slowly from Wichita to Concord than any other place on Earth. Two weeks passed, and still Sister Louise had received no news. We had developed a signal by this time. When I caught her eye at mail call, she would slightly shake her head. But I feared that all my efforts would end in nothing more than shutting the stable door after the horse had bolted.

I was also communicating with Mark, who was writing to me under the name of Mrs. Crescentia Gottfried. His letters were very funny, and mostly he copied newspaper stories about what was happening in Concord society with his messages hidden in the story. He especially included what was happening with Mr. and Mrs. Stillman. When he requested a visit, I wrote him about our visitor Sunday the first of the month. He insisted he wanted to come and see me in February, that he missed our conversations and that he thought we shared something special. I was eager to see him too, but I didn't know how that would work with Sister Louise's surveillance. I begged him to bring his mother and then we could see each other without being uneasy. Then I asked if his mother knew we had been in contact. He pretended not to understand my response in the person of Mrs. Crescentia Gottfried: how could she be expected to have a mother? I knew you had brothers, Sophiny, and Sister Mary Charles always answers the bell on Sunday afternoons. So I told him to use Andrew Mumm's name. That is actually when I got the idea that our changing identities would be a good thing. You were not expecting visitors, so you did not wait in the visitor room. When your name was called, I went in your stead.

Each academy student is so excited about her own visitors that little attention is paid to anyone else's. Except, of course, Mary Clare asked me what I was up to. I was afraid she would say something to Sister Louise or to you, but she kept my secret. Mark and I had so much to talk about. We walked in the grotto. He brought me chocolates. Mr. Stillman had involved him directly in several legal cases, including my own land holdings. He said Mr. Stillman had leased out my father's farms to a large syndicate of some kind, and they had taken over operations, thus releasing the foreman who had been in charge up to this point.

He asked if I remembered about my father's interest in new technologies and farm products for which he had set up the warehouses to accommodate markets as new advances modified farming demands. Stillman had been traveling back and forth to Wichita to conduct meetings and get paperwork signed and filed. In fact, these meetings had all started on Christmas Eve day, when Mr. Stillman had taken Mark by train to visit his mother in Wichita. They had traveled all night in a Pullman sleeping car. I felt such despair at learning about this visit that I had to stop him from speaking. But knowing I might not get another chance to hear what he knew, I asked him to go on. He seemed to regret telling me too much and became very guarded. He did not know how his mother fit into this new arrangement. Again he assured me that he had not told Mr. Stillman anything about our communications, nor did he think Mr. Stillman suspected. Yet Mr. Stillman had taken to writing a monthly statement of his own informing me of the deteriorating conditions of the Dominguez Farms. He said there were even challenges to boundary lines and that he would need ownership documents to present in court. When I showed the letter to Mark, he merely shrugged.

Then he refused to talk about business anymore and pursued his own agenda. He said he had grown to love me, and seeing me again made him want to possess me. He had thought about what we had to do. I was struck by how easy it seemed for him to make a plan and to act on it. He had accounted for minutes, hours, days, and months, as well as the cost of his decisions. But in his plan, was I the object, the ball to be moved from one place to another until the goal was reached and the game won? But for the sake of discussion, I entered into his scheme as something worthy and significant to pursue. I kept thinking about my birthday in March when I would be eighteen, but as long as I remained out of touch with what was happening at my father's farms and warehouses, I could gather no information upon which to make intelligent decisions.

A.D.

Sister Louise had also begun to search for my mother on my behalf, but the addresses and names I had given her from Mr. Stillman's file did not produce the desired results. All my frustrated efforts and the unexpected hindrances—though providing challenges not easily solved—sort of loosened up my brain and came with a mental benefit. Weird connections simmered in my imagination as I started considering a greater range of possibilities. I began to receive weekly notes initialed by my mother: "I shall be passing your way soon, or I contemplate visiting you before long. I hope you are well." They were posted from different locations and seemed cruelly meant to tease me about her very existence.

In February I came across an article in the *Concord Chronicle* that Mr. Stillman had been appointed the county's public administrator. His new position would include managing the estates of people who died without known heirs. The article quoted him as saying, "One really needs to know fiduciary work in order to oversee these important resources, and I have more experience than anyone in the county." I thought of Crescentia Gottfried and her comment on how such estates were used for good purposes to build parks and libraries and other institutions. Somehow the thought did not comfort me. I wrote a letter to the article writer, Mr. Frank Canon, asking if he remembered me from our dance at the Cloud Ball. I wrote of my own growing concerns about Mr. Stillman as my guardian. Could he help me find my missing mother? I inquired straight out. Sister Louise called me into her office when I received his reply that he would contact his network of fellow journalists. She was not upset, just concerned for me.

Sophiny, I have to write my story for me but also for you rather than tell you because writing makes me slow down and take time to get it right. Surprisingly, hand writing my thoughts is changing the way I think and how I remember things. Remember what Sister Mary Charles said about the great philosophers who understood that written discourse was more logical and rigorous than spoken expression? I hope writing this journal will make me wiser. My aim is to keep certain topics (e.g., my future, my Stillman connection, my search for family) in the forefront of Sister Louise's thoughts. I do think her grapevine will eventually turn up something, though it seems to be dormant for the present. Since Wichita has a convent of Sisters of Mary, we even discussed my transfer there. "Let's just wait," Sister Louise cautioned. "These things take time." But how was I supposed to wait patiently for a legal response that might never come? Even the sheriff and public officials do not have to help us women; instead they try to scare us into staying out of their precious institutions and going home. They also work to assure that we cannot take care of ourselves.

Finally, I decided to take steps.

First, I took time to read my Christmas notebook and consoled myself that if I need to see where I am going ahead of time, what good is the journey anyhow? But one thing I am sure of: There is no happily ever after. I do not have that illusion. *Second,* I picked you, Sophiny, as my anchor. Then I had to make sure you would not be in danger as well. *Third,* there are all the details to be considered to get from one location to the next. For that Mark was very agreeable and persuaded me he could take care of certain details. Meeting Mark again at Christmas seemed to have been a stroke of luck, and so I gave myself over to the aid of chance.

A.D.

Sophiny, I know you will recall my strangeness as you are reading my notebook; it must mean you have not heard from me in some months. My elopement did not go as planned. My way is lost, and I am in more trouble than I can get out of. Please use the money you find in this trunk to search for me. Wear my clothes, but be forewarned, they are courtesy of Stillman. A further caution, Stillman is not remote but rather a menacing presence, and I am taking precautions against preemptive panic just in case I need more time to put my plan into action, and so you may find my trail. You were right to stipulate that your promises were only valid if I was able to carry out my own resolutions. I absolve you from your first two promises to me. But the third, which I shall not repeat, I trust that you will keep.

The semester resumes.

A.D.

Chapter 13
Day of Miracles

Tokens echo warnings. Symbols point to other meanings. Allegories hide deeper truths. *Trunk keys, hidden documents, St. Eulalia's thirteen tortures.* Could Antoinette make these things work for her to counter the consequences of trespassing into an unnatural world? Or had she entered the natural world, after all, a world of survival and evolution?

In her continuing search, Sophiny found from Mrs. Dominguez a series of brief activity accounts with the letter threatening Antoinette with an arranged marriage and the short notes promising a visit, from Mr. Stillman few letters regarding property issues in vague lawyer language. A packet of bills and copies of order forms and catalogues with notes in the margins confirmed Antoinette's father's interest in new technologies related to farm products. Mr. Dominguez's account book documented liabilities and assets, including properties in Wichita, Abilene, and Concord. Contracts, along with financial and pricing data provided in Mr. Stillman's and Mr. Dominguez's own handwriting, stipulated consequences if either side reneged on obligations and the laws governing the contract in case of a dispute about the transaction. There was no mention that Mr. Stillman should become guardian of the Dominguez businesses, of her mother or of Antoinette herself, or beneficiary of any Dominguez property. Mr. Dominguez did not seem to be a man who was planning his own demise but rather a man bent on protecting his family's interests.

Indeed the trunk's contents cast a new light on Antoinette's transformation in recent months. Furthermore, the secrets inside created yet another upheaval: the trunk was too vulnerable to sit in the corner of Sophiny's room. Even the confining layers of routine existence would not be enough to keep it safe. But she resisted investigating what was hidden under the paper at the bottom of the tray, knowing from Antoinette's letter and the extracted vow that the contents included the deeds to the Dominguez Farms and other properties now in her possession for safekeeping.

A world created with separations is a world created with order: day and night, life and death, good and evil, men and women, friends and enemies, work and play. How could Sophiny reenter the world she had left behind? Looking for Antoinette would create chaos in her life, even if she did know how to begin the search. She could picture several scenarios, but each presented challenges. What if she told her four brothers? Could they be persuaded to leave the farm and follow her to Concord? But where would her search begin? Even now Andrew and Henry were talking about joining a threshing crew to cut wheat in season and so provide for the summer harvest of the Mumm wheat and the purchase of much-needed new farm machinery of their own. What if she told Martha? Martha could take a photograph, and then what? What if she told Sister Louise? Sister Louise had probably already contacted the sheriff, but she would ask for the trunk. What if she contacted Detective Tyler? Was he looking out for Antoinette's interests? For Mrs. Dominguez's? Or for Stillman's? Which option would do the most good for Antoinette? Sophiny was still undecided when she arrived at the Shaw farmhouse the next day.

In the buggy with Martha to deliver photographs, Sophiny could not keep Antoinette's notebook out of her mind. "Do you think women should have rights separate from men?"

"Are you asking me about a woman's place in society?"

"I guess so."

"There are many theories of women's emancipation, including Mary Wollstonecraft's that men of good will should treat their wives as equals to have better marriages and Elizabeth Cady Stanton's that women must have the right to vote in order to secure all other rights, and don't forget those sisters at your academy. After all, religious orders gave women the idea that they were not children and could do meaningful work outside the home."

"What about you, why didn't you marry?"

"I never really thought I was fit for domestic life. Actually I don't think most women are. How many women have been driven to the brink of insanity? Being a daughter was confining enough. Then I never formed—or cared to, for that matter—an attachment that would induce me to be a wife or mother. After our parents died, Paul took charge of the business part of farming. I settled in to take care of him and bought my first camera. Then it came to me: the only role in which a woman is man's equal in our society is that of sister. So you see, I have no family to abandon me ... but one does have to be careful not to be undermined by intimidation and suspicion for challenging expected roles."

Sophiny was not sure what Martha was talking about, but she was about to find out. When they arrived at the farmhouse, Sophiny set the brake and secured the reins. The woman came to help Martha get out of the buggy and embraced her affectionately, as though she had been a long-lost sister. She seemed overjoyed to see the other woman and said, "Oh, my dear, you seem just like an angel come to me in my loneliness." Then she led the two inside where her husband, a squat, strong-smelling goblin of a man sat, chewing on a cigar, legs outstretched, blocking their direct passage to the table, but he made no attempt to move his righteous bulk or to allow them entry. Instead the woman moved around to the other side, taking a longer path, avoiding a conflict.

As Martha laid out the photographs, the woman came forward eagerly to look at the images of her family. The man said, "I'd as soon have a photograph of my cattle."

"Yes, and I can provide that for you as well." Martha was not to be intimidated.

"And how much would these photographs cost?" asked the woman, no longer smiling but seemingly in a hurry to head off further damage.

Martha handed her a bill as the man reached out to gather the photographs to himself.

"Why should I pay for my wife's own image? You have just copied what is already there, and that I can see every day. How much art does it take to turn a knob? You aren't even producing anything useful." The man dismissed Martha's work just as he had dismissed his wife.

At this point, Sophiny could endure his threatening demeanor no longer. She felt the start of a tear welling up and spilling down her cheek and then another and another. "Because of Martha I have many photographs of my dear mother, and what a consolation it is to me and my brothers to be able to see our mother's image. She died, very recently, you might remember, and now I am an orphan taking care of all these brothers without a mother or father to look after us. All we have left is our grief and these remembrances … not that I would ever wish such a tragedy upon your family for such little consolation." Then she let her grief choke up and close off her voice and rack her body with sobs.

"Oh, you are the Mumm girl." The rheumy eyes turned toward Sophiny in recognition, and the man promptly bought all the photographs to stop her tears. The woman just as promptly picked up her photographs and Martha her money to ensure that the decision could not be reversed.

"You are quite a little saleswoman," said Martha, impressed after they returned to the buggy. "And those tears …"

Sophiny flicked the reins, and the horse started moving. "The tears were real. I do miss my mother."

"I know you do. So do I."

"Which brings me to another point ... I also miss my friend, and I don't know who to talk to about her."

"Do you have a picture?"

"Yes, how did you know?"

"Just thought you might. Let's take a look."

Sophiny handed her the most recent photograph, taken over Antoinette's Christmas stay with the Stillmans. "Her name is Antoinette Dominguez."

"A very pretty girl ... Do you want me to tell you what I see? There are clues in the photograph."

"Clues? What clues?

"She was sitting on the edge of a desk, her skirt above her ankles, flirting with the cameraman."

"You see all of that?'

"She is missing, isn't she?"

"But how did you know?"

"I did not want to say anything, but you seemed very troubled when you came home. At first I thought it was your mother. But the only tears I have seen from you were those when you looked at her in the casket, and those you just shed for special effect. You have grown quite serious over the past year, and I'm curious as to the cause."

Martha's insight was such a welcome relief that the words began to tumble out as Sophiny related the events of Antoinette's elopement and disappearance and the fears she had held in reserve for the past months. She stopped short of telling Martha that she had Antoinette's trunk in her possession and that she had only just opened that trunk and read Antoinette's notebook the day before.

"Is there anything you can do for your friend now?"

"I don't know."

Once at Martha's house they studied the photographs that Sophiny had taken the previous day. "Pick one," said Martha, and when Sophiny pointed, asked, "What is going on here? What is this woman in the photograph saying to the viewer? Doesn't this image just beg for an interpretation?"

"I think she is trying to sell her business," Sophiny noted the cameras and photographs in the background along with the props, the woman's perch on the edge of her chair, looking at another camera she held in one hand.

"Good. Do you think we could use this photograph to advertise? Is that not daring?"

Being daring meant all the things she was beginning to associate with Martha: inventing her own life, pushing boundaries, expressing individuality ... choosing her own companions. "Yes, it is daring, but so are you in a good way."

"It is a good time and a good occupation to get into. Many women are practicing photography equally with men."

"Why do you like this work so much?"

Martha's ready response surprised her, "Because my time is valuable—and so is the record of women's lives and activities."

Sophiny was still thinking about their encounter, "That man was really a tyrant, wasn't he? He lives to make her suffer."

Martha sighed. "One must not only elevate woman in the eyes of men but even in her own eyes. I would have given her the photographs because she is my friend, and he was probably counting on that. Some men refuse to pay women for their work. Thanks for the rescue."

"Glad to. Wish I could help Antoinette so easily."

"Yes, tears, prayers, and persistence are our weapons," Martha said with a laugh.

"And food," added Sophiny, thinking of her brothers.

Martha began to heat water and set out a tea cozy. "There is a traveling theater group coming to town to perform next week in the assembly room above the bank. Would you like to come with me? We'll photograph the company for the newspaper. They might give us tickets in exchange."

"What is the play?"

"*Uncle Tom's Cabin*, now that I think about it. The play is about using tears, prayers, and persistence as arguments to abolish slavery."

Sophiny had read the novel written by Harriet Beecher Stowe, heard the claim that it changed America and moved the world more than any other. Out of what genius did this woman's talent spring? "How did Stowe on her knees in the kitchen, with constant calls to cooking and other details of housework, punctuate her sentences and develop her paragraphs? Even more difficult without leisure in a quiet room, how did she find time to create all those chapters?"

"How indeed? But women are having better lives, learning not to be overwhelmed by the power of the past."

"What do you mean?" Sophiny looked at Martha, absorbed and serious.

"There is a story, maybe an apocryphal one, about one of those cattle towns on the Chisholm Trail that boomed when the railroad came. It seems a gang of ruffian cowboys had been disturbing the town for a month or more with their carousing and bullying before they decided to attend an amateur production of *Uncle Tom's Cabin*. They brought along some prostitutes and carried on in a loud, obscene way, shouting profanities that disturbed the townsfolk who challenged them. Of course the ruffians threatened they would 'fix them' the next day. The show closed, but the next day the local citizens engaged the gang in a shootout in the main street. One of the townspeople was killed. A posse pursued the troublemakers out of town, though they must have caught one because ironically the whole chain of events ended in a lynching. At least we haven't seen that kind of violence."

"A lot has changed since the dark ages of the 1800s."

"Indeed," Martha said with a laugh, "let's hope the civilizing forces continue."

How strange that Antoinette had written about seeing that play in her notebook—coincidence or connection? Though sorting out the details of Antoinette's disappearance began as a kind of accident, the mystery quickly engaged her imagination. Early on she resolved against conveying her findings directly to the sheriff of Prairie Dog. She had promised not to turn over the contents to anyone but Antoinette. That promise she intended to keep to the best of her ability. Somebody was after something in Antoinette's trunk. After reading the accounts of the trunk room break-in, she was sure of it. Perhaps Antoinette's very life depended on keeping the trunk's contents secure.

Where did that leave her? At an impasse, knowing from the little voice inside her head that the trouble coming up was sealed under the paper at the bottom of the trunk tray, she wanted to delay as long as possible a decision about a course of action. When she returned, her brothers were working in the ruins of the old granary, knocking down the gutted building with axes and hammers and shoveling broken foundation and debris into the wagon to haul to the trash heap in one of the pasture ravines. Their attention would be centered for the remaining daylight hours around demolition and then for days in reconstruction. There was no sense attempting to plan beyond that point—no sense burdening herself with situations that might never occur. The enigmatic was Antoinette's tactic, and she knew she herself was not strong enough to bear the weight of not knowing alone. Hadn't Detective Tyler when he was Brother Clause suggested traveling in pairs as a protection against danger?

Restless, Sophiny, took the stairs two at a time to her room. She had to finish what she had started and know all that was in the trunk. Carefully she began to work the paper away from one side of the tray, revealing several large envelopes. These she carefully opened one at a time. The first was a deed to a property listed as a single-family dwelling near Wichita, the second for hundreds of acres of land, several others for business properties around Wichita, including warehouses. Another envelope contained a will designating Antoinette and her mother as beneficiaries. Several bills of sale for land, for buildings, for farm equipment—even an automobile were tied into a bundle. Another bundle included bonds. The last envelope contained birth and death certificates belonging to the Dominguez family, Antoinette's birth certificate among them. March 31, 1892, her eighteenth birthday had passed. So this was what Stillman had been asking for over Christmas: documents for Antoinette's property. Without disguise, truth would be destroyed. How could Sophiny keep Antoinette's truth safe? The trunk no longer offered adequate concealment. These deeds belonged locked up in a safe. Where would she have access to such a thing? Would Martha know? But how could she involve Martha?

The next day Martha's sittings for the actors of the traveling theater company began between rehearsals before the production of the play. "I want something sophisticated but with a little whimsy," said the actress playing the part of Eva, St. Clare and Marie's angelic daughter. Sophiny enjoyed watching Martha work, the way she talked to people, asking them questions, gathering information. She had a kind and gentle way about her that people liked.

"Well, yes, but what you cannot see is the aesthetic that I can bring to your photograph. It won't just be the picture of a woman but a sign of women in many different roles: mother, seductress, muse. Do you want your audience to see you as normal, orderly, reassuring, admirable, virtuous, happy, rewarded?" Martha brought out photographic images to demonstrate her point. "Maybe if you were a bride or pictured with your husband or child, that would be the case." Here she brought out photographs of faces caught like flies in amber to illustrate her second point, "But as an actress, you might sell more tickets if you gave the impression of being just a little deviant, dangerous, seductive, or even ludicrous. Then there is the attention that being depraved, miserable, or punished gets."

"I want my image to be a magnet for my audience, so that they want to come up close and see why I shimmer." She laughed and shook her chest, blatantly provocative, which Sophiny thought delightful. It was not a crime to display bright plumage, though not really in the character of Eva.

"Which I will print in the newspaper, post in the store windows, and leave on display in my studio for all the world to see," agreed Martha.

"All right, snap away," said the actress, striking a pose.

"Life goes on … but click goes the camera and the moment lasts … maybe forever," Martha said.

Sophiny was thinking of the photos of other women and other fates already part of Martha's collection when she became aware of a commotion caused by bicycles going by on the street below. She recognized Janet Adamy and Glenda Sommers in the group. They seemed to be arguing about the rules of the road, whether they should pass on the right or the left. Since they could not settle the argument, they opted instead to sound their bells to warn anyone else on the street. Martha set up her props, positioned her subjects, adjusted her lighting, and prepared to take her masterpieces.

The sounds of bicycle bells and the ordinary traffic of horses and buggies were sharply and suddenly interrupted by pedestrians shouting, "Watch out." Before her very eyes as she peered through the second-story window of the assembly hall, Sophiny saw two women on the sidewalk, a mother pushing a baby carriage coming in the opposite direction, the flash of a horseman endeavoring to cut in between an approaching cart, and the crush of bicyclists causing a terrible accident. The cart overturned, and many of the bicyclists were thrown from their vehicles. By now the cast forgot their poses and came to the window as well. The rider's horse seemed to be badly damaged. Many of the young women were getting to their feet and assessing their injuries as well. Two remained on the ground. A crowd began to gather to give assistance. As Sophiny turned around, she could see that Martha was caught in a dilemma. Should she wait for the actors to return, or should she take her camera outside? But her decision was soon made as her subjects began to spill out, down the stairs, headed for the scene in reactionary mode.

The horseman who collided with the cart and bicyclists was identified as Arthur Gunson. He was so drunk that he was disoriented at the scene, smelled of alcohol, slurred his speech, and had trouble keeping his balance when he got down from his horse. Of the two girls remaining on the ground, Glenda had been killed and Janet severely wounded. Town focus remained on Gunson and his history of alcohol-related incidents. According to the newspaper account accompanied by Martha's photograph, Gunson was only held overnight in jail. His mother said she would give her own life to bring the girl back.

But another account related that people grabbed their children when Arthur Gunson rode into town, sidled away when he strode up the street, lowered their voices when he swaggered into a store. He reveled in the fear he inspired. It made him feel like the outlaw he was on his way to becoming. "He is a strutting menace. Our family can only hope this public spectacle continues until we have justice for the murder of our daughter," Mr. Sommers, Glenda's father, was quoted as saying. "Clearly there are things that need to be changed. He chose to get drunk and ride recklessly in public, and his choice ended up killing someone very close to me. The devil walks unmolested in

Prairie Dog," he said. Janet was expected to fully recover from her injuries, a broken bone, a sprain, and multiple scrapes. The story continued with eyewitness commentary following the incident. Some of those who first ran to the site said they were deeply affected and even suffered from nightmares.

"Who has time to sit around and talk about nightmares?" scoffed Richard as Andrew read the story aloud.

"Which reminds me, Sophiny, can you bake something we can take to Janet's and Glenda's families?" asked James. "Our mother would have done something like that."

His request was followed by some skepticism from Henry. "Good rationale, brother, but I doubt it is Mom you are thinking about."

As Sophiny and her brothers visited Janet and made plans to attend the funeral, the town debate continued. A series of articles in the newspaper appeared bent on educating the townspeople about chronic drinkers with mental problems who used the drug as medicine and could turn violent, especially to family members. Prohibitionists used the event to remind the community that alcoholics and their suppliers often escape meaningful punishment until they kill somebody or do some other horrific act, and the message that gets sent is that they're getting away with it. Also included in the article were the lists of states and counties that had gone dry. Gunson's reckless discord and mindless spree drew the attention of the Women's Christian Temperance Union (WCTU) to Prairie Dog. WCTU circulars began to appear around town as well as an advertisement in the paper about a rally following the funeral.

On Friday morning, about fifty of Prairie Dog's residents, friends, and family members jammed into the Baptist church to say a final good-bye, Sophiny and her brothers among them. They sang hymns, brought early spring flowers, and told stories to honor the slain girl. After the cemetery burial, the family and funeral procession returned to the Main Street site of the accident, which had been briefly closed to traffic. In the downtown lined with bland business buildings and stores, a makeshift memorial with flowers and candles had begun to form where Glenda was killed.

Miss Henrietta Bratley from the Women's Christian Temperance Union waited for them in front of the bank on a dry goods box. Clad in a long, dark cape dress and bonnet, she was armed with a Bible and sweet smile. Her lecture was on the vice and debauchery of prodigious imbibing. No auctioneer at a farm sale had ever drawn together such a crowd.

Miss Bratley said she came from Wichita and that she had been a hero worshiper of Carrie Nation's but that she could no longer help the work of the temperance crusade from afar. She reminded her audience that under the governorship of John P. St. John in 1880, Kansas voters had passed an amendment, the first in the nation, prohibiting the sale or manufacture of intoxicants. However, this amendment did not altogether halt the liquor traffic. After this warm-up, she seemed to point directly to Prairie Dog's failure.

> Just last year Kansas Governor Walter R. Stubbs signed into
> law an addendum to the prohibitory law that did away with
> the granting of permits to drugstores to sell intoxicants. It
> seems you have a lack-of-enforcement problem in Prairie Dog.
> A druggist is still dispensing liquor for so-called "medical,
> scientific, and mechanical purposes." Now I know many local
> sheriffs and politicians are reluctant to enforce the law and
> leave the administration of the law up to the discretion of the
> druggist … and in Prairie Dog the druggist had no discretion.

After this last statement, she paused to acknowledge the audience's reaction. Then she thanked her audience for their civility and reason in listening to her words in a sometimes rough and uncouth world and reminded them again of the moral evils such as fraud, theft, uncleanliness, and murder that resulted from the use of distilled spirits.

Sophiny heard the comments of her brothers at the end of the speech as the crowd was breaking up, "She is not bad looking," observed Henry in mock puzzlement.

"Sure if you like that Mennonite style. Glenda might have had something to say about that," Andrew commented. "Wish she were here to say it."

"She has a fine voice and a great flow of language," praised Richard.

"Did you say flow? It was a perfect torrent. She talked for an hour and never stopped for breath," scoffed Henry.

"I think we can all draw a long breath and thank our stars we were not tied to her for life." James shepherded his siblings toward the wagon.

But at this moment the street drama of the previous week continued. "Whoa! What's he doing out of jail?" James jerked his head in the direction of the drugstore, out of which Arthur Gunson had just appeared. He was not the only one to notice. Glenda's brother had started arguing with Gunson. A neighbor saw the argument and intervened by pushing Gunson away. But the enmity of the two families reached a climax when the dead girl's father walked to his wagon, grabbed a gun, and returned to the area, prepared to shoot Gunson. Each man was too intensely engaged in living the shifting rhythms of violence, of exaltation and despair, of victory and defeat to grasp the whole picture. Sophiny saw them as though through a film of grime as representations of the universal man in a posture of warning, of impending violence, a message transcending language to passersby: *danger, life in danger, intent to kill.*

The townspeople were also interpreting this warning and began backing away, heading in a direction of safety. Sophiny with the clarity of the outside perspective discerned the workings of the violent resolution about to take place. Without conscious thought, she propelled herself to Mr. Sommer's side and gently touching him on the arm, said, "Just wait ten minutes before you kill him. Think of your family." Then she turned and walked to her family's wagon. When she looked back, the scene was miraculously resolved.

"Show's over, folks. There is nothing more to see here. Let's move on." The sheriff, or someone acting in that capacity, began moving the crowd out of the vicinity.

The following days were frantic ones. This so-called miracle day became a mixed blessing. Good things do happen out of bad; unfortunately the reverse is also true. The tragedy and near tragedy to the Sommers family blew a cold wind through the town forcing the residents of Prairie Dog to rethink its decades-old ways of battling alcohol. The town newspaper published a series of interviews with residents on what should be done. Sophiny's photograph and an account of her intervention were included, to her chagrin and her brothers' teasing. The drugstore was closed down and the druggist charged with selling intoxicating liquors and maintaining a nuisance. When the Mumms delivered Sophiny's baked sour-cream chocolate cake with caramel icing, Glenda's mother made a special point to give Sophiny a big hug. She was kind of crying as she said, "Oh my goodness, this little girl did a big thing."

The sheriff was forced to begin criminal proceedings against Gunson, who was caught with a wagonload of liquor. He arrested him straight out for violating the Kansas prohibitory law, arrested him for taking orders, seized his delivery wagon under the nuisance laws, and began preparations to move him from the local jail to Fort Leavenworth Prison. Janet and James became a couple and started talking about marriage. The shift had been gradual, almost imperceptible, but there it was.

Notice did not come without threat. The frightening downside was that while the townspeople began to tackle the practical implications of temperance, state attention now focused on the town because the local newspaper story was picked up by prohibitionist newspapers with uncompromising missionary convictions in their attempt to keep tempers boiling. Prairie Dog had gotten their man but in doing so had stirred up more trouble. Rumors of violent action continued from both factions—wet and dry. Brewers and distillers were beginning to organize with the avowed purpose of making Kansas wet. Mobs had been known to set free operators and distributers, creating a state of anarchy. It took little effort at all to point fingers and make accusations. The interest of outsiders in Prairie Dog's importation, sale, and consumption of alcohol tended to make civilization give way to savagery. The end result was that not only were no alcoholic beverages available for consumption, but a series of ousters and fines of public officials who had shirked their duties with enforcement of the prohibitory law followed. And so people began to blame miracle day on Sophiny.

Chapter 14
Tangle of Weeds

"I wonder how we can cut seed costs for next year." James's brow wrinkled over breakfast as he attempted to ground his siblings in the plowing, planting, and livestock-feeding that had been interrupted by the excitement of the past three days.

Sophiny, though focused on her tasks and distracted by the excitement of the day before, could not forget her resolution to take action regarding her friend. *Dear Antoinette, please do not grow weary of my efforts and confusion here. You are struggling at great cost—in terms of love and legacy—maybe even accused of all manner of impropriety.*

On her morning's buggy run to stop in on Martha and take her eggs to the general store, Sophiny brought along Antoinette's pocket notebook to share in hopes that Martha could direct her course of action. "Your friend seems to have been very concerned with the distinction between having a right and exercising it," said Martha as the buggy started down the hill and the two observed the cattle from a neighboring barnyard pen file into the pasture.

"When you think about it, some women have less freedom than the cows in that pasture."

"I suppose it might seem that way. Without a father or husband's authorization, a woman cannot take an examination, enroll in a university, open a bank account, file a lawsuit, own property, or seek treatment in a hospital. Yet in most cases if the man was incapacitated, banished, or absent for some other reason, his wife is competent to stand in his place."

"Is the same true of being a guardian for her children?"

"Depends on the state, I suppose—I think there is a difference in guardianship of property or an entailment versus guardianship of physical care. Why?"

"What if we cannot find Antoinette or her mother? Does Stillman take over her property? Or what if Antoinette is married? Does her husband now own her property? What action would the courts take? Would she lose what she risked all to recover?"

"I don't know. But you must report what you do know."

"I know—but to whom, and what about my promise?"

"What about Sister Louise? What about that detective? What about the Concord sheriff? Your friend is a missing person. Her life may be in danger."

"Is Detective Tyler on the side of Stillman or Antoinette? Who hired him? It has been almost a month. Why hasn't he found her if he is so good? What if she is in hiding? And as for Sister Louise … what has she been able to do so far but keep secrets?"

"All good questions. Are you going to tell your brothers?"

"Should I?"

"Your friend has some serious enemies. Didn't you say the trunks were broken into at the academy? If someone knew your connection to Antoinette, your family might be in danger as well."

Returning home, Sophiny's thoughts were still on Martha's words. Should she confide in them all or consider which of her brothers would treat her as an equal? With which brother could she develop a sustainable relationship, as Martha had with Paul? Would twenty-two-year-old Andrew be the one? The two stood surveying the plot at the back of the house that had been their mother's garden, their feet sinking into the softened dirt. Within days of her recent cultivation, unruly greenery had grown up around the sprouts of newly planted vegetables.

"Eyesores, menaces, botanical thugs—why are they there in the first place?" Sophiny voiced her frustration as she thought about this invasion even as one thought invaded another in her own mind.

"One year's seeds, seven year's weeds," said Andrew, shading his eyes and searching the sky before dropping to his knees. With ruthless efficiency, he began a devastating sweep of the plot within his reach. "Never walk by a weed. Pull it when you notice it or it will grow bigger."

"But they do not care how hostile you are: they just insinuate themselves wherever." She picked up a rock-hard clod of dirt with a healthy-looking vine to demonstrate. "Wild things—why can't they follow the rules?" Even as she complained, she felt a sneaking admiration for the bindweed, an exquisite white-flowered morning glory and its tenacious powers of survival creeping around the edge of the rows.

"They do have an obnoxious cussedness, especially the sandburs," Andrew agreed, crumbling a weed in his hand.

"Where do all these weeds come from?"

"Seeds."

"Yes, but we killed them several times over!"

"Some seeds can last years, and that pigweed produces millions of seeds," he said, indicating new sprouts along her cultivated rows. "If you pull them when they are small, not only are they easier to remove, but they disturb less soil. When you disturb soil in a bed, buried weed seeds may come to the surface and germinate. And especially don't allow weeds to go to seed."

"How do you know all that?"

"Hard to imagine, isn't it? I think it was something our grandparents passed on."

"You'd think tilling the soil like you did before I planted would have discouraged them, but no … the weeds loved my attack with the hoe even more."

"I think it has something to do with the sunlight hitting the seeds— according to the almanac you're supposed to cultivate a garden on cloudy, moonless nights."

"Hum …"

"Seeds … not just last year's plantings but seeds in the soil wait for the right light to flourish."

"Do you really like this work?"

"We aren't talking about weeds, are we?" Andrew's look was significant.

"Not exactly. I can't seem to get into the whole business of plowing, harrowing, sowing, and other soil-disturbing activities."

"Care to elaborate?"

"Do you think I am a weed?"

"You?"

"Am I growing where I don't belong?"

"Little Mumm, I don't know what is going to happen to any of us, especially if James and Janet tie the knot." Andrew called her by the term of endearment her parents had always used.

"Yeah, that too."

"Then there's always the risk of unintended harm. Farming … gardening is a very boring process, as most processes are; growth lies buried and unknown until a plant suddenly springs forth and becomes what we'd hoped it would be … or not. And it is the process that teaches us what we need to master a task. But I may be all wrong, remember that gospel story about letting the weeds and the wheat grow up together, since pulling the one might damage the other in the growth stage?"

"Thanks anyway for the help weed pulling … and that thing you said about light."

"You have choices, unlike plants. Do you want to be here?"

"I love the farm and all my brothers, you know, and I'm glad to be here. It's just that sometimes it feels a little dull … Do you want to be here?"

"I've got to find a better place to be first … or get my own acres to watch the sun rise up over."

Andrew's honesty surprised her, and so did his industry. *Do I want to be here?* His commentary on the relation of light to the growth of seeds reminded Sophiny of Martha's words on the relation of light to the appearance of photographic images. What was the right light to make Antoinette reappear?

For this reason, when Richard, later that morning, gave her news of a stranger in town asking questions about Miss Sophiny Mumm, she was filled with dread but also hope. "Being noticed as the Mumm girl has a whole new meaning now," teased Richard. He bowed and handed Sophiny a scrawled message. "I made you a business card."

Sophiny read what he had written:

SOPHINY MUMM
Buggy Driver, Camera Operator, Egg Sales
Prairie Dog Heroine
Clothes Washed and Dinners on Time

"I was thinking about adding brave, trustworthy, clean, honest, cheerful … but that places too much burden on the rest of us. Soon they'll be talking about creating a monument or statue in the park. Forgotten heroines tend to be forgotten for good reason."

"Just stop! What did you say about me?" Sophiny queried.

"Don't worry, you can buy my silence as well as my forgetfulness. Dinner ready?"

"Even a monument marking such a wonder would collapse under your pressure."

"Yes, you and that Bratley woman are wonders …"

"I wonder that you think any of this is funny."

"To assure you of my sincerity, I promise that if you get in real trouble, as your brother, I would take a bullet for you … but only in the shoulder after my wrist heals. I can only take one wound at a time."

"Do you have any idea why he is asking about you?" James interrupted.

"You should all know a few things," said Sophiny, heeding Martha's warning to enlist her brothers' help. Her selection of details from the story of Antoinette's disappearance and her involvement included the trading of their trunks, the record of Antoinette's pocket notebook, the contents of the book on guardianship laws, but not the fact that Antoinette's property deeds were included. She was gratified that her brothers had adopted expressions of concentration, as if she were telling them that she loved the sight of germinating wheat, buckets full of fresh milk, and new litters of pigs.

"What a scabby scoundrel to steal from a widow's hen roost. The question is no longer whether you can keep secrets, little Mumm, but whether you can convey the information to the right person," observed Andrew.

"Let's go to town and find out what this stranger is all about—let him make his case," declared James, pushing himself back from the table, decisively ready for action. "Think he will be at the production this afternoon?"

On the ride into Prairie Dog with her brothers, Sophiny observed the pastures of buffalo grass pockmarked with craters. Each crater had a volcano-like cone, an entrance to the little creature's burrow. The prairie dog, for which the town had been named, would gather soil from the surface and pat it into place, forming the cone that served as a lookout post and as protection against floods after heavy rains. Each burrow had many entrances. And each entrance descended steeply for about four yards before meeting radial tunnels. At the end of the tunnels, the prairie dogs would build their nests. Why was someone asking about her? Should she hide?

The production of *Uncle Tom's Cabin,* delayed in the aftermath of Glenda's death and funeral, had returned to town. Sophiny knew the names of all the characters: Uncle Tom, the protagonist slave, Aunt Chloe, his wife, the members of the Shelby family, owners of Uncle Tom, the St. Clare family, new owners of Uncle Tom, Mr. Haley, a slave trader, Tom Loker, a slave hunter, evil slave master Simon Legree, the beautiful slave Eliza, her husband and young son as well, as the minor characters who represented a range of viewpoints on slavery. She also knew the names of all the locations mentioned in the North to represent freedom and the South to represent slavery to support two stories: Uncle Tom's worsening enslavement and Liza's escape to freedom.

She was proud that Kansas had never been a slave state and had even produced some famous abolitionists. She could see that the assembly hall was nearly filled when they arrived. As she wondered if they could get seating together and James looked around to see if Janet had been able to come, she saw the familiar face that she was really looking for. Though in a new disguise, Detective Tyler's dress stood out from the usual farmer uniform of overalls and cotton shirts: sedate blue blazer with dark slacks and a dark plaid tie. She wondered at the light-headed sensation that came over her at the sight of him. For an instant, she simply stared, indulging the hope that he had come to search for her. As though he sensed her, he turned in her direction. When he saw her, he moved like a sunbeam through the crowd, his eyes never losing contact with hers, sending pleasure shimmering down her spine. He had been looking for her!

"What are you doing here?" asked Sophiny as Detective Tyler made his way to her side.

"I have a seat for you." He nodded, taking her by the arm. Satisfaction washed over her. "Pardon me, sir, but can you give this young lady a chair?" he turned to a man seated in the back row, refusing to acknowledge the beginnings of dissent from either the chair holder or Sophiny.

"I am sitting with my brothers." She stood tensely beside him keeping an eye on their locations.

"Would you rather talk to me in private? The sheriff's office perhaps?"

"Would you rather explain to my brothers why you were asking about me?"

"We are on the same side here. I am trying to help your friend."

Sophiny sat. "I do not have anything to do with Arthur Gunson."

"You know that is not the case I am referring to."

"Where do you think she is then? Hiding in a prairie dog tunnel?"

"Is she?" he asked and then winked.

Sophiny struggled not to laugh. "I don't know where she is. What have you discovered?"

"Most people seem to believe that good detective work may be achieved much like popcorn: apply heat for a short time and a fully formed blossom appears instantly. Not so. A good case grows one clue on top of another … and you have provided all the best clues. I need you to talk to me."

"First, who are you really? Why were you in that missionary disguise?"

"Since you asked, I am detailed on many different kinds of operations through an agency out of Kansas City." He handed her a card with the agency's name printed below his name. "Sometimes they overlap. Sometimes disguises help me get in solid with a community. I embed myself in the fabric of the town and then draw the target to me as surely as grasshoppers draw a prairie dog."

By this time all four of her brothers came to surround her and the detective. "What's your business with our sister, stranger?" asked James.

Sophiny wondered at her brother's challenge of Detective Tyler's right to anything. His certainty and self-assuredness gave off the impression that he would not be on the losing side if it came to a fight. "My apologies, gentlemen, an oversight on my part." Detective Tyler shifted around in his chair and stood up, slowly surveying his challengers. There was a silent moment. Then he said, "Perhaps the shock of finding out that this young lady has more substance than her appearance reveals had some affect upon my manners. Shall we take this outside?"

Sophiny's brothers gave him a nod, refusing to leave his presence, so that when he moved, they moved as well. And a good thing too, the play was starting, and people all around were shushing them. She heard someone say, "Is that Mumm girl under arrest?" Again the play would have to wait. Sophiny was surprised not only at her own pluck but also at her brothers' protective stance. The grounds had shifted. She had something he needed.

"What kind of an agency? Are you some kind of a bounty hunter? Or are you working for a liquor outfit?" Henry asked.

"No nothing like that. It takes cash to employ our agency." he handed each of them his card and continued. "As we never work for rewards. The company has to have a good guarantee to ensure their pay *per diem* and all necessary expenses. They rightly contend that a detective working for a reward will often stretch the truth in order to convict, whereas with the *per diem* plan, there is no incentive for someone like me to perjure himself."

"So glad you grasped the heart of the matter. It is always good to have things explained in terms we simpletons can understand," said Henry.

"Now hold on," said Detective Tyler in a soothing voice, "can we wait on the things that we are going to disagree about and start on the things we agree on? I am looking for a missing person, and I think this young lady knows something about that."

"I recognize this name. Your company has a good reputation." James studied the card, as though looking for more information.

"Thank you, sir—"

"First, can we agree on your intentions?" interrupted James. "Maybe you aren't lying to us, but you might be allowing Sophiny here to deceive herself."

"I am not sure I am following you." The detective shifted his weight and smiled with an expression that was part I'm-your-buddy, part confusion.

"Should be easy for anyone who ever killed snakes," said Richard.

"Are you setting up her expectations to find her friend with a very different prospect from what's in her mind to what's in the mind of your employer? To make the sting worse, you are there in the middle and quite active in permitting her to deceive herself by your omission and partial revelation," Andrew offered clarity.

"I can tell you this …" Then he took a newspaper advertisement from his pocket. "I am representing the syndicate who want me to find a missing owner of these properties, as well the property deeds themselves." Andrew read the newspaper headline aloud, "Great Dominguez Farms to be Sold, Local Syndicate to Subdivide."

But as the siblings attempted to crowd in to see over his shoulder, he continued to read aloud:

Great Dominguez Farms to be Sold, Local Syndicate to Subdivide
The great Dominguez Farms of fifteen thousand acres near Wichita has just been placed on the market for hundreds of thousands of dollars. A syndicate of local capitalists has been formed to purchase, subdivide, and sell it in smaller parcels. The properties extend for miles and include a variety of pasturelands and farmlands. The purchase will include not only the land but also warehouses, livestock, engines, wagons, harvesting machinery, and all the other appurtenances of the farms. The operation of the farms will continue for a year as surveyors, land developers, and road projects emerge to suit the buyers.

If there was one thing her brothers understood, it was land. The production of the flyer and its contents calmed them a bit, through their faces reflected their open incredulity. "Just to be clear, is this Antonio Dominguez's land?" asked Sophiny.

"How can land be sold without the owner's say-so?" James's air was no longer grumpy.

"All it takes is a public notice, one month minus one day, to notify missing heirs."

"So you are telling us that you are here to determine what this Antoinette person knew about the sale of her own land?" Andrew put the pieces together. "After she disappeared?"

"This is why you need to talk to me about anything … everything. We have to find Antoinette Dominguez." Detective Tyler looked steadily at Sophiny. He knew surprisingly little about Antoinette, given that he had said he was looking out for her interests. Detective Tyler wanted to know about their friendship, Antoinette's state of mind before the elopement, her family background, what Sophiny knew about the Dominguez holdings and Mrs. Dominguez's whereabouts. He wanted to know things that did not add up. Ideally he wanted a reason why Antoinette had picked the month of March to elope, *before* the public notice of the land sale had been published. So did Sophiny, and getting at the truth was Antoinette's best hope of rescue.

She and her brothers asked to see his badge, his papers, and evidence of his background. They also wanted to know the relationship between the temperance case and Antoinette's disappearance. Antoinette's case had gone cold. He reassured her there was no connection other than that he was assigned to escort Arthur Gunson part of the journey to Leavenworth. In the course of those arrangements he had seen Sophiny's photograph in the local newspaper and became aware that she lived in Prairie Dog. When the Mumms, accompanied by Detective Tyler, returned to the Mumm farm, Sophiny's brothers carried the trunk downstairs, where she could reveal Antoinette's journals, photographs, letters, and newspaper articles on the kitchen table. She had removed the tray with the concealed documents verifying Antoinette's ownership of her father's properties. How could she be absolutely certain that Detective Tyler was looking out for Antoinette's interests and not Mr. Stillman's? And until she was certain, she could not break her promise. She had also removed the last page of Antoinette's pocket notebook conveying Mr. Dominguez's wishes about his documents.

Sophiny talked for the next hour about her findings. It was cathartic, and she plucked courage from telling Antoinette's story. Her voice rose and fell with emotion. Though Tyler injected an occasional question, he mainly listened and made notes. Sophiny illustrated her story with a web of names, ages, places, and connecting ideas, and grouped them together as logically as she could, putting Antoinette in the center. When her tale came to an end, she propped the sheet of paper against a loaf of bread on the kitchen table and remembered to breathe. "What do you think, Detective?" She wanted to see him make a case, tell a story, reveal a pattern that would produce Antoinette.

When that did not seem to be happening, she crossed her arms and watched as Tyler scrutinized the page, reading words aloud acknowledging the points on her diagram that he was familiar with. "This Stillman character seems like a dog admiring a bone, but he wishes the bone to become his so that he may more perfectly admire it."

Sophiny could bear the suspense for only so long and asked again, "Where do you think she is?"

"I think," Tyler said, "your friend got herself in way over her head."

"But?" Sophiny could hear it in his voice.

"But there are still several obstacles to finding her. A major one is if she presents a threat to Stillman, what would he do to her? Another is the intentions of this guy she eloped with or didn't elope with—are they honorable, and who is he? And third, her mother. Was she ever able to contact her?"

"At least we know where to find Mr. Stillman. As for Mrs. Dominguez's whereabouts, perhaps Sister Louise may have discovered something by now." Sophiny bit her lip to keep from saying more. *Don't fall. Don't fall. Don't fall.* Even if Sister Louise and Detective Tyler were on Antoinette's side, Antoinette's property titles were not hers to hand over, and that's exactly what he would order her to do if he knew about them. *What would Antoinette do? She would keep the whereabouts of the documents secret and safe.*

As it was, Sophiny expected Detective Tyler to order her to hand over Antoinette's notebooks, letters, newspaper clippings, and photographs, saying he would take it from here. To her surprise, he had an entirely different solution. He was taking the culprit Arthur Gunson by train to a stop along the way back to Concord, and he suggested that Sophiny make the journey as well. After he handed over custody of the prisoner, they would continue to Concord to pick up the trail where her friend had disappeared. At this point, her brothers voiced their dissent as if signaled on cue, "No."

"She has told you what she knows. Why should she go with you?" said James.

"Isn't it your job to find her missing friend?" said Andrew.

"What's your take in delivering her?" asked Richard as though he were ready to split profits.

"What does she look like—this Antoinette?" asked Henry.

Detective Tyler begged their pardon for the appearance of indecency in his proposal. "We're nowhere done here yet."

"But Sophiny is not the one who needs to be rescued except maybe from you. Don't you have some train robbers or cattle rustlers or bank holdups to tend to?"

"I am taking in Gunson. Sure was bad timing for him to apply the hair-of-the-dog remedy after that girl's death. But detective work isn't just about racing across the tops of train cars, or breaking into or out of bank vaults, or slugging it out in a fistfight. That kind of exercise has been replaced by extra coffee."

"Bad guys to assassinate then?"

"Detectives rarely assassinate people or even get involved in shootouts. We leave sentencing to the courts. The biggest problem is building a solid case and legal accountability. When the foundation is defective, the subsequent trial becomes a house of cards."

"What do you do then?"

"Mostly gather intelligence," he said, smiling slightly.

"Why are you telling us this?"

"Intelligence comes from open sources, information available to everyone, found in newspapers, observations in public, public records, and filed documents. Sophiny has been my best source for this case. Besides, her friend entrusted Sophiny and no one else with her story. The evidence will have more weight when it comes with a witness."

"Thank you, I guess, for letting me know that you think so highly of me." Tired of being talked about as though she had no voice of her own, Sophiny turned to her brothers. "I will go. I need to find my friend. I need to know she is safe, and if there is anything I can do to help Detective Tyler, I want to be there."

"You realize," Detective Tyler said, "I'm just trying to stop a dog fight."

"I am still not sure that is exactly true, the problem seems to have gone beyond a fight over a bone with the little dog missing and all. But just so you know, Henry and I were thinking of heading that way in another week or so for the Dominguez Farm Machinery Hall sale to look at new technologies." Andrew held up the circular promoting the "latest in corn planters, harvesters, binders, threshers, seeders, hay-stackers, reapers, windmills, and even tractors and barbed wire." Trading glances with his brothers in a show of solidarity, he warned, "We'll check up on her and you."

Chapter 15
Process of Selection

ophiny's return to Concord was much quicker and more comfortable than her trip home had been. "All aboard!" the conductor called. The train smelled musty and exciting as it jolted, chugged, jerked, and rolled into motion and eventually chuffed steadily through fields and pastures, past farmhouses and windbreaks, and along the outskirts of country towns. She was thrilled by the scent of oiled wheels, the speed of the train, and the adventure of travel but most of all the proximity of Detective Tyler. His prisoner did not seem so menacing today. She worried that she seemed young, insignificant, ignorant, forlorn, a country bumpkin. She worried that she annoyed, bored, and appalled. Then she worried that she didn't, though all of her instincts told her she was doing the right thing. There was nothing left but to lean her head on the back of the seat, savor the view, and declare a truce with her warring emotions for the duration of the journey. The process of selection was knowledge forbidden to her. In the meantime, she clutched her reticule with Antoinette's property deeds blind stitched into the lining. She intended not to let the cache of documents out of her sight or her reach.

Arthur Gunson was to be handed over to prison officials at a stop along the way. Sadness seemed to have overspread his features, and his deportment was full of mildness and humility following the destruction that his fanatic and obnoxious behavior had caused. His face seemed shrunken from lack of food and his forehead and jaw pronounced, reminding her of a corpse. Could this really be the face of a twenty-one-year-old? Even so there seemed to be more alarming things in the world than this destabilized youth. How well would he photograph? Would Martha be able to capture his mutation? For it was determined that Martha Shaw should accompany Sophiny. Martha was less than euphoric but became more willing, especially when told by the newspaper editor of *The Prairie Gazette* that she would be paid for her photographs of Arthur Gunson. Perhaps even the temperance publications would be interested in her work. When the exchange was about to take place, she began to set up her camera. Not until Martha Shaw volunteered to accompany Sophiny had her brothers resigned themselves to Detective Tyler's suggestion.

Sophiny moved into the vacated seat next to Detective Tyler. He leaned in. Intimacy or the impression of confiding secrets was clearly his mode. He did not touch her, but she felt a thrill of alarm as though he had. "So this is interesting, watching crooks being processed," she said and was rewarded with a strike of golden flint in his eyes.

"You're welcome to clean my pistol while you wait. Chances are we'll find another one very soon," he said, pointing to the weapon concealed under his jacket.

"Or alternatively, we could converse. I could tell you all my hopes and dreams, and you could tell me yours. The hours would fly by." Was she flirting with him?

"Go ahead." It was not an invitation.

"No, you first. You look like you have a lot more interesting life than I have."

The burnished gold of his eyes ignited and then dimmed as he changed the subject. "Stillman may be a dangerous man. If he knew about you, he might have you followed or worse. If Antoinette's suspicions are to be believed, he is not the kind of man to leave loose ends. We still don't know where Miss Dominguez is."

"Are you going to question Stillman? How will you get information from him?" Sophiny queried, imagining Stillman as having Gunson's skeletal appearance, a face that was almost fleshless, so tightly was the skin drawn across the bones.

"Are you thinking of coercive techniques, something painful?"

"Umm," she nodded, "how would you torture him?"

"Nothing like that, my imaginative friend. Interrogation is the best method. It calls for the same skills and approaches probably as your headmistress uses," he said with a deadpan face, but still there was that spark in his eyes.

"I'm sure Sister Louise would have an expertise in that area, but how does she … do you, do it?"

"Rapport … developing personal trust, a bond between the two individuals, and of course, manipulation. Rogues like to talk, and they usually think I have more proof against them than I really have. I am careful not to undeceive until I gain their confidence to such an extent that they admit guilt."

"How does the manipulation work?"

"I find out what he wants, what he values, and I try to give it to him, though usually not the way he is expecting it, in exchange for information. In the end he realizes he has been outwitted and cooperates."

Sophiny was as much surprised at her own interest in Detective Tyler's profession as she was in his patience in answering her. "Remember that time at the academy when we were asking you about your missionary work? You weren't talking about saving souls, were you?"

"Maybe not souls exactly, but people do need saving all the time."

"Like Antoinette?"

"Like Antoinette. Can you walk me through what she did in the days, weeks that led up to the day of her disappearance?"

"I've told you most of it."

"I know, but sometimes we recall details that may have been forgotten. What else do you have to do? We're on a train. That's part of the 'we can converse' you mentioned earlier. I talk. Then you talk."

"Were you following Antoinette? Like tailing her?" Sophiny asked, even though she suspected he was using his manipulation techniques on her.

"What?"

"That night she eloped, someone was following the buggy, in an automobile. I saw from the alcove window."

"You didn't say anything about a mysterious observer when I questioned you at Concord."

"I thought it might be you, and I was waiting for you to say something. I had already told you too much, not knowing which side you were on."

"He must have been working with a team. Somebody else knew the plan. I assure you, I wasn't there that night … wish I had been," he said with regret.

"Why did you leave Mount St. Mary's?"

"Job done. The Antoinette I thought I knew did not seem to be under duress, and I had some work to finish up on another case. I hadn't counted on schoolgirl games." He was looking at her strangely. "Did you think I was that clergyman?"

"Well, yes … it is always exciting to get visitors, especially someone who has traveled." Embarrassed at the memory of her naïve indiscretion, Sophiny turned away to look out the window. "Have you ever even been to Brazil?"

"Not even close, but I did read a story about the trouble they were having with their monarchy. They seem to be going through some kind of military revolution in any case. I always liked Brazil nuts and appreciated the way the country was named after the nut."

"You just picked a place, just like that?"

"Just picked a place that I figured I knew as much about as anyone."

"Tell me about your disguises."

"Can't really tell you that … trade secret. I never know when I might have to take on one of my old identities again."

"How did you think up the Brother Claude disguise?"

"Anonymity and access. Keeping *incognito* as much as possible multiplies the chances of prompt detection. I was able to get a signature—turns out not the right one—and talk to my subject, again not the right one."

"When did you figure out I wasn't Antoinette?"

"The newspaper story brought me back to Mount St. Mary's. I usually stay in disguise without revealing my identity, but I had a little trouble getting the sisters to talk to me about Antoinette, especially since she disappeared and her whereabouts were unknown. Did you tell her about my conversation with you, that I wanted to help her?"

"She wouldn't talk to me much before she left because she didn't want me to be under suspicion after … you know. She didn't trust you either. I thought Antoinette was playing games too, but now I'm thinking her disguises were much more than mischievous fun. By putting on another face, she gave herself courage to take action when all the adults around failed her. You, as a man of disguise, should know all about that."

"How did you figure that one out?"

"Her journal. She just stepped into the center of it all, breaking rules, to catch a rule breaker."

"Indeed she did. You could say crime is a fine art and criminal detection a science. Antoinette seems to be very smart; I just hope she is a match for the smart criminal she is up against."

"At least I did get her sent to you over that faith/doubt argument. She was suspicious of you, you know. The patron saints gave you away."

"Clever girl. Let's just hope that cleverness saves her."

"Why didn't you just tell us who you were?"

"Mr. Stillman told the syndicate that Antoinette knew all about the transfer of her property. Some even met her at the Stillman Christmas party thinking she had been told. I was just at the academy to see that she wasn't under duress."

"Can you at least tell me what's the easiest disguise?" Sophiny asked to break the silence that had settled between them. *Forbidden knowledge. Knowledge forbidden.* If only Antoinette had known then what Sophiny knew now, she wouldn't have veered in the wrong direction.

"Wearing fake bad teeth to draw attention away from your other features."

"What's the best way to forge a signature? It seems Stillman must have done that more than once," she said, remembering her own forgery of Antoinette's name.

"Do you want the easy way? Use your slate pencil. Shade in an area. Turn the paper over. Put the paper with the signature on top. Then press heavily to draw over the signature you want to mimic."

"I can see why you say your job involves saving people," said Sophiny thinking about the role of a *salvator,* "one who saves." What did it mean to save someone anyway? She thought of all the prayers she had repeated on salvation, though none seemed to apply here. Antoinette had been right to question Stillman's salve to a guilty conscience by putting hapless women and children on the hook for his pet causes. No doubt Mr. Stillman's charitable giving had done some wonderful things for Concord. Unfortunately, when it came to a fashionable cause, Mr. Stillman's concern for those same clients, Antoinette and her mother, simply vanished. His approach to gaining money for himself, to securing his elevated placement in Concord society was to get as much as he possibly could from those he made vulnerable.

"Unfortunately criminal minds are darkly twisted. You have to keep up with who you are dealing with and try not to look nuts while you are doing it." Detective Tyler looked out the windows on both sides of the train, assessing the sudden change in landscape. His body tensed in readiness for action.

"See, you are an interesting person." Sophiny shocked herself by how brazenly she had manipulated Detective Tyler into revealing himself. She tried not to look nuts.

As the train came into the station at the line's end, she watched the diversity of humanity on the platform: the isolated people trying to disappear in plain sight, the celebrating people reveling at arrivals, but most especially those whose clothing fads, manners, and class roles seemed to reflect values and attitudes about material wealth and social status that Antoinette had become so conscious of during her stay with the Stillmans. Reading Antoinette's pocket notebook had changed the way she was seeing things. Some passengers debarked, others boarded, and freight was loaded and unloaded into carts and vehicles. Trainmen yelled and signaled. There was some switching, clanking, and grinding of metal. What amazed her was how the whole lot cobbled itself together and how she, Martha, and Detective Tyler fit in. Detective Tyler had made arrangements before coming, and a conveyance was waiting. As soon as their luggage could be packed into the hack, they were taken to Mount St. Mary's.

Sophiny had expected him to say, "But you do not understand these things, you have led a sheltered life. You have not seen what happens in the courts, negotiated complex problems with the banks, or experienced the composite ways of men," and she was ready to resent him. But when he instead revealed some of his own investigation secrets, she felt a compulsive need to test these techniques and definitions on those around her. "Are you going to speak to Sister Louise about Antoinette's letters and what she knows of Stillman? She was at the Stillman home for their Christmas party. She must have spoken to him on occasion. He paid Antoinette's tuition and left directions where she was to spend holidays."

"Start with what you know ... always a good plan," he agreed.

At least she would be on familiar ground. Sophiny could not help blaming herself as the very silence of Antoinette's disappearance continued and seemed a screaming accusation of her failure to recognize the seriousness of her friend's plight. If she hadn't been so enamored with the missionary who had tried to get his message of aid to her friend, that help, in time, could have changed the course of the past month. Why hadn't she just told the detective that she wasn't Antoinette that morning on the staircase?

Sister Louise led them to the guest dining room, where a hot meal awaited. The smell of meatloaf and new potatoes, onions, and peas in cream sauce made her mouth water. Sophiny did not know what to expect of the interview with Sister Louise or of her return to the academy. Speed, such as was necessary for rescuing Antoinette, if she were in danger, was not the custom of the motherhouse. Calm and silence ruled. Movement and sound had to be scheduled. Sister Louise herself usually consumed much time pacing back and forth, carefully planning her sentences before committing her thoughts to words. "The sheriff said there was not much his men could do until there is evidence that a crime has been committed," she replied when asked what had transpired concerning Antoinette since their last meeting.

"Antoinette was not a troublemaker. Quite the opposite, she was an outstanding student with a gifted intellect. She has never given cause or reason not to believe her."

"Then why don't we start with you both telling me what you know about Antoinette?" Detective Tyler placed his notepad and pencil before him when the dishes were removed from the table.

"She stayed with the Stillman family here in Concord over the Christmas holidays," confirmed Sister Louise. "And though they were not related, the families had been close at one time. Her mother had become too ill to look after her."

"What was the nature of her illness?"

"Some sort of depression ... I am not sure, but it was serious enough that she had to have medical care at an institution—not a hospital but a place where she was getting the care she needed."

"Antoinette did not know that her mother was not living in her own home until she found out through Mark. But you knew that she was not well?"

"Mr. Stillman did not want her to worry about her mother. She would have difficulty concentrating on her studies. If there was truly nothing she could do, not knowing was a kindness. I asked him for an address, but he refused, saying he would forward any communication. The patient could not be upset."

"If there was truly nothing she could do, possibly, but for months Antoinette thought that her mother had abandoned her, had taken all of her father's money, in other words deserted her and stolen her inheritance."

"When Antoinette became concerned, I did try to learn her mother's whereabouts. My attempts were unsuccessful. Mr. Stillman is both her mother's and Antoinette's guardian. This I did not know myself until Antoinette disappeared, and we notified the police, who then began looking for contact information. The only contact information we had was Mr. Stillman."

As more of the quiet, shaming secret was revealed, so grew Sophiny's impatience. But this was not the time for recriminations. Antoinette had been lied to by the people she most trusted. What else did she not know? Had Stillman's control of her mother been forcibly taken? And for what purpose? How far did his control over the Dominguez family's affairs extend? And she remembered Antoinette's questions to her guardian about her own future. Though he had not revealed them, did he have plans for Antoinette when she left the academy? Or did he intend that she never leave? Was Stillman becoming ever more dangerous because Antoinette was old enough not to have a guardian?

"He did not say, though he did mention that her reputation, as well as her mother's, must be protected from any hint of scandal."

"What did he mean by that?"

"That her own father's death was clouded by his unseemly business practices and that neither his daughter nor his wife should suffer as a result of what was beyond their control. He sounded very concerned at the time. I thought I was doing what was best for her."

For a second time Sophiny felt a visceral despair. Sister Louise had this nugget of information all that time and had not shared it with Antoinette? "Did *you* inform Mr. Stillman that Antoinette had disappeared?"

"I believe the sheriff notified him."

"What was his reaction?"

"He wanted Antoinette's trunk and belongings delivered to his house."

"Did you?"

"I thought it more appropriate to have Antoinette's things sent to her mother, but when I said as much, he authenticated his claim as her guardian, showing me a document with the court order. The sheriff had already completed his search, and so Mr. Stillman took the trunk."

"What was in it?"

"Mostly a wardrobe that I understand the Stillmans purchased for Antoinette at Christmas."

"Did you speak to him about Antoinette—where he thought she was? What happened to her?"

"He thought she might be trying to see her mother, who he said had lived for a time under a dark cloud of depression but seems to have recovered and been released from doctor's care. She was traveling. He said he would do his best to contact her, but he was vague. Then he asked me about Antoinette's state of mind, trying to determine if she was depressed, hinting it might be hereditary."

"Did he know she was eloping?"

"I am afraid I gave him that news after I had talked to you, Sophiny."

"How did he appear?" interjected Detective Tyler.

"Concerned about Antoinette, her whereabouts, concerned about her present state, concerned that she left anything behind. He also asked who her friends were, especially how close she was to Mary Clare."

"And what did you tell him about her friends?"

"That we did not encourage particular friendships and that Antoinette was generally inclusive in her attentions to others."

"Was there anything else?"

"I told him I had given the sheriff her journal. But her entries were mostly about the readings on the saint of the day, the day's menu, and homework assignments, topics the students usually write about. I also gave him letters that she had sent—one two days after she left saying she was searching for her mother and that she was sorry for any alarm she had caused. A week later she wrote that she was thinking about going to Mexico to look for her father's relatives and expressed some concern about the turmoil going on in the country due to political unrest but gave assurances that she would not do anything dangerous. The elopement had not gone as planned. If she had left anything behind, could I have it sent to her guardian, Mr. Stillman. Then there were other short messages, nothing significant. One came just this morning regarding the transfer of the Dominguez Farms to a land syndicate. She indicated that she was aware of what is going on and her lawyer is handling her affairs. Both she and her mother were too depressed to attend the auction of personal effects and so they have chosen to remain where they are. I have not had a chance to get it to the investigating officer."

"She probably did not write the letters," said Sophiny.

"What makes you so sure?"

"She usually adds a closing—something revealing about what she is up to. Her signature would also include ornamental lettering of the *A* and *D* when she writes her name."

"Did Mr. Stillman mention the whereabouts of his clerk?" Detective Tyler had sat back, taking notes, letting Sophiny ask most of the questions up to this point.

"No, why?" Sister Louise looked startled as Sophiny showed her Antoinette's entry on Mark Weaver's visit to the academy, increasing the probability that he was the partner with whom she had eloped. "I believe I met him at the Stillman Christmas party." She seemed to be conjuring up a face.

"He has also become a person of interest."

Her champion Mark Weaver had failed to liberate Antoinette from her guardian's oppression.

Sophiny remembered that she had first told Detective Tyler in Sister Louise's presence of Antoinette's plan to elope in the days after her disappearance. Detective Tyler had showed surprise, but Sister Louise had revealed nothing. Had she known about Antoinette's visitor all along?

"I too feel that I have a part in Antoinette's disappearance—not providing the security and safety she needed or assistance when she asked for it."

"What do you mean?"

Sister Louise got up from her chair and walked to the window as though looking for another perspective from the pigeons and the squirrels outside. "Let me ask you a question. You seem to know something about Mr. Stillman's economic control over Antoinette. But is he capable of physically harming her?"

"She thought so."

"At Christmas she asked to be taken to the train station to visit her mother in Wichita. Because I had other instructions from Mr. Stillman, I did not listen to her wishes or her needs but to those of her guardian. Again when she returned from the holiday, she made the same request. I had explicit instructions from Mr. Stillman that she was to remain at the motherhouse for her own protection. But I was hard pressed by Antoinette's appeals when she returned from the Stillmans. The church has always tried to help the young, stepping in where we can. Antoinette seemed distraught that she had nothing solid in this world, which is a pretty scary place. She did not feel her mother was safe, and with each lack of evidence to the contrary, her fear grew. What she needed, I could not provide, and her guardian's resistance to a search only increased her rage."

"You told Stillman about Antoinette's concerns?"

"I thought I was doing what was best for her, and he was in the best position to do something, or so I thought."

Sister Louise, her teacher and mentor had failed her.

"How did he react?"

"He said the best we could all do was observe the law, be patient, and remain calm."

"Did you notice anything else unusual about Antoinette's behavior?"

"She wrote a flurry of letters: to the editors of Wichita and Concord newspapers, to Wichita hospitals, to Mrs. Weaver her father's accountant in Wichita—several letters to Mrs. Crescentia Gottfried, to the sheriff's department and the state attorney general."

"Did you mail them?"

"Some of them, like Mrs. Gottfried's, were very gossipy about events in Concord, so I let them go even though they went to two different addresses. Others, unfortunately, no. Mr. Stillman had asked me, again for Antoinette's own protection, to inform him of all communications so that he could better assist her through this difficult transition without getting others involved, to protect her mother's reputation, and not to embarrass herself."

"What did you do with those letters?"

"Actually, I wrote inquiry letters of my own to those same sources, saying that Antoinette was our student, and we were concerned on her behalf. Letters of reference and introduction from superiors often carry more authority than those written by minors."

"Did anyone respond?"

"Not with positive news, but I am assuming, Detective Tyler, that is why you were hired on this case?"

"I was hired by the syndicate formed to purchase Dominguez Farms, and yes, the agency was contacted by newspaper writers from the Concord and Wichita newspapers."

"What about notifying the sheriff? Are Antoinette's pocket notebooks and letters evidence?" Sister Louise straightened with impressive dignity.

"Not unless we know a crime has been committed. This is a missing-persons case, or has been up to now. Authorities have no evidence of a crime and thus no subpoena power to examine Stillman's or Antoinette's bank and credit records in an attempt to track her." Detective Tyler confirmed Sister Louise's earlier experience with the local agencies.

Will Detective Tyler be the next to fail her? With all this failure going around, Sophiny thought she should have been gratified, but she felt just the opposite.

Is he going to dismiss me now? Send me back home to wait? By adding Martha's, Detective Tyler's, and Sister Louise's voices to her own and Antoinette's experiences and observations, Sophiny had gained insight very quickly. The price, though, was that analysis remained in the shallows. So many people were opining that a definite course of action was in danger of being taken without her. Too soon her fears were realized.

"And in the meantime, Sophiny and her friend will stay with us for her own safety and protection. She cannot be left to wander around with you, Detective," Sister Louise declared.

"We need to keep witnesses safe," agreed Detective Tyler as the two of them seemed to study what was to be done with her.

"But Sister …" Sophiny protested, realizing that her activities would be closely monitored. The adults would muzzle her. She stood for a moment, clutching her bag with Antoinette's documents, uncertain of how to act. Doing as Sister Louise suggested, she knew was going to limit her participation in the investigation; but to say at this point, "No thank you, I'd rather not," when the request was obviously harmless and in her interest would have made her feel even more uneasy. Where would she and Martha stay if she refused? After a minute, she found herself turning to Sister Louise, "Will you let me tell the students about Antoinette? They could pray for her. She needs their support, just as I did when my mother died."

"What did you have in mind?"

On better footing, Sophiny decided to go the opposite way and consider the good detective policies Tyler had shared with her on the train in the midst of the uncertainty that surrounded them. After all, she did imagine herself capable of making grown-up decisions. "We know Stillman is capable of forgery. We know Stillman is capable of theft. Could he be capable of murder?"

"Whose?"

"I was wondering, how did Antoinette's father die? Is her mother really still alive? And if Antoinette does not fit into Stillman's plans, will she be next?"

"Is Antoinette's family his only victim?" Sister Louise too sought reassurance.

"That would require an extensive look into his other cases, best obtained from his own files." Detective Tyler gave her none and instead seemed to be thinking about the task ahead of him.

"Has your investigation led to other names and properties? Has anyone else disappeared that he has connections to?"

But the detective appeared either not to have an answer or not to hear her question.

Sophiny leaped to her feet, ready for action. "Why can't you just go to his office and to his house and look through his records like Antoinette did? He must have all sorts of irregularities in his documentation. And don't forget, he has my trunk too. I'm ready to go in disguise if you won't, Detective."

"Well actually, I was thinking along those lines. We have to charge him with something first. Any ideas, Sister?" When Sister Louise did not answer, he continued. "It seems he was not being candid with Antoinette about her mother. She is of age now but missing. At least we might be able to get his guardianship revoked and stop the sale of her property. Is she in possession of her father's land deeds, I wonder?" He looked meaningfully at Sophiny.

"At least that will save me from having to break in!" Sophiny sighed in relief, trying to distract him from that thought. Detective Tyler had regained his stature in her esteem.

"I'll see if I can make some charges stick to take him in for questioning. You'll excuse me. I need to send some telegrams, make some telephone calls tonight to get started on that in the morning." He reached for his hat to leave before turning to Sophiny, "I'll be in touch with you tomorrow. Don't go anyplace. I can't be looking out for two missing schoolgirls."

"Or better yet, do you know where I can get some fake, bad teeth?"

"What do you intend to do with those?"

"I'm just thinking about hiding in plain sight."

Detective Tyler reached into his jacket pocket and handed her a small wrapped parcel. "I just happen to have a spare."

"And by the way, our code word, Antoinette's and mine, was missionary in case you need it. We were paying attention when you told us how to get out of dangerous situations."

Saying good afternoon to Sister Louise, he put his canvas bag over his shoulder and turned to the door.

Sophiny followed to show the detective out of the room, down the stairs, and out of the building. Martha remained with their bags in the dining room.

"Is there anything you still aren't telling me, Sophiny," Detective Tyler asked gently, "before we set in motion a course of action?"

I cannot fail my friend by breaking my vow. "No," she said without elaboration. Sophiny trudged heavily back up the stairs. Though Antoinette's property deeds remained in her possession, she worried about their security. It was important to keep one's treasures scattered. If her connection to Antoinette were discovered, Antoinette's cache might be discovered as well. So she returned to Sister Louise and opened her bag. It was time to tell someone. "When Antoinette eloped, she left her trunk with me and made me promise not to tell anyone of our exchange, or to let anyone look at or have what was inside. I felt bound until her absence continued for so long. What if she needed my help? So I broke my promises and looked."

Sister Louise moved beside her at the table. "Is there something else?"

Sophiny ripped apart the blind stitching of the lining and carefully lifted the string-bound packet from the bag where she had hidden it. Then she hugged it to her body. "Antoinette did not trust anyone, and she had every reason for caution. Because she made me vow, I feel that I cannot give Detective Tyler these papers. The syndicate that hired him may use them against her. Even though they may provide possible evidence that a crime has been committed, they are Antoinette's only protection of her rights, which the courts already have denied in the person of her guardian. Sister Louise, will you secure these in the convent safe? Will you help me keep my vow to my friend? I ask this of you before Martha as my witness, and I submit to you a receipt for your signature." Sophiny stated her case as clearly as she understood it.

"We must uphold the law," Sister Louise answered without a moment's hesitation, but she no longer seemed the picture of composure.

"According to the law, whoever possesses these papers possesses the land. Antoinette's eighteenth birthday has passed. She has no need of a guardian. Will you help me keep possession for the legitimate heirs according to Mr. Dominguez's will? Or must I safeguard them with my own person?"

"You have learned a thing or two about sums and measures, haven't you?" Sister Louise nodded approval and without another word, signaled for them to follow her to the bursar's office. Something had happened. A new force had entered the room. Once the documents were securely deposited and the receipt signed, Sister Louise wondered aloud how best to reintroduce Sophiny and Antoinette to the academy students. Sophiny had a plan of her own.

Reminded of the vigil for Glenda, she thought that Antoinette should have no less and requested that the students be allowed to gather in the grotto for a candlelight vigil. Sophiny was welcomed back and knew herself to be the disruption that they all looked forward to. When the sun dropped below the horizon, candles lighted the girls' faces as they strolled along the grotto path. Spring had come with extraordinary beauty, brilliance of coloring, and richness of life in the trees, bushes, and flowering bulbs of the surrounding grounds. A breeze tried to snuff out the glow. But cupped hands protected the fluttering flames.

The young women fell silent, pondering the absence of their classmate while listening to the grotto's sounds: wind shushing in the boughs of the trees, dying with the sunset, birds chittering and fluttering as they settled, safe for the night. One of the students strummed a guitar quietly. The young women began singing together, in part harmony, to create something both evocative and communicative in a way that their individual voices could not. Though Sophiny knew their voices, no matter how sweet, would not bring Antoinette back, the flame of hope that she was alive remained—Antoinette's disappearance wasn't like Glenda's. When Sister Louise gave the signal for the students to return indoors, Sophiny had still another plan. "What if we let the community of Concord know that one of our students is missing?"

"How?" they asked, and she was gratified by their interest.

"There are lots of ways to get an audience." Sophiny remembered the sequence of events that led to Arthur Gunson's arrest.

"We could put up posters." Theora began to think aloud. "We could tell the newspaper her story."

The vigil for Antoinette gained a momentum that could not be explained simply as a welcome change in schedule. Girls pranced around the music hall chattering like birds as suggestions poured forth. Putting up posters in the downtown area was scheduled into an afternoon walk.

But the creation of the posters themselves stalled over a rivalry as to their design and wording. "You can't be serious," hooted Mary Clare as she examined Sophiny's efforts.

"What's wrong with it?" Sophiny asked patiently, knowing it was unwise to needle a senior girl she needed for resources and credibility of the project, yet sensitive to the howl of ridicule.

"*Simplicio.*" Mary Clare pointed at Sophiny's stick figures and uneven lettering.

"Do you think you could do better?" Sophiny asked, looking at Mary Clare's labors with envy, for she did have talent. Sophiny felt the saliva rise in her mouth and wondered if she could vomit straight in Mary Clare's lap or just over her shoes. Mary Clare had seemed bent on reminding her just who held the title of Antoinette's best friend. For hadn't she kept Antoinette's secret about Mark's visit and passed on Antoinette's letters to Mark by way of her own brothers for mailing? This account had come out in the candle ceremony.

But she had still more to add. "This is all starting to make sense," said Mary Clare.

"What do you mean?"

"Antoinette gave me a letter that she made me promise to send on her birthday, March 31 to Frank Canon of the *Concord Chronicle*. I wasn't supposed to open the envelope, but after she left I read it and made a copy before I sent it." She removed her own pocket notebook and read:

Dear Watchdog,

I would like to report on my investigations of improper activities by Mr. Thomas Stillman, appointed guardians of minors and persons of unsound mind in the case of Miss Antoinette Dominguez and her mother, Mrs. Antonio Dominguez. They include falsification of records, inexcusable neglect of professional duty, failure to monitor properties under his control, waste of funds, and misuse of a minor's resources. Where are they now? Both are missing, and an investigation needs to take place.

Antoinette Dominguez
March 16, 1910

Mary Clare's disclosure of what was going on with Antoinette right under their noses further confirmed how strange was her disappearance. The issues involved seemed to be increasing in gravity, adding significance to their own poster and circular campaign. "Do you want me to try?"

"What?" Sophiny had forgotten what she was about.

"The poster drawing …"

"It's yours then," Sophiny delegated, knowing their feud had lasted long enough. Their mutual outrage could be better spent on another target. But she also sensed that this was the moment to strike as many bargains as she could. "What if Detective Tyler cannot secure his subpoenas for a records search? Will the investigation continue, do you think?" she asked Martha, who was busy photographing their efforts.

"Everything takes so much time …"

"And then there are laws … and rules … and expectations for proper behavior …"

"Should all expectations, rules, or for that matter laws be obeyed?"

"Antoinette will be lost forever if this injustice against her continues."

"Let's think about whether all the laws of this country deserve our respect and obedience. Slavery is immoral—but it took a war that cost six hundred thousand lives to change that law," said Martha, citing from her own article in the local paper following the *Uncle Tom's Cabin* performance in Prairie Dog.

"If this is to be a campaign to rescue Antoinette, then it must go beyond the walls of the convent. Eyes and ears must be multiplied to go right into the thralldom of wickedness where Antoinette has been cratered." Sophiny was thinking of the pit of vices at the base of the chart of virtues hanging on the study hall wall. It was the kind of idea that comes in the middle of something else happening. Sophiny noticed that several of the students were forming a half circle around her and Martha, intent on hearing what she had to say. She herself waited for the revelation.

Martha paused and turned away from her camera. "Even so, if Mr. Stillman hears that there is an investigation, he will move the evidence."

"That's what I am afraid of … not only the records, but Stillman has a basement full of alcohol and medicine bottles according to Antoinette's notebook."

"What are you thinking now?"

"A costume, a masque." And there it was; if Detective Tyler could don a disguise, why couldn't she? But how did one go about getting into someone's basement? There were the Christmas ornaments, the Seelye pharmacopeia products, the intoxicants, the poisons, the safe, and the records all mentioned in Antoinette's pocket notebook. Could she say she was a messenger from Mr. Stillman himself looking for documents in his basement? At least they would know if Mr. Stillman was hiding Antoinette in his home or if he had fled. Martha was happy to entertain the scenario with her.

"All right, so we go up to the door, the Irish maid answers and says that Mr. Stillman is not at home and Mrs. Stillman is indisposed. The basement door is locked. No one has access. Good-bye. Door closes."

"I give her a letter saying it requires Mr. Stillman's immediate attention."

"Maid looks, takes the letter, says she will give it to her employer—good-bye. Door closes."

"What if the letter requires a reply?"

"What message would you send that is so urgent?"

"You are right! But what we *could* do is call Miss Henrietta Bratley from the Temperance Union to give one of her fine talks. From Antoinette's list of intoxicants on the shelves in Mr. Stillman's basement at Christmastime, isn't he as guilty as Arthur Gunson? He gave Antoinette alcohol to drink."

"And where did that apple cider come from? Maybe he had a still in his locked basement room." Theora was in full rumor mode.

Sister Louise had moved within hearing. "Unfortunately, Detective Tyler would have to get even more warrants to search the Stillman house."

"And what standing does a missing woman's diary have in the legal system?" Mary Clare was beginning to get the picture.

"But the diary should count for something …" hesitated Viola.

"In a social setting, it could count. What if … what if …" Sophiny was thinking out loud of Lucretia Stillman's name story, "we had a full-fledged temperance meeting—bigger than Glenda's right here in Concord. Martha, that brings us back to Henrietta Bratley."

"When I took her photograph for *The Prairie Gazette* story, she gave me a contact number. Is there a telephone I can use?"

"And what if we had a street trial like the one Antoinette staged for Dr. Frankenstein? Her guardian Mr. Stillman gave her alcohol while she stayed with him. We have her own words in her pocket notebook as evidence."

"Oh, Sophiny! It is good to have you back." Mary Clare's enthusiasm was genuine. "Mr. Frank Canon would be sure to cover the event in his newspaper as well."

But as she reached out to hug her, Sophiny stepped back, another thought occurring to her. When things are difficult, tension is best maintained. She was not ready to bury the hatchet. "And we could carry hatchets instead of candles."

"What?" Mary Clare showed her confusion at being rebuffed.

"We need to stay angry about Antoinette's disappearance. The purpose of this gathering is not our enjoyment." Sophiny opened the pocket notebook and read Antoinette's New Year's Eve entry to the growing circle. Their silent attention to Antoinette's words was all the support she needed, for her friend's words were taking on a power of their own in the imaginations of her listeners.

"I think my brothers could make the hatchets," Mary Clare volunteered, and Sophiny knew that she wasn't the only one excited by morbid thoughts. "Should we put blood on them, do you think?"

"We need to listen to all of the diary," said Theora, and the reading commenced, with students taking turns. "If you are reading my diary, it must be because you have not heard from me …" Theora began at the beginning.

After morning mass, breakfast, and charges, a convulsion of energy swept from student to student. Spirits, which had at first flagged in learning about their classmate, rose. Labor banished boredom. Work on the posters continued with increasing enthusiasm, imagination, and even tolerance toward getting in each other's way. As Mary Clare penciled out a script for the street trial, another student typed Antoinette's pocket notebook, which Sophiny had reluctantly surrendered. The St. Cecilia Music Hall hummed with activity as groups fashioned their posters, designed their walking campaign, and argued over trial protocol and presentation of evidence. Sister Louise had been dispatched to find library resources on Kansas's prohibition legislation. She was even considering a fieldtrip to the town hall so that the students could see a trial in progress for themselves.

Martha's contact produced Henrietta Bratley, who promised an appearance in Concord two days hence. Sophiny stood on the threshold of the St. Cecilia Music Hall, not needing to go farther into the room, content for a moment merely to stand and watch, remembering the stories they had told themselves about Antoinette's disappearance even as they invented new accounts of what might have happened. She envied their camaraderie and missed even more their security in being part of the academy of young ladies. The sisters were the keepers of ancient boundaries. She was a trespasser.

Students were only too happy after a long month of silence to take action, to make right the damage to her reputation. All they needed was the suggestion. They immediately knew how to take action and form groups patterned after the Dr. Frankenstein trial: prosecution, defense, judge, and jury as the principal set of actors. Sister Louise, who otherwise might have censored their activity, was now fully invested in recovering the academy's missing student.

"But who is the monster bringing charges in this case?"

"Antoinette, of course—she's the one with no rights who has not received proper initiation into the society she has been thrust into. Therefore, she has been made invisible to the law. Because she cannot be here, her diary will speak for her as it cannot before a court."

"What's a monster again?" asked one of the first years.

"A word mostly used to describe what we don't understand," Sophiny answered, thinking of the role she had played in the *Frankenstein* trial. Was she becoming a person of enigma and mystery after all?

"Don't forget. The diary is circumstantial evidence of her being made invisible," Theora contributed with somber voice. She seemed to like playing the role of a judge. The end result was a deft narrative that borrowed gracefully from Mary Wollstonecraft Shelley's street trial in *Frankenstein* and even gave Sophiny some credit for the idea. Evidence of corruption of a minor, her guardian giving her intoxicating liquors, came directly from Antoinette's own notebook.

Chapter 16
Thralldom of Wickedness

"You are still unsatisfied, aren't you?" Martha read her mind. Sophiny felt a curious inner trembling, a shaking she could not quite control. "I can't fix my mind on anything but finding Antoinette. I feel like I'm being sidetracked by trifles, looking at what I cannot do instead of doing what I can. Are we helpless?"

"What do you say we visit the Stillman Law Office on the pretense of offering our photography services ... see for ourselves the thralldom of wickedness as you put it?" Martha smiled, her professional serenity returning to her manner.

Sophiny readily agreed, telling herself that it wasn't because she was hoping to catch a glimpse of Detective Tyler at work. But she did make an effort for the outing. Taking one of Antoinette's street dresses from her bag, she slipped it over her head. They easily convinced the sister who drove the convent automobile to drop them off in the town square. Antoinette's journal gave her a whole new perspective of the main boulevard, which she had previously only experienced by the academy students walking two-by-two following one of the sisters through the town. Martha took the lead in heading toward the town hall.

Detective Tyler raised his hand in greeting but shook his head, discouraging further approach. Two deputies were exiting the building next door marked Concord Sheriff. The interview process, obtaining subpoenas for bank records, did not seem to be going well. "Don't take no for an answer," Tyler snapped at the detectives.

"We will look more like businesswomen if we carry something." From her bag Martha produced a photograph album, writing instrument, and an assortment of papers. She handed Sophiny a camera and writing pad. "You can always pretend you are taking notes if you don't know what else to do ... or better yet talk. Talk about what to do with the head, the lips, gazing at the camera, keeping eyes opened when the flash goes off … the more nonsense you can spout, the better."

Stillman Enterprises, a sign on the door, gave Sophiny pause. Was this the secret lair where Mr. Stillman had hatched his evil plans and where Mark Weaver, his assistant, perhaps a decent man who meant well, had been miscast in his role as hero? Would she see Mr. Stillman the obvious misfit for the title of guardian for herself? And learn the whereabouts of Mark Weaver, whose attempts of rescue seemed to have made life even more hazardous for Antoinette?

But the place seemed deserted except for a young clerk at the front desk who took Martha's card and replied that Mr. Stillman had not been in the office for the past week. "He is conducting important business in Wichita." Viewing the hangings on the walls, Sophiny noted that Stillman had an affinity for photographs of a growing Concord and of himself with various state and city elite. His walls were his own celebrity gallery and record of himself receiving awards and plaques. Sophiny remembered Antoinette's pocket notebook about how Mr. Stillman tried to gain prestige and a place in society by accumulating connections and here installed for all of Concord to see him as he saw himself through his collection.

Instead of witnessing Detective Tyler's supervision of the removal of records from Stillman's office, there was a complete lack of activity. She had not expected Antoinette to suddenly appear when she came into the domain of her friend's guardian, but neither had she expected her investigation to end so quickly. For indeed they were back in the hallway with the door closed behind them.

For its size, the office building had few inhabitants who all seemed to be keeping a low profile behind closed doorways on either side. Sophiny whispered her doubts of a quick resolution to Antoinette's disappearance. "Martha, I don't think Detective Tyler will be able to get started for some time. Antoinette was right to be wary of the inefficiencies of legal processes regarding her case."

"There did seem to be something going on by the sheriff's headquarters."

"Yes … and he will get the records search under control without us. In the meantime, Antoinette is still missing."

"Were you thinking of going to Wichita?"

"Not exactly, I was thinking about looking for Mark Weaver." Despite the closed door, Sophiny could not bring herself to leave the building housing the Stillman suite before making some discovery. "I have Mark's photograph."

"All right, let's see how far that will get you," agreed Martha.

This time Sophiny led the way when they tentatively reentered the

Stillman offices. Remembering how Janet had looked at her brother James, and Antoinette's journal entry praising Mark for his attention to details, she looked at the clerk and said, "I admire how you keep all these papers in such fine order."

"Thank you," he said simply.

"Martha was saying that she'd bet you could find anything quick as a wink too."

He looked at her closely, as though trying to measure her intentions: Friend or foe?

"Uh … I just wanted to ask … do you know where Mark Weaver lives? I wanted to give him a copy of this photograph my friend," not entirely a lie if he mistook the friend for Martha instead of Antoinette, "took of him at Christmas. I was hoping to see him … again."

"And your name is?"

"Antoinette … Antoinette Dominguez." She lowered her voice to a whisper. "Mr. Stillman is my guardian."

"Yes, I know." He looked at her strangely. "Mark no longer works in this office."

"Oh, I am sooo disappointed to hear that." She let her shoulders droop and looked at the photograph as though she had lost something … which she had.

He hesitated for a moment and then opened a book, turned it facing her on the desk, and pointed to a neat script for her to see an address. Sophiny quickly picked up a pencil to write the address, not bothering to hide her jubilation. The clerk grinned in return; clearly she was now a friend.

Back on the street, Martha said to her, "You have a rare knack of making a loyal ally of a stranger instantly. Something about your manner of innocence and complete trust—and youth—as though getting him to help you in a conspiracy, making him think you would do the same for him if he were your friend … You read him very well."

"Thank you?" Sophiny wasn't sure this was a compliment.

But Martha's smile reassured her. "Where are we going?"

"Abilene," she replied with conviction, as though herself following the Chisholm Trail of characters, causes, and effects. Routes once thought impassable were now open, and new enticements for exploration appeared. Living in the scene, experiencing multiple points of view, fitting together the sounds of certain words caused new shifts and depths of her own understanding of the way things unfolded. What course of action would stop the sale of Antoinette's property, revoke Mr. Stillman's guardianship of both Antoinette and her mother, and restore her to her rightful position?

What did evil look like? Sophiny was reminded of the rheumy eyes and the goblin-like appearance of the man who thought cows more worthy of Martha's photographs than his long-suffering wife and life partner. Or the gaunt face of Arthur, wasted by alcohol … about to be turned over to the jailer. Then there was Mr. Stillman who, under the pretense of assistance, of security, of protection, had deceived Antoinette. She had walked into someone else's nightmare. And Antoinette had never described him as a monster promising pestilence and plague.

"Martha, we have to get there first. If he took Antoinette there or if she left anymore of her journals, we have to find her or them before anyone else."

"What about Detective Tyler, shouldn't he go with us?" observed Martha thoughtfully.

"He is investigating Stillman's offices. You said yourself getting permits and looking through all those records will take some time. We cannot be of much help to him on that score," replied Sophiny, still suffering somewhat from the dismissal they had received earlier that morning. "But we might be able to find out … something he couldn't."

Once they returned to the academy, they found the students were beginning to put up posters of their missing classmate in advance of Henrietta Bratley's visit.

Sophiny asked, "How is the street trial script going?"

Mary Clare had much that was positive to report. "We are putting the finishing touches on it tonight after we watch a trial this afternoon. Want to come? Sister Louise arranged it."

"Martha and I have other plans. We are going to see if Mrs. Crescentia Gottfried will attend your event and bring her friends."

Early the following morning, Sophiny and Martha made their way to the train station just in time to purchase boarding passes for the scheduled trip to Abilene. They were still thinking about their long talk with Mrs. Gottfried and her promise to attend the academy students' temperance event. She had provided even more evidence of Mr. Stillman's access to intoxicating liquors. One of the punch bowls at the Christmas Party had contained alcohol, as did another at the New Year's gala. Martha had packed a small hamper of food to eat on the train. Between bites Sophiny offered several scenarios as to what might have occurred on the day Antoinette "eloped." If she and Mark were traveling together, his living arrangements might be part of their plan.

Abilene, the slowed gravitation and a final bang and hiss of the brake shoes as the locomotive slid to a halt told them they had arrived. Their destination was not difficult to find. The clerk behind the ticket counter knew immediately the address and pointed Martha and Sophiny in the direction, saying it was easily walking distance. "You're talking about what locals call the Shutter House. You might miss it behind that large hedge, but you'll know it by its large shutters. There's been some strange activity going on there lately. The neighbors are talking." He remarked in a careless way, "Why are you interested?"

"What kind of activity?" asked Sophiny, taken aback, but the clerk's question seemed to smooth the way toward the two things she wanted so badly—Antoinette's recovery and a good ending to the adventure. It had not occurred to her to trade information.

"Lights and noises … an automobile parked out front. All the comings and goings are … unusual."

"How so exactly?'

"It used to belong to an elderly couple … he died. She lived there … what was the family name? It's been called the Shutter House for so long, I can't remember. Then it was rented out for a time, mostly to Seelye families who worked for the patent medicine company. It's been empty off and on."

Since Sophiny was not forthcoming in trading information, her source dried up. She thought better of her silence. "I am looking for my missing friend. Her name is Dominguez. If we don't report back to you by, shall we say 4:00 this afternoon, would you please contact this person?" She wrote quickly on a ripped-out page of her pocket notebook the name and telephone number of Claude Tyler's detective agency. She decided to omit the detective part.

The sun was high and hot and relentless on one side of a tall hedge. On the other side trees stood motionless, flies buzzed, and bees swarmed around untrimmed bushes and unkempt undergrowth. Sophiny was grateful for the information she had received as she checked for an automobile in front and walked around the parameter before moving cautiously onto the glass-enclosed veranda. To her surprise, the doorknob moved easily in her hand, and the door swung open. The musty smell of damp flagstones outside was followed by a combination of stale smoke, rotting food, urine, and vomit inside. The smell hit her in the face like a physical assault, causing a sensation akin to pain and a strong gag reflex. For a moment she had to adjust to the interior darkness. Once Martha found a light switch, they entered the neglect of what must have been a parlor and stared blankly. A dumb misery deepened as they realized what they were seeing and what the inhabitants had lost before moving warily through dark rooms, searching for clues of Antoinette's presence.

Sophiny rubbed her eyes and whispered to Martha, "This seems the right sort of place, if anywhere, we will find her." But the house though recently occupied appeared empty and unwilling to give up secrets readily. "She must have been here," Sophiny insisted, and the two began to ascend the stairs. All the upstairs bedrooms but one were locked. Sophiny quickly surveyed the burned curtains and bed coverings, the smoke stains on the wall, the window glass broken, though bars remained, until she found the source of the most offensive smell.

"Let's get rid of this, so we can think better," Martha used a pillow case as a protective covering to lift the chamber pot from the stand and carry it outside. How had Antoinette been made to stay in a room with her own excrement? Sophiny moved about picking up clothing and other objects, studying the condition of each. Martha lifted the mattress, opened and turned over drawers, studied the walls and the floors, but hiding places were few, and so the task did not take long. "Someone else has searched this room."

"Find anything?" How terrified Antoinette must have felt, cloaked in secrecy and manipulated by her so-called guardian.

"It looks like she spent some time here," said Martha, surveying the gloom.

"And what did she do with her time?" Sophiny noticed her own sampler, "A stitch in time saves nine," hanging over the electric light switch. She remembered Antoinette's insistence on an exchange object to signal that all was well. But all was not well. Had Antoinette used the square as a symbol to alert her that something important was close by? "Martha, do you think she's hidden something … in the wall … by the light." Sophiny immediately went to the light switch. "Do you have a coin?" With a few twists she easily loosened the screws. After removing the plate, she felt around on the inside wall and found a string—her trunk key cord. She carefully raised it, aware of extra weight. Antoinette had left another diary.

Gratefully she sank to the floor in a swirl of skirts and began to read. Martha sat close enough to look over her shoulder. They were silent for a time. "There does seem more to be done." Sophiny nodded grimly.

Chapter 17
Fabric of Lies

Antoinette's Pocket Notebook: March–April 1910

My first task before retiring was to find a hiding place for my pocket notebook. I looked for loose floorboards, closets, vents, and finally found the hole in the wall behind the light switch, where I secured my money and my writing. I used your trunk key cord, dear friend, to lower my treasure from a nail projected through a beam on the inside. Should such a time ever come, I know you will think of looking near where I placed your sampler. My own hope of being able to go back in time to pick up a lost stitch … well, we'll see where it leads.

A.D.

March 15, 1910, Tuesday, day 1. Mark reserved a hotel room for me near the train station. I did not sleep very well.

A.D.

March 26, 1910, Wednesday, day 2. My original plan was to go to the train station the following morning and purchase a ticket to Wichita with money I had been saving, but before I was dressed, there was a knock on the door. I did not answer until I heard Mark say in a low voice, "Antoinette, I have breakfast for you."

I hadn't realized how famished I was until I saw the eggs and toast on the tray. As we ate together, the plans we were making and my hopes seemed possible. The first stop was Abilene, some fifty miles away, where we would change trains. I was wearing my traveling suit with matching boots and hat. Mark had already purchased train tickets. Though I had not expected him to, he insisted on going with me, saying that he had promised his mother a visit and couldn't imagine me going the distance alone. I thought Mark's assistance might ease the surprise as well when I showed up on the doorstep of my house intending to take up residency. From Abilene, I planned to send a letter to Sister Louise explaining my actions and apologizing for my hasty departure thus, lessening the worry that I may have caused.

The journey was exciting, and Mark and I had no lack of topics to discuss. The most important for him seemed to be our marriage when I came of age. I knew I had led him to believe that being with him was my primary purpose in leaving Mount St. Mary's, and I had spent many hours fantasizing about such a union between us. On the one hand, now that the possibility was imminent, I found myself erecting obstacles. Finding my mother was the most tangible. On the other hand, it was as though I had snatched a thick curtain from my face, allowing air to my suffering lungs, so light and giddy did I feel at the prospect of finally taking action. "Antoinette, how brave are you?" Mark asked as a town came into sight."

"Very," I said recklessly, secure with the notion that I was gaining ground in the miles that we had covered. I say this to contrast with what came later. "Why?"

"I want to cross over a threshold with you and then look out the window and know I am living in my own house away from here. Then, there are things I want to tell you. Will you come?"

I was about to protest that my own plan had to come first. *What things did he want to tell me?* Could he unveil my own hidden past? Or was he trying to prove that he had a crazy side too?

"You have to know a few things. It's not safe for you."

Still I hesitated. *I wanted to know a few things. What wasn't safe?*

"Just for a day or so here in Abilene until we sort this all out. Will you stay with me?"

I don't know why I was even considering his suggestion, but I heard myself say, "Just for a day, perhaps."

Our arrival in Abilene, first of the principal cattle-trading centers, around midday triggered an onslaught of memories. I remembered my father telling me that his entry into the world had been in Abilene a year after the cattle drives began in 1867. The event had launched his own father's independence when he left home by participating in the drives. Abilene had all the requirements of a cattle-shipping town in those early days: a railroad, a river providing water for thirsty cattle, and prairies for miles around to fatten stock at the end of the drives. Fort Riley nearby offered protection from Indian raids until the last big season in 1871, when cattlemen were considered the enemy of small farmers and the big boom collapsed. By that time my grandfather had become a farmer himself, grazing cattle on land he had homesteaded with his cattle drive earnings and convincing my grandmother to leave Texas as well. But after the year of the grasshopper plague in 1874, he moved the family to the new boomtown Wichita, purchasing more land and supporting his growing holdings by becoming an itinerant well driller to support the new economy based on irrigation. As the area grew and water was scarce, his skills were much in need. He had shared his interest in power machines, attended the state fairs, and gone to the farm machinery halls, bringing my father along to tutor him. How much of my family's history was Mark aware of, I wondered, for this industry had supported him as well as me.

Passengers began to disembark from the train with their bags and boxes and trunks. Women sat on benches while the men smoked and waited for the next train or their transportation elsewhere. I suppose the reason that I didn't protest when Mark and I were among those passengers was that I suddenly wanted to see this town, overcome as I was with nostalgia. Street traffic included a fleet of delivery wagons that looked strangely familiar. We talked of inconsequential things: I thought there was time for asking all my questions later. Mark had a plan worked out. I had seen that Seelye delivery truck in front of the Stillman house in Concord. A large barnlike affair with the Seelye Patent Medicine Company sign loomed over the town. Mark noticed my interest. "Seelye manufactures and warehouses their products here. See that house over there?" He pointed to a beautiful, three-story, white mansion, "That's the Seelye family home."

"Where are we going?" I asked as Mark led me away from the train station. I felt a pang of regret that we weren't boarding. My father had taken a special pride in saying, "Cattle came over with the Spaniards. They landed at Vera Cruz in 1521, six heifers and a young bull." After a while I heard the train and saw it slowly move away from the station, Wichita receding with it. Grandfather's photograph of himself wearing a slouch hat, unbuttoned vest, and chaps was among my father's treasures. I pictured him now and could almost hear the echoes of the dust-muffled beat of horses' hooves and bawling cattle as cowboys drove their herds, stopping business, frightening horses, filling eyes, mouths, and clothes with dust until they reached the stock pens. The shouts of command, the creaking of leather saddles, whips and boots, the musket and rifle shot, and with some effort the near silent swish of saloon doors as gamblers, cattlemen, and the city marshal marked their arrival. I imagined the taunt characters with itchy trigger fingers all watching the procession of long-legged, taper-horned cattle having something of a wild look in their own eyes. Abilene had grown quickly to support the cattle drives:

boardinghouses, saloons, general stores, hotels, stores dealing in firearms and boots and hats, and eventually a jail. The pungent odor of the new pine lumber in the buildings must have mingled with the smell of the dust and excited animals. That would have been some forty years ago. Again I was reminded of my father's age: almost forty when he died, he would have been forty-four this year, Mr. Stillman's age as well.

"Not far. I want to show you this house." Mark had hefted my reticule to one shoulder while he carried his bag in the opposite hand. Like Concord, this town was expanding with new building projects along its broad streets.

"There goes our train." I trudged after him, somewhat confused by the disruption of my carefully laid plans but even more confused by my own response. It was as though I had entered a museum filled with exhibits to look at, reflect, look at again, reflect some more, to make connections and thereby … and thereby … What was I meant to do here? All I could think of, my friend, was the sampler you made for me. I truly felt that I had gone back in time to pick up that lost stitch.

"We cannot make Wichita in one day anyway." Mark shifted the strap on his shoulder and glanced to the right and to the left as we stopped for traffic before crossing a street. "We'll stay the night here. It will be more comfortable than a hotel."

The house was quite isolated, standing at the end of a long dirt driveway and partially hidden by an overgrown hedge and tall trees. Though not nearly so grand as the Seelye house, it had its own turreted, gingerbread-encrusted charm. Large green shutters covered over all the windows; an extended, glass-enclosed veranda shielded etched-glass front doors. When the latch clicked and the door opened, I was surprised at the darkness of the entry. Not only did the outside shutters prevent light from coming in, but the etched glass doors had also been covered over with wooden panels on the inside. Heavy drapes covered the windows. Only later, when I tried to pull the curtains, did I notice the bars on the windows inside. Mark switched on the electric light.

We toured the downstairs. A murky coat of varnish gave off a gloomy aspect of neglect. Even Mark's occupancy left few signs of use. "The local kids like to go through empty houses. Besides theft, they can do a lot of damage to a property. The shutters were part of the original design, but other modifications had to be made," he explained. I trailed my fingers in the dust covering the tabletop, leaving four parallel lines. "We could live here for a while, until we get our own place or figure out what to do next."

His suggestion astonished me. "Why would we do that?"

"Just for a few days."

Mark, you have not been listening to me. I must go to my mother as soon as possible, before …"

"Mr. Stillman may have taken precautions—given directions as to who may visit her."

"Yes … I thought of that. That's why it is even more important to begin the search as soon as possible."

"You must allow me some time to make inquiries."

"We do this together." *Had I made a mistake in leaving the train?*

"It is best that I see the lay of the land, so to speak. If we were married, you would have my protection, guardianship wouldn't be an issue. Under eighteen, you risk your freedom and mine if Mr. Stillman discovers what we have done."

My mind careened between hope and despair. I wondered about the journey of my life. What was he thinking to forbid my movement so soon? "Two weeks isn't long until I am of age. We need time to get to know each other. Then we will go to a priest as soon as I am eighteen."

"We don't have to go to a priest. There are other ways to marry … And unless we are married, not only is Mr. Stillman an obstacle, but your mother might object as well. She only sees me as the son of an employee. To lose you would break my heart."

"What is this place? Why is it all boarded up?" I tried to divert him from his reasoning even as a growing dread came over me that we had not really strayed from the point of my search.

"Mr. Stillman's company has taken over its care. The owner is—actually I don't know anything about the owner—but we can stay here for the next month or so until it is sold, or ownership is transferred."

"Make your inquiries, if you must," I said, knowing it was pointless to try convincing him otherwise. He obviously had a plan that did not include me. How had one day, two or three days extended into a month?

"Antoinette, don't you see you must stay here, out of sight and out of danger? If we are found out or discovered living together like this, both our reputations will be ruined. I would be fired for helping you, and you would be accused of who knows what impropriety."

What a sour taste this all left. Further protests that my original intention had been to search on my own and even now need not concern him went unanswered. In spite of my objections, I wasn't afraid of Mark then, or even of having my plan derailed. I had after all come to stand and face the fabric of lies. *A stitch in time.* I could have walked away that morning, taken a path through the back door and through the walled garden, found the sheriff, and told everyone where I was. So why didn't I? Because I couldn't help but think that lost stitch was here somewhere and because I was suspicious. Though I shushed my inside warning voice, my doubts had taken on a dark and ravenous bent more encompassing than any motive of love.

Finally, we each selected a bedroom upstairs as a kind of truce. With a promise to review our situation in the morning, we separated. I was exhausted.

But in the middle of the night, I woke as though in a yawning void, slipped on my clothing, and crept down the stairs in darkness. Somehow my bare foot became entangled in an obstruction (was it a rope strung across a step?) mid-stairs, and I plunged forward in a tangle of my own skirts, twisting my foot so severely that I could not suppress the scream of fear that had gathered in my throat. Sliding painfully to the newel post, I tried to stand. Instead my foot refused to support my weight, and I crumpled to the floor. I heard Mark stirring on the stairs before the lights came on. "Antoinette, are you all right? What happened?"

"I was trying to go to the toilet. I must have tripped. I think I have sprained my ankle."

He knelt beside me then and examined my ankle. It was already starting to swell. I didn't want to deal with the unpleasant fact of the shape I was now in. So I insisted he help me to the toilet and then back upstairs to bed. "It will be all right in the morning." I could see nothing on the stairs that might have caused me to trip.

𝒜.𝒟.

March 17, 1910, Thursday, day 3. In the morning I was awakened by noises from downstairs. My ankle seemed to be worse, and Mark practically carried me downstairs. His travel bag and coat were already settled near the front door. When I looked at him warily, he explained apologetically, "Antoinette, you are in no condition to travel with that ankle. I thought I would go to Wichita myself and have a look around."

When I said nothing, he continued, "I might have to be gone for a couple of days, but I brought you some bread, dried fruits, nuts, sausage, and cheese. There are some jars of canned vegetables and packets of tea and coffee in the kitchen as well."

"You can't mean to do this without me." How convenient that he seemed to have just the right supplies.

"You need to rest your ankle," he repeated. Was his concern masking a more devious motive?

I could no longer see my ally in the set of his shoulders. Was this an act of treachery? He looked at me as though he expected an answer, but suddenly I was eager to have him gone.

"Promise me that you won't go outside. We cannot have neighbors suspicious."

"I'm not entirely clear about your concern." *He can't mean what he is saying. My journey wasn't about him.*

"For your own sake, Antoinette, I am thinking about you—about us, our reputations—and it's just for a short while." He sat beside me, resting his hand on the space between us.

"Do you really mean to abandon me in Castle Doleful?" I sought to tease him. "Surely with a little help, I can make it to the train station. Once we get to Wichita, I will have my own house to stay in."

"Remember my mother is living there. She doesn't know about all this. I don't know what she would do if she did. Certainly she would be obligated to tell Mr. Stillman. Don't feel slighted, Antoinette, my darling. All will work out in time. Is there anything else you need to make you comfortable?" He had brought a blanket and some pillows downstairs and placed within my reach a desk chair with wheels that I could sit in and push myself from room to room. His studied casualness felt about as real as my own.

"No, it seems you have thought of everything ..." I was wondering what he would be doing this morning if I hadn't sprained my ankle and instead suddenly sprang forward and rushed at the front door for my freedom. Would he attack me? Subdue me to the ground? Harm me physically? Did he really think he was doing the right thing? Or was he acting on someone else's behalf? What I didn't want to think about was would he question or oppose another's decisions regarding me? And what was my new course of action? Would I just sit it out? I didn't know.

"If you are seen, I might be accused of abducting you. I could be arrested. This is an awful mess until we are married." Was that blame I saw in his eyes?

"I guess it is, isn't it?" I answered uneasily, trying not to give away my suspicions in my tone or my silence. If I waited just a little longer, could I unravel more than if I resisted?

He turned as though to embrace me; but as his shoulder grazed mine, I felt an invisible armor cover my vulnerable places. The soft spot in the vicinity of my heart had turned to stone. Since I have been able to read, I have devoured stories of rescuers of maidens in distress, fighting off monsters, villains, and evil of every concoction, but the darker stories of the saints, while they maintained their virtue, usually lost their lives. The stakes were steadily rising. Slowly it dawned on me that I was the one who had not been listening. Whether or not I wavered was of little consequence. My studies had left so much undone. Not geography or mathematics or embroidering samplers had prepared me for the situation in which I found myself. Mark might as well have been one of those grotesques with strange cries echoing across glaciers out of Mary Shelley's novel, or enigmatic footprints in the snow, or a bogeyman perverting the shadows, for he had made himself as much a foe whose advances I was unlikely ever to consider again. But was he truly evil? When I did not respond, he spoke to me slowly, as though I were a child without understanding.

"I told you, you are not alone. There is enough food for you in the kitchen for a few days until I get back. The house is plumbed for water in the kitchen and bathroom. I think one of the rooms has a small library and puzzles, games, and magazines—quite comfortable, really. Is there anything else I can get for you?" With that he closed the door, and I heard the desolate sound of the key turning in the lock. In the silence that followed Mark's leaving, facts began to speak for themselves. Even as I went to the door and turned the knob, I noticed the lock was solid and the door unyielding. I considered breaking a window to see how secure the outside shutters were. But when I pulled the drapes, I saw bars built into the window frames fashioned to prevent escape. A door off the kitchen was nailed shut, a basement perhaps? I began to look for tools. Strangely, there were no knives in the kitchen drawers or other instruments to free a nail or a screw. My best weapon was an iron fry pan.

Am I a prisoner, a sad hostage as restricted as a piece of furniture to a house purchased by its owner? I wondered as I sat on the edge of the rolling chair taking in the menaces and prohibitions of my surroundings. Late in the day, I crawled up the stairs on my hands and knees, searching for some security among the things I had brought with me in my reticule. I found a new pocket notebook and began to write, and as the hours increased, so did my sense of the house and my world shrinking. Feeling totally alone and forsaken, I decided to retire, but before I did I found this hiding place. By using a coin, I was able to unscrew the switch plate for the light. Slipping the trunk key cord through the pages, I suspended the journal from a nail on the inner wall, where I could retrieve it easily.

A.D.

March 18, 1910, Friday, day 4. The day was more of the same. I found the library and searched through the paltry offering of books: a Bible, a *Physician's Encyclopedia*, a selection of children's books, mostly fairytales, but wonder of wonders one of my favorites, *The Wizard of Oz*, and a stack of old newspapers. I began to read the Bible beginning with Genesis 1, at first determined to read from cover to cover.

Somewhere into Numbers, I read the story of Mariam. For speaking out against Moses, she was turned into a snow-white leper. I had not kept to my plan of reading cover to cover but instead identified with the stories about women. After Eve, the destinies of Sarah, Rebekkah, Rachel, and Leah so engaged me that I looked for more. Mariam's punishment for seeking independence was so severe that I could not go on and snapped the book shut as though bitten. Why was Rebekkah not punished for changing the plan as Mariam was? How did God create men and women to relate to each other in the first place? Noises from downstairs were almost welcome: doors opening, someone walking about, food preparation perhaps. An overhead fixture and the reading lamp lighted the bedroom. The shutter slats did not allow much light, so I could not determine the hour by the sunlight. Since the start of the new year, I had an image of my independence that had sustained me—that along with the image of finding my mother. Any entry into marriage or society would be as mistress of my property and my person. Had something gone horribly wrong? Had my property become bride dowry and made me a perpetual victim after all?

I made my way mostly by sitting on each step and scooting to the next until I was able to get to the roller chair. In the kitchen I observed that Mark had returned with what appeared to be several packets of food. He offered me a tulip "Don't think the neighbor will miss it."

"Where have you been?" I asked as reasonably as I could. It was not, in truth, a very interesting exchange, as is probably the case with most trapped maidens. There were few surprises; no voices were raised or doubts dissolved. After one glance at my captor's face, I understood his resolve.

"I wasn't able to find out anything about your mother. Then I had to go to work. We don't want anyone to be suspicious."

"I might as well tell you that I have no intention of marrying you until I first know where my mother is."

"Of course, if that is what you wish." His response was chilly, but he continued his food preparation, opening kitchen cabinets and drawers, looking for eating utensils.

"Do you have another plan?"

"We wait." He seemed to have found all that he was looking for.

"We wait? What does that accomplish?" I made no attempt to assist.

"Either your mother will show up looking for you *or* Mr. Stillman will take some action regarding your holdings *or* you will turn eighteen and throw off his guardianship." He set the table, somewhat haphazardly. After failing to find a tablecloth or covering, he substituted two tea towels.

"What do you think my friends are saying about my disappearance? By now they must miss me at the academy."

"Yes, you must write a letter that you are well and regret any distress your leaving may have caused." He filled two glasses with water and brought them to the table. "That you left, of your own accord, and that you are trying to contact your mother. You could say that you are making plans to join her. Do you want me to write it for you?"

I didn't answer. *What an odd question. I am perfectly capable of writing my own letters.*

"Do you want me to write the letter?" he asked again. "Would you like to open the food packages and see what we have here?"

"Sorry?" I stalled, looking straight at him. *Misconceptions.*

He began to open the parcels.

"What I need is to get out of this place. Will you at least open the shutters from the outside so that I know if it is day or night?" *I haven't found a thing about my mother, and already two days have passed.*

"You feeling okay?" Mark seemed to be searching my face for signs of an illness that would soon manifest itself.

"Terrific," I said. *Not a thing.*

"You sure?" He pulled out one of the chairs, leaving room for the roller chair.

I paused. *No clues at all as to my mother's whereabouts.* I deliberately moved to a space opposite.

"Yes, I mean it," I said.

And I really did mean it, because I had just had a new thought. Mark, after all was a key to the whole plot, but was he the cause or merely an instrument? There was something I couldn't quite put my finger on—like watching a landscape from a strange angle, like watching the thread of a fabric unravel. The pattern had changed. A long-submerged memory recurred … once a long time ago.

"You will have your father's money. We'll buy a house like this one— maybe even this one. It's in foreclosure; somebody didn't pay the taxes. We could get it cheaply." He took out a rather large pocketknife, wiped the blade, and began to slice the roast chicken.

"I already have a home in Wichita. Let's go there." *How can I eat any of this?*

"But what do you know about its condition? About what's happened to it? You haven't lived there in a while, have you?" He put a slice of chicken on my plate.

"You have. Tell me, what is its condition?" Roasted potatoes followed, then a slice of bread.

"In danger of foreclosure." He looked into a container of green beans as though they had become emeralds. "Look what we have here!"

"But why? My father did not have a mortgage. He built that house." The beans deserved no comment, and I knew I would never eat another for the rest of my life.

"Taxes were not paid." He raked through his hair with both hands.

"That was Mr. Stillman's responsibility. He established guardianship to take care of the property." He could see my anger rising.

"Things go better with wine." He sighed with exasperation, selecting a bottle of what I knew to be contraband from a cabinet in the kitchen and pouring two classes.

"That doesn't solve anything." I refused the extended glass.

"We will straighten it all out when we are married." He drank his glass in a swallow and was about to do the same to mine. "Don't let these legal matters trouble you. This disagreeable earnestness is changing how you look, how you sound." He looked at me as though considering whether I was worthy of eating his precious green beans. But instead of taking them back, he said, "Let's talk about our futures. I will go to law school … open a practice." I was reminded of an almost exact conversation I had had with Mr. Stillman.

"I want to be a lawyer also," I burst out. *Is there one thing we can agree upon?*

He seemed in a hurry to dash my last hope. "Only men can practice the law. Women cannot even vote in national elections, operate a business, own property, or act without a husband's permission."

"Exactly, and would you give me permission?"

"I … I don't know … I'd have to—"

"Have to what?"

"There are our families to consider."

"You know about my family. My father is dead. My mother cannot be reached. To whom are you tied?" I couldn't help but think of Mrs. Crescentia Gottfried's warning—too late—that I should know his father.

"We are young, Antoinette, and there are others to consider."

Hadn't I used that same argument to delay marriage? "I am thinking about others, my mother in particular. What haven't you told me? You want me to support your dreams for going through law school, but you shrink from supporting mine in finding out what happened to my family."

"You don't understand."

"Then please explain."

"Let's just eat. We can talk about this later." He was reasonable. He was fair-minded. He was even tender and beguiling.

I began to rise from my chair, my plate untouched. "I can't eat the chicken. It's Friday." Then I remembered my ankle and leaned against the table to support my weight.

"I'm sorry. I didn't know. I'll get something else."

But I had more on my mind than the food. "Does your mother know what you are doing?" Could I wait any longer to see what would unravel trusting my future and his to whatever puppet masters held our strings? If only I could walk out that front door now, I could catch the train to Wichita.

"I do have a father."

I returned to my seat.

"If I tell you, will you eat something?"

I nodded and took a bite of the beans to prove how agreeable I could be.

"He wants me to go into business with him after I finish law school. Antoinette, we'll have a family and be happy. I thought that is what you wanted."

"I did want that, or at least I thought I did until you brought me here. Mark, please help me get to the train station."

"You sprained your ankle, remember? You need to stay here right now for your own protection. We have both of our reputations to consider. We cannot be seen together before we are married. Neither of us will ever be accepted into society. For a law student, reputation is everything. How can I go into my father's business? What impact will all this impropriety have on my future? On yours? On our future children?"

"Who is your father?" I asked with more curiosity than had Mrs. Gottfried.

"I can't tell you now."

I spit out the beans, "When *are* you going to tell me?"

"He has nothing to do with us."

"It seems this mysterious person has everything to do with us." I was astounded that he continued to omit the most significant part of his revelation.

"It's gotten so complicated."

"No it hasn't. I have to go to Wichita to look for my mother."

"First thing, after we are married, I promise."

"No one will know us. We'll get on the train. We will check all the hospitals and institutions to see her for ourselves, and then I will marry you."

"Where did you get this fantasy that she's in a hospital? She's left the county ... left you." He settled on cutting his chicken slices with his fork. "But you have already delayed our marriage. What will happen to our plans? What if she talks you out of it entirely?"

"It will not be my mother who talks me out of marriage." I reached my hand across the table expecting him to cover mine with his; instead he turned away as if to look out the window before remembering that the window was covered.

"You aren't being sensible."

"Do you have feelings for me?"

"It is certain that you don't have feelings for me. I am beginning to think that all you wanted was someone to get you out of that convent school."

"I was not locked up there."

"Weren't you?"

"Was I?"

"So we will see, is that what you are saying?" he asked, changing the subject.

When I did not answer, he abruptly pushed back his chair, stood, and turned on his heel. At the front door, I heard the key in the lock and his footsteps running down the veranda stairs. I began rolling my chair around the rooms of the bottom floor and found myself in the library looking through the old stack of newspapers yellowed with age. I noticed that most were from fifteen years ago. Why would someone keep newspapers from so long ago? Then I noticed that each contained a story about the same person, a man named H. H. Holmes from Chicago. With horrible fascination, I began to read the accounts of a man who was called the first serial killer of mostly women. These were young women, like me, seeking something at the Chicago World's Fair—employment, love, adventure. They did not deserve to die. Whatever their reason to leave behind the small protections they had, there was no justification for their deaths. There could be no forgiveness for their murders. A final article described the fire of mysterious origins that burned down the mansion he had lived in and where many of the murders occurred.

When I finished reading, I was hungry enough to eat nearly all the food on the table, excepting the chicken. I felt a raw fury toward Stillman and Mark. I noticed he had not left any wine in the bottle. One image seemed to be imposed over the other as the two blended into one. Were the two one? Was there a stronger connection than employer/employee? Had I been betrayed? Who was his mysterious father—a lawyer? There were moments of wavering, moments when I reversed myself between succumbing to his proposal and vowing for revenge, but that bravado inevitably passed, leaving the stark truth. I could be dead before either possibility could come to fruition because I could not leave the confines of the house, get fresh air, see friends, and even select my own food or plan activities. I needed to focus on my next move, not to think about the wreck my original plan had turned into. My imagination became consumed: initiate a lawsuit, commit a murder, give up, give in, go insane, kill myself, harm myself, bargain for a better position, run away (that option had already proven a failure, and so I crossed it off my list). The kind of learning and resources any of these solutions would take was beyond a problem like poor handwriting that could be corrected if enough discipline and instruction were given. I was too young to have reached the plateau of nevers when doors close, never to reopen, not even when I pushed. Caught in a demeaning spiral from which there might not be a simple retreat, I went to bed with the cast iron skillet at my side. At last I fell into an exhausted, fitful sleep. Somewhere in the middle of the night I began thinking about St. Eulalia and taking comfort that she would watch over me whatever may come. I fell into a deep, restful sleep.

A.D.

March 19, 1910, Saturday, day 5.The following morning I was awakened by many noisy signals: footsteps, rattling of a tray, clinking of china, a cough seemingly intent at allaying my fears, finally a knock. "Antoinette, I have breakfast for you." Did he hope by feeding me to earn my forgiveness? Or was there something in the food to make me forget?

Mark came right to the point. "Antoinette, I am committed to you, and I love you. Nothing has happened to change that."

"Something has happened to change that. You lied to me."

"You lied to me too. But I understand. It's not entirely your fault. We can fix this." The scene of the night before was being played out again. Mark had taken the breakfast things and was setting up a side table for dining. I wondered why he was taking such care. Why not just eat downstairs? Wasn't this indecent for a young man to have breakfast with a woman in her dressing gown in her bedroom?

"There is no hope for a future built on people disappearing. Look at the horror of Dr. Henry Howard Homes."

"Who?"

"A killer who made people, mostly women, disappear during the Chicago World's Fair in the 1890s. There is a stack of old newspapers in the library that somebody seems to have saved from that era. Who do you suppose?"

"It wasn't me."

"I didn't figure it was. You are too young to have been around back then. But do you know who used to live here?"

"Sorry, all I know is that the town calls this the Shutter House."

"Because of the shutters? Or was that a family name?"

"Don't know." He shrugged. "Look, can we talk about something else?"

"This relationship is turning out to be like a train wreck." I felt dull and heavy.

"What do you want from me?" He handed me a napkin and plate of scrambled eggs.

Could he really be so unaware? "Someone who doesn't keep secrets from the one he claims to love. Who is in agreement about essential problems and priorities: that straightening out this legal mess comes first. All other crises come second because they cannot be helped without a family base that is healthy and growing." I ate the eggs and a cinnamon roll, relishing the flavors.

"As you said, this is our marriage, not Stillman's."

"Mark, I cannot have someone in my life who thinks it is okay to destroy mine, either you or him. You have to let me go." I took a sip of the hot coffee then added some milk. Focusing on such ordinary tasks was helping me to keep my emotions in check, as if we were discussing the events of an ordinary day.

"It is too late." Mark seemed about to panic.

"But why? I'll just transfer to another school, probably in Wichita. You can return to your job and your life." A good night's sleep and the food had provided a remedy for my own alarm of the day before.

"I cannot without you." He moved his hand next to mine.

"I do not understand … who else knows about our so-called elopement?" I reached over and patted his, showing that no lingering animosity remained.

"I can't tell you anything more."

"What did you mean about me being a prisoner at the convent?" What had his comment betrayed? I watched him closely, his face near mine, his eyes narrow, reading me.

"Mr. Stillman had hoped you might join that convent, but since you did not and now refuse to marry me, he has other plans for both of us."

"You told Mr. Stillman about our plans?"

"I had to; he found the letters."

"But we had a code …" This elaborate game of innocence and ignorance, how long could we sustain it?

"Codes can be broken." He scowled and reached up, rubbing the back of his neck.

"What aren't you telling me? Your actions do not make sense. We planned this together. What does Mr. Stillman have to do with the plan?"

"He is my father."

"Your father? How can that be? Mrs. Stillman …" Mrs. Crescentia Gottfried's warning voice echoed in my head.

"She's not my mother. They never had children. As a matter of fact, she does not even know about me. I grew up in Wichita with my mother. Your father, of course, knew and acted as my guardian, gave my mother a job and saw that we were taken care of. Ironic, isn't it? My father is your guardian, and your father was mine. Unfortunately, I think your father took better care of me than my father is taking of you."

"Oh, Mark, why didn't you tell me?"

"At first I didn't think it mattered. We had found each other again. Keeping the secret of my birth was an old habit. I did not tell anyone. Why should I tell you? Then I thought it would change everything. But things got out of control, and now I do not have a choice."

"You do have a choice."

"Remember when you promised to marry me? You have broken your promise."

"Mark, do not do this. You can be my true rescuer. Do not let him rule you."

"Would you marry me if I did?"

"How can you ask me that when we are not even married and you are already keeping me a prisoner?"

"How can you go back on your promise?"

"You are not who I thought you were ..."

"No, I am just somebody's bastard ... your father's hired help. Why would you want to marry me? When you come from a family that is as messed up as mine, there is something that happens where that trust of putting yourself in anybody else's hands and letting people love you ... it is not easy. You push people away because that is what you know. Then I come to this town and see a man like Stillman, my father. I have learned so much from him about confidence, about control, about ownership ..."

"That is not the reason I cannot marry you. Like you, I have to be my own person, not property, not an infant or a pet. Don't you see—'The history of mankind is a history of repeated injuries and usurpations on the part of man toward woman.' Elizabeth Cady Stanton wrote in her Declaration of Sentiments. Prove this isn't true. You aren't like him. He has wronged us both."

He smiled at the placation. "Is there any hope for us?"

"Getting married now, like this, will not resolve anything for us. We will both be exactly where he wishes us to be—under his control. Mark, he is inching you toward a cliff. Don't you see? We have to be the grownups to come forward—"

"Much is uncertain; he has his flaws. But then who is perfect? At least he has a plan." He had not eaten anything beyond his first bite of eggs.

"What then? What is his plan?"

"That I can't tell you, but I'll ... we'll have more money than we ever dreamed of."

"What do you have to do?" I persisted.

"I already told you. Take care of you." He looked as if he was about to laugh, but he instead showed his teeth.

"I don't need taken care of. What exactly is your part?"

"Nothing much, just wait ... for the legal process to take effect."

"Wait ... like a moth in a spider web? Does this legal process involve the Dominguez Farms?"

Instead of answering, he rose to go. "Got to get to work."

"I hope you don't think robbery is a way to make a living," I couldn't help shouting at the closed door. My carefully crafted serenity had deserted me. His footsteps hesitated on the stairs. Then I heard him return to lock the bedroom door. In his wake, obscure, disturbing thoughts stirred like dry leaves hiding the ground beneath. *There must be a way out.*

This conversation changed everything between us, marking a shift between *safe* and *not safe*, from hope for independence to despair at increasing vulnerability. My illusion of protection was replaced by the reality of immediate danger. Why had I taken my freedom to roam the house the previous day for granted? I ate Mark's cinnamon roll. I ate his eggs. I stashed the oranges in the bottom drawer of a dresser, along with the iron skillet. That is when I noticed the pitcher on the chamber pot stand was filled with water. I was thirsty, and I had to make use of the commode. I could feel the beginning of a blocked nose and a sore throat. There was nothing to do but crawl into bed. An hour later, the flow from my nose seemed inexhaustible, and I felt sore, sodden, and heavy.

A.D.

Not sure what day it is. It is becoming difficult for me to write every day. I have been sick, but I don't know for how long. Days and nights blend together.

"Influenza is bad this year: headache, fever, muscle aches, followed by difficulty breathing, even pneumonia. Coughing, sneezing, and spitting transmit the disease. The number of the sick is growing," said Mark when he brought a tray of food—food I barely touched. But I could not help drinking the glass of strange-tasting water, so great was my thirst. He had brought fresh linens, but I had no inclination to clean up the prison he had made for me and scooted my way down the stairs to the flush toilet. There I stayed subject to the humiliations of my body until I think I must have lost consciousness. When next I awoke, I was again locked in the room. Sheets had been changed, as had my nightgown, and the contents of the commode removed. This brief check was all I could manage.

𝒜.𝒟.

My recovery seemed to take days, but at least I was allowed to move about downstairs where I could use the facilities for bathing and the toilet. When I asked Mark why he didn't seem worried about catching the influenza from me, he assured me that he was but more worried about catching it from the population in general, so he had decided to stay with me. People were being encouraged to stay at home to stop the spread. The iron skillet and other cookware of heft and substance had been removed. I continued to engage Mark. My attempts did not increase our bond. "Can you bring me a newspaper? Could we get a telephone? Some stamps and stationery? Perhaps a nail file?" I asked with tenderness in my voice that opposed all my feelings until the smoldering glare in his eyes frightened me, and I changed my tone. "What about developing a moral character, self-discipline, willpower, and personal responsibility?" I berated him.

"You think your father was all those things? That he didn't benefit from the misfortunes of others in his business dealings?" Clearly his memory was self-serving.

"He was a good man."

"Depends on who says so. Even his 'best friend' doesn't have much good to say about him."

"You mean Stillman?"

"Antoinette, I know what it was like to be the recipient of charities, so-called friendly societies and moral campaigns."

"I do not understand why you are so angry. You grew up with your mother. You always seemed happy together. You had a place to live."

"She was never there … always working. She barely even knew whether I was still living with her or whether I had moved in with the old lady down the street who would put out a bowl of food for me once in a while. Nobody cared if I went to school. Nobody cared if I had something to eat or decent clothes to wear. Your father's death affected me too. I became rebellious, just wandering around the city, verging on scurvy. I spent a lot of time alone with not much to do. It was easy to get into trouble, smoking, drinking, and sampling other stuff … Oh, I don't begrudge her. She tried to get me a job. Then she turned me over to *him*, and I figured, why not? He could keep me out of jail."

"What were you doing?"

"Enough to keep money in my pocket."

204

"Oh, Mark, I didn't know. How easy it is to let the worst in oneself rise up—some mark, a smear, some little knot of evil."

"You don't really believe that stuff about marks on your soul, do you?"

"You'd rather believe in what? The redemptive power of money … or social status?"

"It makes more sense than votive candles, shrines, and holy cards."

"Mark, what do you want to stay in your mind, your heart, your soul? Those things are reminders not just of the pain but the glory that came out of a tragedy."

"I am not a villain. It is not like I have killed anyone or caused the death of someone. But imitation can give one certain influence."

"What are you talking about?"

"Dearest," he whispered suddenly changing tactics, "stop this resistance. We can have it all …"

"We cannot have it all if you are placing your trust in Stillman. The fact is that he is only good at dismantling. He does not have the vision of my father to build, to create, or to call into being a legacy. Tell me, Mark, does this house belong to a widow—a widow who is living in a sanitarium because of her sudden health problems? Do her relatives know where she is?" Had I hit upon another truth? His silence seemed to indicate that I had. I tried to quell the churning that seemed to have taken over my entire body, but it wasn't happening. "All this solitude and loneliness … I might go mad."

He chose to make light of my fears. "It is always fashionable for a great house to have a ghost in residence."

"Is that what I have become? Ghost girl?"

"You know I am just teasing."

"A woman is not quite powerless despite the law. I still have the right of refusal," I countered, thinking of another kind of being who seemed to lack substance.

"We will see," he said, but his face was grim. Again he locked me in the room. "I cannot have you accidentally falling down the stairs again."

A.D.

One morning I fell trying to get up. A severe fit of weakness and my injured ankle obliged me to return to the bed. Mark must have heard me moving about. He stood outside the room and through a crack in the door declared the source of my illness had been identified. The day after I had left the academy, students had been quarantined due to an outbreak of severe influenza and the report sent to the State Board of Health. There was an article in the newspaper.

"Thank heavens it was properly diagnosed and isolated in time to prevent an epidemic, but it has proved fatal." Then he told me that one of the students, a Mary Clare something, had died. "Getting well is frustratingly slow. There is no easy cure—rest, fluids, and good nursing care." But according to Mark, the newspaper article claimed that laudanum would give pain relief and induce sleep. Vicks VapoRub and a liquid mouth rinse would help the breathing and throat congestion as well. I had never seen anyone die, but thoughts of death, especially Mary Clare's death, extinguished thoughts of escape. I shivered and shook, snuffled and streamed. My head ached and my body burned, drowned in mucus. My heart felt broken for her family, for our classmates, for me. "Where is my stationery? I have to send letters."

"You mustn't read or write. Tell me what you want to say, and I will see that it is done." Nor would he even consider allowing me to strain my eyes by reading the newspaper article referring to Mary Clare.

A.D.

On another morning, I woke sweating, tangled in damp sheets. There was a certain weightless quality in the darkness that made me believe it was close to dawn. I climbed out of bed, hitching up my nightgown. But when I attempted to walk, I staggered like a newborn colt. I was burning up, and every part of me ached. Had I really gotten a fever? Then I felt an unfamiliar wetness between my legs. I calmed myself, thinking I might have started my course, another mark of time, another reminder that a month of my own life had passed. My last period was at the academy. When I turned on the light, I saw there was blood on the sheet but no flow from my body. Was this a new night terror that I would be subjected to, making going to sleep a new fear? I took a drink from the glass left at my bedside, and that's all I remember until late in the afternoon when I was awakened by noises coming from downstairs. Still confused and disoriented, I thought of Mrs. Stillman that December morning at the breakfast table. I forced myself to rise and to dress. Then I noticed that my things had been disturbed, as though someone had gone through my traveling case and clothing. My bed coverings had been replaced, and the gown I was wearing was not one of my own. I tried to push away the worry.

When Mark came into my room, I waited for him to explain what had happened to me during the night, but he said nothing. With quiet sadness, we spent hours talking to each other about the fears that had led to our actions. We even talked about what a real marriage between us might be like, our children, our house furnishings, our favorite foods, how we would spend our days, our weeks, and even years. At times he became the boy I had first had

206

feelings for. At times I thought he was becoming aware of the harm that he was doing not only legally but to his very soul. I appealed on every level I could think of for him to right these perverted actions. I pleaded with him to conduct his own research and find out about his father's activities and what his intentions toward us were. I was too tired to record the conversation fully.

A.D.

As the days passed, my head congestion cleared up, but my weakness worsened. The mysterious malady subjected me to the most excruciatingly horrible dreams when I slept. My waking hours locked in the room were haunted by the visions emerging from the dreams. From there I slipped into what I thought must be a fever that left me so incapacitated that I could not again get out of bed or eat. I was not always lucid during this illness, but there was one incident I remember with absolute clarity. The Stillmans' Irish maid was holding a bowl of chicken soup and encouraging me to eat. "Have you recovered, miss?" she asked.

"Eaglan, is it?"

"Yes, miss."

"Eaglan, can you help me get out of here?" I pleaded, trying to look past the bowl of soup to find a human being inside.

"Oh, no, miss. It is best you stay right where you are and get well. You are still very contagious." I noticed that she was keeping her distance.

My illness had also brought about a change in Mark. As his hopes of securing the exchange of our vows lessened, his threats to the safety of my person increased. He dropped all pretenses that he was anything other than my jailer. His pressure about finding my father's papers became relentless. This wasn't his voice but Mr. Stillman's. My protests that I knew nothing of my father's businesses resulted in his longer absences and my physical care being turned over to Eaglan. I must stop now, for these events are disturbing me, and my eyes are hurting.

A.D.

One day Mark brought a bottle of clear liquor and two glasses from below. He poured one and asked me to drink with him. I shook my head and instead filled a glass from the water pitcher. "More for me then ... He'll send you out of the country on a charge of spousal desertion and not living up to your marriage vows. As to the destination, your guess is as good as mine. I hear there is a war starting in Mexico, a revolution. Perhaps you went to visit relatives and got caught in the crossfire … But I am sure a complete report will be filed, and you will be dropped from the missing persons' list, not that you were ever on one." His tone was grim. Was this Stillman's new plan for my disposal?

"But I did not marry you. There is no documentation on that account, so how can there be spousal desertion?"

"He has his ways."

"This is forgery, kidnapping, and theft." I could not bring myself to ask if I had been violated, nor did he volunteer the information.

"He just wants to know where the deeds are to your father's holdings."

"He asked me that himself at Christmastime. Why would I know? Hasn't he asked my mother? Didn't he have access to her papers and records?"

"She didn't know. And yes, he has gone through all the records."

"What about his own records? Surely your mother would know where my father kept his important papers. She was his trusted bookkeeper."

"Your father kept that information from her. It seems she was not so trusted after all."

"I do not know either. I was only fourteen when he died." The temperature between us was rising. I could feel it coming up like vomit in my throat. And I could feel Mark tensing up across the room. He poured himself another drink.

"Sure you won't have some? If you do have those deeds, no bank will lend you capital. They have no proof that you still own the land to which you claim title. The deed might have been forged, or even stolen, or the property confiscated for mortgages owed. And who can justify the expense of an investigation to check out the records?" He said with such certainty that I could no longer think otherwise than that he was his father's son.

After the third drink, it seemed to strike him that he was a pitiable victim of injustice. He had not meant to kidnap me. It was really just bad luck that he had gotten caught up in the disparity between what I wanted and what Stillman wanted, but no one was going to believe that. There were no witnesses to my leaving and his picking me up at the convent gates to connect us. He began to think of the story he could tell.

"Here's a story for you," I interrupted. "You acted in a wise and courageous manner to help out your childhood friend and to save her from being taken advantage of by her so-called guardian."

"There is no story—only reality. Things work out or they don't." Something disturbing imposed itself over his features.

When had our ripening friendship turned to rot? Why had my suspicions not been raised before I put myself in jeopardy? "Mark, this is an irrational act, a brutal act, an act from which you do not come back. Is that what you want?" I could hear the wind around the house, and it was moaning.

A.D.

My uncharted days made me long for the schedule that had brought such security in our school life: At this hour we wake; at this hour we go to the chapel for morning mass; at this hour we have breakfast; at this hour we begin classes; at this hour we have dinner; at this hour we go outside for physical exercise. This is the first moment during the day that our minds can begin to wonder, and we think about what is happening in the larger world outside the walls as we talk with the other girls about mail from families, or readings in textbooks, or small changes in the seasons or the weather or the food. We cannot talk about what the sisters wore since they always wore the same black-and-white habit, or what was in the newspaper since we have little access.

Here the only diversion had been Mark's comings and goings … and now, more frequently, Eaglan's comings and goings.

Many days passed when I was left alone thinking, of all things, about the comfort a chocolate would bring. I seemed to be passing in and out of consciousness, and the darkness pressing around me filled me with dread. During brief intervals, someone was there. Was it the Stillman's friendly seeming Irish maid? All I know is that I was not myself. I could not rise from the bed. Something was wrong. My head ached, my skin crawled and sweated, small areas beneath my arms and in my neck throbbed. Someone tried to feed me, but my stomach turned to liquid. Nausea bubbled up in the back of my throat.

Time slipped away like sands in an hourglass running down a hole in my head to a still point, turning my thoughts to that measure of duration: time. Time the creator and devourer destroys the world but also destroys truth. What really happened long ago in those mists of history between my father and Stillman? Between Stillman and my mother? When time stops, the breakthrough is eternity. If measured by the sun, solar time is recorded by the interval between two successive transits of that celestial body over the same meridian. Locked in this darkness the light could not warm my soul—nor could I watch the sun come through the window—trying to hold on to the thought of it made my mind shake. But neither could I account for the period of duration measured by the stars, called sidereal time. Sidereal time loses time against solar time. A between time occurs.

Is that where I was? I had not been able to witness either solar or sidereal time for the past weeks of my captivity, something I had so taken for granted all my life up to this point. In my new world, I was only able to study Mark's and my characters in a landscape of his creation, every bit as fantastical as reading the ancient tales from Greece and Rome ... or the suffering of the saints. But I hadn't taken so much trouble, wandering to the very edge of the abyss, just to kill time. The pain seeped into my dreams, and I woke myself screaming, but the house was deathly quiet around me. How could I navigate without the stars or the sun? *Dead reckoning*—I seemed to have lost all resources except my mind for determining my course and position. How fragile is life. I could see that Mark and I would not create a marriage or a family or years together, not because it was not meant to be but because those strands from the beginning of our knowing each other had been so badly frayed that they could never become knotted together. We could not make a life together because one thing and then another had been done in the past that would continue to unravel the fabric of our relationship. Had he been right after all that I had nothing to worry about? The world would end soon? Had Earth passed through the tail of Halley's comet and been covered with darkness?

A.D.

Yet another kind of time appeared on a plate before me when I awakened. Hot cross buns, now stale and hard but which I contemplated eating, reminded me of the cycle of the liturgical year. Had Easter passed? How many weeks had gone by while I was in this state? I continued to refuse to marry Mark.

Was it April yet or still March? The white frosting drizzled in a cross pattern over the buns symbolized the crucifixion of Christ and the calendar year, divided into four quarters: spring, summer, autumn, and winter, all dominated by the cross reminded me of the sermons from three Easter retreats. Every year I had written the same notes in my pocket notebook. Christianity's interpretation of human time depends on the birth of the Christ, of God's ordering of the world, and of time being important to sanctifying the world. The promise was that love or happiness lasts forever. Were the academy students listening to the retreat sermons even now? Ironic how "forever" time gets divided into lifetimes, years, months, even days until the very end, their inevitable end. Not only inevitable but ... would my end be invisible?

A. D.

210

My nightmare continued. The thing that brought me back to wakefulness was something I cannot even describe or even remember very well. It was the beginning of pain like harmony changing to discord; like warmth changing to cold, like shadows changing to monsters. I felt mice-feet of apprehension scurrying over my skin. "What have you done?" I demanded when I opened my eyes to see Mr. Stillman himself sitting beside my bed with a large cigar, the smoke drifting in a long column from the tip. How long had he been watching me sleep?

The expression on his face made me aware of how I must look. "You don't mind, do you?" He indicated the cigar. "Covers up the smell."

My thoughts were too garbled to reply.

He began in a soothing voice. "You are pale, Antoinette, deathly pale. The passage of time in this place has been pitiless to you." He poured a glass of orange juice, which he handed to me. "There is nothing more beautiful than a perfect human form. Every part of it, especially the face, has its praises sung in poetry and fiction. A perfect form means perfect health, and perfect health can only be maintained by care of every individual part. The care of the teeth, for example, or the eyes, perhaps the ears—what if something should happen to one of these parts? If you lost your teeth, you might be reduced to drooling. Such a disturbance might result in the mouth becoming dry and hot, restlessness and loss of sleep and appetite, constipation or diarrhea might follow, and frequently, convulsions, ending in death."

Stillman's tactic was to terrorize me in a cat and mouse game—the soothing quality of his voice belying the terror of his words. My tormenter, with a sadistic imitation of gentleness, helped me up to take a sip of juice. It was cruelty out of the Brothers Grimm, another thread added to the fabric of his lies meant to obscure his illicit dealings. *Do not let him know you are afraid. Keep talking. Do not speed your pace. Do not look back,* a voice inside my head cautioned.

"Under what full-moon, scare school did you learn these creepy tactics? You are indeed a master and master teacher too, as I can attest, being the victim of your son."

"And you are your father's daughter. He could never learn the lesson put before him. He could not just stay where he was." Mr. Stillman seemed bent on bullying me, most probably to tears.

"But here is a scary thought … ghouls don't just crawl from a crypt, ready to instill fear—they have some learning to do first … then they have been known to turn against those closest to them—their mentors. Nor can they be relied upon not to eat their own parents … but I forget, you never were a parent." I could not let him see my fear.

"Any more scary thoughts?" he asked, as though reading mine.

What are the scandals dogging this dark old house? What part did he play in my father's end? What happened to my mother? What are his intentions for Mark? Mark's mother? Mrs. Stillman? But most of all for me? I decided to focus on the immediate relationship. Here was opportunity for discovery. I could not fritter it away by succumbing to my own fear.

"How did the paths of you two—you and Mark—suddenly become twined together?" I asked not expecting an answer but instead answering my own question. "It was not paternity—that you have denied all along. Mark was essentially an orphan except that my father took him and his mother under his protection. Was his mother blackmailing you? Had she finally grown tired of your lies? Was she about to expose you for your fraud? Or did you find Mark had become useful to you, a new instrument in the chamber like the rest of us? That is it, isn't it? You were not just tutoring him to enter your law practice, you were using him to marry me and through marriage gain control of my father's properties. Was he the one intended for the arranged marriage? But what is your plan since we have not married?"

"Your refusal pains me. After all that I have done for you, your ingratitude. We punish those who hurt us." By his differential manner, he intended to frighten me.

In spite of myself, I could not stop the thought that had begun to form in my brain, as though it had plans of its own, and it now ensued from my lips. "I *own* this house. And I demand that you get out—now—or I will have you arrested for trespassing."

Mr. Stillman was a man of steady nerves and did not give an indication that my declaration had any truth. "I would love to sympathize with your lunacy, but for one problem. You yourself are guilty of seduction and a breach of promise to marry. On behalf of a minor in destitute circumstances, namely, Mark Weaver not yet twenty-one, your estate is liable for the reasonable value thereof. It is difficult to commiserate with those who inflict wounds on themselves."

"I also own this person … who is now of legal age and being held against her will. I demand you release me at once." I went on, incredulous at my own acumen. Once I had voiced aloud what I had been thinking, I could not believe I had not seen it instantly. What if despair had not been the cause of Mother's disappearance? Mother had planned to stop in Abilene before she came to see me. Had she become a prisoner in this house as well? Had the house been shuttered and barred, the condition I found it? Or had it been rented out at the time and Mother's questioning of the inhabitants caused her to confront Stillman perhaps about her own ownership? What other discoveries had she made looking over the books with Mrs. Weaver?

"There's no reason to be so upset, Antoinette. Let me just take the time to cover plausible scenarios here. In almost any unexpected situation, but especially where there is fear and trauma, accounts are notoriously inaccurate. Women and infants are poor sources of information. Memory is malleable and can be shaped by events occurring after the fact. Accounts can be corrupted by misleading questions … especially when said person is not of sound mind and must be protected against her own depressed state."

"Is it more plausible that I am imagining things than what is really happening? That I was so unnerved by my mother's rejection of me that I needed your assistance? Or so enamored by your son that I would do something so foolhardy as to forfeit all the claims of my true identity?" I paused and demanded clarity. "Am I understanding you correctly?"

"It stands to reason, and the evidence will support such a conclusion." He put down his cigar without putting it out.

"Actually no, it will not. I am female, Mr. Stillman. I am not helpless, nor am I a mental incompetent," I countered, watching the thin trail of smoke. "Your confidence that the intent of the law can be subjected to your ability to interpret and implement, or should I say manipulate, is misplaced. The text of the law is perfectly clear. I have also left a trail of evidence to the contrary that, if my plans go awry, will come to light."

"Bravo. I would expect nothing less. What you didn't know, however, is that I was obliged to invent bits of news. Sister Louise has been steadily receiving letters from you about your wellbeing and whereabouts. You have moved back to Texas, to be close to some long-lost relative. Isn't that where your father was originally from? And living with your new husband, whose name you failed to mention. For you see, you and Mark did not work out after all, though you did have quite an adventure. You have asked for forgiveness for all the worry you have caused her and your guardian, who you have come to realize was only doing what was best to keep you safe. You have also discounted all your warnings and the trouble you have caused your friends, who are to please forgive your youthful indiscretion. All evidence is of your own testimony, which can and will be used against you. And let me remind you: you are helpless … and looking unconscionably shapeless and draggy, I might add. When I tell you to get dressed and come downstairs, you need to eat. There is food on the table. You'd better do it if you want to keep said person alive. One might think you were considering suicide."

Strange how an image of Mrs. Stillman flashed before me in this familiar description of my appearance. I wondered how she was, and was she still attending equal suffrage meetings without Mr. Stillman's knowledge? "Does Mrs. Stillman know where you are right now or what you are doing?"

"Doing some memory-jogging, my dear?" he said, as though also remembering the same breakfast scene. "Would you like a peppermint?"

"How did you guess?"

"Your concern is misplaced. No one is missing you. It is as though you never existed. The world has gone right on without you. But you do need to worry about yourself." He snubbed out his cigar, rose as though suddenly tired, and left the door open, expecting me to follow.

I went, instead, to the toilet, attending to my bodily needs, which had been neglected for so many days I had lost count. At least my ankle felt almost completely healed, and I could walk without support. I noticed how worn my nightgown was as I stripped it over my head. I washed thoroughly and rubbed my dry skin with a scented lotion that I did not remember being there the last time I bathed. My hair hung wet and long over my shoulders. A gown in a new style that I had not seen before had been placed on the hanger at the back of the door. Stillman's characteristic attention to detail was a poor substitute for his lack of attention to enduring issues. When I came to the table, the food was cold, and Stillman was gone. I again checked doors and windows, but there seemed no escape. So I ate and enjoyed the flavors as best I could, for the meal was delicious. The only changes I noted in my tour downstairs was that the yellowed newspapers had disappeared, but several bottles of intoxicants, including one called absinthe, the green fairy, in a dark green bottle had appeared. I read the label on the bottle: wormwood and other botanicals. Stillman had his own "little helpers."

My plan to pretend to elope had been a thing of beauty—eminently illogical and alarmingly scandalous—an action designed to remove myself from my guardian's influence and assume rule over my own life. Dealing with the particulars was quite another matter. Instead, he not only had legal but also physical custody of my person. His only concern, however, seemed to be custody of legal documents for which he was leveraging my freedom: blackmail, but it was progress. The sky was not falling—not yet. Thus began the showdown, a dry run for real default, if I did nothing.

A.D.

After three days of leaving Eaglan to tend to me, my kidnapper (he no longer deserved the titles used in polite society) returned and made his requests directly. "Antoinette, do you not remember that I foretold what would happen in such a case? As your protector, I will indulge your stupidity, your being a woman, etc., makes it impossible for you to understand. A will of the father can give custody of child and wife to a guardian without court intervention, which is the cause here."

"My father had no such will."

"Can you prove that?" Stillman looked at me suspiciously.

"How can I if he had no such will?"

"Show me what documents you have, and we will clarify this matter."

"I don't—"

"You don't have a copy of the will? As his lawyer, I have in his handwriting his very specific intentions. You see, he trusted me back then to file his papers. That is the way of the law, and the favor of the court is on my side." I had the distinct impression that Stillman was trying to sell something.

"I would like to see your copies of his instructions."

"You are becoming very predictable, my dear. I will be more than happy to go over all that with you when you are of age. Do not distress yourself with tiresome legal details that do not concern you until then," but there was something peculiar in the tone of his voice as though he had spent the night sorting through mounds of his own files.

Had my birthday not passed yet? "What day is this?"

Ignoring my question, Stillman seemed intent on showing me the horrible fate I was about to bring down upon myself. "Examine the social order." His sigh was long-suffering. "You will soon see the landscape is fully armed against any woman who tries to raise herself up to compete for reputation with men."

"You mean because of the concocted lies you have been telling yourselves about the natures of men and women? Of course, we all draw strength from the ties between place and storytelling. But the stories I draw from are not the same as yours. Mine remain faithful to my history."

"You keep adding things, Antoinette. I do see that shut up here you have had too much time to annotate and revise and invent. But your memories are not fact." He gave a hint of a skeptical smile. "We have documents to prove the truth." Stillman began to unwind a history of his own that offered familiar information as if for the first time and unfamiliar information as if it were familiar.

"I'm impressed," I said, but I was not in the least.

"You should be." Stillman turned reprovingly. "Never underestimate the ways in which imagination bends experience. The shaped version becomes more true than the reality raided to make it."

Again, I was impressed by his mastery, how far his deception spread. "Real genius, creativity, etc., has little to do with antics such as faking wills, fabricating businesses for property management, and concocting titles such as guardian to reinvent oneself. It is about inventing something new, and hopefully lasting, right here, taking responsibility for tomorrow … for one's children."

"Really, my dear, your nattering on reveals a depth of cluelessness that boggles the mind. Didn't I tell you about this? I am in the business of telling a story, setting a scene, laying out the facts and assumptions behind a case. You are as helpless as a kitten in the real as opposed to the imaginary world. Do stop this nonsense, the interruption of all of our lives, the expenditure of our energies, and the physical toll this is taking on your own body."

Indeed, my breathing came in labored gasps. "What about Mark?"

"What about him? My son—I do admit he is my son—is a youthful fool who, now that he is coming of age, is looking for a replacement to his security blanket. He thinks he has found it in you. Quit while you are ahead. You do not expect me to really aid these rebellions after what you have done to tarnish him? You are young, though stripped of delicacy, and some would say beautiful even in this pitiful condition."

"I will not die here," I told him with a bravado I did not feel.

"No one is dying," he said with a certain cocky reassurance. "This is just a little drama, happens in the best of families."

𝒜.𝒟.

On his third visit, he opened with a faux-confession. "Sadly, I've been keeping something from you. It is a secret." As usual, his smile was devoid of any real warmth. "But before I tell you the secret, I must warn you that sometimes it is better not to know. Now is the time to escape. The door is open. I will not stop you. I will not even watch you leave. You are free to go, which I have always maintained. You have always been free."

When I made no attempt to move, as though caught in his spell, he continued. "Still here? Stubborn, aren't you? Or curious? Which is it?"

"Doubtful ... that anything you tell me is the truth," I said, twisting around to gaze through the opening, mindful of a tragic heroine regarding her off-stage doom. Could I really flee this place?

"You are not a woman of genius after all." He carefully set down a folder and cleaned a speck of dust from the sleeve of his dark jacket. Even under the present situation, Stillman was elegant, imposing, satyr-like in his expensive suit as he preyed on the weak—those less defended, including my mother and me, and those he placed at the mercy of the world, including Mark. In his own defense he claimed, "Everything I have done is legal, but without a graceful exit, there will be bloodletting."

"In sin, omission is as bad as willful behavior. Isn't that the case with the law as well?"

"Do not worry—or do worry, as you wish. It is all according to plan. Now there will not be an escape. Go ahead, get a pencil and take notes. Oh, but you left all your schoolgirl implements behind? Here, use this new invention

216

just for children, a crayon." He handed me an unopened box. "Mrs. Stillman gives these to the orphans. You remember the orphans, don't you? Here's rule number one: never trust children to do as they are told. If you absolutely must involve infants (that is you), bring along blindfolds, put them in safe space, cover their eyes, and tell them you are playing a game. Then hustle like crazy to wrap up the deal and get out before they realize there is no prize at all."

"What is rule number two?"

"So glad you asked that. When delicate information is at stake, great prudence is demanded so that the information does not fall into reckless hands, so that infants (again, that is you) do not hurt themselves. You should know about prudence. Isn't it one of the virtues you study at that academy?"

"What does any of this have to do with me ... or Mark?"

"Your actions have compromised the reputations of you both. You will save his reputation, at least, by honoring your promise to marry him. I have not spent all this effort and training on him to have you throw it away in an instant."

"You know you are not the sort of tutor to give lessons to some young man or young woman, for that matter, in the school of matrimony."

"And you are not a suitable wife for a young man set to take a big leap in his career. Your father put your family in a direct and grave financial crisis triggered by his failed projects, his bankruptcies, and subsequent damage to his reputation, so severe that your mother teeters on the verge of a mental breakdown. You yourself are not unscathed with your burden of inherited debt."

"All of your creation."

"Regardless of who is to blame, it is best that you suck it up to salvage what is left, or you will find yourself thrown out in the streets—or worse. As I see it, you have three choices: one, marry Mark today; two, sign over the deeds; or three, await your own death. The story goes that all the documents were burned in a fire. That is what will be released to the press, and that is what the documents show.

"Is that really appropriate when you have not done your job for the past three years—if it ever was your job? If you think the bitter cup has passed, you have underestimated the server." For by now my reading of the Scriptures had taken me to the Gospels of the New Testament. And there was no darker study in all of history of a mission to be accomplished. "Perhaps a better headline should read: *The Dominguez family's extraordinary generosity to Thomas Stillman reaches its limit.*"

"And your defender is where?"

It was useless to argue. Truth would not prevail. At that moment, I did not have to go back into the mists of history. The devil did exist not just as a symbol of evil but as a physical reality in the person of Stillman. "And while we are sharing confidences like this, getting cozy and all, aren't you forgetting something—your promise to tell me a secret."

"Oh yes, that," he said with a sniff.

"Yes ... that."

"It all started over this house. You were right about that, as a matter of fact. Antonio and I went into partnership over the tract of land for this development. This particular house belonged to your grandparents. Unfortunately, they only lived here a short time before your grandfather died, followed later by your grandmother. Do you remember? You were young ... six or seven. Your father then rented it out, mostly to Seelye families. When he could not attend to its care, he would call upon me, since I lived closer. Unfortunately, he made a stop in Abilene that final trip to check on things. Always so unhappy, Antonio could not let well enough alone. It was so easy like picking fruit off a tree, taking the deed from his pocket. So you see this house is mine now. But your mother ... not so easy a tree to harvest. If she had just stayed where she was ... But there are other instruments of the law."

"Where is she?"

"Nothing to worry about. She is being well taken care of. You really need to worry more about yourself."

"You can't get away with this ... It's kidnapping."

"Not necessarily. Sometimes it is more profitable to trade products for rent. So you see, you were not held against your will at all but had made the decision to stay in a house that once belonged to your family, relying on my generosity, and you hired my assistant and my maid to provide your needs. You have become a recluse after living at a convent boarding school, etc., and disgracing yourself by running away ... ruined trying to elope. Didn't I warn you about the importance of one's appearance in society? Then, unfortunately, you became addicted to alcohol and laudanum like your mother and had a continuing need of a guardian."

"What did you do to my father?" I whispered.

"Why nothing. He died by his own hand." He pantomimed drinking from a glass so that I could not mistake his meaning. "It has always been a fashion especially among royalty to poison those who become a bother."

"You haven't earned any of this."

"My dear, beautiful, young ward, though it saddens me, my duty is to protect you from yourself. This reversal of the natural order of authority—a citizen to the laws of elected officials, a wife to a husband, a child to a parent or a guardian—cannot continue."

"For that you would have me destroyed?"

"I am simply abating a nuisance injurious to the community."

"I could say the same for you."

218

"Well, then, if that is how you see it, mustn't give the game away before it is started." Stillman made a temple of his elegant fingers. "Mystery breeds interest."

A.D.

After this conversation, Stillman reverted to the old practice of locking me in the room upstairs, where, every time he visited, blowing cigar smoke in my face, he asked one question: Where were the deeds to my father's properties? Each day his patience lessened, and he developed a new scenario for my future life: his latest, going to Mexico in search of a distant relative and getting killed in the civil unrest. Was he still composing letters to Sister Louise, just as he had written to me about my mother? Each day I asked him what had happened to my mother. "For whatever mistakes I have made, or my father made, this feels too brutal a price to pay. I want to see Mark."

"Why? You would not act as wife to him anyway." His contempt was clear.

"You do not have any right to keep us apart. You are not my guardian any longer. What about your promise to let me go?" I was grabbing at straws.

"Just a little longer. Have some of this nice pasta I brought for you."

Persistent hopelessness, rage, and low energy contributed to the dark moods and unrelenting depression that made me want to take my life or his. Was I capable of either? First, with every passing day saying to myself, "Everything will be fine, snap out of it," became harder. Second, my reliance on Mark to be strong, honest, and capable had come to nothing. He wasn't big enough to be aware of the fix we were in or to keep my trust and respect. Third, I may lose the person I was born to be. Knowing that Stillman did not yet have possession of my father's lands kept me alive. Had he used the same tactic to reduce my mother to a compliant state? Then I heard a voice outside myself saying, "Get out of this bed. Get off that chair. You cannot sit here day after day letting someone take your life away from you. You have to go and get your life. Go be a lawyer. Go be a sister. Go be a Seelye patent medicine salesperson. You have to do something. Anything."

A.D.

With each signing of my journals, I had reminded myself that A. D. meant *in the year of Our Lord,* not *after death.* God is present. Not dead. After hours, days of being locked in hellish isolation, I did not welcome death, but life took on a gothic twist. I knew that if I were confined much longer, the terrible thing I had sweated over was actually happening. Death would be coming. I felt myself going mad in earnest. My eyes were red, my nose runny. In the dresser mirror I caught a glimpse of the gaunt look that had settled on my face, like my soul was evaporating. And so it was not hard to act the part when after the door creaked, heralding an arrival, Mark finally appeared. "Close the door. Bats are flying in," I screamed when he appeared.

"I don't see any, Antoinette," he said with a scowl.

"Are you blind? Look there! And there! Is there a cave nearby? A church belfry?"

He closed the door, checked the windows, and picked up objects both to study and to wave around the room. "Are they gone now?"

"Not all of them. They are hanging from the ceiling. They see me. Do not let them get in my hair. Do you have a knife? You will have to cut them out of my hair if they swoop."

"Bats can't see."

"Are you sure? If they have rabies, we will die when they suck our blood."

"I'll chase them out." He removed the quilt from the bed and unfurled it in my direction. His calm was unnerving me even more.

"You let the snakes and bugs out," I screamed at him.

"Where?"

"Coming across the floor … green and black and slimy … on the bed. They are climbing on the walls now."

"The snakes?"

"The snakes and the centipedes, crickets, and beetles. Can't you hear them?" My physical weakness and my hysteria elevated my heart rate as I whirled around the room trying to escape the phantoms of my own creation. The exhaustion I felt as a result of my efforts was very real, and I sank into the chair, bundling my knees into my arms and hiding my face, for I trembled to a degree that disabled me from standing.

Mark continued to humor me. "I have driven them away."

"No … no." I raised my head. "Light some candles. They are afraid of candles." Mark did as I asked. I suddenly had an inspiration to burn the house down and perhaps escape in the confusion. "Look there, spiders. Light more candles. The shadows have come to steal our souls and take us to the netherworld." As he turned away, I held the flame to the drapes and watched them turn to fire.

"Antoinette, what are you doing?"

"Look … look at them scatter. They are leaving now." While he was ripping one curtain from the wall, I lit another and another until the flames and smoke were beginning to make my eyes water. As I was heading for the bed, Mark yanked the candle from my hand and pulled me toward the door. Flinging it open with the keys still in the lock, he shoved me out of the room. I grabbed the keys and charged down the stairs while he was distracted with putting out the flames. Escape on my mind, I raced to the bottom, not daring to take time to look behind me while selecting the key I thought I had seen used on the front door, where I was headed. Mark started to swear, long and hard.

"*Delirium tremens*," said Stillman, who loomed up as a large shadow at the bottom of the stairs. "Or perhaps great acting." After he had stopped my progress and shoved me into a chair, he began to applaud. "Which is it, Antoinette?" He removed a bottle from the sideboard, shook it as if trying to conjure up a different resolution, and began to pour liquid amber into a glass. "A toast to you, but your games tire me." Before he could hand it to me, Mark grabbed the glass from his outstretched hand and swallowed the contents without a breath. Though I had not seen him follow me down the stairs, I did not doubt the danger I was in and so was at the point of agreeing to marry his son. How alike the two looked just now. How could I not have seen it before I put Mark—for I did feel some responsibility—and myself into such peril?

Had Mark at last intended to intervene? "This has got to stop," he said in the seconds after downing the liquid and in the seconds before its effects were revealed. "We have to let her go." Unfortunately, he began to sweat profusely. A new realization propelled his energies. "Antoinette, just so you know, you weren't violated." His expression changed rapidly from fear to sadness to anger. "Not in that way … It was all a trick and … I'm sorry … for my part in all this." His breathing became shallow and his balance unsteady. "Forgive me …" he said as he fell to the floor. Mr. Stillman's eyes took on a sudden change. Had the glass been drugged? Did this poison have an antidote? Would Mark ever breathe right again? Stillman was not the kind of fiend who would hit with his fist or even use a knife or a gun. When he chose violence as his instrument, he removed himself from the scene through the manipulation of specialized instruments, including the law itself. But fiend he was. And fiend he now looked as he dragged me up the stairs, shoved me back into my bedroom prison, and retrieving the keys from my hand, locked the door.

My tremors make writing difficult. The lingering smell of smoke, or is it sulfur, makes breathing arduous. But unless my obscure story survives in some form, what proof is there that I have ever lived at all? Or is this, as I feared, my own Castle Doleful, and I meant to be an inhabitant outliving my time as a fading apparition of dispossession? If this be the haunted antechamber of a world between time and eternity, I call upon the power therein to assist in my delivery. How had my plan gotten so mucked up? Then another thought occurred to me. What if this was a staged crime? Had I again been duped? My anger stopped the tremors, and I felt sanity return.

Shortly, I heard the door below creak on its hinges. It was not again thrust to but appeared to remain open. Footsteps traversed the entry as though much dragging of a heavy burden followed by the automobile driving off and finally, silence. What was in the glass? Was it intended for me? What would happen now that Mr. Stillman's plan had been thwarted? I might not have another way out.

By my signature below I, Antoinette Dominguez, declare that this diary is a written instrument by which I have made a record of the days of my captivity. Signed but not dated, as I have lost track of calendar dates. This house is my witness.

March or April in the Year of Our Lord 1910
Antoinette Dominguez

Chapter 18
Threat of Extinction

T hus ended Antoinette's grisly account of the horror that Sophiny and Martha could not see from where they sat in the empty house—catastrophe relayed from the safety of a piece of paper. The condition effectively proved the wickedness and vice of her guardian. From the damage to her surroundings, it was clear that Antoinette had not wasted time being afraid. Instead she had focused her energies on escaping: windows broken, shutters loosened, the door savaged. But here they were back to where they had started. *The threat of extinction continues. If Antoinette escaped, where is she? If Stillman came back for her, where did he take her? If his son took the deadly elixir intended for her, would Stillman's vengeance know any bounds?* Sophiny remembered her friend perched atop a trunk in the trunk room as schemes ran through her head that wintry day in February. What would she do? Antoinette would pretend she was someone else and focus her terror on playing the role. She would go to Wichita. The end of the diary left a vast emptiness of a house in disarray, of persons missing and of a pen silenced.

"By the wielding of her pen, she has given us evidence enough to unravel all," Sophiny whispered into the purgatory that surrounded her.

Sophiny knew the tale of Stillman's unraveling would set Antoinette at the center of the action. Her fake elopement with his son in the beginning scenes was clearly the beginning of the end, but for whom? Stillman or Antoinette? Had Stillman cradled Mark's body in the final reckoning, aghast that his victim had been his own son, thus rendering him impotent? Had the flames of hell burst dramatically around them? Was he tortured yet unrepentant? Had she succumbed to the same poisonous fate as Mark, her crusade ending in a cold ferry ride to the netherworld? Would Stillman get his reckoning? Was Death taking him on a long journey? Could he find companions? Was Mark the Kindred figure? Would the court take his Goods? Would Knowledge bring Confession? Certainly Antoinette and her mother could have been his Good Deeds, but he had lost the opportunity to do right by them. Sophiny wished she could take the test over *Everyman* again; she would be ready this time. Was Antoinette's way out—to pretend—just as deadly as Juliet's with Friar Laurence's potion and misdirected messages?

"We can only hope that her escape has not led to a worsened state." Martha nudged Sophiny from her numbness.

Indeed, the house was a place scarred by malevolence—besides the destruction to possible exit points, burn marks scored the interior equally as menacing as the gloomy exterior had been. *Had Antoinette secured her own release?* Sophiny began to shiver uncontrollably. Even Martha's comforting arms could not stop the deep chill that had taken over her body. "I think we'd better leave this place. It is evil," Martha said, and Sophiny readily agreed. After picking up the pocket notebook, trunk key, and her sampler, she opened the large wardrobe door. While Martha finished taking photographs of the disarray, she picked out one of Antoinette's dresses and placed all the items she had collected in the reticule that Antoinette must have brought with her on the train. Sophiny then followed Martha down the stairs where she left untouched the opened bottle of amber liquid and picked up instead a dark green bottle with a fairy on the label marked absinthe with wormwood: 74 percent alcohol, she read.

Outside they skirted the shadows of the untended hedge adjacent to the house, concealing the flow of traffic from the street. The hair stirred on the nape of her neck. She glanced toward the entrance of the warehouse across the square. A figure stood in the gloom. The town was an arresting sight, with lights beginning to gleam and twinkle. She suddenly realized it was night. The transformation had taken place in real time. Martha had followed her outside, reluctant to lose line of sight. Neither had missed the venomous poison spurting forth from the account they had just finished. It was a desperate alliance, but her other choices were even more uncertain. "Get your camera, Martha."

"Where are we going?"

"There," she said, pointing.

Sophiny began to walk down the boardwalk. Shadow-darkened and looming against the sky, the largest building in the town began to draw her—a three-story warehouse or production building, she surmised; not many of those on the plains. As she neared, she noticed a number of delivery wagons with lettering painted on the sides: *Seelye Patent Medicine Wagon Wasa-Tusa.* Had Antoinette gone to the train station? Had she tried to contact someone? Had she gone past the warehouse? No matter where Antoinette went, the whole town—the whole state—should be looking for her, and Sophiny was ready to shout from the rooftops.

"Have you seen this young woman?" she asked the man, shoving Antoinette's photograph before him. "This is Antoinette Dominguez, granddaughter of the former owners of that house." She pointed in the direction of the high hedge that she and Martha had just vacated. "She has been kidnapped and held in that house, the Shutter House, for the past month by these two." She shoved other photographs. "Have you seen him? He is a Seelye customer of yours from Concord—Thomas Stillman. Or him?" She produced the photograph of Mark Weaver.

"Can't say that I have, but there was a body found. Could there be a connection?"

A sharp ache like a knife wedged between her ribs, an erratic beating of her heart and then trouble breathing. *No, this could not have happened.* When she opened her mouth to speak, *Antoinette … Antoinette … Antoinette … Dead … Dead … Dead …* a strange gurgle came out.

"Sophiny?" Martha moved to support her, not saying what she was thinking.

"Is she all right?" the Seelye salesman asked.

Martha shook her head, "A bit of a shock. Her friend is missing."

"The newspaper is here somewhere … had the story." He wandered into the building to retrieve the paper, which he handed to Martha.

Sophiny listened as Martha began to read the headlines:

Body Found in Abandoned Building
The body of a man in his twenties was found early this morning, and the Abilene sheriff says he is investigating. The Abilene sheriff's office received a report from a citizen about 7:00 a.m. that a body was found in an empty house near the town center. Sheriff Coleman said, "Right now it's suspicious, but we're taking a hard look at it. We're not calling it a homicide, assault, or anything at this point. We really don't know. We're not ready to call it anything other than we found a dead body."

"It is not her, but it might be him … found two days ago." Martha looked at the date and turned the paper over for more to the story, but there wasn't any.

Sophiny felt her eyes suddenly focus, like the shutter on Martha's camera lens. "Where is the body now?"

"The body …?"

"My friend is a photographer. She will need to …"

But at that moment the wheels of a Seelye wagon rumbled in the dry ruts of a bordering street like thunder, and even in the darkness they could see the driver transformed into a demon piloting a hell cart, setting the Seelye man beside them to yelling. The commotion increased as occupants from the building spilled out to see what was going on, and neighbors followed suit. "What is happening? A wheel?"

"Trying to beat the dark … no moon tonight … dangerous road … horses spooked," said the man in gasps, reminding them all that the country was still not properly traversable. Gradually slowing his horses and stepping down, he said, "What a ride that was." His contact with solid ground was greeted with cheers and much clapping on the back.

"Fortunate for you, the dark kept most other traffic off the road. How's Wichita?" asked the first Seelye salesman as he grabbed the reins and made soothing noises to the horses.

A traveler recently arrived from outlying regions was better than a newspaper. The crowd, disappointed that the wild ride had come to such a tame ending, lingered, like Martha wanting to find out if there was more to the story. The driver obliged. "They are getting all set up for that big syndicate to take over the Dominguez Farms. All of a sudden, they seem in a big hurry to get done."

Martha and Sophiny looked at each other as the conversation continued around them. "Is that the one with the big ad in the paper?"

"Dominguez?"

"That's the one."

"Wasn't there a Dominguez who used to live in Abilene?"

At this moment, the first Seelye salesman they had spoken to turned. "These ladies were just asking about that house."

Sophiny came forward. "Is there a sheriff or deputy we could talk to?" *The body—will someone claim it or worse, bury it before it is properly identified? The house—is someone watching it? Antoinette's pocket notebook—can this evidence stop the sale?* These were her thoughts as she watched the approach of a tall, broad-shouldered man with a thick neck and darting, judgmental eyes.

"Sheriff Coleman, what can I do for you, miss?" His presence lent the aura of authority.

"We were hoping to ask you about what's been going on there." Martha stepped in. "But could we speak to you privately?"

"The office inside is open." The Seelye man pointed the way. The sheriff led, and Martha followed. Sophiny was aware from the groans that the crowd resented the eclipse of their entertainment.

Martha was all business, refusing the chair offered. She handed the sheriff her business card and the newspaper story. "I need to photograph this young man for identification," she said. "I have reason to believe he might be a young man missing from Concord who has been living in the Shutter House referred to by this gentleman here." She turned to the Seelye employee whose office they were occupying.

"Well, now, who did you say you were again?" asked the sheriff, in no hurry to take immediate action.

Martha again identified herself. "Can you tell me where I might find the body?"

"Just who is this Concord man? What business did he have in Abilene?" He had taken a hard-to-dislodge stand blocking the door.

"Mark Weaver, an employee of the Thomas Stillman law firm."

"Why was he living here?"

"He was helping Mr. Stillman manage the property."

When the sheriff continued to hesitate, Sophiny could stand it no longer. "Martha, I think this is a job for Detective Tyler's agency. Perhaps the sheriff doesn't have the right jurisdiction … if the deceased is from out of town and all." Looking around, she found what she was looking for and turned her back on the sheriff to appeal to the Seelye salesman. "We will need to use your telephone."

"All right." The sheriff reluctantly shifted his position. "Let's go take a look. But if our body is your man, you owe me a better explanation of why you are looking for him. This would be a lot easier in the daylight. Sure it can't wait until the morning?"

"No," both said together.

"If I can come along, you can use my telephone," the Seelye salesman bargained.

"Got a lantern? Might need some extra candles too," the sheriff said with a nod.

Sophiny knew that their story would be all over town before morning. But grapevine fuel might be their most effective tool in Antoinette's recovery and gaining the official backing she desperately needed to stop Stillman's clock.

Sophiny thought to herself that under no circumstance would she surrender Antoinette's diary to the local sheriff and hoped that Martha wouldn't mention their finding either. *Will they be able to identify the body from a photograph? Will Martha's photograph be sent to Mark's mother? Will she come to Abilene to identify her son's body? Does she know what he has been up to?*

The sheriff lit a lantern and asked them to stay close as he led the way behind a row of storefronts through animal, tool, and storage sheds. The town's appearance at night and from this angle was rough and unattractive in places. Dangerous and rickety structures everywhere provided evidence of the early boon years of saloons, cattle drives, and railroads usually hidden by the later growth spurts. Had Antoinette found shelter here? The Seelye salesman raised his lantern from behind. "Don't think we'll be able to use this ice cellar for the summer. Seems a terrible waste. Watch your step."

Sophiny removed Mark Weaver's photograph, looking for matching features on the body before her.

"Could I see that?" The sheriff took it from her and began to circle the rough-wood box hammered together from packing crates that served as both storage and burial.

Martha signaled the Seelye salesman for best positions for light placement. Sophiny remembered Antoinette's description. The man was young, in his twenties, with hair that could be called unruly, "sprouting a mustache," and clothing that did not show signs of wear, even stylish. His face had not bloated in death but instead looked like a mask of agony.

"He did not go peacefully," Martha commented and turned his palm over. Clear burn marks showed on his hands and scorch marks on his shirt. Even without the photograph, Sophiny knew that this was Mark Weaver. She had to speak to Detective Tyler.

"I'm going to need to keep this photograph," said the sheriff, indicating the one Sophiny had identified as Mark Weaver. "And you two come along with me for questioning."

"Certainly, Sheriff." Martha gave Sophiny a look that said, *Let me do the talking.* "It will take a few more minutes to finish these photographs. The lighting is making things difficult."

"When you make prints, see that I get a set as well."

"I will. But before we get to your questions, perhaps you should take a look—for not knowing another way to identify it—at the old Dominguez house. You might have some of your questions answered."

The sheriff and the Seelye salesman walked through the shuttered, window-barred house while Sophiny and Martha waited on the enclosed veranda.

"Martha, do you think Stillman knows this sheriff?" She cocked her head to one side, looking intently into the darkness.

"Does he know the Seelye salesman?" Martha raised another question instead of answering her.

"We have to go to Wichita *tomorrow*," Sophiny replied, not hiding her impatience.

"I know. Let me answer the sheriff's questions in case he decides one of us has to stay in town." Martha frowned, as if expecting bad news.

"Martha, he can't keep me here. He already took my photograph of

Mark. What if he takes Antoinette's pocket notebook?" Sophiny could hear the despair in her own voice.

"Don't mention that notebook! The sheriff has a body and a ravaged house. That should be enough evidence to keep him busy for a few days," she reassured her.

"About those telephone calls …" Sophiny hesitated.

"I have the phone number for Mount St. Mary's. Sister Louise can get a message to Detective Tyler at his hotel. He will know what is to be done about Stillman in Wichita," Martha reassured her.

After their search, the sheriff came outside, making his case to the salesman about why he needed time to look into the matter before the public could know what happened. "If there's a circus about us, whatever else I can discover will be savaged." His eyes were now heavy-lidded and sadly immobilized. The salesman seemed to shrink back and surrender.

"Where are you staying the night, ladies?" The sheriff turned in their direction.

Martha and Sophiny looked at each other, so occupied were they with their own search, that everything beyond had been suspended for the duration. Even now Sophiny could think of nothing but contacting Detective Tyler. She was at peace with the truce when somehow between Martha and the sheriff, the arrangements for supper and their night's stay in a hotel with a telephone were made. Martha remained to answer the sheriff's questions, insisting Sophiny go to bed, after she made her telephone call to ease her mind, of course, the harsh realities of the day's events being too stimulating for the constitution of one so young. "There's no need to add her name to a crime report. I can give you a statement."

"Suppose so," the sheriff said, nodding reluctantly.

Martha proceeded with her statement as though reading from an account in her head:

His name is Mark Weaver. His mother is Mrs. Weaver of Wichita. His last hours were spent at a residence in Abilene previously owned by the Dominguez family. He was twenty, thinking of going to law school. He worked as a clerk for Mr. Thomas Stillman in his law practice in Concord. There is some evidence that he was in fact Mr. Stillman's son and working under his directives. Shouldn't Mr. Stillman be brought in for questioning …

Sophiny did not wait for her to finish. She had her own story to tell. The usually reticent Sister Louise had a lot to say. Posters had gone up all over Concord that afternoon, and circulars had been distributed to any passersby who would take one. An article advertising the street trial had been sent to the newspaper, along with Antoinette's and her guardian's photographs. Mary Clare had written the script for the street trial, including accusations and charges, much of it directly from Antoinette's pocket notebooks. Students were practicing their roles. Of course, they would read their parts; there was no time for memory work. Detective Tyler himself had come out to watch the academy students at work. The girls were surprised to see Brother Claude out of his religious garb but determined to make him a character in their drama. He did not seem pleased. His own investigation, unfortunately, had met with resistance. "No outsider was going to tell Concord officials what to do or how to treat their own upstanding citizens." When Tyler heard of the students' intentions to work with the Temperance Union speaker, he was even less pleased. Finally, he was about to leave instructions with Sister Louise that Sophiny and Martha were to … but he never finished. "We none of us knew where you had disappeared until Detective Tyler received a telephone call from a railroad clerk in Abilene saying you were going to the Shutter House."

Sister Louise promised to do her best to make contact with him at his hotel or through his agency. In the meantime, she would notify her sister order in Wichita of the discoveries in Abilene. "Somehow Detective Tyler will get your message," she promised. Before they hung up, Sophiny stated her intent of going to Wichita on the morning train, with or without Martha. To which Sister Louise responded, "Someone will meet you at the station. Look for your name on a paper, if you don't recognize a familiar face. Sophiny, this is not the time to be reckless. God be with you."

Before Martha retired, she made her own telephone calls. "Paul says Andrew and Henry left for Wichita this morning to go to the Dominguez Farms Machinery Hall. The ads are out that it is closing down and machines to be auctioned off. They should be there by now." At least Sophiny knew where Andrew and Henry would be when she got into town. "Now get some sleep. Tomorrow will be a big day."

Chapter 19
Piece of Misinformation

. . . .

As Martha feared, she *was* delayed for more questioning. During the night, the house had been gutted by fire. Concord officials arriving on the morning train requested—no, demanded—her presence. The hotel clerk gave her the message from the Abilene sheriff and stood as if to block her exit. "I'll take the opportunity to write a story for the local newspaper," she said when she returned to the room to warn Sophiny, who was not included in the sheriff's demand.

Sophiny left the hotel by the back door, unrecognizable she hoped, in Detective Tyler's fake bad teeth and Martha's hat, shawl, and face powder. She was wearing her own plain-as-an-unbuttered biscuit frock with pockets large enough to hide Antoinette's pocket notebook and carrying Antoinette's reticule. She hoped she made a seriously lumpy impression. Somehow the roll of string with which she had wrapped Antoinette's documents had also made its way into her pocket. She walked a roundabout route to the railroad station, half checking that she was not followed and half hoping that she was. Was Antoinette still in Abilene? Birds chirping from the trees overhead and young cottontails fleeing before her seemed a good sign. She did have to watch her step with all the holes and uneven outcroppings along the path. Travelers moved into the station chatting amiably. Sophiny blended in with a family observing the sound of brakes being pulled, coupled with the metallic screech of wheels against rails, smoke billowing out of slowing engines and a shower of sparks. As though one of the group, she followed the family to the far end of a passenger railcar.

"Miss, is this your newspaper?" said the old gentleman in a threadbare suit and flannel shirt taking a seat beside her. His shoulder smashed into hers with a sinewy firmness that did not come with age. She had noticed the man's limp on a stiff leg and a convincing downtrodden shuffle as he came down the car aisle, his slight stoop giving him an apologetic look. The brim of his battered felt slouch hat drooped so low that only his white beard and white hair around the edges of the hat was visible. She wondered how he could see at all. As he handed her the paper, he tilted his head up, and snow-white eyebrows curled in a most curious way. The old man's thumb pointed to an article title: "Stillman Shakedown."

"Thank you," she said, doing a double-take and fairly grabbing the *Concord Chronicle* out of the man's hand. Could it be? Something was fishy; that thumb didn't look old at all. But before investigating further, she read the entire article in one gulp.

Stillman Shakedown
Hatchet-wielding Mount St. Mary's Academy students created
the largest stir we've had in Concord since the cavalry came
to take up residency at Fort Riley. They put down their prayer
books, sewing needles, and copy pens to take up another
cause. The most urgent reason for the focus of the talents and
energies of the classmates of Antoinette Dominguez, who
has been missing for the past thirty days, was alcohol related.
Hence the inspiration of the street trial and the involvement of
temperance leader Henrietta Bratley, who knew just how to keep
her calm and carry on to add substance to their demands.

Their grievances? They wanted the illegal alcoholic beverages of
the Stillman basement revealed, Mr. Stillman's guardianship
over Mrs. Dominguez and her daughter Antoinette revoked, and
subpoenas issued for the release of his papers. They wanted his
arrest for an abuse of his position. But most of all they wanted
to know the whereabouts of Antoinette herself. *Their support?*
To do all these things, they recited snippets of wisdom from
Suffragist Elizabeth Cady Stanton and temperance leaders such
as Carrie Nation, who advocate changes to laws that consign
women to the status of chattel. But until women have the
voting power to change the laws, this public demonstration
to raise awareness of "the liquor evil" would have to suffice.

Evidence for their case was taken directly from the missing
student's diary. Academy students took turns reading entries
to prove that Antoinette was not a bad girl, a troublemaker,
the kind of young woman mothers warned their daughters
about. Instead her defiance was spent in a cautionary tale of
another sort: uncovering an unrepentant villain. The event

launched a storm and a signature campaign that swept across the Midwestern town to persuade the sheriff's department, county attorney, and judge to issue the subpoenas.

After the rally, subpoenas for the search of Stillman Enterprises speedily followed. Mr. Stillman was unavailable for comment. "It is too soon to celebrate victory. Antoinette is still missing," cautioned Mary Clare Decatur, one of the academy students. Still let us admire the risk Miss Dominguez took in spurning conventional means to find her mother and recover her assets. The local chapter of the WCTU plans to take up the cause and not stop until Mr. Stillman himself opens the doors of his basement and the gutters run with the decanted liquor hidden below.

Miss Dominguez is the daughter of the late Antonio Dominguez, who died under mysterious circumstances four years ago in Concord. Mr. Stillman, his business associate at the time of his death, denied any culpability. However, in the intervening years, he has taken guardianship of Mrs. Dominguez, Miss Dominguez, and the Dominguez Farms and extensive business holdings in Wichita. A recent notice was placed in area newspapers about the sale of these holdings to a local Wichita syndicate following a month-minus-one day newspaper notice of missing heirs. Should this sale be halted?

The conductor came through, "Tickets, gents, ladies," and eyed them closely. Sophiny had to suppress not only a giggle but worse, saying something unintelligent. Clasping her hands together over the bag in her lap, bowing her head, and jailing her tongue within clenched teeth, she tried to stop the eruption about to spew forth. An untidy bottomland grove of elm and bur oak trees passed by the window. When she trusted herself to look up a moment later, she didn't immediately understand what she saw. Was the man wearing a bandanna over his face an illusion? Or was this a demon sent to kill her? Her brothers had talked about Wichita. Her friend was from Wichita. Moments before she had been desperate to go there, but now that desire vanished.

The robber striding boldly out of the shadow overturned his hat in his hand, his forward motion enhanced by the train's jerking action. Detective Tyler sat slouched and docile in his seat beside her. Had he not seen the threat? "Ladies, gents, hand over your wallets. Nobody will get hurt. Jewelry too, you there, ma'am … and sir, you …" With horrible fascination, she watched his every step until he stood before her. "The bag, miss." Not waiting for her to hand it over, he reached over Detective Tyler to snatch it from her lap. His attempt failed. Sophiny refused to let go, and the robber was thrown off balance.

"Watch out," chided a passenger across the aisle at Sophiny as the hat of loot went flying. Detective Tyler leaped to his feet. Suddenly the portrait formation lost exactness and shifted seismically out of control. The detective and the robber zigzagged toward and away, pummeling each other with their fists: *Thwack! Pow! Bam!* leading her eyes into and out of the cluttered depths of the scene. She found herself scanning the frame in great sweeps and even turning her head to follow the action. Blurs of color defined the space: a citron yellow shirtwaist, a minty green scarf, the strawberry red upholstery clashing with the tomato red bandanna, the speed of the train interrupting the shaft of light through the windows. Sophiny felt herself lurch into the unknown as she stuck out her foot and kicked hard, releasing the explosion she had pent up since first recognizing Detective Tyler. In seconds the robber was down on the floor, not knowing what had happened to him, with Detective Tyler astraddle, snapping on a pair of handcuffs. The sharp-tongued wag across the aisle complained, "Somebody could have gotten hurt."

Passengers scrambling to retrieve their belongings silenced her with a rousing cheer. Inside the thin walls of steel, a fragile alliance had been restored; as long as no robbers or wreckers were on board, everybody prospered. "What were you saying?" Sophiny asked, sweetly turning to her. The robber, his bandanna removed and dragged to his feet, glowered. Where had she seen him before? But even the robber's malice could not dim Sophiny's golden glow.

"Where did you learn that?" Detective Tyler's hat and wig had fallen off in the scuffle, and his lip was starting to swell.

"From you—remember?" Sophiny removed her fake teeth, which were making her drool most unattractively. "Do something unexpected."

Despite the apologetic posture and the mild manner, Detective Tyler had proven he was a fighter capable of subduing a culprit. Unfortunately, for the remainder of the trip his priority became his prisoner. When she tried to compliment him, Detective Tyler pantomimed that she was not to say anything within the robber's hearing. "No telling whose hound dog he is," cautioned Detective Tyler. "Just hope he's worth the irritation he's inflicted."

But Sophiny knew exactly who he was: the Seelye patent medicine salesman who had been so helpful the night before.

As arrangements for separate seating for himself and this unwelcome passenger were being made, Sophiny scrawled a note relaying all her discoveries, including the latest about the Seelye salesman and a possible connection to Stillman. This she handed over with Antoinette's recovered pocket notebook wrapped in the newspaper. Still unsatisfied, she took out her Brownie camera, hoping her photography worthy of Martha's instruction. Emboldened by the technology, she located the robber in her viewfinder and snapped a photograph. Next, with Detective Tyler in her viewfinder, she spent more moments than necessary studying him as he read before she grabbed her chance and clicked five times. In the future, she would be able to summon his image at will. Throughout the trip she looked up at him several times and several times caught his return gaze. What would it be like to gaze at him over a breakfast table like this each morning? She allowed this fantasy a brief bubble of life and then shrugged it away.

As the train came into the Wichita station, Sophiny saw her brothers outside the window before they saw her. When she passed his seat, Detective Tyler handed her the newspaper with Antoinette's pocket notebook inside. "Thank you, miss." He remained on board with his prisoner until all the other passengers had gotten off.

"How was the trip?" Andrew greeted when she alighted.

"We got a little side-tracked."

"What happened?" Henry looked around her.

"Train robbery," responded Sophiny. Their eyes followed hers as she spotted Detective Tyler and the robber descending from the train.

"That's never good," said Andrew.

Sophiny reported Detective Tyler's capture of the robber in heroic detail as the three siblings watched the prisoner hand-off to a Wichita sheriff who must have been waiting for Detective Tyler's arrival.

"Busted lip, some blood, and a short trip to the carpet for the robber." Detective Tyler opted for a less colorful storyline as they waited with him to retrieve his horse and saddle from the stock car.

"Thought you said you didn't pick fights anymore," Henry said with one of his smiles.

"Yes, well, you always have to watch out for those quiet dogs. What's the news from the Dominguez Farms Machinery Hall?"

"We saw so many pretty girls last night that Henry's neck was almost disjointed looking around. He'll be glad to get away so as to give his eyes and neck a rest."

"At a farm machinery hall?"

"It was like some ice cream social going on."

"And a special sale on bicycles."

Suddenly things moved swiftly. Approaching them was the man Sophiny had seen with Detective Tyler in Concord. She recognized the build—slight and weathered, the movements—restless and sharp, the definition of hands, and the thin, bony nose.

How could she be so conscious of Detective Tyler's every move, even without looking at him, and yet be so unaware of Antoinette's? Whether frightened and running or safe and in hiding or dead, consequences would have occurred by now. The elation was passing. She thought how remote it seemed, that unprompted, exalted mood that had brought her into the station. Antoinette, hidden from view wherever she was, was either still alive or murdered by Stillman's poison. Until her appearance in the flesh, a requirement of proof for either result existed separately in the world awaiting their discovery.

Detective Tyler seemed to have forgotten her already. His easy, muscular stride taking him away, he didn't even turn around to notice if Sophiny and her brothers had followed. He seemed to thrive on his return to work, but for him the train ride sitting beside her, subduing the train robber, questioning him had been work—the ultimate badge of who he was. Sophiny could hear snatches of conversation: scheduling a hearing, briefings in a judge's chamber, an exploratory chat laying out options, and getting a gag order to stop the flow of information. "It is a tricky piece of business," said his companion.

Feeling somewhat unhinged and unreasonable and still needing to talk to him, Sophiny said a little more loudly than necessary, "Can I get one?" During the train ride, she had assumed she would be included in the search. Was she now being ignored?

"What?" asked Andrew, not quite following her request.

"A bicycle."

"Why?"

"It's cheaper than an automobile?" Sophiny gave him a deadpan look and turned forward again, noting Henry's wandering eye at the vehicles surrounding them.

They were nearing a livery stable in the process of being converted to accommodate motor vehicles. Outside, trucks and automobiles were parked alongside wagons, buggies, and surreys. A newly installed gas pump stood at one end of the lot, a stack of baled hay at the other. The smell of gasoline mingled with that of hay and manure. Inside, the large wooden structure contained stalls for horses and a section for motorcar repairs: wrenches, grease guns, and a chain hoist.

"So what is the plan? What do you intend to do now that you are here?" asked Andrew of his sister.

"How would you two like a job?" Detective Tyler suddenly seemed to have remembered them. "Nothing dangerous." To which the brothers eyed each other skeptically. The job entailed returning to the Dominguez Farms Machinery Hall, hanging around and talking to people, observing the comings and goings, listening to rumors. "Do you have transportation?"

"Two feet."

"Can you drive?"

"Sure," Andrew and Henry said together. How had they had time to learn to drive? Sophiny wondered.

"The agency will provide a car for you." He looked pointedly at his weathered partner. who had been introduced as Detective Smith. Sophiny felt a pang of exclusion. "Ask about the auction, then go on out and poke around for yourselves. What did you say you were interested in?"

"Plows."

Sophiny, once again cruelly reminded that she was rapidly plummeting below the visibility line, considered how to tip the scales to best advantage. Detective Tyler at last seemed to notice her. "Miss Mumm, I need you and that pocket notebook to come with me. We'll meet up with you at the machinery hall later." He nodded to her brothers as they received instructions on the operation of the automobile. "And buy your sister a bicycle. I think she has earned it, right, Smithy?" He signaled to Detective Smith who again took out his wallet and separated several bills. Her brothers set off down a slope in fits and starts, passed through a strip of cottonwood trees, headed into the main center of town, and disappeared from her view.

It happened when she didn't want to be doing what she was doing, or she didn't want to hear what somebody was saying, or she didn't want to be where she was. If she could not leave a situation physically, she left mentally. *Don't fall. Don't fall. Don't fall,* she said to herself.

Even Detective Tyler could tell she was not paying attention. "Sophiny? Did you hear me?" He touched her on the elbow then to make sure.

"Sorry, what?" A hint of the earlier golden glow returned. Now she knew. She could best get his attention by ignoring him.

"Do you have the pocket notebook?"

They made their way to the courthouse in the middle of the common. Though every county seat had a courthouse, she had never been inside one. This was the place where hand-to-hand fights to resolve quarrels gave way to words. Indeed the interior was washed in a serious, brown, and controlled light; the floors were polished almost to dullness. Diligent men in dark coats monitored offices like cells along the corridor. What was hidden behind the doors and perceived only through cracks was likely to leave visitors unsettled for days after the encounter, perhaps more unsettled than a hand-to-hand fight. As they stepped beyond the vestibule, she heard the tap of her heels on the hallway flooring. Was she safe, she wondered, in this place remote and buried to women's lives? For women did not tread here, even after decades of protests. She clutched the newspaper, with Antoinette's journal as a shield, as she went through the lacquered veneer of public space. "What do you think will happen?"

"Hard to say. The big dog gets whatever he wants." Detective Tyler asked her to be seated on a bench in the corridor when he went into one of the cells. Then she watched the door open and close for others, seven in all. She could hear them talking about her. They spoke in murmurs, making the corridor feel calm, but their muffled voices denied access. Luminous landscapes of Kansas prairie hung on the walls, inviting acts of quiet contemplation. Was the prairie meant to be a path to serenity or a reminder of mortality? She wasn't used to doing nothing, in either case. Waiting could have its own use. She felt a pull, like gravity, to the newspaper on the bench beside her. She had a compulsion to know about the monsters and spectacles of Wichita. An article on the imminent sale of the Dominguez Farms to a land syndicate coming at the end of a month-minus-a-day posting for missing heirs first drew her attention. The dates were in alignment with Antoinette's disappearance. But time dragged on, and she found herself reading through the ads … ask for Mrs. Weaver and a telephone number was included for a retirement home. Sophiny checked the number against the address and telephone list Antoinette had collected in her address book and that Sophiny had taken care to copy.

Detective Tyler at last poked his head through the door. "I'll need Miss Dominguez's journal," and beckoned her to follow him to a special hearing room. "We have to convince a skeptical judge that the sale of the Dominguez Farms should not go forward in light of this new evidence." The congress reminded her of the trial against Dr. Frankenstein that the Mount St. Mary's Academy students had performed. Antoinette's untimely disappearance, the recovery of her pocket notebook, the death of Mark Weaver, and the burning of the house in Abilene were all cited. The key figure, Judge Gregory, with a bulbous nose, pursed lips, strong chin, and deep eyes, took command of the room.

"Miss Dominguez's journal," the opposition countered, "that evidence at best can be factually controverted or worse its veracity challenged. Might not this be the insane ravings or even a sort of novel written by the young lady for the thrill of transgression? Haven't we already heard of her propensity for the dramatic?"

Was that their way of saying the journal could be dismissed or lost, just as easily as Antoinette herself? They could make her appear or disappear by their cloud of words? Hadn't such a cloud altered her fate four years ago, causing her and her mother to fall into the hands of Stillman? Hadn't some anonymous judge been the one who lost her in the first place? The greater part of the argument was given over to chronicling the events of the last month. Sophiny's frustration that she had wasted the entire morning traipsing through strangers' opinions of her friend's life was a continuation of the cruelty and injustice Antoinette had already been subjected to. She was about ready to volunteer this opinion when the judge at last turned to her and asked, "Miss Mumm, what have you to say?"

Sophiny knew there was a lot at stake in that question. Would Antoinette again have to give way when the judge imposed his will and hand another win to Stillman? At last, she was asked for her opinion. "Antoinette is of age—eighteen years in Kansas. She would wish to be given full autonomy and be released from the guardianship of Mr. Thomas Stillman, along with her properties and her mother. The court should act on her behalf to find her, restore her rights, and catch her kidnapper."

When the judge left to write his orders, Detective Tyler leaned toward her in his intimate way, "I am hungry. How about you?"

"Mostly angry. What if he does not give her back what is hers?"

"Well, first we have to find her. Do you want to make some telephone calls?" Detective Tyler led the way to connecting offices on the top floor. After making certain that neither office was occupied, he pulled up a chair to the desk in the outer office. "It is good for me that Sister Margaret was thinking about you this morning." He searched through his bag and pulled out biscuits and cheese, cold-boiled eggs, a jar of applesauce, and bottles of sarsaparilla for two. "Let's eat. We will be able to work better."

"Why can't I go out and look for Antoinette?"

"We have men on every lead on the ground. This is an age of wondrous machines. You can do a lot of detective work with the camera, the typewriter, and especially the telephone."

"I do not know anybody here except you," Sophiny chewed on a biscuit and nibbled on the cheese.

Detective Tyler picked up the telephone and dialed the operator. "To whom am I speaking?"

"Lillian," replied the switchboard operator.

"Miss Lillian, this is Detective Tyler. I would like you to meet my assistant, Miss Mumm. She will need your help to follow some leads for an investigation." Detective Tyler handed the receiver to Sophiny. "Now you do."

"Hello, Miss Lillian ..."

"Sophiny, this is important." The detective was edging toward the door, his lunch finished. "I need somebody who can get in there and get the job done. Creativity is the most fantastic tool you have."

Talking to Lillian was a little like talking to Martha. The woman clearly knew what she was about. After a few minutes, Lillian had compiled a list of hospitals and homes for the invalid and the infirm. Lillian made suggestions for the questions she should ask so that the receptionist did not immediately hang up and might even call back with more information.

When Detective Tyler returned with the judge's ruling in hand, Sophiny stood beside him to read for herself: the sale of all Dominguez properties was blocked until the mystery surrounding the death of Mr. Stillman's assistant be resolved (for indeed, Mark Weaver's identity had been verified), and irregularities regarding guardianship of minors and the mentally competent were be investigated. Thomas Stillman faced a formal inquiry over charges that he had drifted away from criteria for guidelines to guardians in his actions regarding the Dominguez family. Furthermore, the judge ordered a letter to be sent out to all area hospitals, sanitariums, and convalescent homes with Mrs. Dominguez's description. As they stood side by side reading the ruling, he put his arm around her shoulders and drew her to his side, curving his body around her protectively. "The most we've been able to achieve is a suspended outcome; Stillman has yet to comment, as has the syndicate. You okay here?"

Beloved, she wanted to say aloud, not knowing how or why the word had sprung to her lips. Instead she nodded. *Bumpkin.*

"I have to see what's been done about that train robber, what your brothers have been up to, and where Stillman has been hiding out." He seemed reluctant to release her, and when he did, Sophiny realized she had stopped breathing.

"What about Abilene? What about Concord?"

"This case just keeps growing, doesn't it? Somebody will have to inform that young man's mother."

Sophiny had things to worry about too. Would she recognize the Stillman of Antoinette's photograph? He, of course, should have been fitted out with a face that caused children to scream with fright and horses to break their halters and run away when they saw him coming. And sooner or later he would have to show himself.

In the first telephone call, she gave Detective Tyler's name as the contact person. Then she decided the detective would be the last person Stillman would speak to if he had hidden Mrs. Dominguez's identity, as Antoinette suspected. *What association would bring Stillman to reveal Mrs. Dominguez's hiding place or his?* If she did manage to draw him out, how would she know for certain which call had produced the desired results and so locate Antoinette's mother? Also, how could she send a message to Antoinette?

Sophiny sat, closed her eyes, and focused her attention on her body. She began to picture a tangle of tiny roots coming out of the palm of her hand, from her arm, from her shoulder, from the base of her brain. She felt them growing and growing, extending through the telephone receiver and along the cord into the instrument workings … beyond the building from one telephone pole outside the window to the next along the wires all the way up the lines into the air above her. On the next inhalation, she imagined all the energy of the heavens flowing through the top of her head, coursing through her entire being, coursing through the telephone lines to search for Antoinette, unfurling the folds in the road to reveal the silhouette man in his silhouette conveyance. Slowly, slowly in her own time, she felt her heartbeat and listened to all the sounds around her; then she opened her eyes.

The journey wasn't so unlike going down the corridors and stairways of Mount St. Mary's radiating out from the chapel or up and down the hills of a stretch of road. She just had to find the right door using this new conveyance. Moreover, the courthouse itself was a veritable three-story mound of Wichita progress. Busy and industrious creatures inhabited its tunnels, who, though they regarded themselves superior, were after all here to earn their livelihoods and protect their territory just as any self-respecting prairie dog. One door led to another room with another escape. If the court could not be used to bring justice for Antoinette, perhaps she could use the building's warren of tunnels to trap him. What would St. Anthony do? The miracle was not the opportunity she had missed for the past two months but the opportunity she had now. She lifted the earpiece from the candlestick style telephone and dialed zero. "Howdy." Time for the queen of the Wheat Kingdom to prove herself. "Lillian, I am going to identify myself as a different person for every contact on your list to make sure we can locate an institution if no name is given on a return call. I want you to have my list for confirmation and please listen in if someone does call back. Do you have a pencil?"

At least the telephone hid her youth and inexperience. First on her list was Marywood Abbey, operated by a sister branch of the Mount St. Mary's religious order. Her speech was ready when she heard the voice on the other end of the line.

My name is Mary Clare Decatur. I am calling on behalf of Mrs. Antonio Dominguez, a patient who may have been admitted under a false name and false pretenses. Her guardian and lawyer's name is Thomas Stillman from Concord. As of today, Judge Gregory has ruled that Mr. Stillman no longer has guardianship over her or her daughter and claims otherwise constitute fraud. Mr. Stillman himself is under investigation for forgery, theft, and murder. If you knowingly assist him, you are guilty of being an accessory. Mrs. Dominguez's life may be in danger. You will be receiving a letter to that effect from Judge Gregory's office in the mail within the week. Thank you for your cooperation. Please ask for Mary Clare Decatur.

Here she gave the courthouse address and telephone number Lillian had given her.

In between telephone calls, Sophiny looked at the room. She paced the oiled wooden planks. She looked out the two narrow windows onto the driveway of the courthouse where agents were collecting. *Will he make a move? Stillman. Can I bargain with him? Doubtful.* As she stood by the desk, fingertips resting on the phone receiver, her eyes traveled over every surface. The room waited. *There might be violence.* What choice of weapons did she have? There was the desk, a pen, Antoinette's reticule and its contents, two chairs, a hatpin, a desk clock framed in polished stone and matching ashtray, her roll of string, an umbrella stand with one umbrella inside, and a coat rack, and she had Lillian. What unexpected gestures could she make with each? And if there was going to be a big gesture, she wanted to have things ready … like a stage set for a trap. For in spite of all her friend's preparations, Antoinette had not been ready. Now a month had passed since she had bravely taken her stand. That was a long time to leave a being in limbo. Stagnation was death. Sophiny knew she herself was enthusiastic but not very skillful, and her best defense for cleaning up rubbish had always been sunlight and disinfectant.

A great *whump*, the sound of the door flying open, caused Sophiny to send her plan into action. Letting the receiver dangle off the desk, she quickly dialed *zero*. Then, for Lillian's benefit, she announced loudly to her visitor, "May I be of assistance?"

"I'm looking for Miss Theora Graney who called from this location."

Sophiny allowed a confirming nod.

"Ah … I have found you."

She swallowed, finding her throat sticky and dry but trying to keep panic out of her voice. Her disguise did give some protection. "Did you find me? I could say I found you."

His eyebrows swept together in a storm cloud over his face. "Why, of course you did." He smiled, his mouth devoid of humor. Sophiny forced herself not to recoil in alarm. There was no one to intervene, no one to keep madness at bay, no one to bring a halt to his advance. Antoinette's pocket notebook entries of privation: dark rooms, locked doors, shuttered/barred windows strengthening his paralyzing effects came like a blow to her stomach. He was a dangerous man, full of violence, charm, greed, grandiosity, obsession, and deception.

"And you are?" She tried to make her face look disinterested.

He moved toward the desk. "Mark Weaver, an associate of Thomas Stillman." Seating himself in the chair she had placed on the opposite side the desk, he reached into his coat pocket, drawing out a long cigar and lighting it from a large flame that came from a small metal case.

Sophiny digested this piece of misinformation. Whom did he think he was impersonating? The shadowy figure of Stillman had at last stepped out of the shadows. Appalled fascination coursed through her as she studied the man who had plundered her friend of family and inheritance. He appeared tall, handsome, and fit; obviously, he cared how he looked.

"I must speak with Antoinette Dominguez immediately. Time is of the essence. You need to tell me where I can find her."

"You understand, Mr. Weaver, we must respect the wishes of clients. I am sure you can appreciate that." Sophiny lifted her head, raised her voice, and tried to look like the clerk she had talked to in Mr. Stillman's own office. "I do not have that information to give you."

"I have critical information about her mother."

"Perhaps Judge Gregory would be available to speak with you." She rose as though to lead the way into the inner office.

"Sit … down," he commanded as though she were an animal he could root to the spot, paralyzed by the inevitable, rendered helpless in the face of menace. He took a long inhale from his cigar. The embers burned red, and smoke drifted across the desk, irritating her nose.

Pretending not to understand as the urge to be stronger than her opponent swept over her, she took up her pen. "That's fine, you can give me that information. I will pass it on."

"I will only communicate with Miss Dominguez." He looked at her with restrained distaste, waving the cigar.

Sophiny knew she must delay the moment to give Lillian time to react, but at least she knew Mr. Stillman did not have custody of Antoinette's person, and she now knew which location had brought him to her. She had all she needed. "You are lying again, aren't you, Mr. Stillman? You didn't come to give information, you came to get information."

"What would that be?" He registered no surprise at her use of his name.

Sophiny let her eyes drift to Antoinette's reticule in the far corner of the room and noted that his eyes followed hers. She used the distraction to remove the hatpin from the cuff of her left sleeve.

"Did you come from the same school as Antoinette, Mount St. Mary's?"

Sophiny did not respond. Though Thomas Stillman continued to look at her, she could tell he wasn't really seeing her but the dress he had purchased for Antoinette. She was glad she had taken the time to change.

"About now I would expect that you are asking God to send in an angel to rescue you."

Sophiny's immediate thought was that she would like to have a word with St. Anthony because the answers he had sent about Antoinette's disappearance so far had not been so great, but she replied, "Yes … while I don't pour them their own cup of coffee at the breakfast table, I do speak to the saints and angels and ask for their help when I feel overpowered."

"Is anyone listening?" After another deep pull on his cigar, he placed it in the polished stone tray, allowing the smoke to create a veil between them.

She forced herself not to blink. "Mr. Stillman, I think you should go home and call your lawyer. Judgment is possible at any moment." Her right hand of its own accord moved to the stone clock on the desk.

The speed of his strike on her arm was worthy of any rattlesnake. Now was the moment to recoil. With Martha's hatpin, she stabbed the hand that held her, then wrenched away from his grip while she picked up the rock to heave toward the narrow window overlooking the courthouse driveway. The crash of broken glass let her know that her aim had been accurate. Then she sprinted through the door at her back while Stillman was still blocked by the desk. This movement pulled the string tied to open the umbrella and topple the coat rack. She quickly secured the lock on the inside door and sped to the window of the inner room to see a gathering crowd below pointing upward, Detective Tyler among them. *Sunshine.* She heard with even greater satisfaction a string of curses telling her that Mr. Stillman had picked up Antoinette's reticule in his own hurry to get away, upsetting the open bottle of absinthe with its 70 percent alcohol content. A thud let her know the bottle had fallen through the opening where she had loosened stitches in the bottom.

Disinfectant. Then something she didn't expect, cries of terror and the smell of smoke, followed by a great clattering.

Even before she heard the knock, something started swelling or lightening in her chest and began to soar. The weight of fear had lifted. It was a coherent world, everything fitting at last. "Sophiny, you okay in there?" She knew from the commotion that the sounds had brought others running.

The danger seemed to have passed. Recognizing Tyler's voice, she knew it was safe to open the door. Unmistakable pinpricks of tears threatened her eyes as the empty space before her became filled by his form. She could imagine no greater joy than his sudden apparition in the doorway.

"What did you do to Stillman? He just took off running like a scalded dog, but we got him on the stairs. How did this fire get started?"

She looked around, realizing that the embers of Stillman's cigar had somehow come in contact with the spilled alcohol. The falling coat rack or the opening umbrella must have knocked the ashtray onto the floor, igniting the spilled absinthe. "What did *you* do to him?"

"He is out cold for now and under guard, but as soon as he comes to, we'll arrest him. He will be explaining himself to the judge."

"I know where Mrs. Dominguez is," Sophiny whispered. The telephone call with Theora's name had been the Dominguez Farms number listed in Antoinette's pocket notebook as well as in the ad under Mrs. Weaver's name from the newspaper. Was she on the Dominguez Farms?

Chapter 20
Abuse of Bromides and Legal Instruments

"Good heavens, what's been going on here?" A young woman with a halo of blonde curls appeared in the doorway. Red blotches emerged on her cheeks from running up the stairs, and her eyes darted. "Miss Sophiny Mumm?"

"Yes." Sophiny turned and was pulled into a fierce embrace while the blonde curls tickled her nose.

"I'm Lillian. Good work! But there's more. *Mary Clare Decatur* has a phone call." After her introduction, Lillian went immediately to the telephone on the desk and replaced the receiver. The telephone bell rang as soon as she did so. Then she grinned with satisfaction at her own role in Stillman's successful capture. "I've got to get back to the switchboard." She swept out of the room.

Through the doorway Sophiny saw her pass Stillman on the floor at the bottom of the landing, hands bound behind his back. She thought how his teeth looked like a dog's teeth, bared. Two officers were barking orders. She was glad Detective Tyler was shielding her from all the dogs that wanted a fight but sad that Antoinette had not had the same protection.

Sophiny turned her attention to the telephone. "Hello, this is Mary Clare," she said into the receiver.

"Is the *missionary* there?" asked the voice on the other end.

"Yes," though recognizing their code word, Sophiny kept her tone matter-of-fact. "The missionary is here."

"Sophiny?"

"Antoinette? Mr. Stillman is in police custody. Where are you?" Sophiny asked, buoyed by triumph, for she already knew the answer. Antoinette had somehow made it to the security of Marywood Abbey. Antoinette's answer confirmed her insight. In hand signals, she communicated her very great find to Detective Tyler. "Stay where you are. A detective and I will come for you."

"Is Mary Clare all right?"

"Yes, she's fine." Sophiny realized what Antoinette must be thinking. "There was never an influenza epidemic at the academy."

The images of that day played and replayed for hours, but the moments of their taking place went by in a whirl. Everyone was doing several jobs at once. Sophiny had plenty to keep her occupied. While Detective Tyler made arrangements for transportation, for Stillman's custody, and for the collection of evidence, Sophiny informed Lillian of the shift in the case and gave instructions for return calls. At last, Detective Tyler nodded in her direction, and she followed him out the door and down the stairs. A few minutes later the automobile pulled up in front of Marywood Abbey. The streets were quiet. The two of them headed through a cloister to the front entrance of the Abbey. *And there she is.* "What was lost was meant to be found. Thank you, St. Anthony," Sophiny breathed.

Though Antoinette's face in the window appeared thin and haunted, she knew she wasn't seeing a ghost: better than finding the nest of golden eggs, the lamp with the three wishes, the hope left in Pandora's box all rolled into one. One of the sisters, unwilling to let her go out alone, answered the door and protectively blocked the way, with her hands outspread on the door frame. Detective Tyler spoke. The sister spoke. Sophiny could not understand a word they were saying. It was prattle to her. Pounding blood had so filled her brain that no word entered. She could see Antoinette in the background taking deep breaths until something seemed to shift inside her. The young women examined each other in silence, two members of a secret sorority who had just exchanged sign and countersign.

"Don't fall. Don't fall. Don't fall before you're pushed." Sophiny bounced a little on the balls of her feet.

"What does that mean?" asked Detective Tyler, ready to support her if she grew unsteady.

Sophiny didn't realize she had spoken aloud. "I don't know what it means exactly. My mother used to say it. And it's something I say to avoid saying anything really, for fear of saying the wrong thing, I suppose." Though she felt unsteady, she decided to do it before she did anything else. Facing the hard thing first might make it easier. "I had to break my promises." She tucked a tendril of hair behind her ear and pretended she wasn't suddenly nervous, intimidated, shy. Before she lost her nerve, she continued hurriedly, "But not, you know …"

Then, moving through the guard in the doorway, Antoinette signaled with the wave of a hand, as if Sophiny had just passed her initiation test and her invitation to pass through an invisible barrier accepted. A light like life itself began to fill her eyes as clearly as a candle being lit. "My stitch saver," she said to Sophiny and to Detective Tyler. "I wish you had taught us how to pick a lock."

Holy cow. Not what Sophiny expected as the first words out of her mouth.

"Antoinette, this is Detective Tyler, a private investigator. He was on a mission of another kind from what we thought."

"Who hired you? How much were you paid?" demanded Antoinette.

"It is here," Detective Tyler said, holding out a manila folder containing the judge's written decision annulling Mr. Stillman's guardianship rights. "I hope we can set your mind at ease."

Antoinette stared at the folder. She did not move her hand. "Tell me what it says." As she listened to Detective Tyler's explanation, Antoinette seemed to notice Sophiny wearing her dress.

"I trust Sophiny's instincts, but if you have any connection to Stillman, Detective, I have nothing to say to you."

"I will give everything that I have to this case and your protection. Stillman is in custody, where he belongs," Detective Tyler reassured her.

Antoinette paused as though to register the smell of dusk, the shelter of elms falling over their heads and shoulders, the endless hum of crickets in the background. When she spoke, her voice hesitated slightly. "Let's talk no more of Stillman." Then carefully controlled, she asked, "Where is my mother?"

Sophiny had almost forgotten how direct Antoinette could be. "From the location of the telephone call, we think she might be at your farms."

Detective Tyler was at the ready to lay out his plan that Sophiny and Antoinette should wait in the safety of Marywood Abbey until the perimeter of the farms had been secured and the interior searched by his men, to which Antoinette frowned. Resolve showed in the lift of her chin. "I have more experience than anyone of how this thief has kept in charge of his prey through abuse of bromides and legal instruments. I go!"

"If her mother is found, Antoinette should be there. And if we don't find her—Antoinette's come too far to miss any more of her life." Sophiny aligned herself with her friend.

"Let's go then." Detective Tyler turned and headed in the direction of the automobile.

Antoinette was introspective for the few miles to the Dominguez Farms. She openly rested her forehead on the glass, looking at the trees and rooftops that seemed to be flying alongside in a race. Every motorcar or buggy that passed, every tree along the road, every building was a message, a landmark, a mystery of the life that had gone on without her. Sophiny clasped her friend's hand, giving it a reassuring squeeze.

In front of the farmhouse, some kind of commotion was going on with arrivals and departures of vehicles and clusters of people as though in readiness for a rummage sale. Then Antoinette spotted the sign advertising an auction of farm implements and household items. A barrier was hastily being constructed to prevent direct entry to the house. A policeman in uniform was making attempts to clear people away. Detective Tyler slowed the automobile to determine his approach. The path to the veranda was lined with more than a year's worth of weeds, Sophiny judged by the dry seedpods and brambles. The front grounds were completely wild. Vegetation had taken over, climbing up benches and under the veranda, over a fountain with cracked tiles, over a broken statue on its side. Everything seemed covered over with sadness. Antoinette, staring at the neglected garden, looked incredibly defenseless and seemed to be contemplating the irony of stealing, like a thief, into her own home. She pointed at the house and said, "That's mine."

"This must have been a beautiful house," whispered Sophiny.

"It was before the barbarians began the looting and pillaging ... the raiding and the scalping," retorted Antoinette, remembering their early encounter with Brother Claude. He looked at her through the rearview mirror as though remembering as well. Impatiently she opened the door when the automobile came to a stop. But as she unfolded her body and tried to stand, she seemed to lose balance and clutched the door for support.

"Miss Dominguez, perhaps you'd better stay here."

She shook her head and gave a back-off-now-mister stare as Detective Tyler and Sophiny came to her assistance from either side.

At the sound of a discreet cough, the three turned as one to find Detective Smith. His eyes went first to Antoinette then to Detective Tyler. "I think we found something,"

"Smithy." Detective Tyler nodded in greeting.

"Tyler, I need to confer with you on an urgent matter." He indicated his partner should follow him.

"We have found *someone* too. Miss Antoinette Dominguez, Detective Smith. Does the matter concern her?"

Detective Smith started, "Yes it does. The Weaver woman has been taken in for questioning. After we told her what had happened to her son, she gave up Mrs. Dominguez's location—a retirement home operated in a couple of the Dominguez warehouses. She *was* being treated under another name, 'for her own privacy,' according to Weaver. It's not far from the boundaries of the farms but still outside the city limits. The building is unmarked."

Detective Tyler shook his head. "How could we stare right at something and not see what lies beneath the surface?" As the conversation continued, bystanders began to take notice of their arrival.

"I would say we should get out of here before we have that crowd following us," Smithy suggested.

"Get in. I'll drive. You can tell me where, though I think I know," ordered Tyler as Smithy slid into the passenger seat, and Sophiny and Antoinette followed into the backseat.

The traffic coming and going to the farm machinery hall continued, even though the hour was getting late. Sophiny saw the outsized sign over the largest of the warehouse buildings and instinctively looked for her brothers in the surroundings. Several visitors seemed intent on spending the night in automobiles and wagons near their machinery purchases. There were no signs on the other warehouse buildings but other clues gave away its existence. The retirement home was at the far end of a row of red brick warehouses. In fact, it looked like two warehouses had been connected by a third to form a U-shaped compound inside a gated brick wall. Only with some difficulty were they allowed access inside the iron gate. The detectives showed badges and cited their credentials. A young man who said he was the night clerk then escorted the foursome to the entrance at the center of the U. Antoinette and Sophiny pointed out to each other the walls, the barred windows, the steel doors.

"What have they done to this place?" asked Antoinette, overlooking the work of her father's ransacking minions. A modernized entry with a solid oak counter, oak desks, and metal filing cabinets had been installed to give the appearance of preserving vital records, proofs of identity. Seven minutes before seven in the fading light of a long day, they solved the mystery of Mrs. Dominguez's whereabouts.

"Our clients are private and pay for our discretion," objected the somewhat large woman behind the desk as though they were breaking a strict code of etiquette.

"Which is precisely the amount that goes into your own pocket. Isn't there a word for that? It begins with S ..." Smithy placed a hand on the gun in his holster.

"It is nothing like stealing." She gave him a flat stare acknowledging the euphemism.

"I have an order from Judge Gregory in my hand that Mrs. Dominguez or whatever you call her is to be released immediately." Detective Tyler's voice was low and measured, authoritative.

But still the woman would not give way. "Her lawyer has power of attorney and insists that she is to be medicated. Without the medication, she becomes agitated, irrational, resistant—dangerous even."

"Her lawyer is in jail, where you soon will be if you don't tell us immediately what you have done with her."

"Room three," said the woman at last.

"A hurt dog barks," said Tyler, signaling to Smithy to stay with the woman at the desk. She had risen as though to flee. "See that she doesn't go anyplace." Antoinette was already around the corner, with Sophiny close behind. The original warehouse buildings had been converted into several bedroom cells leading off a central hallway.

The trap. The smell in the air of antiseptic, urine, and old-building musk was vaguely sweet. Antoinette stared at the woman sitting in a corner, hunched over herself ... not looking at her ... not looking at any of her visitors, rocking slightly, her hands in fists.

"Hello." Antoinette knelt before her.

Hair tangled, hanging in her face, swallowed up by an ill-fitting white gown, her hands fluttered around her body, her torso twisted in her distress, she blinked. Her keepers had slipped her behind a white fog: As though the woman was meant to fade into the white bedding, surrounded by white walls, white curtains, and white lights, too confused even to respond to her visitor's hello except that her eyes looked like bruises. Faded too, apparently, were the daily rituals of dressing, eating, and speaking to companions.

"Do you know where you are?" Antoinette spoke.

The attendant in the room snapped, "She doesn't respond."

"Get out!" Antoinette whispered. Her voice had force without volume. He went. Her rage at her mother's great change was evident. "Look what he's done to her. He has made her an older, thinner, smaller shadow of herself, and he has taken the shine out of her beautiful brown eyes and hair." Antoinette, her voice barely above a whisper, gently reached out. "Give me your hands, Mother."

At first she shook her head, not ready. She stayed rocking for a moment and then slowly uncurled them from her body and extended first one hand and then the other. Antoinette touched the ends of her fingers.

"What do I do now?" Her voice shook as she asked the question, but she had heard and understood.

"Put on your shoes." Antoinette had spotted a pair under the bed.

"Okay," she allowed. Her whole body was shaking by this time so that she could not perform the task but gave herself over to the care of the daughter she didn't recognize as her daughter. Let it come to her in fits and starts, bits and pieces, snips and snatches from wherever she had hidden it.

Detective Tyler closed the door quietly, leaving them alone. "Do you think you could find your brothers over at the machinery hall? We need to get someone to guard this place. I don't think you are in any danger, but be careful. Don't talk to anybody. There are some strange characters wandering around ..."

As if she needed reminding ... Sophiny did not wait for him to finish, and he was still giving instructions as she turned and sped. She did not have far to go. Henry was riding a brand-new bicycle past the retirement home. Andrew was standing some distance away watching. She was overjoyed to see them both.

The doctor's opinion, when one was called in to evaluate Mrs. Dominguez's condition, "She will need constant supervision at least for a time because of her immobility, which may improve. Her difficulty in walking stems from general weakness and dizziness and confusion, but also one of her legs is packing up from some kind of injury it looks like. With proper medication and nutrition, strength exercises, and loving care … well, we'll see … It could make all the difference. She's nowhere near death's door. There are complaints of impaired vision, which means she's having trouble reading. She'll have to undergo further examination to see what is going on. She is dehydrated and overmedicated. Now, Miss Dominguez, what do you plan to do about her situation?"

"If her mind's all right, she's capable of making her own decisions."

"I am afraid we cannot determine that for now."

"Well then, we are both going home tonight."

A plan soon formed: Detective Tyler and Sophiny would accompany Antoinette and her mother by automobile to the Dominguez farmhouse to tend her there. She did not make a fuss, nor did the two staff members. Antoinette wrapped her tight as a mummy in a blanket, and Detective Tyler put her gently into the automobile. She seemed to crumble when the outside air hit her and became winded by the slightest movement. "You are safe now, Mama. I will look after you." Antoinette spoke to her like she was a child, saying anything to keep her from reconnecting with her fear until she ran out of things to say. When they arrived at the house, she bathed her and rubbed her skin with a lavender-scented lotion, noting that her mother's weight had dropped so precipitously that her bones lacked cushioning, yet another reminder of the carnage of her life.

Sophiny made some tea and found a tin of hard biscuits in the kitchen. First Antoinette dunked the biscuit in the tea and then put it to her mother's lips. She took it in and chewed slowly, coughing slightly. Antoinette waited until she swallowed and then fed her some more, along with a sip of tea. Little by little, bite-by-bite, sip-by-sip, a change came over her, though she remained in a kind of stupor. Then Antoinette read to her from *The Wizard of Oz*, probably the very book that her parents had read to her. Sophiny sat with them until Antoinette climbed into her mother's bed and lay down by her side. When she put her arm over her, her mother curled in like a child. Antoinette wrapped herself around her mother until Sophiny heard them breathing evenly in and out. Then she left the room and closed the door.

Detective Tyler was on the telephone in the parlor looking out the front window as he spoke. When he heard her come into the room, he asked with concern in his voice, "Everything okay upstairs?"

Sophiny nodded and felt her body go slack as she sank into the sofa. "They are both sleeping," she reported.

"And that is what we need to do right now. I have somebody on watch here. Your brothers and Smithy are taking shifts keeping an eye on the retirement home. Just one other thing … you want to tell me what promises you broke?"

"I opened Antoinette's trunk and looked at her stuff—the pocket notebooks." She yawned, suddenly overcome with fatigue.

"And …?" He leaned in close in the intimate way he had.

"I cannot tell you about that." Sophiny thought that this would be a good time for him to argue with her. She might even tell. The next thing she knew, she had leaned against him and closed her eyes for a moment … and made a mental note to chide herself for it later.

She did not know how much later she woke in darkness. A cry that sounded like terror came from upstairs. Sophiny bolted upright, comforted that Detective Tyler had been asleep beside her. Upstairs in the early dawn light, they saw that Mrs. Dominguez had sat up, worrying the hem of the sheet in her hands, gazing around the room, as though hungry for details. Antoinette called to her softly, "Mother."

She seemed to know her daughter right away. "Antoinette, I am home."

"So am I," Antoinette answered. "So am I." The fog lifted as mother and daughter embraced and reaction settled in. Mrs. Dominguez began shaking uncontrollably. Antoinette held her and began to tremble as well, but she was smiling even as the tears slipped down her face.

"What happened to us?" Mrs. Dominguez asked.

Antoinette, as though remembering how difficult had been the journey of her recovery, did not appear to want to embark too soon on those terrors and simply said, "We were robbed, Mother, of each other and Father. But we don't have to keep digging. It's enough that we are together again."

The sight burned its impression into the depths of Sophiny's memory at the backs of her eyeballs so that she could see it when she blinked against the tears. Tyler beside her took her hand and led her back downstairs. "I think they are going to be fine. Can you go back to sleep? I have to check on some things." And he was gone.

Chapter 21
Dreams of Heaven

"It's like I went to sleep ... In my sleep I dreamed I went to heaven and saw my mother, and when I woke up she was here with me." Antoinette answered Sophiny's question about how she was after Mrs. Dominguez drifted off again. Then she patted the top step next to her within view of her mother's open bedroom door. The two girls sat with their heads on each other's shoulders, sipping the tea that Sophiny had made. Antoinette began slowly to tell what had happened in Abilene after her final pocket notebook entry, stopping for sips of tea. She had written about the incident while listening to the commotion below. Then, in a moment of desperation, she had taken Sophiny's trunk key and put it in the lock, turning it this way and that, with no success. Finally she had used the key to pry away the inch of wood molding stopping the door, to reveal a gap between the door and the doorframe. The key just fit, and as she pushed against the lock, the lock suddenly released and the door swung open. Antoinette, set down her teacup, sort of covered her face, rubbed her forehead, and continued as best she could.

"I simply ran like an animal, knowing predators stalked the night. At the end of the street I stopped before the front of the church. Everything was dark. I looked up and down, and no one was in sight. It must have been close to midnight. The doors were unlocked, so I went in and hid myself in a garment closet in the sacristy behind long white robes. That's where one of the sisters found me the next morning when she came to set out the vestments for mass. Somehow she knew that I needed her. I had to trust someone, so I told her a story about running away from my abusive husband who had imprisoned me and asked if she could help me get back to my parents in Wichita; they would compensate her for her generosity. I must have looked a sight, for she noted my appearance and the disarray of my clothing. She said she needed to make a trip to Wichita herself. Sometime later when I was clean and shiny, draped in a borrowed black robe, and fed scrambled eggs and toast with the most delicious apricot preserves, the plan came together. She had gotten permission to lend me her second habit so I could go to Wichita as her companion. The sisters must travel in pairs. No one paid much attention to us on the train.

"When we got to Wichita, the sisters were talking about the Dominguez Farms sale and the missing heirs, and hadn't a Sister Louise from Mount St. Mary's been calling about Mrs. Dominguez? I must confess that I was in a state of panic. I didn't know where Stillman was or what had happened to my mother. I telephoned Sister Louise just this morning before you called Marywood Abbey and pretended to be from your family asking for you. She told me that your mother had died, and you were no longer at the academy. But when she asked, 'Antoinette, is that you?' I couldn't say anything until she said, 'Do you need a missionary?' I knew then something else must have happened. She told me about the detectives searching for me, about you leaving, about the trunk room break-in, about your return to involve the academy students in a rally, about the documents you had put in the safe, about you going to Abilene, about finding Mark's body. So when someone named Mary Clare called, I was informed immediately. Sister Louise is coming by train this afternoon. I told her to bring the documents."

"Antoinette," her mother spoke from the darkened bedroom. Then Antoinette broke off and focused her attention entirely on her mother. Sophiny went to the kitchen to make more tea and to look for something the Weaver woman might have left for breakfast. By now it was light outside, and people were gathering. The doctor arrived to check on Mrs. Dominguez just as the teapot was boiling. Through the open door, she saw that though people were gathering for the auction, they were just as quickly being turned away. Was that Andrew and Henry directing traffic? A paperboy on a bicycle flung a newspaper onto the front porch and looked at her strangely. She was hungry for news, as she knew Antoinette would be. One look at the headlines announced what was happening outside, "Land Syndicate Takeover Is Off." *Flapjacks.* She could make flapjacks for everyone, and there was plenty of bacon and eggs, as though Mrs. Weaver was getting ready for guests. So busy was she that she did not notice that Detective Tyler had come into the kitchen. "And she cooks too."

"What is happening out there, Detective?"

"Nothing as important as what's happening in here." He grinned. "Need some help?"

"Can you make coffee?" asked Sophiny, rethinking the tea.

"I think you could call me Tyler after what happened last night."

At that moment, Antoinette appeared. "I'll set the table. We'll have a party for our homecoming. How many pancakes can you make?"

"As many as you need."

"What happened last night?"

"Nothing!" they said together. Tyler winked at Sophiny, making her smile in return.

The party grew, as did the stories they all had to tell. Once the food was before them, they all seemed to discover how ravenous they were. With all the diplomacy she could muster, Sophiny tried to reconstruct something of her encounter with Stillman the previous afternoon that would bring consolation to the ward he had so cruelly held against her will, robbing her of love and legacy.

"For a month, all I could think of was, if I die locked up in that room, I sure wasted a lot of time worrying about getting a summer job." Antoinette trailed a bite of egg around her plate with her fork. She hadn't eaten much.

"Speaking of which, the big dog just tossed me into the can—looks like I am out of a job," announced Detective Tyler.

"I don't understand."

"Since the takeover is off, the land syndicate says they have no further need of my services."

Sophiny thought maybe they could be friends living on the street together; she didn't have a job either.

"How did you find out?"

"I read about it in the papers, just like everyone else."

"Would you work for me?" Antoinette asked.

"I believe I would strongly consider it."

"Give me your gun," Antoinette demanded.

Without questioning her, he handed it over and then followed as she rose from the table and set off outside with purpose. Her intention soon became clear, as all at the table were not to be left behind. Antoinette took aim, announcing, "I need a new sign." The gun exploded, and the sign promoting the land syndicate crumpled.

She looked directly at Andrew. "I need a new foreman too. Interested?"

Andrew nodded.

Still pointing the gun at the sign, she said to Andrew, "Replacing this will be your first task. Your second task will be to tell any of Stillman's or Weaver's hires that they are fired and escort them from the premises." She took the gun by the cylinder, handing it back to Detective Tyler, handle toward his hand. "Thank you for the gun. How do I go about getting you hired?"

Detective Tyler turned to her. "We have a lot of complications to sort out. Now tell me everything."

Antoinette nodded and led the way to her father's former study. "Sophiny, Andrew, you need to be in on this too."

"I guess that leaves me to do the dishes," Henry complained.

Sophiny wondered at his uncharacteristic generosity until she saw that Antoinette had rewarded him with a smile. "Would you?"

"How else am I going to find out the ending to this stem winder?"

Sophiny was relieved that at last they were having a conversation about the Dominguez documents. Full disclosure would have to wait until Sister Louise's arrival. About Antoinette's kidnapping and escape, she had difficulty remembering things that happened days and weeks before, people's names, the daily routine of living, but she was well on her way to accomplishing what she had set out to do, and that was all that mattered. It was her way of emerging from the nightmare. The journey was like breaking the spell of a dark enchantment until the past months receded like another world, like the nightmare it was.

The talk and the explanations went on for a while, until it seemed they had talked themselves out and silence fell, but it was a pleasant silence. They all knew that Antoinette would encounter a difficult task, which was that of confronting the events of March and April and committing them to court documents. For that she needed Detective Tyler's help to gather evidence, Sophiny's support in many categories, and now Andrew's assistance in unraveling the operations of the Dominguez Farms. But after the legal process was over … They agreed to think about that stage when they got to it. "In the meantime, shouldn't there be a meeting to let everyone know what is happening?" Sophiny asked, thinking of the chat in the judge's chamber to stop the syndicate takeover. Her question was left up in the air as other threads developed.

"As for Stillman … to ask what motivates a man like Stillman is to ask why you put on a jacket when it snows or eat supper when you get hungry. When he wants something, he takes it. There is no way to justify or understand what he has done. He is just plain evil," reflected Antoinette.

"It's best just to take the curs away and lock them up where they can't do any more damage. They are another species." Detective Tyler nodded in agreement. "But it does makes you wonder … if you were able to unravel the mystery of his murderous mind, would you then be capable of committing his actions as well? Perhaps some gaps in understanding are better left unfilled. There is a place where doubt stops or all is lost."

When they finished, Antoinette set out to arrange one of the rooms downstairs as a sort of recovery room, with pillows and quilts, photographs, and flowers where her mother could lie all day in the warmest part of the house. Whoever was about could take a turn reading to her, talking to her, encouraging her to eat something, or to move about. But her mother, who was restless, not much given to chatter, and still fatigued by the ordeal she had been through, frequently drifted off to sleep. She did, however, take an immense interest in her clothes as the least threatening of all the changes that had gone on around her. And so Antoinette scheduled a shopping trip for her mother.

Detective Tyler pulled Sophiny aside. "You are right about the chat. Are you up to making more telephone calls? Let's get this town's top dogs involved and introduce Antoinette properly. No sense in us camping out at the sheriff's department demanding answers or in Miss Dominguez getting jerked around like she's the one on a leash. Let's see who has what pieces of the puzzle and swing as many as we can around to her side."

Sophiny's flapjacks had accomplished what she intended. "Just tell me when, who, and what do I say."

"How about meeting here in a couple of days? Call the mayor, the city attorney, the sheriff's department, and who is the head of the new police department? See if that judge will come and anyone else you and Lillian think should be here. Tell them Mrs. Dominguez is unable to come to them. She may not have been Stillman's only victim. They can have a tour of the retirement home if they like. Stemming crime is in their best interest, and enhancing their reputations might come as a bonus."

"How about newspaper reporters?"

"No reporters. Let city officials take care of statements to the newspaper. Miss Dominguez has a trial to go through. That way, city officials won't get all political. Oh, and tell them there will be coffee. It is no substitute for the Dominguez bone they were all planning to gnaw on, but at least it is something."

Over the next couple of days, Sophiny and Lillian had several telephone conversations about the meeting. To the requests from reporters for interviews with Mrs. and Miss Dominguez, Sophiny replied, "Not at this time." Martha arrived with news from Abilene. Mark Weaver's body had been placed on the same train, so she witnessed the transfer. Sophiny was sure she had gotten in a few photographs of better quality than their night visit to the ice cellar as well. Late in the day, Sister Louise came carrying a black leather bag with a split handle and single clasp. Antoinette turned to the leather bag and pressed the clasp, opening it with a snap. From the inside she removed and weighted the packet with her hands. Then she carefully untied the string that bound the documents. Sophiny wondered at their power, the temptation and desire they had inspired. "Are you ready to talk to Judge Gregory?" Detective Tyler asked Antoinette, knowing that this was his area of expertise. "There may still be dangers attached to those papers."

When Frank Canon of the *Concord Chronicle* made a request, Sophiny carefully wrote down his telephone number and interrupted Antoinette. It

Barbara Mueller

was his arrival that caused Antoinette to put down her papers and hurry from her mother's side. Upon their meeting, they simply stared at each other with wonder, each as if not quite sure the other was the same person. Everything else could wait, Sophiny thought. Some things are vastly more important ...

Chapter 22
Variations of the Unraveling

"Yesterday's news." Frank Canon insisted they all call him Frank as he filled them in on the talk around Concord. "It is increasingly likely that the law firm of Stillman, Inc., most recently Stillman Enterprises, will close its door."

He passed around copies of his own and other newspapers' articles, which mainly focused on who was most damaged by Stillman's criminal activity. The first, admittedly earnest answer was Concord. The muddle over Stillman's far-reaching activities would continue for some time. The second party most damaged by Stillman was the mayor, whose public prestige and reputation had been associated with Stillman's ability to make departments work. A man can be brought low merely by association. Frank Canon, who seemed to have eyes only for Antoinette, offered variations of the unraveling. "It is important that you are aware of what is happening and what is being said out there in spite of what you have been through." He began to read his own article.

No Easy Clean-up in Concord
At the center of the scandal is a haunting, painful question:
If the mounting allegations—including fraud, forgery, filing
false documents, theft, and even murder—against Thomas
Stillman are true, how did his activities go unnoticed and
his deeds unpunished for so long? County sheriff department
agents raided the law office of Thomas Stillman in Concord,
carting away boxes of documents as part of an investigation into
whether its executive knowingly misled clients to secure holdings
worth tens of thousands of dollars, said people familiar with
the matter. The raid was conducted at the behest of the sheriff's
department following the disappearance of his ward, Antoinette
Dominguez, and the death of his clerical assistant, Mark Weaver.

Cannon did not press Antoinette for information, seemingly understanding that it would take some time before she would open up to him. Instead, Antoinette sat quietly listening to his accounts of how the raid had jolted Concord, where Stillman was a respected member of the community. Some city officials were calling for Stillman to answer questions before a city council hearing in the aftermath of the Mount St. Mary's Academy students/Temperance Union accusations of giving intoxicants to a minor. "They have been dithering for years on the alcohol question. But with that public temperance meeting staged by school girls ... now all of a sudden, city officials decided enough is enough."

Sister Louise gave her version. "It is serious business maintaining equilibrium in a community. Privacy really does not exist. In spite of our walls, the convent is deeply connected to the people and events in Concord. I am proud of what our students did."

There were all the usual disclaimers by anyone associated with Stillman, maintaining that the raid was a "total surprise" and they had no idea what the sheriff's department was looking for. And the "We are cooperating and giving them access to whatever they want" kinds of statements followed. Of course, Mr. Stillman himself was nowhere to be found, but the newspaper phrase, "Anyone knowing his whereabouts is asked to contact the sheriff's department," set fire to rumors. Frank submitted another account from the morning's newspaper for their shared reading.

Stillman Collapse a Pockmark on Concord Business
Give Thomas Stillman credit; he knew how to live. The Stillman's three-story, four thousand–square-foot house had all the turn-of-the-century conveniences of the 1900s. He drove a new motorcar, enjoyed season tickets at the theater, and held multiple club memberships, where he hobnobbed with Concord's elite. His rented office space, now eerily quiet, is located in Concord's newest downtown city building. Best of all, other people paid for his lifestyle. At least that's what county and state officials hint. He covered up investment losses for years and scalped the assets of his wards as his own to clean up his books. An ongoing investigation hopes to clear up some of the mystery surrounding those deals and reverse statements by Stillman defending the transactions. The size of the losses and the cover up has not yet been determined. Forensic accountants are needed to do a thorough investigation into what happened. This is not the first time Mr. Stillman has attracted attention for his finances. Five years ago, as part of a settlement with partners, he agreed to buy

back with interest a collection of properties whose value had been misrepresented. Investigators said they traced accounts and withdrawals back to Mr. Stillman. A further review of Concord bank records found the misappropriation of city funds back to three years, according to a US attorney. Federal authorities said the investigation is continuing. Mr. Stillman didn't return a phone call seeking comment, and no one answered the phone at the number listed or the door at the Stillman residence.

A pockmark? thought Sophiny as she scanned the news article. At least she knew what was happening in Concord, the raider and the scalper finally identified. But she was relieved that serious business was taking place in Stillman's office. Court officials were finally going through all his papers—every folder, file, and book—looking for clues to his business practices.

"Should we be there, do you think?" asked Antoinette.

"They won't let you in," said Tyler, "not until they are finished and have carted away whatever it is they think they need."

"All we girls can do is get dinner on the table. Funny how the secrets come out over a full stomach," commented Martha, but there was a glint in her eyes.

"What has happened to Mrs. Stillman?" Sophiny wondered out loud as she finished reading an article on the orphanage.

Charity under a Cloud

The future of the charity founded by Mr. and Mrs. Thomas Stillman to support a Cloud County orphanage is unclear. Mr. Stillman, who faces multiple charges of fraud, forgery, and abuse of his minor clients, would not comment. In the past week, some board members have resigned and some donors have said they can no longer continue their support because the allegations against Stillman are so "egregious" and "diametrically opposed" to the charity's mission.

"She has not been seen around Concord. There is a rumor that she is traveling for the summer," said Frank

"How long has she been missing?" asked Sister Louise.

"Now that you mention it, she may be in danger as well," Frank said, confirming her fear.

"'It is hard to figure what it all means." Antoinette turned the newspaper with the largest headlines before them and took a turn at reading.

Marked for Closure

The dissolution of Stillman Enterprises comes with startling swiftness. A year ago, Concord inhabitants viewed Thomas Stillman as a vibrant, consequential, rising local star, someone who knew something, setter of trends, marked for success. Now the company's operations have been suspended and its founder ordered to respond to questions about alleged abuses and secrets of his own. Stillman's last appearance in Concord was for a bankruptcy court hearing with his trademark good looks, crisp suit, and grooming, but his expression was dark and brooding. He was broke.

According to bankruptcy court papers, he had amassed tens of thousands in debts. His assets, including his business and his home, plus multiple properties over which he claims conservatorship, are facing foreclosure. According to documents reviewed by *The Concord Chronicle* and a person familiar with the matter, an entity created by Mr. Stillman received a loan of upward of one hundred thousand dollars from local lenders (mortgages on the Dominguez properties, which in turn was used as equity for the Concord Resources company). The loan was to Concord Resources LLC, which lists Mr. Stillman as president and shares an address with Stillman Enterprises. Critics say Stillman let his ego get the best of him, that he got reckless, spent excessively, and failed to see the looming day of reckoning. He has gambled on his client's resources for far too long.

The atmosphere in the room had shifted dramatically to a buzz of restless anticipation. "What happens next?" Antoinette turned to Frank. Their familiarity with each other had grown, and by the time she read through this last account, an uncommon understanding seemed to have developed between them. He had the knowledge of Stillman's activities and past that she had been seeking. Frank, in his turn, asked more and more questions of Antoinette, and Sophiny was amazed by how readily and openly she answered, as if she had known him for a very long time.

"For now, Stillman has been asked to surrender to authorities voluntarily all his files and documents, and I suspect the state attorney general will be adding the weight of their office to that request based on an indictment accusing him of submitting documents containing forged signatures that have been fraudulently notarized. If he fails to act voluntarily and cooperate, more charges will follow."

"So it is happening then—Stillman is finally coming undone?" asked Antoinette, endeavoring to sort out the effects of events on her own life.

"For now, but Dominguez properties enmeshed in Stillman's criminal activities will all take some sorting out," cautioned Frank.

"And who knows what will happen when the court battles begin?" Tyler said, glancing at Antoinette. "There is one other thing you should know … something Judge Gregory asked our agency to look into after he read the Abilene pocket notebook. It seems Mr. Stillman had a connection to H. H. Holmes. He was a distant relative treated cruelly by Holmes as a youngster."

"Crescentia Gottfried was right to warn me! There was madness in the family." Antoinette looked stunned.

Chapter 23
A Pretty Age

"Sixteen, such a pretty age, too soon to introduce tragedy." Detective Tyler's smile, slow and finite, suggested endings when Sophiny had told him about her part in their academy reenactment of Romeo's and Juliet's untimely deaths. She was trying to keep him talking, keep him from leaving, and keep him thinking about her on that last night. Instead he had asked how old she was. A feeling of alarm sharp as electricity shot through her. *"Pretty age": how could such a pleasing term come with such unsettling signifiers?*

Now waiting at the train station, looking through dancing dust particles and the shapes of people walking past, Sophiny felt bereft. She had been getting on so well with Detective Tyler. For her, those first conversations had been the hardest, but the more time they had spent together, unfolding the pieces of Antoinette's case, the easier the small talk that followed. But still she knew she had to shock him to really get his attention. Would declaring her love have the discomforting affect on him that she was seeking? She stared at the sunlight burnishing the train engine and caught the noise of the passengers moving around them. But Sophiny heard only bits: a newspaper story, a sighting, a run-in with the law, a complaint about a neighbor, a coarse joke. All his nearness went right to her brain and heart, scorched her throat, and prickled her skin. She could not say, *Hold my hand.* She could not say, *Please stay.* She felt disappointment sink down through her. She wanted to lay her head against Tyler's shoulder and feel his arms slip around her as she had that night on the Dominguez sofa.

More perplexingly, there were entire chapters still missing from her book of experience. She did not know what was meant to come next in a relationship between a woman and a man. Here was the problem with posing as a person of knowledge—Tyler would see past the brief flash of excitement in her life to what she had been doing before and what she would be doing after. And while she had been a loving sister, a true friend, a so-so student and had acted on a good imagination, she could not claim to have accomplished much else. The only tangible things she seemed to have produced were a few samplers. The whole backdrop of violent, chaotic, apocalyptic events she had gone through on behalf of her friend was about to come down. She waited for her stomach to drop, her heart to stop, and her lungs to empty, but cruelly, every part of her was still waiting.

Martha and Henry exchanged final reminders with Andrew before they boarded. Returning to Prairie Dog would have felt strange. Sophiny thought of the effect of sudden high temperatures putting an immense stress on plants that had not been adequately watered. For her the excitement of spring gardening had waned, and she would rather sit in the shade than go out and water the garden in spite of knowing that all her hard work preparing the soil and planting could be undone in one day of super-hot weather. But she hoped Janet was taking care of the weeds and the watering, as the garden was soon to be hers anyway. She would go back for James and Janet's wedding in another month or so; in the meantime, she and Andrew were staying on with Antoinette. Sister Louise had left the week before, carrying letters from Antoinette and Sophiny for the academy students. She had been able to contact Mrs. Stillman, and the two had arranged to meet.

"Got a second?" Detective Tyler finally turned to her. His arrangements for the transport of his horse and saddle in the train stock car completed, he drew her over to a bench apart from the others. Tyler's work for Antoinette had been taken over by local law enforcement. Judge Gregory had taken a special interest in Antoinette following their meeting in his chambers. He assured her that she would have justice at the highest level. And Tyler's assignment to a new case was taking him in another direction.

"Nothing good ever starts with that sentence." Even so her heart was doing that little squishy thing it did every time Detective Tyler came near. In a second, a gust of wind could come along and scatter the drying seeds all ready to take flight. She wanted to say, *I think about you all the time, or else I think about thinking about you and the fact that I shouldn't. But if I stop thinking about you, my life is just a plain after all.*

The heat of his gaze made her heartbeat quicken, her skin tingle. For one brief moment, everything seemed possible. Then he spoke. His voice was low and enigmatic. "Don't get attached to me, Sophiny. That sweet image you have will just get tarnished, tearing your life to fragments like what happened to your friend. Instead I would like you to think that there are good men in this world left to fight the villains and protect our future." She felt like she had fallen off the edge of something solid. It did not make sense. *He does care about me, yet he is leaving.*

"Are you married?" she asked in one last desperate attempt to stop him.

"Marriage? Most of us see settling down as compromising our promise."

"You made a promise?"

He continued cautiously. "Not an actual promise. Most of us see ourselves as making a mark, shaping the future, changing lawlessness."

"That is great." Sophiny blinked, alert to a stinging pain in the region of her chest.

"And family ... gets in the way of all that."

"Yeah, that is true, families get in the way of civilizing society." Was there a contradiction someplace? Sophiny was no longer listening. Then she raised her hand as if to shield off what was coming. What were those stories about wind schooners sweeping across the prairies, or had the buffalo returned in a stampede? The roar in her ears was making her dizzy. Smithy appeared, interrupting. Somebody wanted Tyler's attention elsewhere. He didn't respond to the request immediately, saying something about having something to take care of. Detective Tyler had always seemed to be a man who knew what he wanted.

The despair she felt was from the knowledge that he didn't want her. "I think I might become a photographer. But of course, there are my brothers to think about and finding paying customers, and getting equipment, and what if I am no good at it?" She waited for an argument.

"I think that is pretty great," he said. "There is plenty to be afraid of, but don't let that stop you." There was nothing ironic in his tone.

"Of course, it is nothing to what you will be doing." The flame in her heart had turned to a lump of burning dread in her throat. She could feel the tears coming to her eyes at his rejection, sums and ... "I will never measure up ... will I?" Her voice crackled ... dry ... so dry.

He caressed her hair and swooped to drop a kiss on the top of her head. "Oh you do ... it is all just timing." With a gallant nod, he pushed himself up. "Well," he said, "try to be good."

"I am not planning on growing old any time soon, just growing up," she retorted crisply. "Sometimes it's wise to keep mum; sometimes it isn't."

She thought he looked ruffled. There was something aggressive about the way he had pushed away from her. "Got to get to work. I would advise you to keep those brothers close, but should you ever need my help, I am at your service. I would wager we will have another use for you."

"Remember when you asked me to write? Will you write to me?"

He touched his hand to the brim of his hat, nodded, and was gone.

Her eyes still blurred with the salt of her tears. Happiness and Detective Tyler were linked together. It helped a little that his rejection had been gentle. And the fact that he had taken her feelings seriously, that helped too. But she mostly felt cheated. Should she start planning an accidental meeting? A stray thought came into her head: one day she would come back, or he would come back. A right time might occur when he had *another use for her* or he could be *of use* to her.

"Ready to go?" asked Andrew as the two were left alone on the platform.

"Will you teach me how to drive an automobile?" Sophiny asked to stop herself from drawing conclusions too soon. She could not just be a crack buggy driver in an age of automobiles. And she was not going to spend any more time blaming herself or anyone else for things not working out the way she wanted. Another procession was about to start.

CPSIA information can be obtained at www.ICGtesting.com
Printed in the USA
BVOW071641270113

311649BV00002B/6/P